Dianne Blacklock has been █████████████████████████
out chick, and even one of t██████████████████████
avoid in shopping centres. ████████████████████████
one by staying home and writing █████████████████ ‹,
and by the time you read this, she'll be wo████████ ›.

www.dianneblacklock.com

DIANNE BLACKLOCK

Crossing Paths

PAN
Pan Macmillan Australia

First published 2008 in Macmillan by Pan Macmillan Australia Pty Limited
This Pan edition published in 2009 by Pan Macmillan Australia Pty Limited
1 Market Street, Sydney

National Library of Australia
Cataloguing-in-Publication Data:

Blacklock, Dianne.
Crossing Paths/Dianne Blacklock,

ISBN 978 0 330 42514 8

A823.4

Typeset in 12.5/14pt Bembo by Post Pre-press Group
Printed in Australia by McPherson's Printing Group

Papers used by Pan Macmillan Australia Pty Ltd are natural, recyclable products made from
wood grown in sustainable forests. The manufacturing processes conform to the environmental
regulations of the country of origin.

To Cate Paterson

Acknowledgements

It occurred to me as I came to write these once again, that trying to find a new angle on the acknowledgements is akin to coming up with a new storyline using the same characters. The same faithful band of long-suffering friends and family members buoy me up, keep me laughing, and give me some really good material, albeit unintentionally. Anyway, you know who you are, and I love and appreciate you all every day.

There are, however, a few new twists to the plot. This book would have struggled to get off the ground if not for a stimulating and intense workshopping session over a bottle of something or other with Jeska Allan. I had all the separate ingredients but had stalled trying to put them together. Jeska is smart and insightful and quick as a whip, and we had it all sorted by the end of the night and the end of the bottle. Her input was invaluable, and I am genuinely indebted to her.

Her partner and my son, Joel Naoum, is always one of my first readers, and always, always, a patient and intelligent sounding board. Second son, Dane, was studying in Portugal virtually the entire time I was writing this novel, and was sorely missed, but I couldn't possibly mention him in the acknowledgements. Sons three and four, however, had to live with me, so they deserve a special commendation; in fact, Patrick sat his HSC and completed the transition to university smoothly, which is how Pat does things; and Zac persevered valiantly through his own particular teenage trials (he'd be embarrassed if I mentioned puberty).

Cate Paterson makes an appearance around this point each time, because I wouldn't be here still if it wasn't for her. She is a peerless publisher and a dear friend, and I am eternally grateful that she brought me into the Pan Macmillan family, which really has come to be more and more of a family each year. Thank you particularly to the delightful and highly competent Louise Bourke for looking after all the details, and supremo publicist Jane Novak for looking after me in various locales around the countryside, till all hours (sorry Jane!). Julia Stiles has been my copy-editor since the beginning, and now I am incredibly privileged and thoroughly spoilt to have her as my structural editor as well. And thank you to the wonderful, hardworking sales team who actually get the books out onto the shelves – see, I do appreciate you all, Maria!

Finally to all the lovely readers who write to me asking for the next book – here it is, I hope you enjoy it.

Wednesday

Jo decided she was getting old. She used to think moving was fun, a bit of an adventure, but that was when she was a student and she could fit everything she owned into one or two cardboard boxes and a couple of garbage bags. Now she had too much stuff. And she hated that. She had always vowed never to have so much stuff that it would weigh her down. She'd managed to keep that vow through her twenties, but inertia took over once she hit thirty. You had to stay put for a little longer. And staying put meant you needed certain things you'd never bothered about before. A dining table for example, once eating off a coffee table became too uncomfortable, and frankly, a little ridiculous. And matching plates and cups and glasses suddenly took on new importance. Jo didn't want them to, they just did. Gradually her cast-off furniture was replaced with simple, quality 'pieces'. However, the day she sent the futon to the tip and bought a Sealy Posturepedic queen-size bed instead, was the day she knew she had crossed over to the other side. But what was she supposed to do? Despite her twentysomething spirit, she had a thirtysomething body and it needed good lumbar support.

And now she had bought her first apartment. She'd not only crossed over, she'd signed up for life. She was going to live here for a long time, longer than she had lived anywhere, more than likely. You didn't go through all the rigmarole of purchasing a property to up and move any time soon after. Buying the apartment meant she was resigned to staying put, that erstwhile dreams of travelling the world would remain just that – dreams. It probably meant she was resigned to a whole lot of things that would no doubt make themselves known to her over time.

Her mobile phone began to ring and Jo slipped it out of her pocket and peered at the screen. She smiled, sinking down onto the floor and resting her back against the couch.

'Hiya Ange.' Jo had lost count of how many times she'd called today.

'How's it going? Are you okay? Are you hanging in there?'

The tangible concern in her friend's voice always caught her

by surprise. Jo had never been one to make friends easily. She
put it down to her itinerant childhood; though her sister Belle
had lived through the same childhood and didn't seem to have
any trouble making friends. She had hordes of them. Jo had met
Angie when she first came to work at the *Sunday Tribune*. She
had been given the sandwich orders, not officially, but stealthily,
one by one. 'Jo, you're going down to Earl's? Could you pick me
up . . .' By the end of the week Jo was taking nine regular orders
and she felt like the office gopher. When Angie smiled at her
from across the counter, saying something to the effect of 'Hey,
it's you again! What would you like today?', Jo suddenly blurted,
'A little respect wouldn't go astray!' and proceeded to blather on
about how she was a fully-qualified journalist and had done her
time on regional newspapers and now she'd finally made it to the
city, with a job at the *Sunday Tribune*, which while not a broadsheet, was nonetheless a reputable Sunday newspaper, and all she
wanted was the opportunity to work hard and be taken seriously,
not to have to fetch lunch orders like a kid on work experience.
Was that too much to ask?

Angie had been patient enough to sift through the babble and
get to the gist of the problem. 'I know how to fix it so they never
ask you to fetch the lunches again,' she'd told Jo, as she calmly
proceeded to garnish each of the sandwiches with a generous
smear of wasabi.

Just as Angie had predicted, Jo was never asked to fetch the
lunches again. And her wasabi-wielding accomplice turned
out to have many more strings to her bow than just sandwich-
making and vengeance-wreaking. A long-aspiring actress, Angie
was working at the Earl of Sandwich while she patiently waited
for her big break. Or even a medium-sized one would do.

'Is the power on yet?' Angie was asking.

'Just,' Jo said wearily. She'd planned this move with typical
military precision, not leaving anything to chance; but much to
her chagrin, chance had a way of tagging along regardless. The
removalists had already been running behind schedule when
a brief but significant downpour in the middle of the day had
brought proceedings to a complete halt. On top of that, she'd discovered that the power had not been turned on at the apartment,

necessitating a series of irate calls till Jo was finally put through to where the buck stopped and demanded something was done immediately. Which ended up being barely half an hour ago.

'But it's nearly ten!' Angie exclaimed. 'Jo, that's a nightmare. You won't have any hot water. You'd better come and stay at my place tonight; have a warm shower, get a good night's sleep, and then you can go back and face it tomorrow.'

'But I have to go to work tomorrow.'

'Can't you take a sickie?'

Jo was shaking her head, despite the fact that Angie couldn't see her. 'Everyone knows I was moving, I got my one day of leave, I'm not expected to require any more than that. Besides, Leo has called some extraordinary meeting first thing. I don't want to miss it.'

'You do realise the world keeps revolving even when you're not there to spin it?' said Angie.

Jo ignored that, taking a swig from the bottle of champagne she'd opened. She hadn't been able to find a glass, not that she'd spent all that much time looking.

'Tell me you're having a drink, at least?'

'I'm having a drink,' Jo confirmed. She'd bought the bottle to celebrate, a reward or incentive if she actually had managed to pull the place into some semblance of order. But when the lights finally came on and Jo surveyed the cardboard landscape of her apartment, she decided she needed a drink then and there.

'Do you want me to come round?' Angie asked.

'No, it's too much of a mess here. I'm not going to get much done tonight. I think I'll just have to make my bed and then go lie in it.'

'What do you want to do about breakfast?'

'The usual. But let's make it seven-thirty.'

'Eew, do we have to?'

'Look, you can get to Oliver's whenever you like, Ange, but I have no milk and I'll never be able to find the coffee –'

'Okay, okay . . . I'll see you at seven-thirty.'

Jo hung up, slipping her phone back into her pocket. She gazed around the flat. No – *apartment*. She was only going to refer to it as an apartment. Her apartment. For every uncomfortable, niggling thought that crossed her mind about home ownership, there were three other secretly gleeful, slightly smug ones that stopped to dance a little jig. Angie didn't quite get it, neither did Belle when she trekked all the way into the city with the twins in their hummer-pram to have a look. 'It's very . . . stark, isn't it?' was all she could say.

Exactly. What you saw was what you got. There had originally been a three-storey department store on the site, one of the finest examples of Art Deco architecture in the city, apparently. Council bureaucrats insisted the façade be maintained, so the developer set about accommodating their request. Some kind of engineering miscalculation resulted in half the building collapsing when the interior was being gutted. It was naturally suspected the miscalculation was intentional, but that proved impossible to substantiate. So after some unavoidable delays, the developer was permitted to demolish what was remaining of the department store and erect a clean, soaring, symmetrical tower, free of its Art Deco shackles, like a sleek phoenix rising out of the rubble.

And that's what Jo loved about it. There was no history to this building, there were no features to preserve. There had been no other occupants. It was a blank canvas. She could paint the walls, hang pictures, put locks on the doors. Extra ones. And one of those chains. She could invite people over and keep people out. No one could tell her what she was allowed or not allowed to do in her own apartment.

Her mobile phone rang again. Jo looked at the screen. 'Not even you, Mr Barr.' She pressed the button to answer and held the phone to her ear. 'Hi Lachlan.'

'How goes the move?'

She grunted dismissively. She didn't want to relive it.

'I was thinking of coming over,' said Lachlan.

'Well think again.'

'But I'm going away tomorrow.'

Jo frowned. 'Where are you going again?'

'The premiers' conference . . . in Tasmania,' he said, in that exasperated 'I've told you this several times' tone. Lachlan rarely remembered anything going on in her life, but she was expected to remember every detail of his.

'I'm really tired, Lach.'

'But I won't see you for nearly a week,' he protested. 'Come on, it'll perk you up, I'll bring some food, a bottle of wine . . .'

'I have food here,' she half-lied, rummaging through a box and unearthing a packet of pretzels. 'And I'm already making my way through a bottle of champagne.'

'Is Angie there?'

'No.'

'Is anyone with you?'

'No, I'm on my own.'

'Well, you can't be drinking on your own, what will people say?'

'You see, the beauty of drinking on your own, Lach, is that people can't say anything because there's no one here to see you doing it.'

'Come on, Jo.' He was getting frustrated now. 'Let me come over, I'll help you unpack or something.'

'I know what the "something" will be.'

'Jo –'

'Lachlan, I said no,' she repeated, sounding a little like a parent. She cleared her throat. 'I just want to go to bed –'

'Fine with me.'

'Lachlan!' she scolded, sounding exactly like a parent.

'Let's talk about this when I get there. I'll see you soon.'

'No you won't.'

'You can't stop me coming over there, Jo.'

'But I don't have to let you in. You don't have a key to this place, remember.'

'Then I'll be forced to stand outside and knock on your door until you open it.'

No wonder she was sounding like a parent when Lachlan was behaving like a child.

'And I'll just have to ring your wife and ask her to come and collect her pathetic husband.'

She heard Lachlan breathe out heavily. She had him there. Popular wisdom seemed to suggest that having an affair with a married man gave him all the power. But Jo didn't see it that way at all. She wouldn't be in it otherwise. She had relinquished her power in too many relationships to ever let it happen again. Jo knew where she stood with Lachlan, she had no expectations beyond that; and likewise, he could have no expectations beyond what she was prepared to give. It was a perfect arrangement. Lachlan was good for sex, very good for sex as a matter of fact. And he was intelligent, which was a huge plus for Jo. She could talk and discuss and argue and debate with Lachlan on almost any topic. He was good company, most of the time. But that didn't mean she wanted him to leave his marriage for her. Not that there was any risk of that happening. Sandra Barr was a trophy wife of the highest calibre and Lachlan enjoyed nothing more than to walk into a crowded room with her on his arm. And there were two kids. Really sweet kids they were as well, entirely to Sandra's credit. Lachlan was barely there to kiss them goodnight.

'I'll see you next week, Lach,' said Jo.

'You're sure you don't want me to come over?'

'Quite sure.'

There was a pause. Lachlan did not like being turned down, he wasn't used to it. Jo had to admit to a secret thrill knowing she had the power to disappoint him.

'I'll miss you, Jo-bloh,' he said finally.

'You'll survive,' she returned breezily.

'Sleep tight.'

She intended to. One smart thing she had done was pack herself an overnight bag with toiletries, an outfit for work tomorrow, pyjamas and bed linen, and bring it along separately with her. Very clever thinking. She surprised herself sometimes. Not that she wasn't an organised person. Jo was highly organised, focused, disciplined, but generally only about one thing at a time. When she was working on an article she was not conscious of anything else. She'd run out of clean clothes, not answer the phone, the place could collapse around her ears. Then once she'd submitted, she'd suddenly notice the mess and go into a frenzy, not resting until it was hospital-grade clean. Angie said she was obsessive, but Jo wasn't the obsessive type. She had focus. Single-minded focus. Lachlan said she was a bit like a man in that way.

Jo pushed some boxes out of the way to clear space in the bedroom so she could make up the bed. She was too tired for a shower and the water would only be lukewarm at best, so she just changed into her pyjamas and climbed in between the sheets, smiling indulgently. Bugger, she hadn't thought of pillows. She frowned, considering the boxes marked *Bedroom*. They were sure to be in the last box she'd open, so Jo decided not to put herself through the frustration. She went back out to the living room and grabbed the seat cushions off the sofa. They would have to do.

Sitting propped up against the cushions, still swigging the champagne from the bottle and munching away on pretzels, Jo sighed contentedly like a self-satisfied cat. Maybe she would get a cat. She'd call it Apostrophe or Metaphor or something writerly and witty like that.

What was she thinking? She wasn't going to get a cat. She didn't even like cats. This whole home ownership thing put funny ideas into one's head.

The best part about it was living in the city. All the way in. She had hovered on the fringes for a long time; the bohemian, cheaper, grotty regions, because Jo had always had the feeling if she dared to live right in the city, it would up and evict her, like a hapless competitor on one of those survival shows, the first to get booted off because they so obviously didn't make the grade.

But now she felt so goddamn urbane she could spit. This would put her in the thick of it. Jo intended to spend so much time at the office, Leo was going to get sick of the sight of her. Sooner or later he had to start giving her real assignments, important stories. Not the fluffy 'human interest' pieces he considered fitting of her abilities. He treated her like a cadet. Despite consistently impressive results, it had taken Jo years longer to finish her degree, due to interruptions and delays beyond her control. So when she finally started working as a journalist she was a few years behind her peers, and she felt as though she'd been playing catch-up ever since. Okay, she had her column, but even there she was censored. Write your opinion, Leo had told her. But heaven forbid she had an opinion about anything that mattered, like government policy or police corruption or global terrorism. No, being a woman she should only have an opinion about things that supposedly mattered to women. The length of skirts this season. The price of real estate. The demise of cooking. The rebirth of knitting. But since when was that all women cared about? And besides, who said because she was a woman no one except women would read what she had to say?

Leo might have been a fossil, but he was also her boss. Jo knew she had to find a way to appease him and get what she wanted at the same time. She had started at the *Sunday Tribune* as a real estate writer, then environment, then science, which had bored her stupid. It was like swotting for an exam in a subject she had no intention of pursuing after she finished school. She even had a go at sports; in fact, Jo took to it with relish. She had visions of becoming Sydney's pre-eminent sportswriter, perhaps even Australia's. Men would have to concede to her spectacular wealth of knowledge. She would be cool. There was just one little problem. Jo didn't like sport; she thought it was stupid.

'That's because you don't understand it,' Lachlan had once made the mistake of saying.

'I understand it, I just don't see the point of it,' she'd retorted.

'Explain the rules of cricket then.'

And so she did, in such meticulous detail that Lachlan was forced to concede to her spectacular wealth of knowledge, if only to shut her up.

Jo had continued to bump around like a pinball from one section to another, till the day she submitted a feature piece about the leader of a minor political party. She'd worked on it for weeks, in her own time of course. That was the only way she could do it. The first time she'd handed Leo an article he'd dismissed it without a glance. 'It's not your job, Jo. I have senior journos who know what they're doing writing this stuff. Can you imagine how Don McAllister or Lachlan Barr would feel if I said, "Here, the lass from real estate has written an analysis on the economic summit."?' Somehow, Jo had prevented steam escaping from her ears long enough to assure Leo that she wasn't expecting him to run her pieces, not right away. But how would she learn if she didn't try? And it would mean so much to her if he could give her feedback. She needed a mentor, and a mentor of the stature of Leo Monaghan would be – take a deep breath – more than she could ever hope for. That got him. Men were so vain. And so predictable.

Of course, he rejected one article after the next for about a year. Good effort, kid. But –

'No room this time.'

'Don's just finished a piece on this.'

'Lachlan's researching the very same as we speak. In fact, pass on your notes to him, would you?'

Then she submitted the article on Andrew Leslie, who, despite being highly qualified, was leading his party straight into the political wasteland of irrelevance. Jo had constructed a whole Macbeth allegory, with Leslie's wife a kind of Lady Macbeth who had pushed her husband so far that he had overreached himself. Leo loved it, and then proceeded to pull the guts out of it. Gone was the analysis of the man's political contribution and instead the focus became entirely on his wife. He turned it into a catty hatchet piece. Jo had felt conflicted for a while, until she saw her by-line. *By Jo Liddell.* The response when it was printed was astonishing; the floodgates opened and suddenly everyone was attacking them. Jo never forgot the press conference where he announced his retirement from the leadership and the party, and then crossed directly to his wife, took her hand, and together they walked from the room.

Jo had gone home and got drunk, very drunk, and proceeded to pen a wordy, self-righteous resignation, berating journalism, politics, the *Tribune* and herself. But when she arrived hungover at work the next morning, Leo had offered her the column. It had come to him overnight, apparently.

'Bitch! We'll just call it Bitch, as in having a bitch, but it's a clever play on the word, don't you think? Subtle.'

As a sledgehammer.

She didn't hand in the letter of resignation.

Jo drained the rest of the bottle and dropped it down next to the bed, and then twisted the top of the foil packet of pretzels and tossed it on the floor as well. Snuggling down under the sheets, she gazed up at the ceiling. Her ceiling. She turned and looked out the window. At her view. She was bristling with the feeling that things were going to be different now, that her time had finally come . . . that she was verged on the precipice, about to fly . . .

But that was just champagne-fuelled nonsense. She had moved house – of course things were going to be different. That wasn't extraordinary, it was to be expected. She should write a piece on this, how people con themselves into believing that normal, natural feelings are loaded with significance, almost mystical. Jo had learned the hard way that life was not mystical, or magical; it was hard and grey and cold most of the time. Much better to see it for what it is than to be perennially disappointed.

Thursday

Joe decided he was getting old. He used to be proud of the fact he could fit everything he owned in the world into a backpack and an overnight bag or two. He had vowed never to have so much stuff that it would weigh him down. But it was certainly weighing him down now as he trudged up the final flight of stairs to his flat.

As he arrived at the top floor landing, he experienced no surge of sentimental feeling at the sight of his front door, only relief that he could put these bags down. He dumped them on the tessellated tiles and crouched down to check under the mat. No key. Bloody useless Will. He'd offered to pick him up from the airport, but Joe had argued that the flight was arriving too early and he didn't want to inconvenience anyone, though it was really because he knew his younger brother all too well. The chances of Will actually showing up at the airport were slim to highly improbable.

'Just put a key under the mat,' Joe had told him on the phone from Boston a couple of days ago.

'No way,' Will had protested. 'You can't arrive in the country after nearly two years away and not have a familiar face there to meet you.'

'Honestly, Will,' Joe persisted, 'I'll jump in a cab and I'll see your familiar face fifteen minutes later. Leave a key under the mat and I'll wake you when I get in.'

There had been a pause. 'You don't trust me, do you, Joe? You think I'm not going to show.'

'It's not that –'

'Well, I just might surprise you.'

But of course he hadn't, which was no surprise either. And although Joe had emailed from his stopover in LA only yesterday, urging him once again to leave a key out, Will hadn't managed it. His brother was all good intentions with no follow-through. Joe put it down to his being the youngest of a big family; he'd had too many people looking after him so he'd never learned how to look after himself, much less anyone else.

Joe knocked lightly on the door and waited. There was no response, not a sound coming from inside, or from the entire floor it seemed. He glanced either side of the landing at the doors of the adjacent apartments, reluctant to knock too loudly at this time of the morning, given their close proximity. It was only a small block, a three-storey walk-up, one of the last of the liver-brick Art Deco buildings still standing this close to the city. So it did have some charm, unlike the stark apartment towers that had sprouted up all over the city in his absence.

He hadn't planned to buy the flat; his job involved way too much travelling, as well as the probability of extended posts abroad. Owning real estate equated to settling down in his mind, staying put, and Joe was not resigned to staying put anywhere at the time. Besides, when he eventually did settle down, it would never be in a city. Though by necessity he spent a lot of his time in cities, his dream was to settle somewhere up in the Blue Mountains, the only place in all the world he truly considered home.

'You've always got a room here at the house, and you always will,' his dad had assured him. 'But you need a place close to town, close to work, where you can hang your hat between trips. And you won't have to worry about it while you're away. If you take an overseas post, you can rent it out and forget about it. But for godsakes, son, you're earning decent money now and you need to spend it on something more substantial than beer and smokes.'

He was right of course. Joe had quit the smokes when he turned thirty, cut down on beer in favour of a good red with dinner, and he had come to appreciate the convenience of having a place in the city. But it had never felt like home. Joe knew he would only feel like he had come home once he made his way up to Leura. He would have liked to have gone there directly, but he wanted to sort work out first so that he could spend at least a few uninterrupted days with his father.

At this moment, though, he'd just be glad to get inside the flat, have a shower, change his clothes, maybe grab a quick nap. Joe generally travelled well, but he'd had to share the plane with the Australian water polo team and they were a rowdy bunch. He was yet to come across an Australian sporting team that wasn't.

Joe knocked again, not loud enough to wake the neighbours, so it was unlikely to wake Will either. He considered his options. He couldn't even phone Will because the SIM card in his mobile wouldn't function here. He could go back down onto the street, find a payphone, maybe grab some breakfast. But he felt grimy and tired and not up to schlepping around the streets hunting for a phone. Right now he just wanted to rest his weary head. Joe stared at his luggage, thinking. He crouched down, stacking the bags on top of each other and wedging them into a corner of the alcove. Then he propped his backpack up against them, and lowered himself onto the floor, sinking gratefully into the padded backing. This would do; he'd slept in worse conditions, a good deal worse. He just hadn't expected he would have to once he was home in Australia.

And he was home to stay, at least for the foreseeable future. He didn't want to leave his dad again until ... well, he didn't want to think about that. Joe was aware the old man had deteriorated significantly since he'd last seen him, but it was hard to imagine. In his almost daily emails he was still as sharp and quick-witted as ever, but it was the mind that went last with this sadistic disease. His muscles would gradually atrophy to the point where he would be unable to swallow or, ultimately, even breathe. But his brain would still register every helpless, painful moment, even though he'd no longer possess the ability to communicate it. He had assured his son over many philosophical online exchanges that if it had to be this or losing his mind, he'd choose this. Joe didn't agree with the premise: why did it have to be anything? Why couldn't his father just pass away peacefully in his sleep in his nineties? They'd already lost their mother too early; she was only fifty-nine when the aneurism burst in her brain, killing her instantly. At least she hadn't suffered, which was the only solace the family had throughout the shattering grief that followed.

Joe had often wondered how his dad had been able to bear her loss. Joseph and Nancy Bannister were an extraordinary couple by any estimation. They met when they were both covering the Vietnam War. She was a feisty reporter from New Jersey who didn't take crap from anyone; she wouldn't have got to where she was otherwise. Joseph was a senior correspondent for a Sydney newspaper, still single pushing thirty, and he fell hopelessly in love with her. Though she took some coaxing, according to him, he eventually won her over. Nancy told it differently. In her version, she fell hard from the get-go for the laconic Australian reporter who hid his intellect under a bushel but let it shine on the page. As Vietnam collapsed into an unholy mess after the Tet Offensive, Nancy discovered she was pregnant. She knew she had to get to safer ground, and though Joe would have followed her anywhere, Nancy couldn't abide Nixon and didn't want to live in the US under his presidency. They married in the embassy in Singapore on their way back to Sydney, where they set up home. Over the years Joe travelled back and forth, their anniversaries forming a timeline of the conflicts throughout south-east Asia during the seventies and eighties, each pregnancy a marker of his sabbaticals home. When baby William made five, Nancy decided they needed room to spread out, and she moved the family up to the Blue Mountains while Joe was in Cambodia covering the fall of the Khmer Rouge in Phnom Penh. She wired him their new address so he'd know where to find them next time he came home.

Nancy was fiercely independent and self-sufficient, but the bond between his parents never waned. Joe was happiest when his dad was home, and he'd hang on every word as his parents debated the state of the world. They had intellects to match, but his mother was fiery, perpetually frustrated, always worked up about injustice and inequality, while his dad was quieter, considered, calling himself a 'compassionate realist'. When Joe was old enough to twig, he realised their differences only served to fuel the passion between them. Despite all the places he'd travelled and all the people he'd met, he'd never come across a couple quite like them.

Which Joe reckoned was the reason he was still single pushing forty. He had a tendency to regard his own relationships through the prism of his parents' marriage, so they always came up wanting. It probably wasn't fair, but he didn't know how to avoid it. His sisters suggested that he had to let a relationship develop on its own terms, give it time, but he'd been with Sarah for three years and their relationship had simply run its course. In fact, it had probably been over for a while, given they were apart more than they were together, so it took them longer to notice. That's why he'd found it hard to get too upset about their split. But it hadn't stopped Sarah putting on the usual histrionics. She said a few bitchy things about wasting her time, the tired old biological clock sore point. Joe was so over it. He wanted to have kids, but he didn't treat every woman he dated as little more than a prospective incubator and therefore a waste of his precious time if it didn't work out. Okay, he realised men had a few more years up their sleeves than women, but surely if the relationship wasn't right, then it wasn't right to bring kids into it, no matter how loudly the blasted clock was ticking.

Joe sighed heavily, rubbing his eyes. His brain was firing in odd directions; lack of sleep didn't help, but he knew it was more than that. He felt restless and on edge, and not just because he was trying to take a nap on his doorstep. It was coming home and everything that went with it. He hadn't worked steadily in Australia for years, he hadn't lived in this flat for an extended period ever. He hadn't spent enough time with his dad, and now he had no say in it, the time had been apportioned and this was all he was going to get. And then what? Back to more of the same? Joe wondered if he had it in him any more.

He drifted off to sleep, his head filled with images of the house in the mountains, the voices of children, the silhouette of a future he had no idea would ever eventuate.

*

8:20 am

Dry ... parched ... arid ... desiccated ... Desiccated? Hmm, maybe not. Dehydrated? Definitely, but that was a little prosaic. Jo's brain had a habit of doing this, sometimes it was like a thesaurus on speed. It was a hazard of the profession, she'd decided, constantly having to come up with 'another word for –'. Angie said she was a wordsmith, but Jo was not so sure, when half the time she couldn't recall the name of everyday things like spatulas.

Whatever, her throat was dry and parched while her tongue felt as though it was carpeted in a slimy fuzz which Jo imagined to be not unlike moss. What was that stuff anyway? There was no word for it, as far as she was aware. Her teeth were coated with the same foul substance. This was what you got for quaffing champagne and pretzels right before falling asleep.

She stumbled out of bed to brush her teeth, kicking her toe on a box on her way to the bathroom, then nearly tripping over the same box as she turned back to get her toiletries bag from beside the bed. She then proceeded to spend an inordinate amount of time brushing her teeth. Eventually her mouth didn't feel like the inside of a vacuum cleaner any more, but she was still stranded-in-the-desert thirsty. She needed hydration, irrigation, reconstitution ... she needed something with fizz. It was the only cure for this particular kind of thirst. She made her way out to the kitchen and opened the fridge door with a vague hope she'd find something cold and fizzy therein, despite the fact that Jo was well aware she didn't actually put anything in the fridge last night, and wishing wouldn't make it so.

A buzzer went off suddenly, giving her a start. There it was again, louder this time. What was that? By the third time Jo finally twigged – it was the security intercom. She wasn't used to it yet, she hadn't had one in her previous building. She dashed over to the receiver on the wall and picked up the handset.

'Hello?'

'Hi Jo, it's Angie.'

'Oh, hi,' she said, rubbing her forehead. 'I thought we were meeting at Oliver's?'

'So did I. I waited for forty-five minutes –'

'*Forty-five minutes!* What's the time?'

'It's after eight-thirty, Jo.'

'*What?*' she almost shrieked. 'I'm going to be late, I'm going to be *so* late, I have to go, I'm sorry, Ange, I'll make it up to you –'

'I brought you breakfast, and coffee,' Angie broke in. 'It's rocket fuel, just the way you like it. Oliver made it specially.'

'Oh, jeez Ange, I don't know if I've got time.'

'Jo, can you at least let me in down here?'

'Sorry!' she said, pressing the security button.

When she opened the door to Angie a few minutes later, Jo was holding up her mobile phone. 'It's flat. There was no alarm.'

'I figured as much,' said Angie, walking past her, 'when I tried to ring and the recorded voice said your phone was turned off.'

'God, I'm so sorry, Ange. And I was the one who insisted we meet early.' Jo winced. 'Are you very pissed off?' she asked, knowing full well nothing ever pissed Angie off. Jo didn't know how she did it. So many things – too many things – seemed to piss Jo off.

'Don't worry about it,' said Angie, handing her a cardboard cup and a paper bag. 'After yesterday it's a wonder you woke up at all. Look at the state of this place.'

The floor was covered with boxes, some opened, their contents spewing out onto each other. The larger pieces of furniture had been plonked in approximately the right places, but everything else was in disarray.

Jo took a gulp of the coffee. Far out, it was strong. But it was effective. She reckoned this was what those electric paddles the doctors used on medical shows must feel like. Defibrillators. She should tell Oliver to call it his defibrillator brew. 'What's in the bag?' Jo asked, taking another cautious sip.

'One of those savoury breakfast muffins. I figured you could eat it on the run.'

'And I really am going to have to run. What's the time now?'

'A little further past eight-thirty.'

'*Jesus!*'

'Don't forget you're only a walk away from work now,' Angie reminded her.

'That's right, that's good, okay, I might just make it.' Jo looked around the room. 'Can you see any boxes marked *Linen* or *Bathroom* maybe?'

'What are you after?'

'A towel. I should have had a shower last night, but I was just so exhausted, and besides, the water was barely warm.'

Angie had dropped to her knees and was tearing the masking tape from one of the boxes. She fished out a towel.

'I should call you Radar,' said Jo. 'You're amazing.'

'And you're late,' said Angie, standing up and passing Jo the towel as she took the cup and bag back from her. 'I'll put these in the kitchen and see myself out. You'd better get a wriggle on.'

'Thanks, Ange,' she said, walking backwards towards the bedroom. 'I'll call you later, okay? I owe you a drink, or three . . .'

'I'll hold you to it.'

8:35 am

'What the hell are you doing, Joe?'

He jumped, startled, staring up at his accuser. He blinked a couple of times, his eyes adjusting to the apparition of his brother gazing down on him from above.

'It's a wonder the neighbours didn't call the police or something,' Will went on. 'You look like you've come in off the street.'

Joe rubbed his eyes, sitting upright. His heart was still pounding in his chest. He had to calm down, breathe, remember where he was . . . He was home in Australia, he was safe.

'Why are you sleeping in the doorway?' Will persisted.

'I didn't have much choice, Will. You forgot to put the key under the mat and you didn't answer the door.'

'Because I wasn't here,' said Will.

Joe was still in a fugue of sleep, he was not quite following.

'You should have waited at the airport, I told you I'd be there,' Will added, a little petulantly.

'I didn't see you.'

'Well, I was a bit late . . .'

'How late?'

'I dunno, half an hour . . . or so . . .' he shrugged. 'I was going to stay up all night so I didn't miss you, but it kinda turned into a party at Jake's . . . I ended up crashing and nobody woke me. Retards, they knew I had to get to the airport.'

That was the Will he knew and loved. Everyone else's fault but his own. 'Give me a hand up,' said Joe, raising his arm.

'Thing is, if you trusted me, you'd have waited –' Will grasped his brother's forearm, '– and then you wouldn't have had to sleep on the landing,' he said, pulling him to his feet.

'Yeah, but then I wouldn't have got any sleep at all waiting around for you at the airport.' Joe drew level with him. He still wasn't used to them being the same height. Will was slighter though; he hadn't filled out like Joe. Give him another decade. 'Good to see your not-so-familiar face.' He chucked his brother under the chin. 'What's this feeble excuse for a beard?'

'Fuck off,' Will grinned, knocking his hand away. 'Look at you. You know the three-day growth thing went out with metro-sexuals, Joe. You're living in the past, old man.'

'I've been travelling for twenty-something hours, and this is the welcome I get?'

'You started it.'

They paused, smiling at each other.

'Good to have you home, Joe,' said Will.

'Good to be home.'

The brothers proceeded to hug in the way men do, punctu-ated with a couple of good hard slaps on the back.

'So, are you going to let me in?' Joe said finally.

'Sure, sure.' Will dug for his keys in his pocket while Joe hoisted his backpack up onto his shoulder.

'Now just so you know,' said Will. 'Rancid hasn't quite moved all his stuff out yet, but he's promised to by the weekend.'

Joe didn't want to think about how Will's friend had earned that moniker. 'Renting and forgetting' had turned into providing his itinerant brother and assorted hangers-on with somewhere to stay for little to no rent. Will was an aspiring actor, though as far as Joe understood, 'aspiring' usually involved some ambition, goal-setting, hard work, and he had the feeling that Will was waiting for his big break to be handed to him on a platter.

'Where do I get to sleep?' Joe asked him.

'In your room, in your bed,' Will assured him. 'I even changed the sheets.' He unlocked the door and swung it back to allow Joe to walk through. The place had all the signs of a hasty tidy-up. There were various 'neat' piles around the room, newspapers, books, clothes hanging over the backs of chairs, dishes peeking above the sink.

'Let me put these bags down,' said Joe, crossing to the bedroom. The bed had been freshly made up, a mound of dirty linen in the corner testimony to it. Joe dumped his bags on the floor, frowning at the bedside alarm clock. 'Is that the time?'

Will walked in behind him with the second overnight bag. 'Ah, yeah, probably. Close enough anyway.'

'Fuck,' muttered Joe, blinking at his wristwatch. 'I'm still on US time. I've got to get out of here, I've got a meeting up town in about twenty minutes.'

'Jeez, Joe, you didn't organise that too well.'

He gave Will a withering look. 'Can you please go make sure that is the right time while I wash my face and change my shirt?'

Joe was rummaging through his bag when Will reappeared in the doorway.

'Clock's dead on,' he announced. 'Hey, old man, getting a bit of a gut there,' he added, giving Joe a gentle whack across the middle as he pulled a clean T-shirt over his head.

'What are you talking about,' said Joe. 'It's all muscle.'

Will snorted. 'Coffee's on.'

He slipped a collared shirt over his T-shirt, the least crumpled one he could find. 'Do you still make it like rocket fuel?'

'Yep,' Will said proudly.

'Never mind, I don't have time anyway, I have to get out of here,' said Joe, feeling for his wallet in the pocket of his jeans.

Will was regarding him, frowning. 'This meeting, is it about work, like an interview? 'Cause you know you look like you slept in those clothes.'

'Funny about that.' Joe walked past him into the living room. 'It's not an interview, just a chat with an old friend. Putting some feelers out.'

'Well, I hope for your sake he's a really good friend, understanding, you know . . .'

Joe stuck out his hand. 'Key, please.'

'I'll be here,' he said.

'Just to be on the safe side,' Joe persisted, beckoning with his fingers.

'Fine.' Will shoved a hand into his pocket. 'Take mine, 'cause I'm not going anywhere.' He dropped the keys into Joe's hand.

'I'll buy you a beer later,' said Joe as he crossed to the door.

'I'll hold you to it.'

8:55 am

Jo was finally on her way to work, setting a brisk pace. She'd dressed in the outfit she had packed separately, twisted her damp hair into an approximation of a French roll and slapped on a little make-up. That would have to do.

Three blocks and five minutes later, she arrived at the building that housed the offices of the *Daily* and *Sunday Tribune*, and various other sister publications. It was an ugly edifice, its prominent concrete ribs and brown detailing placing it undeniably in the building boom of the seventies. Jo hurried through the revolving door and skittered towards the lift bay.

'Hold it!'

The elevator doors blithely ignored her, Jo couldn't see from the angle of her approach whether there was anyone inside.

'I said hold the lift, please!' she cried as she careered towards the closing doors. They touched, barely, before miraculously parting again, gliding open to reveal a tall, scruffy man smiling out at her.

'Sorry,' he said cheerfully.

Why was he saying sorry? He'd held the lift, she hadn't missed it. What was there to be sorry about? Jo gave the man a cursory nod and stepped inside.

'Which floor?' he asked.

'I've got it,' she said brusquely, reaching across to press the button herself. Did he think she was incapable of pressing a button? Moron.

He nodded, still sporting the goofy grin. He really was tall, freakishly tall in fact. Jo was used to everyone being taller than her; she'd lived with that reality the whole of her adult life. But she could still tell when someone was exceptionally tall. And this guy was tall. And big. Not overweight – he was what her mother would call 'a big bear of a man'. His presence seemed to fill the elevator, which was a little intimidating in such a small space. Just as well Jo was not easily intimidated.

She fixed her stare on the buttons as they lit their way to her floor. They seemed to be moving at a painfully slow pace. In fact Jo's hackles were rising faster than this elevator. At this rate she was going to be late for the meeting and Leo would make her suffer for it. He wouldn't let her slip in quietly and take her seat. No, Leo could never let an opportunity like that pass without getting some mileage out of it. That was Leo's way – lead through humiliation.

Oh come *on* . . . what the hell was wrong with this thing?

Jo glanced sideways at tall scruffy guy; he was watching the buttons too, frowning curiously. Had he noticed the lift was barely moving as well? She thought about asking him, but she had never been one to do the small talk thing with strangers.

Clunk.

'What was that?' Jo gasped as the floor beneath her hiccupped. There followed a loud wheezing groan, another *clunk* and the elevator came to a shuddering halt.

'Shit!' she exclaimed, pressing her hands against the walls for support.

'Are you okay?' Scruffy asked her.

'Of course I'm okay. What's wrong with the lift?'

'Looks like it's stopped.'

He was clearly a genius.

Jo stepped gingerly away from the wall and approached the control panel. She pressed *OPEN DOOR, CLOSE DOOR*, then the buttons for the floors above and below, then the open and close buttons again, but nothing happened. 'This is ridiculous,' she muttered. 'Why isn't anything responding?'

'I think it must be pretty well stuck,' he declared.

'It can't be stuck,' Jo snapped. 'People don't get stuck in lifts these days, everything's computerised, right?'

'Mm, and computers are foolproof.' He folded his arms and leant back against the wall. 'Nothing ever goes wrong with computers.'

She glanced at him, slouched against the wall like a vagrant at a bus shelter, and about as useful. 'Well, aren't you going to do something?'

Joe raised an eyebrow. He knew her type. All feisty and independent, but they still expected blokes to fix everything. Demanded it, in fact. Equality meant payback: men owed women for all their years of oppression, even if most of the guys he knew had never oppressed a woman in their lives. They were too scared.

She was still standing there, hands on hips, all self-righteousness, waiting for an answer.

He shook his head regretfully. 'Gee, if only I'd packed my emergency elevator repair kit . . .'

No, he wasn't a genius, he was a smart-arse. Jo had met his type before, too often. Useless males who had decided that equality between the sexes meant they didn't have to do blokey things any more. Women could look after themselves if they wanted their independence so badly. Problem was, they didn't make up for it by taking their fair share of 'women's work'. So in the end they did bugger all, but still managed to be self-righteous about it.

'What I can do,' he said, pushing off the wall and stepping across to the control panel, 'is press this button that says *Help*.' Joe was pretty sure she could have worked that out for herself eventually, but hey, he was happy to oblige.

'*You have reached the Otis emergency helpline.*'

'I don't believe it!' Jo exclaimed. 'It's a recorded message?'

'*This line is exclusively to report service difficulties, breakdowns and malfunctions of the elevator, and cannot be used for any other purpose. Heavy penalties apply . . .*'

The voice droned on as Jo tuned out. Her heart had started to race and her stomach was churning, which was not a good thing considering that she'd just scoffed a cheesy muffin studded with globules of bacon and then washed it down with industrial-strength coffee. God, what if she threw up in this small space with this strange man? She felt a cold sweat break across her forehead. No, no way, she simply could not throw up. She had to steel herself . . . focus on something else . . .

She tuned in again as a voice – a live one – was saying something about 'an hour and a half'.

'What was that?' she cried. 'Did they just say an *hour and a half?*'

'Is everyone okay there?'

'No, we're not okay!' Jo shrilled. 'We're stuck in a friggin' elevator.'

'I'm aware of that, ma'am, and I've logged you into the system. I was just telling the gentleman that we'll have someone out there within an hour and a ha–'

'You're kidding me?' Jo had had just about enough. Random downpours, power failures, batteries dying, now lifts breaking down? It was like a comedy of errors, except there was nothing funny about it whatsoever.

She shoved scruffy boy aside, leaning her hands against the wall and talking straight into the intercom. 'Just how many people are stuck in lifts across Sydney right now?' she demanded. 'There can't be so many that it takes you an hour and a half to respond to a call, unless you have the shoddiest elevators on the planet, or the most incompetent technicians. But they're not incompetent, are they? They're just lazy. It must be morning smoko –'

'I wouldn't –'

'– and there's a pair of them there right now, isn't there, the work ethic of a three-toed sloth between them –'

'Miss –'

'– slurping on milky tea and stuffing oversize muffins down their throats while they scratch their balls –'

'*Miss!*'

'– and read the form guide, refusing to get off their arses till they've had their "break" from doing nothing all morning anyway!'

'*Lady!*' Joe raised his voice above hers this time. He finally got her attention. 'I think you've made your point.'

'Not until they guarantee they'll get out here ASAP.'

'Well, they hung up back at "scratching their balls", so I think the only guarantee we have is that we'll be waiting a lot longer now.'

Jo blinked. 'Why do you say that?'

'Oh, maybe because of the way you just spoke to them,' he suggested. 'Why do you think they'd hurry out here now to release a caged lion? They're more likely to forget to come at all.'

'What are you saying?' Her eyes grew wide. 'They won't just leave us here all day? They can't do that.'

'No, but they might wait till another call comes in.'

'So we'll call again!' She lurched at the *Help* button, but he beat her to it, covering it over with his rather sizeable mitt.

'It's not going to help matters you calling again,' he pointed out. 'In fact it'd probably only make things worse.'

'Well who else is going to call?' she cried shrilly. 'No one even knows we're here, no one's going to call, no one's going to come!' Her voice rose hysterically with each phrase.

'Someone from building maintenance will report it as soon as they realise.'

Jo wanted to ask him how long that was likely to take, but she couldn't find her voice or catch her breath. Her chest felt as though it was caving in and she had to gasp for air. 'I can't do an hour and a half, not an hour and a half,' she muttered. 'I can't do it, it's too long.'

'What's wrong?' he was asking. 'Are you claustrophobic or something?'

'No, of course not,' Jo retorted, recovering her voice. 'I just get nervous in confined spaces and I have trouble . . . breathing.'

'I think that makes you claustrophobic.'

'Look, I'm not crazy.'

'I didn't say you were.'

'I just feel . . .' but she couldn't finish what she was going to say. Her head had gone cloudy, and dizzy, and she could feel the panic rising in her chest . . . along with her breakfast. But worse than that, she had a dreadful sensation that she might possibly burst into tears. There was a tightness in her throat, a lump pushing upwards. She'd never *burst* into tears in her whole life, not even as a child. She used to dare Bradley Peters down the street to pinch her harder and harder, and she bet him he couldn't make her cry. He never won the bet.

But right now her body was out of her control, and there was nothing that made Jo more anxious than being out of control.

'Hey, hey, look at me,' the scruffy man was saying. He had his hands on her shoulders but his voice felt as though it was a long way away, like he was calling her from the other end of a tunnel. Jo focused on his eyes, because everything around them seemed to be spinning. But his eyes were very steady and blue and unblinking.

'You have to slow down and breathe,' he was saying. 'Not so fast, there's plenty of air in here. Look, there are vents, we're not going to run out of air.' He steered her into a corner of the elevator as he spoke, gently easing her down to sit on the floor.

'What are you doing?' she said breathlessly.

'If you sit in a corner it gives you the greatest perspective, see?' he said, straightening up again. 'Everything seems bigger.' He certainly did, looming above her even taller as he reached up to the ceiling, feeling around.

'Now what are you doing?' Jo asked, watching him nervously.

'I'm just going to try to open up your perspective even more,' he said as his fingers traced the edges of the panels that made up the ceiling, till he finally pushed against one and it dislodged.

Jo gasped. 'I don't think you should be doing that.'

He slid the panel out of the way and glanced back down at her. 'It's okay, see, now you're not closed in.'

'It's not being closed in that's the problem.'

'Then what is the problem?'

'It's . . .' She had no idea, this had never happened to her before. But it wasn't being closed in, she didn't see how it could be that. She and Belle had always felt safe being closed in, shut away in their room together, out of the way. The problem was what was going on outside, the voices getting louder, the first few thumps as fists hit walls, doors slammed, the sound of glass smashing. Jo remembered the fear, and unfortunately so did her body.

Joe crouched down in front of her. She had drawn herself up into a tight little ball, shrinking back into the corner, still panting for breath. Her eyes were filled with fear. He'd seen that look often enough, usually on the faces of small children huddled alone behind a mound of rubble that used to be their home. She was right on the edge, and he did not want to have to deal with a full-blown panic attack with rescue more than an hour away.

'I've got something that might help,' he said, leaning on one knee so that he could reach into the pocket of his jeans. He drew out his wallet and opened it, slipping out two small square yellow tablets in blister packing.

'Oh no, I don't think so . . .' She shook her head. She wasn't good with drugs.

'They're very mild, just a relaxant,' he persisted.

Jo was suspicious. 'Why do you carry them with you?'

'I don't usually. Only on long-haul flights.'

'Are you afraid of flying?'

'No, they help if I can't sleep –'

'I'm not taking something that's going to knock me out!'

'They won't knock you out. They just relax you enough so you can get to sleep.'

She looked at him warily. 'Do you think I'm crazy? I'm not accepting drugs from a stranger. I don't even know you . . .' Her heart was pounding painfully in her chest. She wished she could just take one full breath. 'How do I know . . . you didn't plan this . . .' Jo realised how ridiculous that sounded the second the words left her lips.

From the look on his face, so did he. 'Yeah, you're right. I lie in wait in elevators during daylight hours, till a woman happens to walk in, alone, and then I make sure it breaks down – I can't reveal how I manage that, it's a trade secret – and then I wait for her to panic – don't ask me how I know she will, I just do, years of experience – and I drug her and have my way with her. That's why I knocked out the roof panel, so I can make a quick getaway afterwards.'

Jo had stopped listening; she was staring at the pills in his hand, her heart still racing sickeningly in her chest as the air seemed to become thinner and harder to breathe. 'Are they like Valium or something?'

'Yeah, except they're so mild they sell them over the counter in the US. They've never knocked me out, I promise you, but they just might get you through this.'

Her head was throbbing and her eyes were stinging. She wasn't going to make an hour and a half. She snatched the pills from his hand and popped them out of the blister pack onto her tongue.

As soon as Jo swallowed them she began to feel calmer simply from the knowledge that she wouldn't have a complete break-down trapped in this steel box with a total stranger. That was the problem with anxiety: the more anxious you felt, the more anxious you became. Now that she didn't feel anxious about being anxious, she was feeling less anxious. So now she had to regain full control. She began to focus on her breathing, closing her eyes as she consciously slowed it down.

'Are you all right?' he asked after a while.

'I'll be fine. I'm feeling better already.' Jo took a deep breath, finally, all the way into her lungs. There, much better. She opened her eyes again.

He'd settled himself back against the opposite wall to her, stretching his long legs out in front of him. It occurred to Jo that she should take a mental note of his description in case she had to give details to police later. Perhaps a little paranoid, but she felt it prudent nonetheless. He was late thirties, maybe forty, a hundred and ninety-five centimetres and ninety kilograms. She'd developed estimating skills from her time doing the police rounds at one of the regional papers out west; it was quite a handy party trick. He had blue eyes; light brown, unkempt hair growing over his collar; unshaven appearance. He was wearing faded jeans, which inci-dentally looked like he'd slept in them, and a loose short-sleeved blue-checked shirt over a long-sleeved off-white T-shirt. And a pair of shabby Volley sandshoes that had seen better days, quite some time ago now. He looked like an overgrown uni student.

'So I suppose we should introduce ourselves,' he proposed, breaking her reverie.

She held up her hand, stopping him. 'No names, no pack drill, okay?' she said.

He looked a little stunned. 'You mean we're going to be stuck in this elevator for an hour and a half and not speak to each other?'

'I didn't say that,' she returned. 'It's just that you and I don't know each other from Adam. We never would have laid eyes on each other again if the elevator hadn't broken down, so let's not do the whole thing and swap email addresses and vow to keep in touch out of some sense of . . . I don't know . . . what do they call it? Siege mentality? Like we have some special connection because of this. We're not fighting a war together, we're just ships pausing in the night, okay? Let's leave it at that.'

Joe listened dumbfounded to her spiel. She was a real piece of work, this one. He wondered what had made her so narky. Broken heart? Broken family? More likely she was just a spoilt little princess who did not tolerate even the slightest inconvenience because of an expectation that the world should pretty much revolve around her.

Jo was beginning to feel uncomfortable. He was just staring at her, and he had this look on his face . . . knowing . . . judging . . . whatever it was, she didn't like it.

'I'm going to be late for a meeting,' she said to break the impasse. 'What am I saying,' she sighed. 'I'm not going to make it at all, am I?'

'I wouldn't count on it. But I reckon you've got a good excuse.'

Jo shook her head. 'You don't know my boss. I could be trapped in a mineshaft and he'd still want to know why I didn't call in – oh *jeez*, why didn't I think!' She grabbed her bag and started digging around in it. But as she finally retrieved her mobile phone she remembered that it wasn't charged. 'Fucking worthless piece of shit!' She glanced over at him. 'Sorry.'

He shrugged.

'My phone's dead,' said Jo. 'Do you mind if I use yours?'

'Can't help you, sorry. Mine's not working either.'

'You're kidding me. How did you let that happen?'

He raised an eyebrow. 'Maybe the same way you did?' *Princess*.

'I doubt that,' she said airily. 'I moved house yesterday, the battery ran down and the recharger's still packed away.'

'I flew in from the States this morning,' Joe informed her. 'My phone won't operate locally until I get a new SIM card.' He paused. 'Do I win?'

'Let's call it a draw,' she said drolly. So he'd been on a plane overnight. At least that explained the drugs, and the rumpled get-up.

'So, was it a business trip?' she asked.

'Pardon?'

'Were you away on business?' Jo repeated, like it was any of hers.

Joe wondered what had happened to the 'no names, no pack drill' policy. Apparently she had appointed herself chief presiding judge of the territory and would decide what was on or off limits.

'I've been working overseas for a few years,' he said finally. 'I had to come back for family reasons. My father's ill.'

She didn't want to know that. Why was he telling her that? Did he expect her to ask him all about his father now? Well, she wasn't going to. Next thing he'd be asking her about her family and she wasn't going *there* with a complete stranger.

'So do you work here, in the building?' Joe prompted after a while.

Good, back on track. Work was a much safer subject. 'I'm with the *Sunday Tribune*.'

Jo noticed the slight surprised raise of his eyebrow.

'In what capacity?' he asked.

Of course he would never imagine she was a journalist. Not a print journalist anyway, though the term itself was tautological. Only real journalists worked in print, the others were just performers, show ponies. And real female journalists were brunette, medium to tall, preferably with those black-rimmed serious specs perched on the end of serious noses that could sniff out a story anywhere. Serious stories. Real journalists weren't short and blonde and, groan, *cute*. Unless they were newsreaders, and thus back to her original point, not real journalists. Jo hated being cute. No one took her seriously.

She squared her shoulders and cleared her throat. 'I'm a journalist,' she said, attempting an authoritative tone.

Joe hadn't expected that, he wasn't sure why, she was just too . . . cute, really. Had he known she was in the industry, he'd have picked her for a newsreader, maybe.

Okay, so he was stereotyping big-time and his sisters would slap him on the wrist and have every right to . . . but by definition stereotypes had to have some truth to them.

'Well, what do you know?' he remarked in an attempt to sound interested but not surprised.

'Don't say it with that tone,' Jo returned curtly. She'd seen right through him. 'Just because I'm blonde –'

'Hey, wait on,' he interrupted. 'I didn't mean that, it's only –'

'– a stereotype, is what it is. You shouldn't judge people on appearances, you know.'

'You're absolutely right.' Joe decided it wasn't worth going fifteen rounds with her when he didn't have a leg to stand on anyway. 'So what do you write about? Do you have a specialty?'

'I'm a staff writer,' said Jo. 'I graduated with first-class honours from Charles Sturt University, which is considered the best school of journalism in the country, and then I did my time around the regional papers, till I was offered a position with the *Trib*.'

He looked a little taken aback. 'Well, congratulations.'

What the hell was she doing? She sounded like an idiot. She didn't have to prove her credentials to him. Though for some reason Jo always felt she had to prove herself. Maybe it was the cute thing. She cleared her throat. 'Anyway, I was saying, I'm a staff writer, so I've written for just about every section of the newspaper.'

'And you won't tell me your name?'

'Nope,' she shook her head.

'But I might recognise it.'

There was every chance, and that was another reason to keep it to herself. She had mixed feelings about having her own column. Serious journalists didn't have columns called 'Bitch'. Though why she should give a rat's what he thought, she had no idea. He was a stranger. At least as soon as their incarceration was over, he'd go back to being a stranger, as long as she didn't tell him anything else about herself. It had probably been a bit of a slip revealing she was a journalist with the *Trib*. If she was completely honest she'd have to admit she was probably trying to impress him, prove there was a brain under this blonde pelt. But no matter. It wasn't too late, he couldn't trace her without a name. And Jo had flatly refused to have her picture at the top of her column, no matter how hard Leo had pushed for it. That had been a deal-breaker. She was not about to have her face labelled *Bitch* and then have to put up with any crazy on a train or a bus or in a nightclub calling out 'Hey bitch' across the crowd. No amount of column space was worth that.

'Hello, is anyone in there? Is there someone in the elevator?' a voice came over the intercom.

Joe sprang up to crouch in front of the speaker. 'Hi, yeah, hello. There's two of us in here.'

'Are you both okay – not hurt or crook or anything?'

He glanced at his cell mate and she just shrugged, yawning. The pills must have started to kick in. 'No, we're good.'

'Glad to hear it.'

'So how long is it going to take you to get us out?' Joe asked hopefully.

'I can't actually get you out, mate,' said the voice. 'I'm Mick, the building maintenance supervisor. We've just reported the breakdown. They said it could be up to an hour and a half before they can get a technician out.'

'But we already called . . . a while ago now.'

'They didn't say anything about that.'

Joe raised a vaguely accusing eyebrow at her, but she just shrugged again. 'Bastards.'

'So d'you reckon you're gunna be all right in there?' Mick continued. 'Do you need me to get a message to anyone?'

A message? Contact with the outside world? Jo went to speak up but she stopped herself in time. Bugger, she'd painted herself into a corner now. She didn't want to lose her anonymity in front of Scruffy. How would she handle this? She was trying to think of some kind of anonymous coded message that would make sense at the other end, when it occurred to her that no one knew where she was, and more than that, no one could reach her. Leo couldn't rouse on her for being late, Lachlan couldn't lecture her about keeping her phone charged. This wasn't her fault, she wasn't responsible, and she couldn't do a thing about it. There was something quite liberating about that.

He was watching her expectantly, waiting for an answer. She shook her head. 'No, no message.'

'Are you sure?' he asked. 'What about your meeting?'

Jo shrugged. 'I've got a pretty good excuse, right?'

He smiled, nodding. He turned back to the intercom. 'No, we'll be right, Mick, but we'd appreciate if they could hurry it along.'

'I'll call 'em back, see if I can't put some wind up their sails. I'll keep you posted.'

Jo was beginning to feel very relaxed. Unusually relaxed. In fact she was so relaxed, her head was becoming heavy. But her lower back was getting stiff in this position and her bum was going numb. She sidled away from the wall and swivelled around to lie flat on her back in the middle of the floor. The outside border of the floor was tiled but here in the middle it was carpeted, and much more comfortable.

'Are you feeling okay?' he asked.

'Wow, look at that . . .'

'What?' He shifted closer, craning his head to peer up the shaft.

'No, you have to lie down to get the full effect,' she said, grabbing hold of his shoulder and pushing him down so his head was beside hers, but he was lying in the opposite direction.

'Look how far up it goes.' She raised her arm and pointed up into the shaft, one eye closed. 'How far would that be, do you reckon?'

'Well, the building's thirty-two floors,' he said. 'And we're stopped, what, at around the eighth, tenth floor?' He paused for a moment. 'So I'd say . . . about . . . seventy-four metres.'

She glanced at him. 'How did you figure that?'

'Standard floor-to-ceiling height is around 2.7 metres, ceiling-to-floor cavity is a little under half a metre, times that total by the number of floors and it comes to approximately seventy-four metres, give or take.'

'Wow.' Jo was impressed. Numbers were not her thing, she was a wordsmith, after all. 'Are you an engineer or something?'

'No, I'm not an engineer.'

'But you sure are something!' Jo broke into a gentle rolling giggle. She turned her head to look at him. 'Oh dear, sorry about that. Are lame lines a side effect of those pills?'

He smiled. 'Not that I'm aware.'

She really was feeling incredibly relaxed now, as she stretched her arms up over her head. It was as though the stress of the last few days was unfurling up into the elevator shaft, like those twirling ribbons gymnasts used in their routines. That was a nice image, Jo mused, twirling whirly ribbons unfurling upwards into the shaft, taking all her cares and woes . . . What was that song . . . da da da . . . da da . . . da da . . . 'Bye Bye Blackbird'. Who sang that?

'Who sang 'Bye Bye Blackbird'?' she asked him suddenly.

He turned his head to look at her. His face was upside down. How did he do that?

'Sorry?'

'You don't have to be sorry,' said Jo. 'You held the lift.'

He was frowning now. Upside down. Which should have looked like a smile. Wasn't that how the saying went? A frown is an upside-down smile. Or was it a smile is an upside-down frown? What was the point of that saying, anyway?

'Are you all right?' he was asking her.

Jo blinked a few times. Had she said any of that out loud? She roused herself, looking at him. Upside down. She felt dizzy again. 'Would you mind turning around?' she asked. 'I'm going a little cock-eyed.'

He smiled, then shifted out of her view, returning to lie beside her, right side up, still smiling. That was better. He had a nice smile, Jo decided. And nice eyes. Very blue, very striking. Maybe that was only in contrast to their setting. If he cleaned himself up, had a shave, washed his hair and got it cut properly, put on some decent clothes . . . well, he might not be half bad looking, she suspected.

She sighed contentedly, gazing back up the shaft. 'What if the roof wasn't in the way,' she mused. 'How far do you think we'd be able to see then?'

'I read somewhere that the most distant galaxy is over thirteen billion light-years away.'

'Mm, was that in *Geek Weekly*?'

He glanced at her sideways. 'You don't find stuff like that interesting?'

'Vaguely, but I can't even comprehend what thirteen billion light-years is,' said Jo. 'People get all worked up about the universe and what's out there, but what about what's right here. The world is enormous. Forget about outer space, you couldn't even get around this planet in a whole lifetime.'

'That's true.'

'I wish I'd seen more of it.'

'We're not going to die in here, you know.'

'I know,' she elbowed him. 'But I'm still not going to see much of it in my lifetime, I reckon.'

'Why do you say that?'

'I think I've left my run a bit late.'

'What are you talking about? What are you, late twenties, thirty?'

He was playing it safe, underestimating, but she wasn't going to confirm or deny.

'You've got your whole life ahead of you,' he insisted.

'Which should give me just enough time to pay off my mortgage,' she said. 'I just bought a place, moved in yesterday.'

'So you said,' he nodded. 'Where did you move to?'

'The city, a few blocks away in fact.'

'Congratulations. You must be feeling good?'

She shrugged. 'The mortgage part's a little daunting.'

'You shouldn't let that bother you,' said Joe. 'I was a bit the same when I took out my first mortgage, but after a while you don't even think about it any more. The money comes out of the bank the same as if it was rent. It's really not that big a deal. What's the worst that could happen?'

'What's the worst that could happen?' Jo repeated, incredulous.

'Yeah,' he said guilelessly.

'Oh, let me see,' she began, 'I could get sick or have an accident or lose my job and default on the repayments so I'd have no choice but to sell. And if any of that happened in the next few years before I've been able to recoup my costs and increase my equity, and without a considerable boom in the property market, then I would in all likelihood end up out of pocket. But what's probably the very worst that could happen is interest rates going up so high that I can't afford the repayments. If I was forced to sell when there's high interest rates, property prices are more likely to slump, so I probably wouldn't even get back what I paid for my place, which means I'd still owe money but I wouldn't have anywhere to live.'

'Wow.' He was shaking his head. 'You've really thought of every possible thing that could go wrong, haven't you?'

'I think it's wise to be prepared for the worst.'

'I don't know about wise,' he muttered. 'Pessimistic maybe.'

He was hardly the first person to accuse her of that.

'You should chill a bit,' Joe went on. 'Most people would be happy to own their own place . . . actually, most people in the world would be happy to have a meal once a day.'

Well, that was certainly putting her in her place. But when she glanced at him, he didn't look like he was judging her. He looked . . . like he was trying to reassure her.

'So what did you say your name was again?' he asked.

Jo smiled. 'I didn't.' She looked sideways at him. 'You're persistent.'

'So I've been told.'

She gazed back up the shaft. 'Funny thing is, I don't even use my real name.'

'Pardon?'

'I don't go by the name I was given at birth.'

'Why not?'

'Because I changed it.'

'Really?' He turned his head to look at her. 'Why would you do that?'

'You'd understand if you heard it.'

'Okay . . . let me have it.'

'I'm not telling you,' said Jo. 'I never tell anyone my real name.'

'Oh come on, how bad could it be?'

'Oh, it's bad.'

'I don't believe you.'

'I don't care.'

Joe regarded her thoughtfully. 'You don't strike me as someone who'd be bothered by something like that. I would have thought you'd wear it with pride and challenge anyone to make fun of it.'

'Not this name,' she muttered. 'There's nothing you can do but make fun of it.'

'You're not being a little dramatic? I bet you most people wouldn't even blink if they heard it.'

'Yeah, because their eyes would be popping out of their heads in disbelief.'

'Oh, come on,' he said dubiously. 'So it's Gertrude or Ethel or something –'

She grunted. 'I wish.'

He looked at her, shaking his head. 'I'm sorry, I just don't believe there's a name so bad that it's worth changing it. It's your identity, after all. It shapes you, to some degree it –'

'It's Bambi,' she blurted.

Joe blinked. 'I'm sorry?'

'My real name is, or was, Bambi.'

He looked at her, incredulous. 'You're kidding me.'

'This is what I've been trying to tell you.'

'I don't believe you,' he said. 'Show me your driver's licence.'

'I will not. I told you, I don't go by that name now.'

'So you changed it legally?'

'Wouldn't you?'

'Well, I'd look pretty ridiculous with a name like Bambi, but you could get away with it.'

'If I was an exotic dancer. Not if I want to be taken seriously as a journalist. Can you imagine the by-line?'

He smiled at her. 'So what's your by-line now?'

Jo opened her mouth and then stopped. 'Aha, nearly got me.'

He sighed. 'Bambi. That really is bad.'

'My sister had it worse.'

'Don't tell me she's called Thumper?'

Jo laughed. 'We used to joke about that, but no, she was named Tinkerbell.'

'You're making that up.'

'I swear,' she said, holding her hand to her heart. 'Clearly my mother should never have been allowed to have children.'

It was true. Charlene Liddell had had no idea how to parent her girls – she was barely more than a girl herself when she had them – but she had certainly loved playing with them. And dressing them up, like they were dolls. She used to put them in matching outfits with ribbons in their hair and frills on their socks, but Jo complained so relentlessly that her mother finally gave up when she was about six and let her choose her own clothes. But it wasn't till she read *Little Women* that she found a female character she could relate to. She wanted to be just like Jo. She would be a writer. She would travel the world. She would be strong and independent. She would cut off all her hair. Jo had never seen her mother's face so white as the day she came into the bathroom to find her blonde curls littered all over the floor. The curls never grew back, and Jo never answered to Bambi again.

'Do you really mean that?'

'What?' said Jo, stirring.

'That your mum shouldn't have been allowed to have children?'

Did she say that? 'Oh, she was just too young . . . and stupid,' Jo dismissed. 'I shouldn't complain, I wouldn't be here if she hadn't been. Nor would most of us . . . be here, you know, if people weren't young and stupid . . . generally.' She probably could have put that better.

'What about your father?'

'He left when I was four.'

'Oh. Did you see him after that?'

Jo shook her head. 'According to my mother, he left because we didn't behave. I'd try to be good so he'd come back, but we were always butting heads, my mother and I. She used to say "See? This is why your father won't come back. He never wanted you in the first place, you think he's gunna put up with this behaviour?"'

He was just staring at her, his eyes drowning in pathos.

'Oh, don't look like that,' Jo dismissed. 'I know it's crap, I've had the therapy. My mother was a nut job, still is.'

Jo had consoled herself for a while there with the idea that she must have been adopted; nothing else would explain the utter disparity between her and Charlene. It had been suggested more than once that the problem was they were too much alike, but Jo would not have a bar of that. They certainly looked nothing alike. Jo reckoned she looked like her dad, in the one picture she had managed to salvage before her mother burned the rest. 'The bastard's never coming back,' Charlene had declared as she lit a cigarette then tossed the match onto a kero-soaked pile of his stuff in the backyard. Jo's dreams shrivelled up in the flames that day too. Dreams of a tall, handsome father who'd come back from the war – not that she knew of any particular wars that Australia was involved in at the time, but it had to be something noble to have kept him away so long. He would stride into the house and scoop up his girls, one in each arm, and take them away from the cheerless, tenuous existence that was their childhood. Different towns, different houses, different schools, different men. A lot of different men. But because her father was quite extraordinary, he would forgive Charlene and give her another chance, and they would be a normal family again.

'Did your father keep in touch?' Joe asked.

'He phoned a few times,' said Jo, 'but Mum wouldn't let him speak to us, she was too busy yelling at him. He soon stopped calling.'

Not such a princess after all. 'So your mother brought you up on her own?'

'In a manner of speaking,' said Jo. 'She got over being a single parent pretty quickly, and she decided she wanted her life back. She started going out at night, leaving me to look after Belle.'

'How old were you?'

'Eight or nine.' Jo shrugged at his incredulous expression. 'It wasn't so bad, it was better than when she brought men home. It was when she didn't come home – sometimes for days at a time . . .' Jo's voice trailed off. The first time it had happened she was eleven. When she woke up and realised her mother wasn't there, Jo felt the greatest sense of panic. What if she never came home again, like their father? What if she was dead? What would happen to them? But she couldn't upset Belle, so she closed their mother's bedroom door and said she was sleeping in, which was certainly not out of the ordinary. Then she made breakfast and packed their lunches, and surreptitiously unlocked one window before they left for school so that they would be able to get back in, just in case. But Charlene was there when they got home, and when Jo held onto her for a long time, she firmly detached her and told her not to make such a fuss. So Jo never made a fuss after that. She taught herself to cook, use the washing machine, iron, and forge her mother's signature for school notes. She became adept at pilfering small amounts of money, undetected, from her mother's purse so she always had emergency funds for food and school excursions and the like. And she had a key cut. By the time she was twelve, Jo had the routine down pat and could manage quite well on her own for up to three or four days at a time.

'Your mother left you on your own for *days at a time*?' Joe was asking.

She saw the mixture of horror and pity in his eyes. Jo had seen that look before, which is why she never talked about it any more. She wasn't sure what had made her talk about it now. Probably those pills, they were like a verbal laxative. Well, that was enough personal disclosure for one day. For a year.

She shrugged. 'Who hasn't had a crappy childhood?'

'Me,' Joe said without hesitation.

She looked at him. 'Not even a little crappy?'

'Not even a little. Not one minute of it.'

Jo had an idea he was seeing the past through a pretty powerful pair of your rose-coloured variety glasses. Nobody's childhood was *that* happy. But who was she to shatter his delusions.

'So, I guess you were lucky then,' was all she said.

'It shouldn't have anything to do with luck,' said Joe. 'It should be a birthright. I've seen people in the third world who have nothing, yet they give their children everything that matters – their time, love, attention. And here we have everything, but parents can't seem to give their children what they need the most.'

Jo was watching him. She didn't know what to say, she'd clearly hit a sore point.

'Sorry,' he said, noticing the expression on her face. 'I'm preaching, aren't I?'

'Little bit.'

Joe smiled self-consciously. 'Hazard of the profession.'

She frowned. 'Are you a priest or something?'

He laughed then. 'No, I'm not a priest, or anything.'

'Thank God for that.'

'You're thanking God that I'm not a priest? That's a little ironic.'

'Is it?' Jo mused. 'Strictly speaking, I mean. I shouldn't admit this, being a writer, but irony's a hard one to pin down, don't you find? I can never quite put my finger on it.'

'Best example I know is Alanis Morissette's song "Ironic".'

'No, that's the thing,' said Jo. 'It's not ironic if it rains on your wedding day, it's just bad luck. That song isn't about irony at all.'

'Which makes it ironic, don't you think?'

She grinned. She'd have to remember that one, she could probably get a column out of it. 'Okay, so, ironically or otherwise, you're not a priest and you're not an engineer, and you're clearly not an elevator technician, or a stalker who preys on unsuspecting women . . .'

'Definitely not.'

'So what do you do?'

He looked at her. 'What happened to "no names, no pack drill"?'

'I'm not asking for your name, and I told you what I do for a living.'

Joe sighed loudly, stretching his arms out in front of him before tucking them behind his head. 'You know what, I bet you couldn't guess if we were here all day.'

'Oh?' He'd done it now. Jo could never resist a challenge, especially when she was told she couldn't do something. Besides, she'd written a feature piece on unusual occupations only last year. He didn't stand a chance. 'You're on.'

'Okay, what are the stakes?'

She pulled a face. 'We don't have to actually bet, do we?'

'I think it makes it more interesting,' said Joe. 'How about if you guess I have to buy you a drink when we get out of here?'

'This time of the morning?'

'It doesn't have to be as soon as we get out,' he said. 'I'll take a raincheck.'

'What if I don't guess?' Jo asked,

'Then you have to buy me a drink.'

That sounded like he was winning either way. What did it matter, no names, no pack drill. She was never going to see him again anyway. But that didn't mean she didn't want to win.

'Deal,' said Jo, offering her hand to shake on it. He smiled, gazing at her with those very blue eyes in a slightly unsettling way, as he took her hand in his and held it just a moment longer than was altogether necessary. Jo turned her head to look back up the shaft, slipping her hand out of his at the same time.

'Private investigator?' she began, starting with the uncommon but not exactly weird.

He shook his head.

'Undertaker?'

'No.'

'Greeting card writer?'

A faint chuckle, followed by another 'No'.

'Department-store Santa Claus?'

He slapped his stomach. 'I could be offended, but the answer's no.'

'Condom tester?'

'I certainly hope not. No one told me if that's what I was supposed to be doing.'

Jo rolled her eyes. 'Stand-up comedian?'

'What do you think?'

'Circus performer?'

'Nope.'

'Chicken sexer?'

'A what?'

'I'll take that as a no.'

'At the rate you're going you might as well assume no unless I say otherwise,' Joe said dryly.

'Okay . . .' Jo ran through the list. 'Beekeeper . . . bull inseminator . . . snake-venom milker . . .'

He rolled onto his side, propping his head on his hand so he could look down at her. 'You're a journalist and this is how you go about it?'

'What do you mean?'

'Well, you may as well go through the alphabet to find out what letter it starts with.'

She hadn't thought of that.

'Where's your investigative skills, woman?'

'I've got investigative skills,' Jo defended. 'In fact, I did an article on unusual occupations once –'

'No kidding?' he said drolly. 'Look, just because I said you'd never guess, doesn't mean my job has to be bizarre. You made a pretty huge assumption there.'

Jo frowned. 'So it's not bizarre . . . or unusual?'

'Not at all.'

'Well, you could have said.'

'I believe I just did.'

Okay, this was a whole new ball game. 'Are you here in the building for work?' Jo asked.

'That's more like it,' he said, lying flat on his back again. 'I'm actually here to catch up with an old friend.' He was still going to make her work for it.

She sighed. Then she glanced sideways at him. 'Would you dress like that for work?'

'Like this?' he said, looking down at himself. 'Sure, maybe, it all depends. Sometimes I wear a suit, sometimes I work in my pyjamas. I've had to wear all kinds of get-ups in the line of duty. I've even worn a wetsuit.'

'To work?'

'*For* work might be a better way of putting it.'

'You're not a marine biologist or something?'

'No, the wetsuit was a one-off.'

Jo thought about it. 'Are you an actor?'

'No, not an actor,' he smiled. 'Funny you should say that, my brother's an actor, or at least he wants to be.'

'Aren't they all wannabes?' said Jo. 'I did an article once on employment rates in the entertainment industry . . . or should I say, unemployment rates. It's woeful, it's like ninety-seven percent. Why would anyone go into it? All those poor sods paying a fortune to go through NIDA just to staff the hospitality industry. My best friend's an actor. She's been working in a sandwich shop for years, going to auditions, waiting for her big break, for any break. I can't believe how blindly optimistic actors must be.'

'I don't know if my brother's all that optimistic,' said Joe. 'Unrealistic, idealistic, nihilistic maybe. Definitely hedonistic.'

'That's a lot of tics,' Jo remarked.

'He's all right, he's just a little irresponsible. Youngest of five.'

She nodded, watching him. 'And you're the eldest, right?'

He glanced at her. 'How did you know that?'

Something about the way he snapped into responsible mode when she freaked out, Jo thought, but all she said was, 'Takes one to know one.'

Joe smiled. So that explained why she was so bossy. 'How many siblings?' he asked.

'Just my sister.'

'Tinkerbell.'

'That's the one. Though she prefers to be known as Belle these days.'

'So is she an irresponsible youngest child?'

Jo shook her head. 'No, she's married with three kids under three. She hasn't got time to be irresponsible, so she keeps telling me, ad nauseam.'

'Do I detect a little sibling friction?'

'No, not really,' said Jo. 'I love her to death, I think she's amazing. But she thinks I look down on her for being a stay-at-home mum, which is absolutely not the case. But for some reason, people think that if you make different choices to them that means you don't approve of their choices.'

Joe turned his head to look at her. 'You don't want kids?'

'I don't know,' she sighed. 'That's the sixty-four thousand dollar question, isn't it? For women at least. I know I'm not ready right now, I still have things I want to do . . . I guess it depends if all the planets align at the right time.'

'And if they don't?'

'Then *c'est la vie.*'

'That's an unusually healthy attitude for a woman.'

Jo looked at him. 'What does that mean?'

'Only that most of the women I meet are obsessed by their biological clocks without ever thinking through their options.'

She shrugged. 'Maybe I'm just avoiding the decision. Sometimes I'm at my sister's place and the kids are all jumping around and screaming and banging things, and I just want to scream back at them to shut up. But Belle and her husband seem oblivious. I don't know if I could do it.'

Truth be told, Jo was a little terrified of having babies. Newborns particularly freaked her out, she was not at all sure she wanted that kind of responsibility. She often wondered why hospitals didn't keep babies till that hole in their heads closed up at least.

But her real fear was that she wouldn't be able to love a baby, wouldn't know how to be a proper mum; she hadn't exactly had the best role model.

'You're one of five, did you say?' Jo asked him. 'Your mother must have been a saint . . . or was she the one who put you onto those drugs?'

He laughed. 'No, she was great, my mum. We lived in a big rambling house on a big rambling block up in the Blue Mountains. My dad was away a lot for work, and she let us run free. But she could pull us into line with a single word. Sometimes she didn't even have to say a word, we could tell by the look in her eye.' Joe was smiling fondly, remembering her . . . missing her.

'So if you're the oldest, and the thespian's the youngest, who's in between?' Jo asked.

'Three sisters.'

'Three sisters from the Blue Mountains? Are you making this up?'

'No, I actually have three sisters,' he assured her. 'Hilary comes after me, she's in the US, teaching at MIT in Boston. Corinne lives in Melbourne and works in publishing, and my baby sister, Mim – Miriam – she's a poet.'

'Wow, that's an impressive line-up,' Jo remarked. 'So you're the big disappointment of the family?'

'Huge,' he replied without missing a beat. 'They don't know where they went wrong with me.'

'Maybe if they'd taught you how to iron your clothes . . .'

Joe just smiled. He liked her sense of humour, even if he was the punchline most of the time. He decided he could have done a hell of a lot worse than be stuck in an elevator with Ms No-name-no-pack-drill.

'So, are you married?' he asked.

'Pardon?' said Jo. Where did that come from?

'Are you married?'

'What kind of a question is that?'

'Just the regular kind. What's the problem?'

'It sounds like a pick-up line.'

Joe laughed then. 'Yeah, well, see, I couldn't use "Do you come here often?".'

'I do, as a matter of fact,' she replied archly. 'Tuesday to Saturday, morning and afternoon, often in between as well.'

'So you're not going to answer my question?'

She sighed. 'No, I'm not married . . . any more.'

'Oh, so you have been married?'

Why the hell did she say that? Hadn't she vowed no more personal disclosure? Okay, keep it brief and vague.

'I was one of those young stupid people,' she said, 'but fortunately I didn't bring a child onto the sinking ship, and I bailed out before the ink was dry on the marriage certificate. What about you?'

'What about me?'

'Are you married?'

'Nope.'

'Never?'

He shook his head. 'Does that make me sound like a hopeless loser or a commitment-phobe?'

'You tell me,' Jo returned.

'I wouldn't say I'm either, I think I'm just a victim of circumstance.'

'Interesting way of putting it,' she said. 'Sounds much better than hopeless loser or commitment-phobe.'

He grinned. 'Honestly, I'm not afraid of commitment; in fact, I think I'd really like to commit to someone. It just has to be the right someone.'

Jo wasn't sure why he was giving her the sales pitch. And it was making her slightly uncomfortable. 'It's all a bit of a furphy though, don't you think?'

'What is?'

'Marriage,' she said simply. 'It started off as a commercial arrangement, but once women no longer needed a dowry to get a bloke, Hollywood had to invent another reason to be bothered. Thus the notion of falling in love and finding your soul mate and all that hooey.'

'I think "all that hooey" was around long before Hollywood,' Joe suggested. 'What about Jane Austen, all the Romantic poets, Shakespeare . . .'

'Shakespeare wasn't romantic.'

'What do you call *Romeo and Juliet*?'

'A tragedy,' Jo declared. 'They're both dead at the end, and for no good reason.'

'You're missing the point,' he exclaimed. 'Romeo and Juliet is all about love, the kind of blinding passion that will make you risk everything, even your life.' He paused. 'Have you read any of Shakespeare's sonnets?'

'Probably, under duress, at school.'

'Well, I challenge you to read number twenty-nine and still believe that love is a fabrication of Hollywood.'

'Are you an English teacher?' she asked suspiciously.

He smiled. 'No.'

Jo yawned loudly and stretched. She was suddenly feeling quite sleepy, but she wasn't throwing in the towel yet.

'Is your job your dream job?' she asked, taking a different tack. 'Is it what you always imagined you'd do?'

'Yeah, pretty much. What about you?'

'Hmm, pretty much as well,' she mused. 'Though I did always dream of becoming a foreign correspondent.'

Joe turned his head sharply to look at her. 'What?'

'You don't have to look so shocked,' she returned. 'It's the blonde thing again, isn't it?'

'No, no, it's not,' he said. 'Really. So why didn't you become a foreign correspondent?'

She sighed. 'Long story. Belle and I moved down to Sydney when I was only about a year into my degree. I had to support her till she got a job, so it took me a lot longer to graduate, then I had to start to build my career . . .'

And then she'd settled in at the *Trib*, and now she'd bought the apartment, and dreams of being a foreign correspondent had drifted into a dusty corner of her subconscious. Until something like an Iraq or a Hurricane Katrina made her wonder all over again what it would be like to be over there in the thick of it, where she couldn't help but be regarded as a serious journalist.

'So what's stopping you now?' he was asking.

'Hmm?'

'I imagine your sister can probably look after herself at this stage, so what's stopping you from becoming a foreign correspondent now?'

'Well, I have a mortgage . . .'

'I've got a mortgage and it's never stopped me from travelling and working overseas.'

'Ahah!' said Jo. 'Another clue.'

'I already told you that I just got back from working overseas for a few years.'

'So you did.' She was beginning to have trouble keeping her eyes open. She gave her head a little shake. 'Okay,' she said, 'I'm thinking you must do something creative, coming out of that gene pool. Are you a musician?'

'I can play a little guitar, but no one would pay to listen.'

'What about an artist?'

He shook his head.

'A sculptor?'

'Same diff, isn't it? But no to both.'

Jo yawned again. Her eyes were starting to sting in this fluorescent light. She might close them, just for a moment, give them a rest. Where was she? 'Mmm . . . web designer?'

'No way,' he said with a sudden hearty laugh.

'What's so funny?' she said sleepily.

'The idea of me being a web designer,' said Joe, shaking his head. 'I'm only as technologically proficient as I absolutely have to be to get by. Beyond that I haven't got a clue. Computers, mobile phones, satellite phones even, all useful, essential in fact in my line of work, which by the way you haven't guessed yet. That drink is looking like a sure thing.'

She didn't say anything.

'And don't think I'm going to let you get out of it,' he went on. 'A deal's a deal, after all.'

When she still hadn't said anything for a moment, Joe looked across at her. Her face was turned away from him. He lifted himself on one elbow and looked down at her. Christ, she'd passed out.

'Hey, hey . . .' he said, giving her a gentle nudge. No response. 'Hey . . . *hey princess*,' he said, a little louder, with a slightly firmer nudge. But she didn't stir, not so much as a peep. She was out cold. Joe sat upright and took hold of her wrist to check her pulse. He hoped she wasn't having some kind of reaction to the drugs. He watched her breathing steadily, and after a minute was satisfied that her pulse was normal. He supposed he should just let her sleep it off. But this was certainly going to look interesting when someone eventually came to the rescue.

'*Hello in there.*'

Speak of the devil.

'Is everything all right?' It was Mick. 'Technician's arrived. We should have you out of there in no time.'

5 pm

'So did you bang her?'

Joe was opening a bottle of beer and he looked up with a jerk. 'What?'

'You're stuck in a lift with a cute blonde,' said Will. 'You're both consenting adults with an hour and a half to kill and no chance of being caught . . .'

Joe passed his brother the beer, speechless.

'Never let an opportunity pass you by, old man,' Will added with a wink.

'Now I feel old,' said Joe, shaking his head.

'Don't get so holier than thou, Joe. I still remember you, all the girls. You would have banged her ten years ago.'

'No, Will, I wouldn't have.'

'Why not?

'Because I've got class, little brother. Something you can only dream about.'

Will grinned. 'I think I know who's dreaming.'

They clinked their bottles together.

'To coming home,' said Joe.

'Happy landings.'

Joe had bought a slab on the way back to the flat because he knew if he didn't show up with beer, Will would drag him out to some noisy pub, and he wasn't up to it. Maybe he was getting old, but it had been a tiring day – surprising and unexpectedly pleasant in parts, at least the part inside the elevator – but tiring nonetheless. He wasn't used to long lunches any more, and he was still jet-lagged. He had to get a good night's sleep tonight. Because of the hiccup today, he was going to have to go back to the office again tomorrow to meet the staff, at least those he hadn't met already, and be formally introduced. He was expected first thing, and then he'd finally head up to Leura. Joe glanced at his watch, he really should give Mim a call soon.

'So how was Dad last time you saw him?' he asked Will as they settled themselves on the couch.

He shrugged. 'The same.'

Joe narrowed his eyes. 'The same as what?'

Will hesitated. 'Oh, you know . . .'

'No, I don't know. I've been away for two years, remember.'

'But you write to him, like, every day, don't you?'

'Yeah but I haven't seen him, Will. I want to be prepared.'

Will sighed. 'He's the same, what can I tell you? He's pretty thin, he can't get around much. Stays on the computer all the time, seems to keep him happy.'

Joe met his gaze directly. 'When's the last time you went to see him, Will?'

'I dunno, a while, I've had a lot on . . .'

Joe rubbed his forehead. He wasn't going to start scolding Will like he was still a child. He just wished he didn't so often act like one.

'You haven't been leaving everything to Mim, have you?' he asked.

'What else has she got to do anyway?'

'She has her work.'

'The world will go on if she doesn't finish one of her poems, you know.'

'Don't be a dickhead, Will, it's her thing.'

'Yeah, well how come no one takes my "thing" seriously?' said Will. 'Mim can waste her life in an ivory tower writing poems no one's going to read, but I'm treated like a fool when I want to follow my dream of being an actor.'

'You're being a jerk, Will. Mim isn't wasting her life. That's unfair and you know it.'

Mim Bannister had won a swag of poetry prizes in Australia, as well as some overseas, and her work had been published extensively, but it was hardly a lucrative industry. Most people in her situation would be teaching at university, but Mim was far too timid.

'No one's treating you like a fool, Will,' Joe went on. 'You can follow your dreams and still do your share with Dad.'

'Unlike you, or Hil, or Corinne. You all get off scot-free.'

Joe sighed heavily. 'I wanted to stay. You know it was Dad who insisted that I go.'

'Yeah, because what you do is so "important",' said Will, making the quotation marks with his fingers.

'I'm not so sure about that,' Joe muttered, picking at the label on his bottle.

'But Dad is,' said Will. 'Whereas he thinks I'm just wasting my time.'

'He loves you, Will. He's only worried about you.'

'He still treats me like the baby.'

'He's your dad, he's never going to stop worrying about you. That's his job. And your job, if you don't want to be treated like the baby, is to start acting like a grown-up and take some of the responsibility from your sister.'

Joe took a swig of his beer. God he hated when he realised he was lecturing, such a typical big brother thing to do, and he slipped into it so easily around Will. He looked across at him. He was a man; Joe had no right telling him what to do. 'Okay, end of lecture. That's my one and only, I promise.'

'Thank Christ for that,' Will muttered. 'So when are you head-ing up home?'

'Tomorrow. Wanna come?'

Will sighed, considering. 'I'll give you a few days, might join you later.'

Joe nodded, taking another swig of his beer. 'So, what's going on for you? Been treading any boards lately?'

Will launched into a scattered account of the past few months: this audition, that call-back, helping out a friend who was mak-ing a short film, plans for an amateur theatre company he and a bunch of other actors were attempting to get off the ground. Joe knew he was only giving him the edited highlights, and that a lot of Will's time was spent sitting around consuming alcohol and other substances and bemoaning the lack of funding for the arts in Australia. Which was probably a fair point, but it was unlikely to change any time soon, so Joe just wished he would get over this and get a real job . . . God, that really was his inner big brother talking.

As Will rattled on, Joe found his mind drifting. Her friend was an actor, she'd said, the girl in the elevator. He wondered if Will knew her, had ever come across her. That would be a weird coincidence. He wondered where she was now. Had she woken up? Surely she had by this time. He hoped she was feeling all right, he should have called the office to find out. Maybe he still should? Would she remember him . . . she must remember him, but what would she remember *about* him? Would she be self-conscious, upset, outraged? He wondered what she was thinking right this minute . . .

5:17 pm

Jo opened her eyes suddenly, blinking. She'd woken herself up with a snore. Her mouth was open, her throat felt dry, though there was a little dribble spilling over the edge of her lip. Her cheek was pressed against a smooth, leather-like surface. Or more like stuck. Jo moved her head slowly to allow her skin to peel off. Where was she? She squinted, blinking some more. She rolled over onto her back, waiting for her eyes to adjust to the dimly lit room.

Was this Leo's office? Jo sat bolt upright, but then she felt light-headed. She swung her legs off the couch and dropped her head to her knees, breathing slowly and deeply till the sensation subsided. She lifted her head again, gradually this time, and looked around. This was Leo's office. What was she doing asleep on the couch in Leo's office?

Images slowly began to come back to her. The elevator, it broke down, and the scruffy man. The big, scruffy bear of a man. He was nice though, she remembered, he was kind to her . . . they were talking . . . lying on the floor, looking up through the shaft . . .

Then what happened? How did they get out? She couldn't remember anything more. She closed her eyes tight, as though she could squeeze the memory out, but nothing came. Go back to the beginning. She got in the lift. The man was already there, he held the door for her, but he said sorry anyway. One ninety-five centimetres tall, ninety kilos, checked shirt, old jeans, blue eyes. Very blue eyes. Why did she look so deeply into his eyes? That's right, she started having a panic attack, he knocked out the ceiling panel and . . .

He drugged her!

Oh my God! Jo's heart started to race. He drugged her! She remembered taking the pills from his hand. Okay, so he didn't exactly force them on her, but what were they anyway? They must have knocked her out cold . . . What happened after that?

Jo jumped to her feet, checking herself over frantically. She was fully dressed, everything seemed to be in place, her shirt wasn't on inside out or anything odd, her buttons were all done up properly. She noticed her bag on the floor by the couch and she snatched it up, rummaging through the contents. Her wallet was still there, cards, cash, everything, her phone. She sank back into the couch, staring out in front of her, trying to remember . . .

Where was Leo anyway? What time was it? She glanced at her watch but her eyes were still hazy and she couldn't see the hands clearly in the dim light. Was it nearly half past two, or ten past five? Surely it couldn't be . . . she'd lost a whole day? Doing what? Lying here on Leo's couch? Lying on the floor of an elevator? How did she get out? A repulsed shiver ran through her. She hated the thought that she had been watched, that people had gathered around, that someone had hoisted her up, maybe two people, one holding her arms and one her legs, with her slung between them like a hammock . . .

Enough. She stood up, straightening her clothes and smoothing back her hair. She had to find out, and if that meant some amused looks, raised eyebrows, even sneers, then so be it. She couldn't hide in here forever. She picked up her bag and walked briskly to the door.

'Oh, you're up!' said Judith, swivelling around in her chair as the door opened. Judith was Leo's perpetually good-natured and highly efficient assistant. How she remained so determinedly sunny working directly under Leo had always been a mystery to Jo.

'How are you feeling?' she asked.

Jo cleared her throat. 'Fine, I'm fine,' she said, crossing over to Judith's desk. 'Um, how long . . . Have I been out, um, asleep, for long?'

'Yes, most of the day, Jo,' Judith said brightly. 'You must have needed it, after your move, that's all I can say. Exhaustion catches up with us all. You can't outrun mother nature, I've always –'

'Judith,' Jo interrupted.

She looked up, eyebrows raised, waiting.

'Um,' Jo began, rather cluelessly. She wanted to know how she had got to the couch, but she also didn't want to know. 'Where is Leo, by the way?' she asked instead.

'Long lunch,' said Judith with a conspiratorial nod. 'You know what it's like with old friends. We won't be seeing him back at work this afternoon. That's why he suggested his office was the best place to let you sleep it off.'

Jo nodded. That didn't tell her anything. There was nothing she could do but just come out with it. 'Well, here's the thing, Judith, I'm a bit unclear as to how I even got there . . .' She waved her hand vaguely towards Leo's office.

'Oh, he carried you, of course.'

'Leo?' Jo was stunned. Leo was not a big man. In fact, Leo was a small man. Bigger than her, of course, that was no feat. How on earth had he managed to carry her?

'No, not Leo.' Judith was clearly amused by the idea. 'Leo could never pick you up, let alone carry you all the way through the office. Not that I'm suggesting you're heavy in any way,' she was quick to add. 'Of course not, Jo, look at you, you're just a petite little thing, but your friend's quite a big fellow. "Built" I think they call it, don't they?' She almost swooned. 'He carried you through here like you were barely more than a child in his arms.'

Jo felt nauseous. 'He's not my "friend", I don't even know him, he's a total stranger,' she blurted.

'Oh, I hardly think you can call him that. After –'

'After what?' she said indignantly. 'I don't know what he told you, but nothing happened, absolutely nothing. We just talked, that's all, filled in time. That's all there was to it. And as I'm a trusted long-time employee here I think it's my word that should be taken over anything he might have said.'

Judith looked a little perplexed at her outburst.

'Anyway,' Jo went on, composing herself. 'I barely remember him and I have no interest in remembering him. I don't want to talk about him, I just want to know why I had to be . . . carried, exactly?'

'Because you couldn't be woken, of course,' Judith said matter-of-factly.

'So I was asleep?'

'Well, yes . . . no, not asleep as such,' she said. 'Mr . . . um – the person you don't want to talk about – explained that he gave you some pills to help you calm down.'

Jo groaned inwardly. She saw a circle of her colleagues, people she still had to work with, standing around as he regaled them with her panic attack, perhaps even acting it out, everyone laughing hysterically . . . But he wouldn't do something like that, would he?

What the hell did she know? Nothing, she knew absolutely nothing about the man. And she'd taken drugs from him, drugs that had knocked her out cold and erased her memory. Or part of it. She had to find out what he had given her. And she had to find out how many people had seen her wasted and probably drooling, slumped in his arms as he carried her through the office.

'He left a note,' Judith was saying, holding up a scrap of paper.

'What?' Jo stirred, snatching it from her a little too eagerly. But there was just two words written on it: multisyllabic, virtually unpronounceable pharmaceutical terms. Inexplicably, her heart sank.

'That's the name of the pills you took,' said Judith. 'He thought you should know, so you can look them up on the Net, reassure yourself. He said you should check with your doctor if you're not feeling right though.' She paused. 'He did seem genuinely concerned . . . and really, well, very nice.'

And all he'd written on the note was the name of a drug.

'Jo, is everything okay?' Judith asked.

'Sure, I'm fine,' she said vaguely. 'Um, I'd better go, get some work done.'

'Leo thought you wouldn't be up to it,' said Judith. 'And it is nearly five-thirty. But he did want me to tell you that obviously the meeting had to be rescheduled, so it will be at nine sharp tomorrow morning. I think he said take the stairs if you have to. But I'm sure he was only joking.'

Why was it *obvious* that the meeting had to be rescheduled? He wouldn't have rescheduled it just for her, never. Unless he planned to make some kind of example of her. That would be just like Leo.

But she'd been trapped in an elevator, what kind of an example could he make out of that? Maybe taking the stairs wasn't a joke after all.

Jo caught the lift to the floor below, and wandered listlessly across the news floor maze to her desk. The place was almost deserted. It was only Thursday, the pressure wasn't on yet, it would start getting frenetic tomorrow when everyone realised there was only one more day after that to pull the paper together. By Saturday it would be mayhem. But now there was just the odd person working quietly away, oblivious to Jo passing by. She plonked down on her chair and stared at her computer monitor for a while, before it occurred to her to turn it on. She sat back, her mind drifting, inevitably, to the man in the elevator. A little more detail, some flashes of conversation, were coming back to her. His job, they'd talked about his job. What did he say it was? Something unusual, a private investigator . . . an actor maybe?

She looked down at the scrap of paper still in her hand. Two words in block letters, so she couldn't even discern much from his handwriting. The lettering was large and the hand heavy; you'd assume it was probably written by a male, but that was about all you could assume. Couldn't he have added something a little personal? Even 'Regards . . .' What was his name? Had he said?

No names, no pack drill. Jo had insisted that, she remembered now. But considering how things had ended up, couldn't he have left his name and phone number on the note, in case she wanted to contact him about the drugs? Would that have been such an invasion of his privacy? Or was he just relieved he could remain anonymous and get the hell out of there before she woke up?

Jo looked up as the computer screen came to life. It suddenly occurred to her that he probably did leave his details with Judith. Of course he did. He didn't have to write them on the piece of paper, Judith had already taken them down, as a matter of course. He'd only written the name of the drug to save spelling it out to her. Why hadn't Judith just said she had his name and phone number?

Because Jo had told her to stop talking about him.

So, if she went back now and asked Judith for his details, would that seem odd? Maybe if she waited till tomorrow . . . She could look up the drug now, she decided, typing the words into Google. And tomorrow she could go casually to Judith and say she had some questions she wanted to run by him.

Jo sighed as the results appeared. The references ran into the millions; she doubted there was going to be anything sinister about it. She clicked on the first listing, which led to pages of information. It was a mild form of Diazepam, used to treat anxiety, amongst other things. It was also an effective pre-med, known

to induce sedation or amnesia prior to certain medical proce-
dures. Well, there you go.

She read on, unsurprised to learn that she had had what was
described as an overreaction to the drug. Jo had realised from an
early age that she was never going to be a user, recreational or
otherwise. She was highly susceptible to drugs; even Panadol had
been known to make her drowsy. She'd never even gone through
a pot-smoking phase in her youth because the couple of times
she'd tried it she just passed out. For some reason alcohol didn't
have the same effect – praise the Lord – so it had remained her
one and only drug of choice.

Jo closed the page on her computer screen. She didn't need
to contact him for information. She wouldn't ask Judith for his
number tomorrow. What she would do was leave well enough
alone.

But she felt odd . . . bereft, somehow, that she wasn't going to
see him again. Why? She had only the vaguest memory of him;
he was very tall, and okay-looking, though a little unkempt for
her tastes. He had been extremely kind to her, really, very gallant.
She probably wouldn't have got through the episode without
him – not that she would admit that to another living soul. But
they'd spent barely an hour together, she estimated. She knew
nothing about him. They were ships pausing in the night . . .

Where had she heard that expression before?

This was not like her. Jo was not a romantic, not in the least,
she prided herself on that. She was pragmatic, ruled by her head
not her heart, persuaded by facts, not swayed by emotion.

And the fact was, the man in the elevator was only intriguing
because she wasn't going to see him again. There, that was it. It
was easy to think favourably of someone who was, for all intents
and purposes, unknowable; to fantasise, to build him up to be
something he wasn't. That was what celebrity worship was all
about. And holiday romances. That was it, Jo had had a holiday
fling, but it had only lasted one hour.

She leaned forward, chewing on the end of her pen. Maybe
there was a column in this . . . Her mind drifted back to the elevator, and she felt an uncomfortable pang in her chest. She was
getting flashes of conversation that were a little unsettling, about

Belle, about her marriage, about having babies even . . . but surely she didn't go there with a total stranger? She must have had some weird dreams lying on Leo's couch.

Clearly she wasn't going to be able to achieve anything productive today, she might as well just answer her emails. But as she scrolled down her inbox, nothing caught her eye, nothing inspired a response, until she came to 'RE: the 29th'. Jo frowned. What was it about the 29th? The email was confirmation of an interview she had set up for next week, but that wasn't it. There was something else about the 29th. Or the number 29 . . .

Sonnet 29, that was it.

Jo went back to Google and found it immediately. She sat with her chin resting on her hand as she read it.

> *When, in disgrace with fortune and men's eyes,*
> *I all alone beweep my outcast state,*
> *And trouble deaf heaven with my bootless cries,*
> *And look upon myself and curse my fate,*
> *Wishing me like to one more rich in hope,*
> *Featured like him, like him with friends possess'd,*
> *Desiring this man's art and that man's scope,*
> *With what I most enjoy contented least;*
> *Yet in these thoughts myself almost despising,*
> *Haply I think on thee, and then my state,*
> *Like to the lark at break of day arising*
> *From sullen earth, sings hymns at heaven's gate;*
> *For thy sweet love remember'd such wealth brings*
> *That then I scorn to change my state with kings.*

What had he said? It was about true love and passion . . . and risking everything . . . or was that *Romeo and Juliet*? How had they come to be talking about Shakespeare? Jo sat there, staring at the computer screen, but she couldn't see the words, she could only see his face, becoming clearer, those eyes . . .

What the hell was she doing? She closed the page and quit all the programs. She was obviously not going to get over this weirdness till she left the building and re-entered it fresh tomorrow. She switched off her computer, picked up her bag and headed out through the office to the lift bay. As she stepped into an elevator, she had an overwhelming sensation . . . was it déjà vu? No, that wasn't quite right. Her heart started beating faster as the doors closed, sealing her in.

Jo didn't know if this was *the* elevator, she hadn't really been paying attention when she rushed headlong into it this morning. Besides, they were all peas in a pod, shabby and dated like the rest of the building, with tired, fake wood-panelled walls, and a square of mustard carpet inset into the centre of the floor. She turned to look at the space beside her, seeing him there, so tall, she remembered feeling a little intimidated. She glanced up at the ceiling, a grid of flimsy acoustic panels. He knocked one out, so she wouldn't feel closed in. He was very practical, obviously, the type who takes over in a situation and knows just what to do. Though Jo had spent all her life being self-sufficient, fiercely so, there was something appealing about that.

The doors opened. She had arrived at the ground floor safely, swiftly and uneventfully. As she stepped out, Jo felt a sense of release. It was over. She wasn't going to see Tall'n'Scruffy ever again. And just as well; in real life, she wouldn't be able to stand his take-charge attitude. Jo was in charge of her own life. She had not allowed a man to have a say in it for a very long time, and she wasn't about to start now.

So that was that. It was an interesting little episode, a pleasant interlude of no great significance. She would put it out of her mind and never think of him again.

7:20 pm

'The best things always happen to you!' said Angie.

'They do not.'

'Do too,' she insisted, topping up her glass. Jo had fulfilled her earlier promise and bought Angie a drink, in the form of a bottle of sparkling to be shared at her place. Her head had started to clear during the walk home, and she began to feel upbeat. She didn't want to be alone tonight, she wanted to celebrate her new apartment and her new lease on life, and put today's little hiccup behind her. So she had called Angie to come over.

'What good things happen to me?' Jo wanted to know.

'Heaps of stuff. You've been to the Logies and the AFIs, you've interviewed the entire cast of *Home and Away*, you met Will Ferrell –'

'At a press conference with a hundred other journalists.'

'You got to tour the Big Brother house,' she went on. And on. Angie had been starstruck when Jo did a reluctant stint as entertainment reporter a couple of years back, and she'd never really got over it when Jo had dropped it to work on Business and Finance instead.

'That's part of my job, Ange, it's not like it just happens to me out of the blue for no reason.'

'This did.'

'What did?'

'Being trapped in an elevator,' said Angie. 'That's never happened to me out of the blue.'

'What's so great about being trapped in an elevator?'

'The part about the really cute guy trapped along with you.'

'I never said he was cute,' Jo protested. 'He wasn't *cute*. You'd never call this guy cute.'

'Sorry, I forgot, big and manly and heroic –'

'Oh, for crying out loud, where are you getting this?'

'From the way you talked about him.'

'I didn't say he was big and manly and heroic. I said he was big and scruffy, and that he turned out to be quite a nice guy. That's all.'

'But he was heroic, wasn't he?'

'Heroic how? That tag gets bandied about so much it doesn't mean anything any more,' said Jo. 'Footballers are heroic, a movie star who does a stage play is heroic. He didn't save me from a burning building or a raging sea, he didn't even save me from an elevator –'

'He saved you from yourself,' Angie nodded sagely.

Jo rolled her eyes. 'Give me that bottle,' she said, reaching across the coffee table. Angie handed her the bottle of champagne. It was already half empty, Jo realised as she poured some into her glass. Of course Angie would say it was half full. And there was the basic difference between the two of them.

'What is that tune you keep humming?' asked Angie.

Jo stopped abruptly. She had been humming on and off since she woke up this afternoon.

'I think it's 'Bye Bye Blackbird',' she mused. 'I don't know where I heard it but I can't get it out of my head.'

'Perhaps it was playing in the elevator?' Angie suggested.

She shook her head. 'They don't pipe music into the elevators in our building.'

'Maybe he sang it to you to help you calm down?'

Jo looked at her. 'I think I would have remembered that, Ange.'

'Well, you can't seem to remember a whole lot else,' she said airily. 'What a bummer you weren't conscious when he was carrying you through the office. I bet it was like that scene from *An Officer And A Gentleman*.'

Jo groaned. 'How was it like that scene? I was unconscious, Angie. If I hadn't been, he wouldn't have had to carry me.'

'It's still romantic,' Angie swooned.

Jo crossed her arms in front of her. 'I'd passed out from the effect of a drug I'd taken to control a panic attack whilst being trapped in an elevator. The total stranger who had the misfortune of finding himself trapped in said elevator with a crazy woman having a panic attack then had to lug me, unconscious, through the offices where I work in front of all my colleagues and deposit me on the couch in my boss's office. That is not romantic. It's humiliating and pathetic.'

Angie pulled a face. 'Why do you always have to do that? Take away all the magic, the fantasy?'

'Because there is no magic, and fantasy is just that. It's not real. In fact, I'm beginning to think it's hormonally induced in women. They concoct fantasies to explain the most mundane of everyday events so they can believe that men are acting with romantic intentions, while in actual fact the dimwits are going about the whole time with nothing much more registering in their brains than the footy score.'

'Sucks to be you, Jo, if that's how you look at the world.'

'Well, it's better than kidding yourself.'

Angie narrowed her eyes. 'Is that a dig at me?'

Jo sighed. 'No, it's not a dig at you, Ange.'

'Because I'll have you know that Rocket-Pastrami and I had a moment today.'

Four years working in a sandwich shop had left Angie with the curious practice of identifying customers according to their choice of filling. Angie had had her eye on Rocket-Pastrami for months now. He was probably a merchant banker, she'd decided, not that she'd know one from a bar of soapless skin cleanser. But he had to be some kind of highly paid executive on account of the dead gorgeous suits and silk ties he wore, and the fact he nearly always paid with a fifty-dollar note, leaving the coin change on the counter as though it was flotsam. Angie had to revise his moniker frequently, because he tended to amend his order every week or so, 'whenever some gourmet food magazine tells him what he's supposed to be eating' Jo had sniped. She didn't like the sound of Rocket-Pastrami at all; she suspected he was a pretentious snob.

'And FYI,' Angie went on, 'Rocket-Pastrami has changed as of today. He will now be known as Roasted-Goat's-Cheese-With . . .' She hesitated, frowning. 'Hmm, it's quite a mouthful, I'll have to abbreviate . . .'

'You know, it might be easier if you just give him a generic name. Like "wanker",' Jo suggested. 'Then I'd know exactly who you were talking about.'

Angie ignored her. 'Anyway, *he* asked *me* which garnish I'd recommend with his new combination.' She paused to allow Jo to digest the significance of that.

'That was your moment?'

Angie was mustering a comeback when the phone started to ring. Jo picked it up and flipped it open. It was Lachlan.

'This'll only take a sec,' she said to Angie. 'Hi Lachlan, how's the conference?'

Angie pulled a face and got to her feet.

'I'm wasting away from tedium,' Lachlan was saying. 'You have to rescue me.'

'How do you expect me to do that?' said Jo as she watched Angie saunter off to the bathroom.

'Hop on a plane and come join me.'

'Huh?'

'Come on down to sunny Tasmania,' he said. 'I'll make it worth your while.'

'It's Thursday, Lach, I can't just run out on work.'

'Sure you can. Find something to write about here. Do a column on apples or roadkill or something.'

'I've done my column for the week, I've already had a day off moving, and I didn't get any work done today.'

'Why not?'

'I got stuck in an elevator.'

'You did what?'

'I got stuck in an elevator,' Jo repeated.

'How did you manage that?'

'It wasn't my fault, Lach, these things happen you know.'

'With alarming regularity to you, I've noticed.'

'No way,' she protested. She was not one of those people. 'I'm not one of those people.'

'We both know you are,' he said. 'But that's beside the point.'

'What point?'

'The point that I miss you and I want you to fly down here and do dirty things to me all night long.'

'In your dreams,' said Jo, 'because that's the only place it's going to happen.'

'Come on, Jo,' he whined.

'Now you're whining.'

'Is it helping my case?'

'Not even a little.'

'Then what do I have to do to convince you?'

'Lachlan, I couldn't get a flight now if I tried,' said Jo as Angie walked back into the room. She must have heard the last comment because she was pretending to gag.

'So come tomorrow,' Lachlan was saying.

'Lach, I have to go, Angie's here and I've got a ton of stuff to do –'

'Angie's there? Good, let me talk to her. She'll back me up, she loves me.'

It was part of Lachlan's charm that he was oblivious to what people really thought of him. Angie couldn't stand him. Oh, she understood the attraction; her distaste was purely on moral grounds. She was very disapproving of the whole extramarital affair business, and while Jo tried to tell her that she knew what she was doing and the arrangement suited her perfectly, Angie chose not to believe her. Lachlan was using her, Angie claimed. No more than I'm using him, Jo countered. You can't have a future with him, she shot back. I don't want a future with him, Jo maintained. Angie groaned, 'Of course you do!'

It was no use trying to explain it to her, because Angie was a Hopeless Romantic. It was like a cult or something. She believed in love and marriage and happily ever after and one person fulfilling your needs for the rest of your life. Jo had long ago discarded such notions. Marriage was not for her. She'd tried it once and it didn't fit.

'I'm hanging up now, Lachlan,' said Jo.

'Take pity on me, Jo-bloh.'

'Oh, don't worry, I find you quite pitiful.'

'Very funny.'

'Talk to you later.'

Angie was still standing, and now she was rummaging through her handbag.

'You're not leaving?' Jo asked, hanging up the phone. 'There's still half a bottle left,' she added, picking it up. 'Nearly.'

'Sorry Jo, I have an audition at eight in the morning. I'm going to have to get up at the crack of dawn to make myself beautiful, which is Mission Impossible at the best of times.'

Angie was bright and round like a bubble. Everything about her was round: her cheeks, her eyes, her belly, her breasts. Even her hair fell in spirals around her shoulders. Jo said she was like a ripe grape. Angie was rather more prosaic – she just said she was fat. It was the bane of her life. She could barely find a bad word to say about anyone because she kept them all for herself.

'Anyway, it's ten-thirty, aren't you feeling tired yet?' asked Angie. 'With everything you've been through in the last few days, I would have thought you'd be dead on your feet by now.'

'I was comatose the whole day, don't forget,' Jo said. 'I'm wired.

I couldn't sleep now if I tried. I'm going to have to tire myself out by pulling this place into order.'

But it didn't work. Jo packed away all the kitchen and bathroom gear, and most of her clothes, shoes, underwear. She stacked her books, CDs and DVDs onto shelves and set up her desk. There were still more boxes but now they were lined up against the wall, out of the way. The living room was neat, though a little bare. She had ornaments and whatnot packed away somewhere, as well as pictures to hang, but she didn't think her neighbours would appreciate hammering at two in the morning.

Yes, it was two in the morning and Jo didn't feel tired. Not a bit. She took a long hot shower and, though she felt more relaxed, she still didn't feel sleepy. When it was going on 3 am, Jo made herself go to bed. But as soon as she was lying there in the darkness, elevator man loomed into her thoughts. She'd kept him at bay all night as she bustled about, whistling, singing to herself . . . though she finally had to put on a CD to drown out 'Bye Bye Blackbird' which had been playing on a continuous loop inside her head the whole time. Now there was nothing to distract her, and her brain was working overtime, processing the day, piecing together what she could remember till she had passed out in the elevator. She could see herself lying on the floor. She could hear his voice close to her ear. *Princess.* She felt his fingers trace a line down her arm, pausing at her wrist. And then his lips on her shoulder, moving up to her neck. She opened her eyes and he was above her and his mouth came down on hers. She wanted to protest but she couldn't. And then she didn't want to. She could feel his hands reaching up under her skirt, his fingers hooking over the top of her pantyhose, pulling them down with a rough urgency, sending a jolt through her body. And then he was inside her, and somehow at the same time Jo could feel his lips, his tongue all over her . . . she was breathing hard, her heart pounding, throbbing . . .

Jo lurched up in bed, panting, her head damp with perspiration. Shit. *Shit!* He had sex with her? While she was out to it? Surely not. But it was so vivid. She could feel him, feel his skin against hers, his lips, his tongue . . . *Stop!*

She took a few deep, slow breaths, willing her heart to stop racing. She flopped backwards on the pillow. What the hell? He couldn't have had sex with her . . . no way. She would know, she would know for sure. Unless that drug was something like Rohypnol, which wiped your memory, she'd heard. No, she did have some memory of the events, snatches of conversation, or did she? Jo couldn't trust her memories any more, she wasn't sure what was real and what was a dream. But her clothes had been intact when she woke, there were no signs to suggest anything untoward. Jo breathed out heavily. This was ridiculous, she was being paranoid. She was just imagining things.

Why would she do that? Why would she imagine – *dream* – about having sex with a total stranger? It wasn't all that odd, she supposed, it was the premise of just about every cheap porn film. Eew, she was having erotic dreams about this man? How desperate was she? She didn't feel desperate. She got enough sex from Lachlan, she was quite satisfied in that department.

That was it! Lachlan had talked about having sex when he called. Her brain was simply processing the events of the day and got them muddled. The relief she felt was overwhelming. Clearly the dream was nothing more than the purging of her subconscious after a very strange and unusual day. Jo turned over onto her side and closed her eyes. Now she could get some sleep.

Morning

Jo woke up with a start. She reached over to her bedside table for her phone, but she couldn't feel it. She sat up, rubbing her eyes as she swung her legs off the bed. The phone was definitely not on the table. She slipped down onto the floor and felt under the bed and around the carpet. What the hell? It couldn't just evaporate. She knelt up, sliding her hands and arms under the covers and sweeping them across the mattress. She reached further up under the second pillow and finally her hand connected with the slim casing. She drew it out and flipped it open, peering at the time.

Oh, *no*! Not again! How could this happen? She must have turned the alarm off in her sleep. She couldn't even remember doing it. Bugger it! She was going to be late again. Leo would have her head on a stick.

Half an hour later, she was literally running along the footpath to work. She was even less organised than yesterday. At least she'd had an outfit ready then. But she'd had no time to iron anything, her hair was flying behind her, she hadn't even managed lipstick. As she dashed inside the building, she did have a momentary pause at the elevators, wondering if she oughtn't take the stairs after all. But she doubted she could manage nineteen floors in her present state of fluster. In any state, for that matter. An elevator arrived and she jumped in, pressing the button for her floor furiously, despite knowing it didn't make things work any faster. Images from yesterday flitted across her brain but they were already starting to break up, like the fragments of a slightly disturbing dream. And not a moment too soon.

But then the sex scene landed with a thud. Jo shook her head to disperse it. It was just a dream, the construct of an addled brain, that was all. She arrived at her floor and bolted out of the elevator like a horse out of a starting gate.

'The meeting's already begun, Leo said you should go straight to the conference room ...' The receptionist's voice trailed behind her as she sped up the corridor. Jo could never remember the name of the receptionist, they seemed to change every three months or so. It was something that started with an E or L – Elizabeth, Emily, Emma, or Laura, Louise, Liz ... She stopped outside the door for a count of three, as she smoothed her wild hair, straightened her jacket and took one deep breath. She placed her hand on the doorknob and turned.

'Good of you to join us, Jo*ANNE*,' Leo's voice boomed from the far end of the table.

Leo had sarcasm down to a martial art. And calling her Joanne was one of his trademark moves, despite the fact Jo had told him repeatedly that it wasn't her name.

'I'm sorry I'm late,' she said, heading for the closest free seat.

'You look like crap,' Leo remarked. 'What happened to you?'

'Um, I didn't sleep very well,' Jo muttered, not meeting any of the eyes she could feel trained on her.

'Well, you've already met Joe, at least we don't have to go through introductions again.'

'Met who?'

'Joe.'

'Yes?'

'Yeah, yeah, ha ha,' Leo said in a monotone. 'I think it's a bit early in the day to be playing "Who's on first", isn't it?'

Jo wasn't following, but then she stopped trying as her eyes were drawn to the man getting up from his seat to the left of Leo. She hadn't noticed him till now. He had been sitting on the same side of the table as her, but there were four or five others between them, so Jo literally couldn't see him until he stood up.

'So we meet again,' he said a little sheepishly.

Jo's heart shot up and lodged in her throat. 'What are you doing here?' she managed to squeeze out.

'He's going to be working here,' said Leo matter-of-factly. 'Didn't you tell her yesterday, Joe?'

'Tell who?' Jo was completely confused. 'I didn't even know.'

'What the hell did you two talk about the whole time?' muttered Leo, shaking his head.

But Jo had just registered. 'You're going to work here?'

'Some coincidence, eh?' he said lamely.

'On so many levels,' Leo muttered, shuffling the papers in front of him.

'What does that mean?' Jo frowned.

He looked across his glasses at her. 'You know, 'cause you're Jo as well.'

'As well as what?' She felt as though she'd fallen down the rabbit hole. Nothing was making any sense.

'Jo,' said elevator man, reclaiming her attention. 'My name is Joe, Joe Bannister. You said "no names, no pack drill" yesterday, remember? So I didn't get the chance to introduce myself properly, and then later, well, you know, you . . . um . . . you weren't conscious, exactly.'

Jo glanced around the table at the amused faces of her

colleagues. They were clearly enjoying the show. Time to bring down the curtain.

'Right, okay,' she said briskly, pulling her chair in closer to the table. 'So I guess you know by now that I'm Jo Liddell. We'll have to figure out something about the names, of course,' she added, taking her notepad out of her bag.

'What do you mean?' he frowned.

'Well obviously we can't both be called Jo,' she said simply.

'But we both are . . . called Joe.'

'I realise that, but it's not going to work. We'll just call you Joseph.'

'No one calls me Joseph,' he declared, taking his seat again. 'Not outside my immediate family, anyway.'

'Well, bad luck, we have to avoid confusion.'

'I'm not confused, is anyone else confused?' asked Joe, scanning the table. Everyone shook their heads. He leaned forward a little so he could see Jo at the end of the table. 'We have different surnames and, besides, I do have an "e" at the end of my name, and I'm guessing you don't.'

'You can't see the "e" when it's spoken,' Jo pointed out. 'It's going to be a problem every time someone calls out "Jo".'

'I don't see the problem,' said Joe.

'Well, I do.'

'Then change your name.'

She shrugged dismissively. 'I was here first.'

'But it's not even your real name.'

Jo froze. How did he know that?

'It's not her real name?' said Leo. 'I knew it.'

She had to change the subject, and quickly. 'Surely you've got more important issues to cover at this meeting, Leo?'

'Which we were doing, Joanne, or whatever the hell your name is, before you made your grand entrance and interrupted the proceedings,' he reminded her. 'I was saying that the plans for the new premises have been approved . . .'.

There was a collective groan around the table. No one wanted to move in the first place. Sure, the building was in need of a revamp; it was daggy and outdated and inefficient, not least the elevators. But management in its wisdom had brought in a team

of consultants to design a vast new office space in a swanky building down in the foreshore development. Which was all well and
good, but what they had come up with was a cutting edge, entirely
open-plan space, which would supposedly reflect the new multi-
platform delivery of news and current affairs. Problem was, no
one had bothered to consult the people who had to work there
and deliver said news and current affairs. The journos hated the
whole concept – no offices, no interviewing rooms, meant no
privacy. They were copying every other paper on the eastern sea-
board, and they hadn't met one journalist from those other papers
who liked it either.

But Leo could have been talking about moving them into
a tree-house for all Jo was taking in. She was having too much
trouble dealing with the piece of sky that had just fallen on her
head. Elevator man was going to *work* here? He was a *journalist*?
Why hadn't he said? Or had he, and she just didn't remember?
No, she would have remembered that. She would have remembered a proper introduction, she would have remembered if he'd
told her they weren't just strangers who were never going to see
each other again. Why wouldn't he have said that he was going to
be working with her? What kind of creepy game was he playing?
Or was it all just a bit of fun at her expense? Jo felt uneasy and
rattled, and she did not like feeling uneasy and rattled.

Lachlan just got a mention, hauling Jo's attention back into
the room.

'. . . and he said it's the most boring premiers' conference
in the history of premiers' conferences, which is really saying
something,' Tim, the picture editor, relayed. 'So unless there are
dramatic developments today, we can't expect anything from
Lachlan for the front page.'

Art for the front page became the focus by Friday. There was
only another day and a half to pull the paper together, and the
front page had to sell it.

'We're keeping an eye on St Alban's, because they're about to
deliver the 250,000th baby born at the hospital.'

'Is that really front-page news?' Leo asked dubiously.

'It is when the birth rate is only 1.75.'

He shook his head. 'It'll do for page three . . .'

'A few of the league results will be significant,' said Glen Nicholas, the sports editor.

'Any chance of some biffo?' asked Leo.

Glen looked blank for a moment. 'We are talking rugby league, boss.'

'Okay, stupid question, but it's still only a maybe for the front page,' said Leo. 'Okay, people, I guess there's nothing for it but to pray for a major political scandal, or else a natural disaster . . . a tsunami, a Katrina, something.'

The whole assembly groaned in disapproval.

'For Chrissakes, I'm joking,' he retorted, though everyone knew that was only half true. 'Get back to me throughout the day with any developments. I'll meet the subs at three.'

Jo hovered outside the room after everyone had filed back to their desks. Well, not everyone. She could hear Leo and whatsisname inside still, talking, their matey, jokey voices muffled, punctuated with an occasional hearty guffaw. Things were going to be impossible around here if she didn't assert her position, it was bad enough he was an old friend of Leo's. But Jo had seniority. She'd been here more than three years, she was a columnist, she was entitled to some respect. She didn't know his background, except that he'd been working overseas for a time, she remembered now . . . he'd only just got off a plane . . . that's why his phone wouldn't work locally, and why he'd looked like he'd slept in his clothes. Had he been working overseas as a journalist? What was his surname? She didn't catch it, she had been somewhat distracted when he introduced himself. No matter, she'd find out and Google him later.

The door swung open suddenly and Leo walked out, looking back over his shoulder. 'So whenever you can make it in, Joe, don't stress about it. We'll see you when we see you.'

Jeez, she would have been dragged over the coals if she'd taken more than one day off to move, but golden boy clearly got to call his own shots. He came into the doorway, or rather, filled the doorway, his eyebrows lifting slightly as he spotted Jo.

'Do you want something, Jo?' asked Leo, noticing her at the same time.

'Um,' she cleared her throat, 'yes, I was hoping to grab a word with, um, Mr . . . um . . .'

'Bannister,' said Joe, 'but you can call me Joe. I won't confuse myself with you.'

He was a smart-arse as well. Joe Bannister. That sounded familiar.

'I'll see you, Joe,' said Leo, walking away up the corridor. 'My best to the old guy, yeah?'

'Will do, Leo.' He turned to look at Jo. 'What can I do for you?'

'I just have a few questions . . .' she faltered, '. . . about yesterday.'

'Sure.'

He stood watching her expectantly, but Jo felt suddenly self-conscious.

'We could go into my office if you like,' he suggested.

'You have an office?' Jo exclaimed. 'You haven't even started yet and you have an *office*?'

'Apparently it was vacant,' he said, guileless.

Oh it was vacant all right. And just about everyone on staff had been angling for it since Alan Dutton retired and, instead of filling his position, management had done a reshuffle.

Jo turned on her heel and marched down the corridor into the vast maze of partitioned pens, one of which she was proud to call her own. Bloody jobs for the boys, it made her want to spit. She weaved her way across the floor to 'his' office, waiting outside for him to catch up.

'It's open, go on in,' he said from behind her.

Jo opened the door and walked inside. He obviously hadn't moved in yet, the room was still bare but for a standard-issue suite of well-worn furniture.

'Just so you know,' she turned around to face him as he closed the door, 'this is going to put a few noses out of joint.'

He frowned. 'What is?'

'You getting this office,' she said, leaning against the window frame and folding her arms, gazing out. There was a decent view as well.

'Do you want it?'

'I'm sorry?' she said, turning abruptly to look at him.

'Do you want the office? I don't want to put anyone's nose out of joint, so you can have it if you want.'

'I wasn't talking about me,' Jo said archly.

'Whatever,' he shrugged, perching on the edge of the desk. 'You're welcome to it, I'm not going to be around much anyway.'

'Oh?'

'A journalist can't journalise from a desk in an office,' he said. 'Not this one anyway.'

Oh God help us, a self-anointed maverick who coined his own words.

'I'm really only here on a freelance basis,' he went on to explain. 'I'm not even on a salary.'

'Yet you get an office,' she said tartly.

'Oh for . . . Take it,' he said, standing up and spreading his arms out. 'It's yours. Please, I want you to have it.'

'I don't want it.'

'I'm serious, it's yours.'

'And I said, I don't want it!' Jo repeated through gritted teeth.

He dropped his arms again. 'Then can you build a bridge?'

'Pardon?'

'And get over it.'

She groaned inwardly. He probably thought he was witty.

'So,' prompted Joe, 'did you want to discuss our problem?'

'Our problem?' she frowned.

'Well, I happen to think it's your problem, but I don't want to start off on the wrong foot,' he said. 'So I was thinking, we could try Big Joe/Little J–'

'Don't finish that thought,' she interrupted, holding up her hand. 'In fact, don't even think it, ever again, and especially don't say it out loud.'

'Okay, okay,' he surrendered, but she could see the glint in his eye as he sat back on the desk again. 'So what did you want to talk about?'

Jo took a breath to compose herself, then looked him straight in the eye, no matter how disconcerting that was proving to be. 'Look, the thing is, whatever happened in the elevator –'

'What do you mean?'

She hesitated. 'I mean, regardless of what might have happened –'

'I don't understand what you're getting at.'

Jo was confused. He was confusing her. 'I haven't said anything yet.'

'Yes you have,' he insisted. '"*Whatever* happened", "what *might* have happened"? What happened happened; there's nothing more – or less – to it.'

Jo's heart started to thump uncomfortably against her rib cage. What was with the double-talk? It was unsettling. So was the way he was looking at her. Intently, with those blue, blue eyes. He was clean-shaven today, she just noticed, but his clothes were still on the rumpled side. Not that she could talk, the way she was dressed.

'Are you okay?' he was asking. 'You do remember everything, don't you, Jo?'

She flicked her hair back defiantly. 'Of course I remember,' she scoffed.

'Because I was kind of hoping,' he went on carefully, 'considering *everything*, that we were going to be friends, at least.'

What the hell did *that* mean?

'Well, um . . .' Bugger. He didn't know what she didn't know, but if she didn't say something soon, he'd know there were things she didn't know, and she didn't want him to know that. All she could do was bluff, and hope he didn't call her on it. He knew her name, allegedly, that much he'd admitted. 'Okay, if you wanted to be friends, why did you go blurting my business to everyone at the meeting?'

He was frowning. 'What are you talking about?'

'You told everyone my real name.'

'No, I didn't.'

'All right, but you told them that Jo isn't my real name.'

'Sorry,' he relented, bowing his head. 'You were pushing the point, it just came out. But I would never actually tell anyone, I promise. I realise you wouldn't want to let that get around.'

Jo felt her face burning. Did he really know, had she really told him? If that was the case, she might have said – or done – anything.

'Why didn't you tell me you were going to be working here?' she tried next. She was sure he hadn't told her that. Pretty sure. He wasn't denying it, so she must be on solid ground. 'There was I thinking that we'd never lay eyes on each other again, and you knew perfectly well that we would, so you did everything you could to get as much information as possible on me.'

'That's not how it happened,' he protested. 'You were the one asking the questions, trying to guess what I did for a job. I was completely honest with you.'

She remembered now. 'No, you offered to let me guess,' she said, 'because you knew I'd never think you had the same job as me.'

'Look,' he said, getting to his feet, 'I'm not going to wear this, Jo, no way. I wanted to introduce myself from the beginning but you did the whole "no names, no pack drill" speech, and if we had just introduced ourselves like normal people it would all have come out and none of this would be happening now.'

Jo just stared at him. He was right. She remembered.

He sighed. 'What do you want from me, Jo?'

She wanted him to fill in all the gaps, so she had a complete picture of what had happened in the elevator. So they were both hitting off the same handicap. Knowledge was power, and right now he had all the knowledge, so Jo had to restore the balance of power.

'I don't want anything from you,' she said plainly.

'Then what's the problem?'

She took a breath. 'I'm just not . . . entirely comfortable, with the way things . . . concluded yesterday. As you could probably tell, I'm not very good with drugs, and I don't know what I might have done while I was under the influence.' She couldn't make eye contact with him. 'I mean, I told you my birth name. I've never told anyone that since I changed it. I don't know what other . . . inhibitions those drugs might have . . . released.'

She finally dared to look at him.

'What do you think happened?' he asked, feigning a kind of wide-eyed innocence. He was so enjoying this.

'Nothing, I don't think anything happened,' she returned firmly. 'In fact, I know nothing happened. I was there, remember?'

'But you just said you don't know what you might have done.'

She did, didn't she. 'I wasn't speaking literally.'

He looked vaguely baffled. 'Then how were you speaking?'

'Not literally.' She was getting annoyed now.

'You're worried you lost your inhibitions,' he persisted.

'No, I'm not.'

'But that's what you just said.'

'Well it's not what I meant.'

'Oh, right, you were speaking "not literally" again?'

'And you're resorting to sarcasm, the lowest form of humour.'

He raised his eyebrows a little at that. 'Look, something's bothering you,' he said. 'What is it, what do you remember, or not remember?'

'Nothing's bothering me, and I remember everything.'

'Obviously you don't,' he insisted. 'You said yourself you don't know what you might have done.'

'Of course I know what I might have done. I certainly know what I wouldn't have done, so I'm not worried about that.'

His eyes narrowed as a sly grin formed slowly on his lips. 'You had a dirty dream about me, didn't you?'

Jo blinked. 'What?'

'About you and me, alone in that elevator ...You're only human after all.'

'Don't be ridiculous.' She started to feel claustrophobic, as though suddenly there wasn't enough air in the room.

He was watching her closely. 'Problem is, you're not sure if it was a dream or not, are you?'

Jo feigned indifference, at least that's what she was aiming for. She doubted she was pulling it off, especially as she felt like she was struggling for breath.

'We could always try a re-enactment, see if that helps jog your memory.'

She shook her head in disgust. 'You know what I do remember? That you seemed like a pretty nice guy, but clearly I was mistaken on that count,' she said, walking past him to the door.

'Oh come on, Jo, I was only kidding around,' he cajoled. 'Nothing happened. You passed out and then about two minutes later the cavalry arrived.'

She didn't respond, grabbing the handle of the door and lurching it open. She could breathe again.

'The way I remember it, you were a lot more fun yesterday,' he muttered behind her.

Jo spun around, glaring at him. 'Looks like we were both mistaken then.' She turned her back on him and marched determinedly out of the room. That was probably a tad melodramatic, but she was pissed off. And she had to assert herself somehow.

She sat down at her desk and turned on her computer. There was one more thing she had to do before she filed Mr Joe Bannister away in the very back of her mind, along with the other occasional work colleagues who were of no particular interest to her. Jo opened Google, typed in his name and clicked on search.

Twenty-two thousand seven hundred results came up. She scanned the list with increasing dread. Walkley award-winning foreign correspondent . . . one of the most experienced journalists reporting on the war in Iraq . . . highly respected . . . erudite . . . informed . . . brilliant . . . insightful . . .

He was *that* Joe Bannister? No wonder the name sounded familiar.

She clicked on 'images', and sure enough there he was, with the three-day growth, the smart-arse grin, wearing khakis and a flak jacket in a war zone, then in a suit before a UN hearing on WMDs . . . a couple of head shots . . . no wetsuit though . . . Jo remembered the conversation now, the challenge. In hindsight it seemed rather obvious.

She returned to the list and clicked on the next page, her eyes immediately drawn to an entry for Joseph Bannister. Ah hah! So he did go by 'Joseph' sometimes. She clicked on the link which took her to Wikipedia. *Foreign correspondent* . . . blah, blah, gush, gush . . . *winner of a Walkley Award for his stunning coverage of the Vietnam War* . . .

What the?

Jo scanned the article to get to the biographical details. *Joseph William Bannister was born in* . . . that couldn't be right. That would make him over seventy. Her eyes raced down the page where 'Joe Bannister' was highlighted . . . *his son, also a highly regarded correspondent and Walkley Award recipient. They are the first father and son to have both received the award.*

His father was ill. That's why he'd come back. She remembered. Jo closed the page, feeling a little queasy. Karma and his mates, Fate and Coincidence, must be having a great big belly laugh at her expense right now. The fact that he was a foreign correspondent was just salt for the wound. She stared at his image on the screen. What was a big fish like him doing swimming in a little pond like the *Trib*, anyway? A Sunday paper was a bit lightweight for someone of his stature, she would have thought. They had their serious features, but Don and Lachlan took care of them, monopolised them, in fact.

Lachlan, what would he have to say about this development? Quite a bit, Jo imagined.

She closed the pages about Bannister, senior and junior, and glanced through her emails, clicking on one Lachlan had sent early this morning. *When are you going to get that tasty little piece of arse down here?* was all it said.

Jo stared at the words for a moment. The last thing she felt like dealing with was another man and his inflated ego. She promptly deleted the email, she wasn't even going to credit it with a response. Instead she opened a document and began to type.

> Why do you think this column is called
> 'Bitch' anyway? Because it's opinion and
> it's written by a woman, and if a woman
> has an opinion she's immediately consid-
> ered a bitch. Why are men never called
> bitches? I mean, never, unless one is being
> ever so slightly ironic.

Hold on, what was that anecdote she'd heard about irony the other day? It had something to do with Alanis Morissette . . . Never mind, it'd come to her later.

> Lately there's been a movement to take the
> name on proudly. Just Google 'bitch' and
> see what you come up with. Everything

from online groups with names like 'Heartless Bitch', to bitch blogs, bitch quizzes, bitch merchandise (of course), to supposedly serious academic discussions on feminists reclaiming the title for themselves.

But isn't this just playing into the same sexist paradigm that says women clad in next to nothing and dancing like strippers is somehow empowering?

Councillors in the City of New York seem to think so. They proposed a symbolic ban on the word more than a year ago. They want people to think twice about using it so freely to replace girlfriend, wife or partner. The councillors went on to state that 'bitch' is as offensive and degrading to women as the 'n-word' is to people of colour.

Notwithstanding the name of this column, I get where they're coming from. I mean, would men ever take on the title 'arsehole' proudly? No way, yet way too many of them could wear that name with ease.

That was an understatement.

Same as it's only women who are ever accused of nagging. Men rarely 'nag' because they rarely have the need. Does a man have to nag his wife to help out around the house? To pay a bill, to call a tradesman, to tend to the kids? I think not. So women are called nags, yet they wouldn't have to nag if men did what they asked in the first place.

Where was she actually going with this?

> The thing is, it's way too easy to label people. Sticks and stones will break your bones and get you charged with assault. Yet names, well, names can be bandied about willy-nilly. But don't believe for a second that 'names will never hurt me'. No one really knows what motivates a person, what their particular heartaches are. Yet we're all too ready to smugly stamp them with a label. But what about not judging others lest you be judged yourself? Next time you're about to slap a label on someone, stop and think for a second what label someone may be putting on you. It's a sobering thought.

Jo read over what she had written. She wasn't sure what her point was, or even if there was a point. Maybe she'd save it for a day when there was a libel case in the news. For now she'd just put it away in her file of column ideas. She had a feeling she was going to need them for a long time yet, with another 'serious' journalist on board, pushing Jo further down the ladder.

And that was a bitch.

2 pm

Joe settled his head against the window as the train lurched and listed its way out of suburbia towards the mountains. He was dog-tired; he still hadn't caught up on his sleep, nor had he adjusted to the inverted time zone. It had been a while since he'd travelled across hemispheres, and he'd forgotten how it was a little tougher on the body clock.

However, he didn't like his chances of getting any sleep now. His mind was too agitated; it had been agitated pretty much since he touched down in Australia. He had not got off to the most auspicious of beginnings. Joe had hoped writing for a Sunday paper would be relatively relaxed and free of the usual pressures, but he had failed to take into account what it would be like to work in a newspaper office again – the internal politics, the prickly egos, the constant compromise. It was why he tended to freelance these days; he could work to his own schedule and he didn't have to mix with anyone he didn't want to; he didn't have to go to meetings, and he didn't have to be careful about treading on anyone's toes. Joe had an unfortunate history of toe-treading, not that he meant to, but it seemed to happen regardless. He'd already managed to rub the lovely – if tempestuous – Ms Liddell the wrong way, which was a pity. He thought they'd clicked in the elevator, made a connection, he was hoping to get to know her better . . . at the very least he thought he'd have an ally in her. And he was going to need as many allies as he could get on the ground, because he had no doubt his appointment with the *Trib* was going to upset a few of those prickly egos.

Joe sat up straight and gave his head a vigorous rub to clear the cobwebs. Bugger them, he had as much right as anyone to call in favours and take advantage where it presented itself. Leo was an old friend of his father's. He had started as a copy boy during Joe Senior's heyday, and had even taken up an overseas post for a while in the hope of emulating his mentor. However, the life of a foreign correspondent was not for Leo and he returned to the news floor, slowly but surely making his way up the editorial ladder. He was much more suited to management, he never would have stuck it out as a correspondent, but that was not to say he didn't admire those who did. That was the reason for Leo's success: while he could be gruff and cranky and didn't appear to possess the essential people skills for management, he could recognise talent, and in his own way he knew how to nurture it, or at least get the most out of it. Which explained why Joe found himself with a job his first day home, when all he'd intended was to establish contact, let Leo know he was back and freelancing. Now he had an office, and a deal to remain exclusive to the *Trib*, though he had stopped short of going on salary. He didn't want to be tied down; he was home to be with his father, that was his priority and no job, no story, was going to come before that.

Joe Senior had been feeling the effects of his advancing condition for years before he was diagnosed, but he'd never said anything, never complained. The doctor said it was not unusual in late-onset motor neurone disease. The symptoms were so gradual that many people thought it was just age catching up with them. The hands trembled; muscles cramped after a bout of gardening or a long walk. But when climbing stairs became difficult Joe did mention it to his doctor. At his age, with a prior history of smoking, the regular battery of heart tests was duly ordered, but the results came back within the normal range. He was monitored after that, but it was only when the weakness in his limbs became more pronounced and he had a few falls that alarm bells started to go off. He was eventually diagnosed with a form of spinal muscular atrophy. It wouldn't kill him, but it would decrease his quality of life to such a degree that death might almost come as a relief.

That was some years ago now, but Joe still remembered how distraught he had been by the news. Hilary had only just taken up her position at MIT, and Corinne was newly married and relocated to Melbourne. So Joe had promptly left his post in the Middle East to return home. He couldn't leave it all to Mim in her honours year at uni, she'd certainly get nothing in the way of support from Will. He had bummed around since leaving school, wasted a 'gap' year, dropped out of two different uni courses, only to talk his father into footing the bill for Drama at UWS.

Although he had his flat in town, Joe worked almost solely from the house in the mountains, which was not so difficult to do, foot-leather journalism being largely an anachronism since the Internet had taken off. He could get in touch with anyone, any time, by phone or email; he had access online to government departments, company reports, statistics, whatever he needed. Of course, it curtailed his subject matter to some degree. He disseminated and analysed rather than reported breaking news, and while that had its frustrations, it meant he could be close to his dad. Joe Senior gradually became more disabled by his illness; he could not walk far, and had to reluctantly surrender to a wheel-chair when they were out of the house. The weakness in his arms and the tremor in his hands made it an effort to type, but that didn't stop him. He still had pieces published occasionally, and Joe involved him in whatever he was working on, running through ideas, getting him to proof final copy.

And then 9/11 happened and everything changed. His father could barely stand it; he insisted that if he couldn't be there, then Joe had to be there for him. He wanted to know what was going on from a source he could trust. Besides, Joe had gained vital insight from his time in the Middle East, and his father said he had a duty to put it to use.

He emailed his son every day, and Joe replied almost as often, certainly as often as he was able. He initially went to the US with the paper he was working for at the time, commuting between New York and Washington, but when the war began he returned to the Middle East bureau. Soon after he took a post with Reu-ters so he could have more autonomy, and eventually he went completely freelance. Joe didn't like being told what to write, what would fit into any given newspaper's agenda. He wanted to report the stories that were happening in front of his eyes; he wanted people to know what it was like on the ground, for ordi-nary people like them whose country had been invaded, whose everyday security was constantly under threat, whose way of life had changed forever.

But that was variously considered too inflammatory, too sen-sitive, too confronting, not of interest . . . Joe was given as many excuses from editors as he had stories to tell. It was wearing him out, and once he could see the writing on the wall with Sarah, there seemed little reason to stay on one side of the world while his father's life was dwindling away on the other.

Joe gazed out the train window, at the endless grey-green expanse of bush, the landscape so familiar and so comforting to him it tugged at his heart. It didn't matter how often he was away or for how long, this always felt like coming home.

*

Mim was waiting for him at the station, Joe spotted her standing on the platform as the train pulled in. She didn't look her thirty years, there was a translucence about her that made her seem ethereal, or fragile. Asthmatic as a child, Mim was perennially thin and pale, her huge blue eyes staring warily out at a world she didn't quite fit into. But her family adored her, cosseted her, made it easy for her to stay within the sanctuary they provided. So she had stayed; through a bachelor degree, an honours year and a masters, she'd made the long commute from the mountains to Sydney University almost every day, never entertaining the possibility of living anywhere else.

As Joe stepped from the carriage onto the platform Mim spotted him and smiled. She stood where she was as he strode across to her, dropped his bag and scooped her up in his arms. He heard her soft little giggle as she returned his hug. They had formed quite a fearsome bond, the two of them, when Joe was back living at home. He had missed a lot of her teenage years, so it had been a good opportunity to get to know the adult she'd become. He read her poetry avidly; as someone who could only use words to explain and expand, he had great admiration for the way she used so few words to say so much.

Joe released her after a moment and smiled down at her. 'Hey Mim, look at you. You never change.'

She set her head on an angle, considering him. 'But you have, Joe. You're starting to look older.'

He shook his head, grinning. 'Thanks, Mim. You could have been a little more poetic about it.'

'No, I don't think I could,' she returned, the faintest glint in her eye. Joe picked up his bag and Mim put her arm through his as they walked out of the station to the car. 'Dad's so excited to see you, he can hardly contain himself.'

'How is he?'

She didn't answer right away. 'He's pretty good, today's a good day,' she said, unlocking the car doors.

Once they drove out of the town centre and were on their way to the house, Joe shifted in his seat to look at his sister. 'So how is he, Mim, really?'

'He has good days, and bad.'

'In what ratio?'

She seemed to have to think about it. 'It's a good day . . . whenever he hears from you, or Hil, or when Corinne calls and he gets to talk to the kids, he loves that . . .'

'I meant his health, Mim.'

Of course she knew that's what he meant. 'It's a good day when he can manage to swallow an entire meal without incident. He gets game then,' she added, smiling faintly, 'and asks for a glass of wine.'

Joe frowned. 'And what's a bad day?'

'When he has one of his episodes.'

'Episodes?'

Her eyes didn't leave the road in front of her. 'Sometimes it's an effort for him to breathe, he needs a spell on oxygen most days, that's not a problem. But if he has a cold, or even just a case of the sniffles, it gets tricky. We can't have fluid building up in his lungs or he'll get pneumonia. But we have the coughing machine now, that's made a big difference. We had a few scary moments before . . .'

Joe felt like he'd been whacked across the head with a cricket bat. 'Why didn't you tell me, Mim?'

She glanced over at him. 'He asked me not to. Sometimes when he's struggling for breath and he can barely speak, he still manages to say don't tell your brother, don't tell Hil or Crinny. I'm not allowed to call anyone except the doctor. As soon as he's right again, he'll point out how he got through that, and imagine if I'd called everyone and made a fuss and they started flying in from all over just to find him okay again.'

'But he's not okay at all, is he?'

'Depends on your frame of reference, Joe. He has good days and he has bad,' she repeated calmly. 'I just thought you should be prepared.'

But Joe didn't feel any more prepared when they pulled into the gravel driveway, though his heart lifted at the sight of the house. As he got out of the car, the pungent smell of eucalyptus hit him, mingled with the smoke from indoor fires, freshly lit. Much as he'd been waiting for this moment, Joe found himself hesitating, one foot paused on the step of the verandah while

Mim unlocked the front door. This was it, he wouldn't be able to pretend after this, he wouldn't be able to kid himself that his dad was doing okay, that he'd be around for a long time to come.

Mim was watching him. She reached out her hand, 'Come on, Joe, he's waiting for you.'

The house didn't change so much as evolve, it had been evolving ever since he was a child. His mother had been a mad fossicker and she had loved scouring the antique and second-hand stores throughout the mountains, picking up an old chair for next to nothing and doing it up, then another, then a small occasional table, a desk, a hallstand . . . till the place got so cluttered she couldn't find any more space no matter how she rearranged things. So then she'd send some of it off to the second-hand dealer, only to make room for whatever she'd bring home next. She had kept that up until the day she died; the last couple of pieces awaiting refurbishment had remained, no one had wanted to change anything afterwards. The colour of the walls was the same, the dark-stained woodwork, the view from all the windows, changeless, and deeply comforting.

'Joe?'

He turned around. A stout middle-aged woman was standing next to Mim. 'This is Janice, one of Dad's nurses,' she explained.

'Oh . . .' Joe was momentarily taken aback. He had nurses, plural?

'It's so wonderful to finally meet you, Mr Bannister,' Janice said warmly, the barest trace of an accent in her voice, Scottish perhaps. 'Your father never stops going on about you. He makes me read all your pieces, not that it's a chore, mind you.'

Joe roused himself, offering her his hand. 'Janice, thank you, thank you for all your help.'

'It's my pleasure, Mr Bannister.'

'Please, call me Joe.'

'Joe.' She dipped her head. 'Your father is an absolute delight . . . an inspiration really.'

Joe smiled faintly, aware of an uneasy pang in his chest.

'Well, I'll be getting out of your way,' said Janice.

'Let me walk you out,' Mim offered.

'I think I know my way by now, thank you, Miriam,' Janice

smiled, patting her arm. 'Your father's anxious to see Joe. You should go on in.'

She retreated up the hallway and they heard the front door open and close.

Joe turned to look at Mim. 'He needs nurses? More than one?'

'Well, obviously he can't be left alone, Joe,' she explained. 'We have a night nurse, three actually, on a rotating roster, and he also has regular physical therapy, as well as respite care a couple of times a week.'

The enormity of his father's disability was dawning on him, or rather, caving in on him.

'I couldn't leave the house at all if we didn't get some respite care,' Mim added in a quiet, tentative voice.

'Of course, Mim,' Joe touched her arm reassuringly. 'Whatever you need. This is just a lot to take in.'

She looked at him. 'Are you going to be all right?'

He took a breath. 'Absolutely. Let's do it.'

Joe Senior was set up in the north-facing sitting room permanently now. Clearly he needed the extra space. It looked like a hospital ward. Joe tried to disguise his alarm as he took in the plethora of machines and contraptions and equipment, his eyes gradually, reluctantly almost, drawn to the state-of-the-art hospital bed, and the withered, pale figure reclining there. He felt Mim's hand on his back, gently propelling him forward.

'Dad . . .' Joe fixed a smile on his face, hoping his voice didn't sound strangled.

His father's eyes lit up, but Joe noticed that though his lips moved into the approximation of a smile, his face was oddly expressionless. It occurred to him that he may not even have the control of his facial muscles any more. He remembered reading about that when he was first diagnosed. He leant over his father, taking his hand and kissing his cheek.

'Joe, my boy . . .' His voice was raspy and weak. 'You look good, son.'

Joe couldn't say the same. 'Mim said I look older,' he told him, pulling a chair closer and sitting down.

'She's gotten cheeky, that one.' He nodded faintly. 'Tells me what to do all the time.'

Joe glanced at his sister, who had stepped back a little, but remained watchful. 'So what's going on, Dad? Taking things a little easy, aren't you?'

He let out a weak laugh. 'Yeah, that's it, I've got lazy, son.' Joe noticed he had to take a breath every few words. 'I'm so lazy, I even got a new computer, does everything for me.'

'Oh yeah?' Joe leaned over to reach the computer on its mobile stand, wheeling it closer. His dad proceeded to take him through the various bibs and bobs he'd acquired to help him work the computer more easily. His speech was so halted and laborious, it was like listening to someone with a severe stutter. Joe wanted to interrupt, fill in words, or tell him to stop when it seemed as though he was struggling, but of course he didn't. He listened patiently, hoping his father did not sense his distress at seeing him like this. He was demonstrating a one-handed keyboard that strapped onto his arm, so he only had to move his fingers, though it did require a whole new approach to typing.

'Have you tried voice recognition, Dad?' Joe asked him.

'I bought the software, but it wasn't as effective, I get too breathless these days.'

Joe waited while he wheezed, catching his breath.

'I want to try out a headmouse next,' he managed after a while.

'What's that?'

'Attaches around your head . . . has a wireless sensor . . . means I can just turn my head slightly, point to a keyboard on the screen. Tedious, but the time will come . . .'

Joe didn't know what to say, it was beyond his comprehension that his dad would eventually be unable to write. How would he go on living then?

His father was watching him. 'So what are you up to, son?'

'Looks like I'm working for Leo Monaghan. He said hi by the way.'

He nodded. 'Little Leo, that lad had an ego . . . short men . . .' He gave a weak laugh, but it made him wheeze again. Mim was instantly at his bedside, and had strapped an oxygen mask to his face before Joe knew what was happening.

'You need to rest now, Dad,' she said. 'You can talk later, Joe's not going anywhere.'

Joe squeezed his hand gently. 'I'll see you in a little while, Dad,' he assured him, leaning over to kiss his forehead.

He walked out of the room, shaken. He turned down the hall, striding past the kitchen and out onto the back verandah, where he bent over, his hands on his knees, catching his breath. His chest ached, and he could feel his eyes filling. He sniffed, shaking his head as he stood up tall again. He rubbed his eyes and took a few deep breaths, gazing out at the view he loved, the purple haze enveloping the ridge beyond. But the ache from his chest was rising into his throat. He wanted to shout out, to yell at someone, to kick something.

'Joe? Are you okay?'

He swung around as Mim came out through the back door. 'Why didn't you tell me? I mean, fuck, look at him, Mim, he's dying.'

She quickly closed the door behind her. 'I know.'

Joe frowned, dropping his voice. 'Does he?'

'Of course, Joe.'

'Then why didn't you tell me?'

'What could you have done about it?' she said calmly.

'I could have been here sooner.'

'He didn't want that. I told you.'

'Bullshit, Mim! He was just saying that, he doesn't want to put anyone out. You should have told me. You should have let me make the decision.'

'I think Dad has a right to make his own decisions.'

'Oh, sure, even if he can't take himself to the bathroom.'

'Joe —'

'I get emails almost every day, smart, informed, witty emails,' he went on. 'What, have you been writing them for him?'

'No, he writes them himself.'

'Oh come on, the state he's in? It'd take him all day.'

'It does,' she said in a level voice. 'His mind's as sharp as ever, Joe. He can still read as fast and as much as he ever did, but writing takes a huge effort. But I'm sure it's helped keep him alive.'

Joe just stared at her.

'This is the way he wanted it, Joe,' Mim went on. 'He still had his dignity while he could write to you, while you couldn't see how much he'd deteriorated. I didn't want to take that away from him.'

'Are you saying I shouldn't have come home?'

'No, of course not,' she said. 'It's time. But you have to find a way to deal with the reality of his condition, Joe, not make him feel self-conscious. He's at peace with it, you have to be as well.'

He sighed. 'You're right. It's just a shock,' he said quietly.

She stepped closer and put her arms around him. The lump rose all the way into his throat and he wept silently, holding his sister tight. It was really happening, they were going to lose him and there was nothing Joe could do about it. The grief, the help-lessness, was overpowering.

He drew back to look at her. 'How do you manage, Mim?'

'I'm okay. Question is, how am I going to manage without him?'

Sunday

Jo was waiting on the west side of Sutherland station as usual, and as usual Belle was running late. She supposed with three littlies that shouldn't be surprising, but it was the weekend, which meant Darren should be around, so how hard could it be for two adults to look after three toddlers and be on time? They always had the same arrangement, so Jo was more than a little frustrated that her sister couldn't get her act together when she went to the trouble of coming all the way out to visit her. If Jo could get to her place any other way, she would, but Belle had insisted on planting herself out here in the 'the Shire', in the shadow of a nuclear reactor, for godsakes, and the train only came as far as Sutherland. There was a patchy bus service on the weekend, and Buckley's of getting a taxi, without taking out a second mortgage at least, so Jo really didn't have any alternative but to rely on a lift. It was Belle who always gave her such a hard time about not visiting enough, not that Jo could ever get her to come into the city, so you'd think she'd at least make an effort to be here on time to pick her up.

As Jo went to check her watch again, Belle's thumping big, gun-metal-grey four-wheel drive careered around the corner and pulled up in front of her, its giant tyres scraping against the kerb. Jo opened the door to be met with, 'Caelen, I swear, if you keep tormenting your sister, I will put you right up the back seat. Now keep your hands to yourself and not another word. Hi Jo, sorry I'm late, I was going to leave the kids with Darren, so what does he do? Starts the mower up five minutes before I have to walk out the door. I said, "What are you doing?" And he said, "What does it look like?" and I said, "But I'm going to pick up Jo", and he says, "So?" And so I go, "What about the kids" and he says, "They'll be fine." Bloody typical. I said I'm not leaving the kids here in the house with you outside with the mower going, you won't hear a thing. So he's trying to insist it's all right, they'll be okay, what could possibly happen? And I'm going "*Are you serious*? Falling down, banging their heads, running with scissors, choking, broken glass, stitches . . ." and you know what he says? "No worries, I'll whack on a DVD and they won't budge." Oh if it was only that easy. What does he think I do all day? He's got no idea, honestly. Are you right there, Jo?'

She had finally managed to clamber up onto the front seat. Bloody oversized cars were not suited to undersized girls. 'Yeah, I'm fine,' she panted, leaning across to kiss Belle on the cheek.

'Say hello to Aunty JoJo, kids.'

There followed a warbled chorus from the back. Jo turned around to smile at her nephews and niece and experienced that familial tug of the heartstrings, a kind of strange pride in the knowledge they were related to her, combined with an enormous sense of relief that she wasn't responsible for them.

Caelen thrust a sticky lollypop towards her. 'Wanna thuck, Arnie JoJo?'

'Tempting, but no thanks, Caelen.'

It never ceased to confound Jo how Belle had chosen to name her children, considering what the two of them had been through. But Belle insisted that Caelen, Cascey and Carsyn were a far cry from Bambi and Tinkerbell. Still, Jo had persisted, why make up something when there are so many perfectly good traditional names to choose from, names that everyone could spell and pronounce . . . John or Jane or Tom or Anne, for example. Belle had turned up her nose. If they had names like those, she maintained, they would stand out around here.

Belle weaved the bulky vehicle rather inelegantly through the streets, routinely hitting roundabouts, corners and anything else apparently outside her peripheral vision. They attempted conversation, but it was virtually impossible with the constant stream of interruptions coming from the back seat. It didn't seem to faze Belle at all. She could be halfway through a sentence and veer off to correct one of the children, solve a dispute or answer a seemingly bottomless well of inane questions, and then pick up again where she'd left off without missing a beat. Jo was the one struggling to keep up, so she did what she always did and gave up trying. They'd have time enough to catch up as the day went on, so Jo decided the best tack was to ask Belle a question that would keep her going for the remainder of the trip home and not require any input from her.

'So how's things with the in-laws?'

'Ugh, don't get me started.'

But that's exactly what she did. Jo tuned out almost immediately, she'd heard it all before. They crossed the bridge over the Woronora River and officially entered the aspirational mortgage belt. Jo found suburbia unsettling; she'd heard it said that people go to the suburbs to die. But that wasn't quite accurate; they go to the Central or South Coast to die, preferably to a small fishing village with a bowling club. The suburbs could be called the destination du jour of the middle-aged, and that was even more depressing. Jo stared out at the houses parading past the car window. McMansions all: super-sized, mass-produced, all the same but for a choice of standard variations, like a brick veneer McValue meal. Faux-Tuscan, Neo-Georgian, Fediterranean, a couple had the facade of a suburban shopping mall. Good God, there was even one with a turret. Did they need to maintain surveillance on enemy forces in the next cul-de-sac?

Jo had never understood what attracted Belle out here, and since she'd moved they didn't get to see each other as often.

When Belle still worked in the city they used to meet regularly for lunch, even after Caelen was born and she went part-time. But when the twins came along, she stopped work altogether. Jo used to try to talk her into coming into the city for a night on her own, but Belle always dismissed the idea. She couldn't leave the children yet, they were too little, Darren would never cope. Jo loved her sister dearly and respected her choices, but in the end they were living markedly different lives, with very little in common any more. Except the past, and that would bind them forever no matter how little they saw each other, or how far apart they lived.

Jo suddenly became aware that Belle was driving into some kind of SUV convention. But no, it was just the carpark for the local shopping mall. Jo held her breath as her sister swerved into a space that didn't look nearly big enough to contain the tank. Miraculously, she somehow managed to avoid hitting the adjacent cars, despite the weird angle she ended up on.

'I'm just going to run in quick, I'll be two secs,' said Belle, leaping from the car.

Jo blinked. 'What?'

'Gin or bubbly?'

'Huh?'

'I'll just get both, ay? Darren is *so* on duty for the *entire* afternoon.'

And then she vanished. Jo didn't even see which way she went, she was swallowed up in the sea of oversized cars. Jo slowly turned around to look uncertainly at the children, just as Caelen jabbed Cascey with his lollypop stick. She opened her mouth, wider than Jo thought possible, and let out a wail that was similarly louder than Jo thought possible from a person of her size.

'Caelen, why did you hurt your sister? Look, you made her cry.' But he would have been hard-pressed to hear her over the siren wails. Jo gingerly reached out a hand to pat Cascey on the knee, but that was just met with more wails. She tried a feeble 'Shhh' which had no effect either. Carsyn was blocking his ears and trying to outbellow his twin with pleas of '*Qui-yettt, Cay-thee!*' and so Caelen started yelling '*You be quiet butt-head!*' and pretty soon people were staring.

Jesus. Jo unbuckled her seatbelt and went to open the door, realising just in time that there was only a whisker between them and the adjacent assault vehicle. She opened a crack in the door and slithered out, sidling to the rear of the car, then dashing around to the other side where there was enough space to open the door. She climbed up and leaned across Caelen to reach Cascey's seatbelt as the little girl screamed like a banshee. Surely she'd have to take a breath eventually?

'Ow! Arnie JoJo, you're squishing me,' Caelen whined. 'I can't *breeeeve*!'

'Yeah, well, you should have thought of that before you poked your sister, bud,' Jo said through gritted teeth.

'I didn't mean to, it was juss a assident!'

'Caelen, jabbing your sister with your lollypop was as much an accident as two planes flying into the World Trade Centre towers.'

Now Caelen was crying, but at least it made Cascey stop long enough to gawk at him. Jo finally managed to undo the buckle, wrestle Cascey's arms free and scoop her up before performing a kind of abseil movement backwards out of the car.

'There now,' she said, flipping her niece around to inspect her. Yuck. Her face was covered in tears mixed with snot, thick and green oozing from both nostrils. Jo instinctively thrust her out at arm's length, which only served to set her off again.

'Oh for . . .' Jo groaned. She looked in the back seat for tissues, a baby bag, an old rag even, but there was nothing. She went around to the back of the car, propping Cascey on her hip facing outwards as she opened the heavy rear door. No nappy bag there either, dammit. She supposed Belle didn't bother to pack a survival kit when she was only popping out briefly. A little oversight that Jo might point out to her for future reference.

Just then the car parked next to them reversed out of its spot, giving Jo room to open the front passenger door wide and get to her bag, where she managed to find a few stray tissues. She turned Cascey around again and attempted to wipe her face, while she squirmed and grizzled and generally made hard work of it.

'For Chrissakes, C, would you just give me one small break!' Jo cried.

But Cascey could cry louder, and she did. They were getting looks, smug 'bad mother' looks. Well, they could look all they wanted. She wasn't a bad mother, she was a childless aunt, so she wasn't even part of their stupid club anyway. Nor did she want any part of it.

She started jiggling Cascey on her hip. 'You have to help me out here, C,' she tried to reason. 'Us girls have got to stick together, you know. I'm telling you, you're definitely going to want me on your side when you hit your teens.' Cascey sniffed, gazing up at her with what could only be described as big blue eyes. When she wasn't screaming, she was actually very cute. 'You're going to be a stunner, *yes you are*,' Jo continued in the saccharine sing-songy voice that even normally intelligent, unsentimental people seemed to revert to automatically when talking to infants. 'And I'm going to be the cool aunt who talks your mum into letting you wear low cut or high cut or whatever the hell cut is in fashion in another decade, *oh yes I am!*'

A small curly giggle escaped from Cascey's lips, followed by a big tremulous sigh. She leaned into Jo and dropped her head on her shoulder. Well, what do you know . . . Jo started to rock slowly back and forth, just like she'd seen mothers do. This wasn't so bad, there was even something a little Zen about it. Jo peered up into the back seat and both boys were quiet, Carsyn actually looked like he was dozing off. Everything was back under control. Now Jo felt smug. Then she got a whiff of something . . . something really foul. Jo walked around to the rear of the car to escape it, but it seemed to be coming with her. Oh no. She lifted Cascey's top to check her pants but she didn't need to, there was poo oozing up her back. Jo gasped, jerking her in her arms. Cascey shot upright, looking at Jo through bleary eyes.

'It's okay,' Jo soothed her, patting her back down with one hand while she kept the other arm firmly lodged behind her knees, so her offending bottom was arched out right away from Jo. She felt queasy. Where the frick was Belle?

Finally she spotted her coming towards them. Jo hurried to meet her, thrusting Cascey at her. 'Your daughter is leaking from every orifice,' she grimaced, swapping her for the Liquorbarn bag. She felt like breaking open one of these bottles right now.

'Well, that'll be a nice surprise for Daddy when we get home, won't it!' declared Belle.

'Have you ever been claustrophobic?' Jo asked Belle.

They were sitting alone outside at the barbecue setting, far from the madding crowd, nursing a chilled G&T each and crunching on chips from a wooden bowl. For all Belle's complaining, Darren wasn't so bad. He'd never exactly impressed Jo with his towering intellect, in fact he was a bit of a goof. He used the same line every time they met – 'How's life in the fast lane?' And Jo would answer, 'Fast and furious', and he'd get a kick out that. Every, single, time. On the other hand, he seemed to do whatever Belle told him to do, that had to be a bonus. Currently he was inside, under strict orders to keep Caelen out of their hair, while tending to the disgusting nappies and putting the twins down for a nap, after which he was to serve lunch. And that meant they didn't have to budge off their backsides for the next couple of hours.

'What do you mean, claustrophobic?' asked Belle.

'You know, anxious in small spaces.'

'I know that . . . I mean, what makes you ask?'

Jo put down her drink. 'I got stuck in an elevator the other day.'

'Really? I didn't think that could happen any more.'

'That's what I thought, but trust me, it can.'

'Yeah, but it's all computerised, right? They just press a button in a central control room and you're on your way again?'

'Not even close. Not in our crappy old building anyway.'

Belle frowned. 'How long were you stuck?'

'Over an hour.'

Now her eyes were taking on a faraway look. 'Wow, a whole hour to yourself. What must that be like . . . ?'

'Ahh . . . vaguely terrifying,' Jo suggested.

'I dunno, it sounds kind of appealing to me. Being stuck in an elevator, not with the kids of course,' she added, rather unnecessarily. 'But it'd be so quiet, was it quiet? I bet it was,' she nodded, answering her own question. 'No one could get to you, there'd be nothing to do but sit and stare at the walls . . . God, do you realise how rarely I get to be completely alone? I mean, they come in to bed if I stay too long, they come in the shower, they come in the toilet, for godsakes. They hunt me out wherever I am. Sometimes I hide, it's true, I hide from my own children when they're looking for me. Behind a door, in the pantry . . . not for long, not if they're crying or anything, just for a minute, when I realise they don't know where I am, I just take that minute to be alone . . . Oh, Darren makes a grand gesture some Friday nights, "Have a bath, love," he says. "Relax, I'll handle everything." And not five minutes passes before he's walking in the door, one of them on his hip, asking where this or that is. I've thought about locking the door, seriously, but what if something was to happen? I mean, I could quite conceivably slip getting out the bath, hit my head, cut myself, even twist an ankle or something. Then could you imagine the to-do – Darren trying to break the door down with all three under his feet? One of them would get hurt, for sure. So I don't lock the door. I don't reckon I'm going to be able to lock the door for another ten years. It's like a prison sentence, only the other way around.'

Was she finished? Jo wondered. She had to be finished. There couldn't anything more to say on the topic, surely?

'So anyway,' Jo ventured tentatively, 'I guess you don't get claustrophobic then?'

Belle roused out of her reverie. 'Oh yeah, what happened? Was it bad?'

'Pretty bad. I had a full-blown panic attack.'

'Wow,' Belle seemed thoughtful. 'What exactly happens in a full-blown panic attack anyway?'

'Oh, you know, gasping for breath, heart palpitations, breaking out into a sweat . . . panicking. That's why it's called a panic attack.'

'I didn't know you had panic attacks.'

'I don't. But I've never been stuck in an elevator before,' said Jo. 'I have felt . . . uncomfortable, I guess, in confined spaces. But I've never been trapped, so it hasn't got out of hand.'

Belle propped her chin on her hand. 'I suppose it could be scary if you were on your own.'

'I wasn't on my own.'

'Oh, well, it'd be even worse if you were feeling claustrophobic and you were surrounded by people.'

'There was just one other person,' said Jo.

'Someone you knew?'

'I'd never met him before.'

'*Him?*' Belle's eyes lit up. Jo rolled hers. 'What was he like, was he cute?'

Why was that always the first question? 'No, he was definitely not cute.'

'Oh, so you got stuck in a lift with a fugly guy?' Belle pulled a face. 'No wonder you had a panic attack.'

'He's not ugly, he's just not cute, okay?' said Jo. 'He's very tall, and big, you know . . .'

'Ooh, a big bear of a man, eh?' Just like their mother used to say. 'Okay, so I see where you're coming from now. He's not *cute*, but was he *handsome?*'

'Oh, I dunno, Belle,' Jo groaned. 'Does it matter?'

'Of course it matters!' she cried. 'You got stuck in a lift with a big bear of a man and I want details. What was he like?'

Jo shrugged. 'He was all right, I suppose. A little scruffy for my tastes.'

Belle lifted an eyebrow, grinning wickedly. 'Ooh, so he was a bit edgy, eh? More Viggo than Orlando.'

'What are you talking about?'

'You know, Orlando Bloom was the pretty one in *Lord of the Rings*, whereas Viggo Mortensen . . .' she sighed '. . . all unshaven and unwashed. That hair . . .'

God, she was as bad as Angie. Jo had never done the fantasising thing, not even as a teenager. She'd always felt it was a pointless exercise. Why waste your time hankering after someone who didn't even know you were alive, and would not be interested if he did. She supposed it explained why she'd ended up a journalist instead of a novelist. She wrote from facts, not from her imagination.

'Okay,' Belle was saying, 'I have a mental picture now, go on . . .'

'He doesn't look like Viggo Mortensen, Belle.'

'He does in my head,' she declared. 'Which is making this a

whole lot more interesting. Now, how did he handle your panic attack? What did he do?'

Jo shrugged. 'He was just very kind, calmed me down . . . you know . . .'

Belle was hanging on her every word. 'No I don't know! That's why I'm asking you. I don't have a life, remember, Jo? I thought getting stuck in a lift sounded exciting even without a bloke thrown in. Give me something.'

'I'm sorry, Belle, but nothing happened.' No way was she going to tell her the part about him carrying her through the office, not after what Angie had made of it.

Belle took a slurp of her drink. 'All I can say is that for a journalist you sure don't know how to spin a yarn.'

'Journalists don't spin yarns.'

'Yeah, right.' She rattled the ice in her glass. 'Well, this is becoming a dry old argument, where's our drinks waiter? *Dar-ren!*'

A moment later the sliding door opened and he stuck his head out. 'What?'

'We need refills here.'

'What did your last slave die of?'

'Insubordination, as I recall.'

'I've got my hands a bit full in here, you know, Belle. You could get it yourself.'

'Yeah, and you could get sex again before you die, but it's not looking good.'

He uttered some kind of expletive, but sauntered out a minute or two later with the bottle of gin and a bottle of tonic. He plonked them on the table. 'Do you think you can manage to pour them yourselves?'

'Thanks Darren,' Jo called after him as he went back inside.

Belle was making them another drink. 'Suppose I'd be pushing it to tell him he forgot the ice?'

Jo grinned. 'I think we can manage without it.'

Belle passed her back her glass.

'So, you've never been claustrophobic?' Jo asked in a last-ditch attempt to get back to the point.

'Nuh,' Belle said plainly. 'In fact I like being shut in, blinds down at night, doors closed, sometimes I even put a pillow over my head to block the light. Freaks Darren out,' she added, with a vaguely malevolent chuckle.

Jo frowned. 'You don't have any negative associations at all?'

'Why should I?'

'It's just, you know, when we were kids, all those nights we had to spend locked away in our room . . .'

Belle shook her head. 'I don't know how you remember it, but I remember the picnics on the carpet, and that magic stash of treats that seemed to come out of nowhere . . . the games we played . . . you reading to me till I fell asleep. I used to love those nights, Jo.'

Those nights were when Charlene would pull Jo aside and tell her the two of them were to keep out of sight or else. She was 'entertaining' and if they made so much as a peep there would be hell to pay. Jo didn't want to frighten Belle, so she tried to make it fun. She kept up a hidden stock of party food purchased from her stolen emergency funds. She made up games they could play in silence, variations on charades, or hangman, making a game out of trying to stay as quiet as possible. When the music was turned up, Jo would read aloud to Belle, who then seemed oblivious to all sounds, raised voices, smashing glass, slamming doors and, the worst, the headboard banging against the adjoining wall accompanied by orgasmic cries. Not that Jo knew they were orgasmic at first, she just knew she didn't want Belle hearing any of it.

'It was our safe place,' said Belle. 'The way I remember it, we liked being holed up in our room. And she never *locked* us in, Jo.'

'Only because the doors usually didn't have locks.'

'I think you're being a little dramatic.'

'Belle,' Jo sighed, 'our mother hid us out of sight because she didn't want the blokes she brought home to know she had kids.'

'Well, it was better than when she dragged us out to show us off,' said Belle. 'Remember what that was like? There was this one guy I'll never forget . . . so creepy . . . what was his name? Barry, maybe?'

There were a lot of Barrys over the years.

'He made us dance for him and Mum, remember? He was missing teeth, and he had gross tattoos all the way up both arms, this was before they were fashionable. He smelled of grog and cigarettes and he kept slobbering on us. Ugh,' she shuddered. 'I'd rather stay shut up in the room any day.'

Jo was casting her mind back . . . remembering . . . Belle was right, but even if they were safe in the room, there was an ever-present feeling of fear, of foreboding, for Jo at least. She was always hypervigilant, anxious that some drunk was going to burst into the room and discover them.

And that was something she obviously couldn't shake off. It had become imprinted into her psyche like an instinct, turning her into a claustrophobe, apparently.

'Speaking of Mum,' said Belle.

Jo's brain came hurtling back into the present.

'Why do you always have to get that look as soon as I mention her?'

'I don't get a look.'

'You so do,' Belle said flatly. 'Anyway, she's coming down next week.'

Jo tried very hard to set her face in such a way that she couldn't be accused of having a 'look'.

'There you go again,' Belle declared. 'Don't look like that!'

'I'm not looking like anything,' Jo insisted. 'So Mum's coming down. What does it have to do with me?'

'Oh, I dunno, I just had this crazy idea that maybe you might want to drop in and say hello to the woman who gave birth to you?'

'You mean the woman who accidentally fell pregnant with me and found out too late to do anything about it?'

'Jo . . .' Now Belle was the one with the look.

'What? It's the truth, isn't it? At least she purposely meant to fall pregnant with you because she was trying to hold onto Dad.'

'Here we go again,' Belle sighed. 'Okay, Jo, we know Mum made a whole lot of mistakes, but she was really young and it was a long time ago. I still believe she loved us, and that she did the best she could in the circumstances.'

'Well, go ahead and believe what you have to, Belle. Doesn't make it true.'

Belle shook her head sadly. 'I'm sure you'd have a different perspective if you had kids of your own.'

Jo groaned. 'That is so patronising, Belle! As if I can't have any insight into my life, or recognise good parenting, without having kids of my own? How would you like it if I said you don't have any understanding of the big wide world because you stay home with your kids?'

'Well that's what you think, isn't it?'

'No it isn't!' Jo insisted. 'I admire you, Belle, I'm not sure I could do what you're doing.'

'And when you say it like that, what you're really saying is that you wouldn't want to do it.'

'Oh, is that what I'm saying, is it, Belle? When have I ever criticised your life choices? You're the one sitting there telling me I don't know which way is up because I haven't had kids.'

'I didn't say that,' she insisted, her voice softening. 'At least I didn't mean that, JoJo. I just wish you could put things in the past and move on with your life, that's all.'

'I have moved on, Belle, you're the one who keeps insisting on dragging me back. Why do you care so much about me and Mum getting along?'

'Because I love you, and I want you to be happy.'

'I'm happy, what makes you think I'm not happy?'

She shook her head sadly. 'Jo, come on . . .'

Jo was perplexed. 'What's that supposed to mean?'

'You're having an affair with a married man, and not for the first time.'

Oh Jesus. It always came back to that.

'How happy can you be, Jo, when you only have relationships with men you have no future with?'

Jo wanted to say, very happy. That was the whole point. She didn't want Belle's suburban dream with all the trappings, emphasis on 'trap'. But she couldn't say that, because while it was perfectly fine for Belle, or any married person, to sit there and tell her where she was going wrong in her life, it was a whole other box of dice for a single person to tell a married person that they wouldn't want their life for quids. That just sounded bitter. Or jealous. Or – a favourite – like you were 'protesting too much'. Or any number of other perverse and unhealthy emotions that poor partner-deficient people were apparently riddled with.

Belle leaned in closer. 'All I'm saying is that you're kidding yourself if you think you can go through life detached from your own mother. Do you know what Bob Geldof said?'

'That he didn't like Mondays?'

She ignored that. 'He said he had a mother-shaped hole in his heart because his mum died when he was young, and no amount of love or success or anything else can fill that because it's mother-shaped.'

Jo was picturing the Charlene-shaped hole in her heart – big hair, tight dress, tottering stilettos.

'Frankly, Jo, I think you're in denial,' Belle went on, 'and until you reconcile this relationship, you won't really feel . . . complete. And if you do end up having kids . . .'

Jo stifled a yawn. Her sister watched way too much Oprah, or Dr Phil. She hoped her glazed expression was giving Belle the hint that she wasn't taking anything more in.

'Anyway,' Belle said finally, 'she's going to be here for a week or so, surely you can fit us in somewhere in your busy schedule?'

The very idea aroused a sense of dread in Jo. It was not that she refused outright to see Charlene, or that they weren't speaking as such. She just avoided contact where possible, and her mother certainly made no overtures in that direction either. It had ever been thus. Jo was well and truly old enough to make her own decisions about how she wanted to spend her time and who she wanted to spend it with. But Belle had this annoying compulsion to mark the milestones of her life with a celebration – getting married, having babies, that kind of thing – so Jo and Charlene had been thrust together over the years, lined up in the same photo, clinking glasses to toast the occasion, playing happy families when really they were barely more than strangers.

'It'll depend on work . . . and that,' said Jo, clutching at her last straw.

'Of course, we'll fit in around you,' said Belle sweetly. 'We could even come into the city to meet you.'

Jo thought about that, her mother coming to her flat, the sneers, the criticism. 'Well, we'll see.'

'And if I don't hear from you, I'll give you a call.'

Jo didn't doubt it.

J O   L I D D E L L

BITCH

I thought it had peaked, I honestly did. I knew that the eighties were the real boom time for the self-help industry, but I thought it had well and truly peaked, and it had been on a steady decline ever since. I truly thought we'd moved on, that we were looking outward, trying to explain the big picture instead, to solve some of life's more pressing issues – like how to save the planet, perhaps.

Surely, I thought, we've all had enough of naval-gazing and blaming our parents, our teachers, our peers, the place we were born, the method of our birth, whether we were breastfed, our religion, our lack of religion . . . I could go on, but I'm sure you get the drift.

But a quick squiz the other day at my local bookstore revealed otherwise. Shelf upon shelf of self-help, self-healing, self-growth, self-fulfilment. In fact, it appears we don't even need an obvious problem any more, if we can't find something wrong, we probably have repressed a memory of some hideous, childhood trauma. Puhlease.

When are we going to get over ourselves? When are we going to stop obsessing and get on with living? I know you've heard this before, but really, what about the starving children in Africa? Have they got time to grizzle about being the middle child? I think not. But we don't have to go all the way to Africa. In your own street there are people with real problems, who have to get up every day and wonder how they're going to get through it. Really.

The fact is, everyone has crap from their past they have to deal with, but do you want it to be what defines you?

My grandmother used to tsk tsk, and mutter she was glad she had teenagers before they invented 'adolescence'. I think I understand what she was getting at now. She used to say, don't pick at scabs, or else they'll never heal. She also said stop whining. I think it's about time we all did.

bitch@thetribune.com

Tuesday morning

It was the first editorial meeting for the week. Sunday's paper was already lining guinea pig cages across the metropolitan area, and they had another edition to put out in five days' time. Everyone generally attended this meeting to get an overview of the direction and flavour of next week's paper, and to make sure there were no major conflicts of interest.

Don McAllister was in the middle of outlining his progress on a series he was compiling on the continuing saga of the war in Afghanistan. He was a nice man, and he knew his stuff, but he was dull as dishwater. Not on the page, thank God. On the page he was thought-provoking and ground-breaking and award-winning. Which was why he was a print journalist. His personality didn't have to sell the story, his words were more than up to the task of doing that.

Lachlan was the one who got invited onto *Meet The Press* and *Lateline* and anywhere the paper did need a personality to sell a story. The meeting had moved on and now Lachlan had the undivided attention of the assembled dilettantes. Which was how he referred to his colleagues, though he'd never say it to their faces.

'I assure you, Leo,' he said, 'there's nothing to the rumours. I've spoken to my contacts at the highest level in state government, and I've personally examined scads of confidential documents. The whole process is above board and completely open to scrutiny.'

'So why do the rumours persist?' asked Leo.

'Because the average punter has a fundamental distrust of Public Private Partnerships,' said Lachlan, 'fuelled by the usual suspects, the Opposition and the Greens amongst others. People can't see why if they pay taxes to fund roads, they should also have to pay a toll to drive on them.'

Jo used to be able to listen to Lachlan all day. She loved the timbre of his voice, the cadence of his speech, his turn of phrase. He was mesmerising, even when he was talking about the current account deficit.

But today Jo was distracted . . . aimless . . . discomfited . . . She couldn't even say which word best fit her mood, she was so discombobulated. Now that was a great word, you didn't get the chance to use a word like that every day. But it was exactly how she felt. She'd spent the whole day yesterday doing nothing much. She had plenty of unpacking to do, and she could have knocked most of it over in a day if she had really set her mind to it, but she felt strangely unmotivated. She fiddled about, poking into boxes and pulling things out at random, but then she couldn't make up her mind where to put anything. Truth be told, the mood she was in, she just didn't care enough. So now the place was in a mild state of disarray. A bit like her head. Lachlan had rung a few times since he got back from Tasmania. He wanted to see her; translation – he wanted sex. Jo didn't pick up when he called, so he left long messages, ranging from eager and insistent at first, to miffed and annoyed a day later. She wasn't sure why she was avoiding him. It wasn't that she was against the idea of sex, it had been more than a week, after all. But she just didn't feel like dealing with him, and his ego, and his needs. And it wasn't just Lachlan. Jo really didn't feel like dealing with anyone. Sometimes she found her mind drifting back fondly to that elevator – sans the panic attack part – when no one knew where she was, and no one could get to her.

This morning she'd woken up hours before her alarm went off. She'd just lain there, staring up at the ceiling. The new ceiling in her new apartment. Wondering when her great new life was going to begin.

'It's what's called an anticlimax, poppet,' Oliver had told her authoritatively, when she arrived on the doorstep of his café, right on opening. What with the move and the late starts, she'd missed Oliver this past week, and not just for his silky scrambled eggs and that defibrillator brew. He was the mainstay of her working week, a bizarro voice of reason who somehow made sense of the world by flipping it on its ear. He had inadvertently helped frame literally dozens of her columns. She didn't know how she'd get by without him once the *Trib* moved to the new building.

'You put way too much stock into this whole moving thing, Josephine,' he went on. 'You've been a bore for months. No wonder it hasn't lived up to the hype.'

'I suppose you're right,' Jo said wistfully, taking the coffee he passed her across the counter. 'But even so, I have a brand-new apartment in the middle of the city, which is literally a dream come true for me. I have a great job, I have good sex on a regular basis –'

'Stop skiting.'

'My point exactly. Isn't it a bit self-indulgent for me to be feeling anything less than happy with my lot in life?'

'One would think. But happiness is an elusive thing, petal, the more we pursue it, the further out of reach it gets,' Oliver mused. 'It's the next big thing, you know, everyone's clambering onto the happiness bandwagon. It seems now that we've all got jobs and we're richer than our parents ever dreamed of being, and we have every convenience, diversion, sexual freedom, you name it, well, we're finding it's not all that it was cracked up to be. People are not happy, and they want to know why.'

Jo sipped her coffee. 'Mm, that's what that positive psychology movement's all about, isn't it? I'm pretty sure we did a feature on the guy who started it over in the States. All about mindfulness and wellbeing and having a life purpose –'

'Yes, yes, blah de blah, blah and blah,' Oliver waved his hands in a dismissive flourish. 'You want to know what I think?' he said, leaning over the counter towards her. 'I think people think too much. Apparently during wars and famine and other major catastrophes, depression is all but nonexistent. Everyone stops contemplating their navels because they're too busy just trying to stay alive.'

'Are you saying we'd be better off if we were at war, Oliver?'

'Last time I looked, we were at war,' he had declared. 'Don't you read the papers, sweetie, or do you only write them?'

Jo stirred, sensing she was being watched. Lachlan was frowning at her from his place further up the conference table. He had finished his spiel, and from the look on his face, it was obvious that he knew she hadn't been paying attention. She gave him a wan smile but he was unmoved, his gaze lingering long enough for her to get the full measure of his disappointment, before he gave a wounded sigh and lowered his eyes to the notes on the table in front of him.

'Haven't we done real estate to death?' Glen Nicholas was

saying. Someone had obviously suggested another startling exposé on the price of real estate, the real estate crisis, the urban sprawl, the urban squeeze, the property boom, the property slump . . .

'You can never do too much real estate in this town,' said Leo. 'Show me what you've got in a couple of days, Kylie, and I'll decide if it's got legs. Next.'

Kylie Chen was a new recruit and her eyes were shining with anticipation of a Walkley. Jo remembered a time when she used to get that excited. She wondered if she was getting jaded, and there was nothing worse than a jaded old hack.

'. . . wait for it – offal!' Hugh Moncrieff, the food editor, was beaming, his hands outstretched as though he had just announced he'd located the holy grail.

'No way,' Leo said flatly.

'But Leo, it's making a comeback, all the best restaurants are serving simply exquisite offal dishes. It's the new black, if you will allow me to borrow a metaphor from the world of fashion.' He nodded deferentially towards Carla Delacqua, who rolled her eyes with unconcealed disdain.

'I don't care,' Leo was adamant. 'Liver is liver, no matter how you dress it up. And tripe is tripe and kidneys are kidneys and they all taste, well, like offal. If you do a feature on it, people will give it a passing glance before they come over nauseous when they remember being force-fed sheep's brains as a child. And next week they'll buy the *other* paper. What else have you got?'

Hugh looked anxious. 'Nothing. I didn't expect –'

'Bring me something by tomorrow. Next.'

Carla launched into a rundown of her list of engagements for the week. As social editor that was pretty much all she had to do. Show up, keep her ears open, remember everyone's name and especially the name of whatever designer they were wearing.

Brett Bowman was next, slumped over in his chair, his chin propped in one hand. As media editor, he had an encyclopaedic knowledge of TV and films, if that wasn't an oxymoron, but he always sounded bored.

'I'll be doing a double page of the new US releases and what the networks are likely to pick up,' he said wearily.

'What's the buzz?' asked Christine, one of the senior editors.

'There is no buzz, that's the problem,' Brett replied. 'In their increasingly desperate attempts to hold onto ever-decreasing audiences, the only thing the networks seem to be able to do is keep reinventing the wheel. Case in point is *Case in Point*, a new legal drama-com that's being touted as a cross between *Ugly Betty* and *Grey's Anatomy*, with a smattering of *The Sopranos*, as it involves a girl who's somewhat plain in the looks department, whose father was put away for mob-related activities, and now she's sharing his house with a bunch of law students, including a pretty blonde former Miss Idaho who falls in love with a guy on death row, as well as an uber-smart Asian woman, an arrogant black man, and, in another breathlessly original concept, a love-able gay guy.'

'That sounds familiar,' Christine mused.

'You think?'

A lull descended on the room. Perhaps everyone was thinking about the new show, more likely they were thinking about lunch. Jo was up next, and she didn't know what she was going to write about in her damn column . . . and worse, she didn't much care. She did wonder, however, why Joe Bannister wasn't at the meeting today. Would he ever come to meetings? Were they beneath him? Was he really not going to be around much, like he'd said? Maybe she should have taken his office –

'Jo*ANNE!*' Leo boomed from the far end of the table.

Jo hurtled back from inner space, to find everyone's eyes trained on her.

'Now is when you tell us what you're planning for this week's column,' he finished in his best patronising tone.

She cleared her throat. 'Well, I was thinking . . . maybe something about . . . um . . .' Nothing, nothing, nothing, then *click!* That glorious little switch inside her head turned on the light bulb hovering above it. 'Happiness,' she announced.

Leo sat back. 'Could you be more specific?'

Damn, he wanted details. 'Well, you know, this whole movement going on now, the search for happiness. Why despite our apparent wealth, low unemployment and, well, everything, people just don't feel happy.'

'Positive psychology,' blurted Kylie. Everyone turned to look at her, and she shrank just a little in her seat. 'I went to a seminar last week, actually,' she added in a smaller voice.

'It's quite a booming industry, boss,' said Christine. 'It's the new black.'

'I thought offal was the new black,' Leo grunted. 'Christ, I'm sick of that expression. What's your take gunna be, Jo?'

'Huh?' she stirred. She'd started to drift off again.

'What the hell's going on with you?' asked Leo. 'Big night last night?'

Jo didn't look at Lachlan, but she could sense his jaw clenching from here.

'What's the angle, Jo?' Leo said slowly. 'Are you going to bitch about happiness itself?'

'Oh . . . I don't know.' She wasn't sure how one would do that.

Leo tapped his pen on the notebook in front of him. 'Have a bitch about the industry growing up around it, people profiting out of it, that it's self-help by any other name . . .'

'That's not exactly what I had in mind –'

'Well that's what I have in mind. Next.'

As everyone filed out of the boardroom Jo felt a hand on her elbow, and then Lachlan's voice in her ear, 'My office.' He pushed past her and everyone else, and she just saw the back of his head disappearing up the corridor.

She didn't appreciate being summoned, but she couldn't keep putting him off either. As she walked towards his office he appeared in the doorway.

'Have you got a minute, Jo?' he said, loud enough for anyone nearby to hear. 'I'd like your input on some research I've been looking into.'

'Sure, Lachlan.' She didn't know why he made such a to-do about the subterfuge, she was quite sure everyone at the *Trib* knew or at least suspected they were having an affair. It was pretty obvious when he closed the blinds every time she went into his office. Besides, who would seriously believe that Lachlan Barr wanted her input on anything?

As she stepped into his office, he closed the door behind her and had her pinned against the back of it in one slick manoeuvre. As his lips came down on hers, Jo realised he'd not so much as said hello, how are you, or engaged in any of the usual polite pleasantries.

'Morning Lachlan,' she said matter-of-factly when he eventually drew back. 'How are you today?'

He considered her curiously. 'Missing you. Why haven't you been answering my messages?'

'I've been caught up with everything, you know, trying to unpack and get organised.'

'So you can't even reply to a text message?'

She paused, thinking about all the unanswered messages she had sent over the course of their relationship. There was an understanding that if he didn't answer, he couldn't. That was that. Apparently that didn't apply both ways.

'There was no point answering,' Jo said finally.

'What's that supposed to mean?' he frowned.

'Look, I knew you wanted to come over, and I still had too much to do around the place, and I would have had to argue the toss with you for ten minutes. So I decided to spare myself the hassle.'

His expression suggested a begrudging acceptance of her excuse. 'So can I come over tonight?'

Jo winced. 'Everything's still a mess.'

'You know I don't care how the place looks.'

She groaned. 'I'm not worried about impressing you, Lachlan. I just want to get it done. If I stop now, I know what'll happen. It'll stay how it is for months.'

He pressed in closer against her. 'I could help,' he said, brushing his lips against hers.

'But you won't,' Jo said plainly. 'You'll get in the way and you'll pout if I don't pay you attention.'

'Sometimes I think you don't have a very high opinion of me.'

'Maybe I just know you too well.'

He pulled back. 'You really think I'm so self-centred and inconsiderate that I wouldn't give you a hand when you needed it?'

He looked sincere, and just a little miffed. So now she'd hurt his feelings. She reached up to kiss him softly on the lips. 'I'm just tired,' she said. 'There was a lot happening while you were away.'

'Mm, so I hear,' he said, perching back on his desk. 'Did you meet the new guy?'

Jo had a sensation like blood rushing to her face. But that was impossible. She didn't blush. Ever. Blushing was not in her repertoire. She cleared her throat. 'Briefly. At the meeting on Friday.'

'Yeah, no offence, hun, but I think your flight path would be well under his radar,' said Lachlan. 'I don't know what Leo was thinking. Like we need someone with his ego around here.'

That Alanis Morissette song popped into her head again. That was it! The most ironic thing about the song 'Ironic' was that it wasn't ironic at all. Unlike Lachlan bitching about the size of someone else's ego.

'What are you smiling about?' asked Lachlan.

Jo blinked. 'Nothing.'

He paused for a moment, frowning curiously at her. 'You'd tell me if you were seeing someone, wouldn't you, Jo?'

'Where did that come from?' she asked. 'What, because Leo made that crack about me having a big night? He was just baiting me.'

'I know that,' he said, drawing her towards him and clasping her backside with both hands as he pulled her hard in against him. 'You would tell me, though, wouldn't you, Jo-bloh?' he murmured, nuzzling into her neck. Damn, he knew just the spot.

'Maybe . . .' She caught her breath as his tongue curled around her earlobe.

'You know, we haven't had sex in over a week,' he breathed into her ear.

'Uhuh.' Just over a week . . . weak in the knees . . . weakening . . .

'We could do it on the desk right now.'

Jo steeled herself. 'No we couldn't, Lach.'

'Wouldn't be the first time.'

'Would be the first time in daylight hours with the office full of people,' she said, easing back from him.

He groaned. 'You sure I can't come over tonight?'

Jo reached behind and removed his hands from her backside,

holding them out from her as she took a step away. 'Maybe tomorrow . . . or the next night. I'll call you.' She leaned forward to give him the faintest peck on the lips before releasing his hands and backing to the door.

Lachlan folded his arms, watching her glumly as she straightened her jacket and smoothed her hair. She blew a kiss at him but he remained sulking as she slipped back out into the main office.

9:30 pm

Joe had his key this time, but by the sounds of things, he wouldn't need it. As he climbed the stairs to his flat he could hear music and voices and laughter, and his heart sank. Will was obviously entertaining. Joe didn't need this tonight, he didn't want it tonight. He was going to have to have a talk with his brother and establish some ground rules, and parties on a Tuesday night would not make the cut.

Acceptable music volume would be on the agenda as well. Joe unlocked the door and stepped inside. There were probably twenty people strewn about, in various stages of inebriation. The air was thick with cigarette smoke laced with pot, which really pissed him off. Couldn't they do it outside? The place would stink tomorrow. No one had even noticed him, let alone acknowledged him. Joe walked over to the stereo and turned it down, not quite to angry old fart level, but getting there. That raised a few eyebrows, just as Will came out of his bedroom.

'Hey, Jo-*seph*,' he riffed. 'Everyone, this is my big brother, Joe, whose hospitality we are now partaking of . . . in . . . This is his place.'

There was a chorus of 'Hey Joe' and the haphazard raising of glasses and beer bottles.

'What are you drinking, Joe?'

He regarded his brother's red eyes and wondered if there was any point saying anything at all tonight. 'Nothing right now, thanks, Will. I just want to dump my stuff, clean up.'

'Sure, sure, go ahead,' he said expansively, throwing his arm towards Joe's room. 'Right that way, brother o' mine.'

Joe escaped to his room and closed the door, only to find the bed completely dishevelled. Someone had been sleeping in here, and whatever else he didn't want to know, and now he was going to have to change the sheets.

Fuck.

He tossed his bag on the floor just as Will burst through the door behind him. 'Oh, I just remembered, wanted to tell you, that was me,' he said, pointing at the bed. 'Me and Em slept in your bed last couple of nights.'

Joe was beginning to have difficulty containing his anger. 'Why, Will?' he asked, his tone brittle. 'Why'd you have to sleep in my bed, and if you did, why didn't you change the sheets at least?'

'I didn't know you were coming back tonight.'

'But why did you have to sleep in my fucking bed at all, Will?'

'Well, I thought you'd prefer us to Rancid. I made him sleep in my room. I was thinking of you, bro.'

'No, you weren't fucking thinking of me at all, Will.'

'What's up with you?' he frowned. 'Why are you being so aggro?'

'Because I've only had one night in my own place since I came back and I wanted to have a quiet one tonight.'

Will went to say something, but hiccupped instead, which made him chuckle. 'That's not going to happen,' he slurred.

Joe sighed. He'd had enough. 'You know what, yes it is.'

'What?'

'Go ask your friends to leave, Will. I'm tired and I want to go to bed.'

'No one's stopping you.'

'Will, I want them out.'

'Jesus, Joe, why are you being such an arsehole? You know what your problem is? You've spent too much time in the Middle East. You do realise that in Australia it's legal to drink and be with women and have a good time?'

Joe took a deep breath. He was not going to get sidetracked

arguing with someone who was out of it. 'Go ask your friends to leave,' he stated calmly, but in a tone that made it clear not to mess with him. 'Or I will.'

'Fuckin . . .'

Joe didn't hear the rest as Will sauntered unsteadily out of the room. He looked back at the bed. The music abruptly stopped.

'Everyone, you have to go,' he heard Will announce. 'My brother's turned into a complete arsehole and he says he doesn't want you in his place.'

Joe reached down and grabbed the bedding, reefing it off and tossing it across the room.

Wednesday

'How's the old man holding up?' Leo asked Joe after he'd taken a seat in his office.

Joe hesitated, he hadn't thought about how he was going to deal with that question yet. He didn't think he could face going over and over the details, describing his father's incapacity, his rapidly advancing decline; he hadn't come to terms with it himself. Besides, most people didn't want to know, they were just being polite. Leo had some history with his father, but he wasn't one for shared intimacies. Joe could keep it vague.

'He's doing all right. Says hello, by the way.'

Leo nodded with a faint smile. 'And what about you?'

'What about me?'

'Are you settling back in okay?'

'Sure,' Joe brushed it off.

'I remember what it was like when I came back from Cambodia, I was a bit of a head case for a while, and I was only there a few months.'

'I've been doing this for a long time, Leo,' Joe dismissed.

Leo paused, considering him for a beat longer. Then he sat forward. 'Fine, are you ready for some work?'

'What did you have in mind?'

'Have you heard about ASoCC, the big Australasian summit on climate change?'

He nodded. Joe had finally had the chance to look at a few newspapers over the weekend, take in the state of play. It never ceased to amaze him how much things changed, and how much they stayed the same.

'So you know it's bipartisan, federal and state, public and private sectors; just about every man and his dog with some barrow to push is going to be there.'

Joe nodded again.

Leo looked at him across his glasses. 'You seem less than enthralled?'

He shrugged. 'You know what they say, if I had a dollar for every summit . . .'

'Ours is not to reason why, Joe, we just have to report on it. You're aware it's being held on your home turf?'

'Now that you mention it.'

'So you could base yourself up there for the duration, spend time with your dad, file a few stories.'

Joe nodded. 'Sure.'

Leo sat back in his chair. 'I was thinking of sending another journo as well, to fill in the gaps.'

'You don't need to do that, Leo, I can handle it.'

'I know that, but the thing is, there's two birds I'd like to stone,' said Leo. 'Your mate from the elevator, she's not a bad little journo, hounds me all the time about being taken seriously. But her column works, it's a very popular feature, gets a lot of mail.'

'So you've been stymieing her?'

'Nah, just not actively encouraging her. Thing is, women get all antsy if you want them to report on women's issues, but who else is going to do it? Blokes haven't got a clue.'

Joe shook his head faintly. Leo really was a fossil in a lot of ways.

'So how do you feel about taking her under your wing?'

'Sorry?'

'I was thinking Jo could stay on site with the press, and you could stay with your dad and come and go as you please, check on her stories, write your own op-eds. Whatever you think. We'll do pretty extensive coverage of it, so it'd be good to have a couple of different angles. I'm sure Jo'll appreciate the opportunity to work with you.'

'I don't know, Leo,' Joe hesitated. 'I don't think I'm exactly her favourite person in the world.'

Leo shook his head. 'What happened in that elevator?'

'Nothing. I think she's just embarrassed about passing out.'

'Maybe this'll get her over it.'

Joe didn't know what to say. If he refused outright, it would seem odd, and it would be. He didn't have any reason to refuse. He didn't have a problem with her, he was still open to a relationship . . . as in a working relationship. He was quite happy to work with her, was all he meant.

'It's okay with me,' he said. 'I suppose you have to run it by her.'

Leo pressed the intercom on his phone. 'Tell Jo Liddell I want to see her, please, Judith.'

'Right now?'

'If not sooner.'

Jo picked up her phone on the second ring. 'Jo Liddell.'

'Judith here, Jo. He wants to see you.'

'Oh?'

'Right away.'

'Okay.' Jo put down the phone and walked briskly through the maze of desks and out to the elevator bay, pressing the button to go up. She couldn't shake a feeling of guilt. This was like being summoned to the principal's office.

She took the lift to the floor above and walked around to Leo's office. Judith looked up as she approached. 'You can go right in, Jo. They're waiting.'

They?

Jo went to the door and opened it gingerly.

'Come on in, Jo,' Leo muttered, frowning at his computer screen.

As she stepped inside, Bannister turned around in his seat on the other side of Leo's desk, giving her an awkward smile. What was he doing here? What was this all about? Jo took halting steps further into the room. Leo had still not looked up from the screen, but she could feel Bannister's eyes on her. She was beginning to feel a little claustrophobic. She wondered if that was destined to be her reaction around him from now on.

'How's it going?' Joe asked.

She glanced at him. 'Fine. Okay.' Should she say something else? Some nicety, to be polite? He was only just back from over-seas, should she ask how he was settling in? Or about his sick father? But she didn't particularly want to know, so why did she have to ask?

'Okay, Jo,' said Leo finally, turning his attention to her. 'The Australasian Summit on Climate Change, ASoCC, is being held up in the Blue Mountains at the end of the month.'

'Yes, I'm aware.'

'Do you want to cover it?'

'Sorry?'

'Do you want to cover it?' he repeated. 'You'll have to stay up there for a few nights. Interested?'

Jo blinked. 'So you don't just mean a column?'

'No, I don't just mean a column,' Leo said in a monotone. 'Don't you know what it means to cover an event, Jo?'

'Yes, definitely. Of course. I would love to.' But what did Joe Bannister have to do with it?

'Okay. Joe here is going up as well, but he has some family responsibilities to attend to so you'll be the constant. We'll be sending a photographer of course, and you'll both stay with the press contingent, accommodation's on site. Judith will look after your registrations. Any questions?'

Yes, whose idea was this? But she couldn't be quite that blunt. It might look a bit obvious.

'I don't understand why we both need to go,' she tried instead.

A look passed between Bannister and Leo. It was definitely a look.

'Jo,' Leo began, 'I wouldn't send you up there alone, it's too big for one journalist. Like I said, Joe has family commitments that take him up that way. Besides, you could benefit from someone of his experience.'

Jo pressed her lips together to stop herself from groaning. This was excruciating. After everything, now she had to treat him like some kind of a mentor? Bannister must be loving this. She glanced sideways at him, he had half his face covered with his hand, kind of peering out, like he was embarrassed. What the hell did he have to be embarrassed about?

'I'm sure Mr Bannister has enough on his plate without having to worry about me,' Jo said tightly.

'I really wish you'd call me Joe,' he muttered with a sigh.

'What are you saying, Jo?' asked Leo, frowning. It was not a curious frown; on the frown scale it was heading more towards annoyed. He was getting frustrated with her. So what *was* she saying?

'It's just, I'm not quite sure how you expect this to work. Maybe you should send someone else you think could handle it and they won't have to bother Mr Ban – Joe. Um, it seems to me that if he's got family stuff going on he doesn't need the responsibility of mentoring me, or maybe I could go with someone else and we could work it out tog–'

'Christ, Jo,' Leo cut her off. 'You're always harping about not getting something to sink your teeth into, and I give you this opportunity and you baulk at it. If you don't want it, fine, I'll give it to someone else. I'm sure Kylie Chen would jump at the chance.'

'I'm sorry, Leo, of course I want it. And I'll take it.' What was the matter with her? This was a major event that would be given wide coverage and she would get a by-line. She was allowing personal feelings to get in the way of her work. Not that she had any personal feelings, as such.

'I'm glad that's settled,' said Leo, returning his attention to the computer screen. 'Judith has the press packs.'

Jo just stood there. Was she supposed to say something to Bannister? Thank him? Kiss his feet?

Leo glanced up at her. 'You can get one on your way out.'

'Oh, right.' She cleared her throat. 'Thanks, Leo.' She nodded at Bannister – that was all he was getting – and quickly left the room.

When the door closed behind her, Leo looked over at Joe. 'What the hell happened in that elevator?'

*

Jo was sitting back at her desk, scrolling through her emails but not taking in anything. She felt agitated. It was a good word, agitated. Almost onomatopoeic. Agitated, twitchy and tense, that's what she was feeling. God, the kowtowing women had to do in this industry made her want to spit. But it wasn't acceptable for a woman to spit. Men get to spit, sleep around, drink like fish and be arrogant arseholes, and what do they get? Their own offices. Women get mentors.

'Jo?'

She literally jumped in her chair. She looked up to see Bannister gawking at her from his lofty height. Where did he get off, being so tall?

'Sorry, I didn't mean to startle you,' he said.

Jo's heart was still racing. 'Did you want something?'

'Uh, yeah,' he said, glancing around. He seemed vaguely uncomfortable. Finally he crouched on his haunches, which brought him to her eye level. She felt like a child.

'I just wanted you to know that the mentor thing was not my idea,' he said.

She should hope not. How arrogant would he have to be to suggest being her mentor? But she was relieved to hear him say it.

'Look, I don't really care,' she said airily. 'You can call yourself whatever you like, but I think you'll find that I know what I'm doing.'

'Of course you do.'

She frowned. What was he up to?

'Your column's very sharp, very well written.'

Part of her was flattered, but most of her was pissed off. She didn't need his validation.

'So you read Sunday's?' she said in a tone that suggested she couldn't care less.

'I've probably read a month of Sundays',' said Joe. 'And other stuff besides. I like the way you write, the way you think.' He paused. 'Maybe not all the cutting stuff about blokes,' he added with a faint smile. 'There was one piece, a while back, on that politician and his wife, it seemed a little vicious, not like your other stuff, didn't have the finesse . . .'

Jo was about to blurt out that it was Leo who'd butchered it, but then she bit her tongue. She didn't owe Bannister any explanations, and what's more, she wasn't going to give him any.

'Where did you come across all this?' she asked instead.

'I Googled you.'

He Googled *her*? This was definitely tilting the balance of power in her direction. 'You're kidding me?' she scoffed.

'Oh, like you haven't Googled me?' said Joe.

She raised an eyebrow. 'That ego must be quite a burden to lug around.'

He didn't say anything to that.

'Look,' she said, getting up out of her chair, 'I realise you've been given carte blanche around here, but some of us still have to work. So if you'll excuse me.'

With that she circled around his still crouching figure and strode off. Joe grabbed hold of the desk to pull himself upright. He was getting too old for this. Not just crouching on the floor, but dealing with this kind of crap. What had he done to offend her? It wasn't his fault the elevator had broken down, or that she'd passed out, or that they had the same name, or that he'd been given an office. He'd even offered it to her, for Chrissakes. What did it take for her to like him? Or at least not loathe him?

Joe shoved his hands in his pockets and wandered around to his office, when he saw that woman leaning provocatively in the doorway, smiling at him. What the hell was her name?

'Hey Joe,' she purred.

He nodded. 'Hey, how's it going?' How come he could remember the name of every single member of the Iraqi parliamentary assembly, and it had changed three times in the last two years, but he couldn't remember this woman's name?

'How are you settling in?' she asked.

'All right.' Lousy actually, but he wasn't about to share that with her.

They stood there, feeling awkward. At least Joe felt awkward, he couldn't say what she was feeling, but he didn't like the predatory look in her eye.

'Well . . .' he said by way of a lame segue, 'best get on with it.'

'Have you got a minute, Joe?' she said. 'I have a proposal for you.'

He fixed a smile on his face. 'Sure. Come on in.' He opened the door for her and she walked through, or rather slithered her way over to his desk where she propped herself as though on a side-saddle, arranging her long legs to achieve maximum exposure. There were definitely guys who got off on this kind of carry-on. He wasn't one of them. Not that he didn't find her attractive. Clearly, she was very attractive; it was just that he didn't particularly enjoy the sensation of being circled by a tigress before she came in for the kill. He leaned back against the doorway to keep her at a distance.

'So I have these tickets,' she began. 'VIP passes, invitations, I get them all the time. Comes with the territory.'

Karen . . . Carol . . . no, it was more exotic . . .

'There's a funky new bar opening,' she went on, 'you know, one of these "holes in the wall" that are popping up all over the place since the government finally had the balls to toss out the old licensing laws.'

Joe looked blankly at her.

'You have been away for a while, haven't you?' she said. 'Anyhow, it's tomorrow night, invitation only. All the cool kids'll be there.'

Jesus.

'You know,' he said carefully, 'I don't think I'm one of the cool kids . . .' *Carmen . . . Cara?*

'You are so wrong about that,' she said. 'But okay . . .' She seemed to be contemplating her next move. Obviously he presented a challenge. 'How do you feel about art? There's an exhibition by a hot new installation artist Friday night.'

Joe would rather have his toenails pulled out with pliers. He cringed in a way he hoped was charming, not insulting.

She got it. 'So I suppose a fashion parade is out of the question? Even if it is Isogawa?'

'I'm guessing he doesn't make martial arts movies?'

She smiled, but it was strained. He didn't want to offend her, or make her feel foolish, and he had a sense it was going that way.

'I'm afraid I'm a bit of a hopeless case . . .' *Carla . . .* Carla! That was it. '. . . Carla.'

She regarded him through a veil of unnaturally long eyelashes.

'Well, I'm not going to give up on you,' she said, sliding off the desk and onto her feet. 'We've got to get you out there, Joe. You really ought to take advantage of your celebrity while it lasts.'

'My celebrity?' he frowned, mystified.

She smiled indulgently at him as she came closer, so close that Joe had to breathe in. She started to adjust the collar of his shirt. 'Don't be so coy, Joe. "Award-winning, rugged war correspondent, returning home like the proverbial prodigal son after a lengthy stint in the Middle East"?' She almost smacked her lips. 'You might have been surrounded by sand out there, but it's time to get your head out of it. War is very sexy right now, you can pretty much write your own ticket in this town.'

Only someone who'd never been in a war zone would say that war was sexy. Correct that. Only someone with half a brain and no idea would say anything remotely like that. Joe flinched a little as she reached into his breast pocket for his phone. She flipped it open.

'I tell you what, Joe, I'll program my number in here,' she said, and proceeded to do just that. 'And if you change your mind, you give me a call. Any time, day or night.' She slipped his phone back in his pocket and gave it a gentle pat. 'See you round.'

She slinked past him and out the door, and Joe breathed out. What the hell was that about? She'd given him her number, just like that. Some women didn't need any work at all. And then there were women like Jo . . . not that he could remember meeting a woman quite like Jo before.

8 pm

'Looks kind of bare,' Angie decided.

'Mm, that's what I was thinking.'

Jo and Angie were considering the living room from another angle. They'd looked at it from the front door, from the doorway into the bedroom, and now from the kitchen.

'Where's all your stuff?' asked Angie. 'You know, pictures and that?'

'All packed away,' said Jo.

'Still?'

'Well, I did pull them out the other night, but I couldn't decide where to put anything. And then they were all lying around and I couldn't stand the mess any more, so I packed them away again.'

Angie frowned at her. 'Why would you do that?'

'I don't know,' Jo groaned, walking across the room and flopping onto the sofa. 'My stuff doesn't seem to belong.'

'But it's your stuff, it belongs to you. This is your place, so it belongs here.'

'Then maybe I don't belong.'

Angie came over and plonked herself in an armchair. 'Are you all right?'

'Of course I am.' She'd always dreamed of having a brand-new place, somewhere without history, without a past. Probably because of all the dives they lived in when she was a kid, up and down the tackiest stretch of real estate on the planet, at least it was back then. Surfers Paradise. You were asking for trouble when you called a place 'paradise'.

Jo wanted to settle somewhere that was unsullied by grubby tenants, grubbier landlords, shady pasts. She wanted a clean slate where she could stamp her own personality. But as the days went by, this place just felt sterile and empty. What did that say about her personality? Ugh, that was a depressing thought.

A knock sounded at the door. Jo frowned. 'That's not supposed to happen.'

'Why not?'

'This is a security block,' said Jo, getting up from the sofa. 'You have to buzz downstairs first, like you did.'

'Maybe it's a neighbour?' Angie suggested. 'Someone from inside the building.'

Jo doubted it. She didn't imagine this was a very neighbourly block – once a building got over six floors it rarely was – which was another thing that had attracted her to the place. She walked over to the door but hesitated as she reached for the handle. She wished she had one of those peepholes.

The knock sounded again, giving her a start. She opened the door a little way, peering out.

'Hi.'

Jo felt her heart jump in her chest. 'What are you doing here?'

'Just passing . . .'

'You were not,' she said dubiously. Jo wasn't sure whether to be flattered or suspicious. She usually went with suspicious. It was safer. 'How did you find out where I live?'

Angie had raced over and positioned herself behind the door, her eyes wide with intrigue.

Joe shrugged. 'Judith looked it up for me.'

So much for confidentiality.

'How did you get up here?' Jo persisted.

He looked a little confused. 'In the elevator.'

She pulled a face. 'But how did you get through the security door?'

'Oh, someone was coming out at the same time.'

So much for security as well.

Angie was poking her, mouthing, *'Who is it?'*

'Anyhow,' said Joe, taking a breath, 'I ah, I thought, since we're going to be working together, we really need to get over this.'

Angie's eyebrows lifted so high they looked like they could quite possibly fly right off her forehead.

'Get over what?' Jo asked guilelessly. 'I don't know what you're talking about.'

'Sure you do,' Joe said wryly. 'Look, I even brought a peace offering,' he went on, holding up a bag obviously containing bottles. 'Red and white, I didn't know which you preferred.'

Angie was nodding her head furiously while Jo stood there, unmoved.

'We had a wager, remember?' said Joe. 'If you guessed what I did for a living, I had to buy you a drink.'

'But I didn't guess.'

'Only because you passed out first.'

'Is this elevator guy?' Angie blurted loudly.

He craned his head. 'Who was that?'

Jo sighed heavily, opening the door wide. 'This is my friend Angie.'

Angie was grinning her face off as she grasped his hand enthusiastically. 'Hi, nice to meet you. I thought you said Elevator Guy
was a complete stranger, Jo?'

'He was at the time, but turns out Joe here has started working
for the *Trib* as well.'

'Who?' said Angie, confused.

'My name's Joe, Joe Bannister,' he explained, still shaking
Angie's hand, or rather still having his hand shaken by Angie.

She snorted a laugh. 'You've got the same name? That's pretty
funny.'

'Hilarious,' said Jo, deadpan.

'So, you're coming in?' said Angie somewhat rhetorically as
she dragged him by the hand which she couldn't seem to bring
herself to part with.

'I think that's up to Jo,' he said as Angie yanked him over the
threshold.

He was persistent, Jo had to give him that. Besides, she was
intrigued. And probably a little flattered. 'Sure, come on in.'

Angie took the bag from him. 'So I'll get us a drink?'

'I'll do that, Ange –'

'No no, you entertain your guest,' she dismissed, bustling off
to the kitchen.

Jo glanced over her shoulder at Bannister as she closed the
door. 'Take a seat.'

'Thanks,' he nodded, wandering slowly over to the sofa as he
surveyed the room. 'Still haven't finished unpacking, eh?'

She came to stand beside him. 'You can tell?'

He shrugged. 'It's a little bare. Doesn't have that lived-in look
yet.'

That was it, that was the look she was going for. And she suspected the only way to achieve it was to live in it, put out all her
stuff and get over herself.

'Jo,' Angie called from the kitchen, 'I can't find your
wineglasses.'

She glanced at Bannister. 'Excuse me. Make yourself at home.'

Jo crossed the few metres to the kitchen which was largely
open to the living room, but for a nook at the end where the wall
wrapped around the fridge and a bifold door concealed the tiny

laundry. Angie was huddled in the alcove out of sight from the living room, beckoning furiously.

'What are you doing?' Jo asked in a low voice.

'Do you want me to go?' Angie whispered urgently.

'Go where?'

'Go, get out of here, leave you two alone. I'll make an excuse.'

'What?' Jo was momentarily confused. 'You don't have to go.'

'But do you *want* me to go?'

'Don't get weird, Angie. He's just a guy from work.'

'Yeah, and you never told me that part either.'

'I didn't know myself till he showed up at a meeting the next day.'

'And now he shows up on your doorstep.' Angie arched one eyebrow suggestively. 'What do you think that means?'

Jo sighed. 'That you have a fertile imagination.'

'Oh, come on, you really can't be that thick,' said Angie. 'He's obviously courting you.'

Jo tried to suppress a laugh but it came out as a snort.

'Mind if I put on some music?'

Jo and Angie both jumped, turning around. Bannister was leaning over the bench, smiling at them. She hoped he hadn't heard any of that.

'Yeah, sure, of course,' said Jo. 'Go ahead, the player's –'

'I've got it,' he smiled, before turning away again.

'He's *cute*,' Angie swooned.

Jo rolled her eyes.

'Oh, okay, you've got some literal fixation with the word cute. He's hot then.'

Jo frowned. 'Seriously?'

'Seriously. Ruggedly. Rough-around-the-edges, eat-him-up-for-breakfast hot,' she drooled. Music started up in the next room and Angie let out a stifled squeal. 'And he likes Jeff Buckley!'

Jo groaned. 'Maybe I should leave you two alone.'

'Don't be daft, woman, you're the one he's courting.'

'Would you stop using that word?' said Jo, reaching up into a cupboard for the glasses. 'We're not in a Jane Austen novel.' She turned around to see Angie's eyes glazing over. Jeez, she was replaying Darcy's wet-shirt scene in her head right this second. 'Snap out of it, Ange.'

She stirred. 'Well I think courting's an excellent word,' she declared, 'and I'm bringing it back. As in – Joe has clearly come here with a couple of bottles of very expensive wine to court your favour. And that's more than El Cheapo would ever do.'

'El Cheapo?'

'Who do you think I'm talking about? Lecherous Lachie.'

'Lachlan's not cheap,' Jo said defensively.

'No, I'm sure he isn't, with anyone but you.' Angie paused. 'Hey, does Joe know about Lachlan?'

Jo was beginning to frame a response when she realised it didn't credit one, and she wasn't going to encourage Angie any further. She poked her head past the dividing wall. 'Red or white?' she called to Joe, who had ensconced himself in one of the armchairs.

'Whatever you open,' he called back.

'Either,' she persisted.

'Okay, red.'

'Can we open the white as well?' said Angie, turning up her nose. 'You know I'm not all that fussed on red.'

Jo slid the bottle towards her. 'Help yourself.'

'We should have a signal,' said Angie in a conspiratorial tone as she opened the wine.

'What?'

'If you do decide you want me to leave after all, you know, if things are going well, we should have a signal. He'll never suspect, I can pull it off, I am an actor. What do you say?'

Jo was shaking her head as she poured the wine. 'I say you're nuts.'

Angie pulled a face.

'He's just a work colleague extending the olive branch of friend-ship,' Jo said calmly. 'That's all there is to it, Ange. There will be no signal, and nobody will be going anywhere.' And with that, Jo picked up the two glasses of red and walked out of the kitchen.

Truth was, Jo felt much more at ease with him on her own territory, especially with Angie providing a very effective buffer. She knew what Angie was like; she would barrage him with questions and monopolise his attention, which would give Jo the perfect opportunity to sit back and observe. Bannister was right, they were going to work together, they should at least try to get along. He was clearly going to heroic efforts to do just that, and despite some lingering suspicion as to his motives, the balance of power was continuing to swing back in her favour, so the least Jo could do was give him a hearing.

'So how do you two know each other?' he asked when they were all seated in the living room, sipping on what was a damn fine red, Jo noted. That scored him a few points.

'I work at the Earl of Sandwich, not far from the *Trib* building,' Angie explained. 'We met right back when Jo first started there. But that's just my day job. I'm an actor,' she added importantly.

'Ah,' said Joe. 'So you're the actor friend?'

'Ooh, my reputation precedes me?' Angie remarked, chuffed.

'You got a mention in the elevator. All good,' he assured her.

Jo found it a little unnerving that he knew so many snippets about her life; she never knew what little snippet was going to pop up next.

'My brother's an actor,' said Joe.

Mm, she remembered that. Now that he said it.

'What's his name? Would I have heard of him?' Angie was asking.

'I doubt it. Will Bannister?'

Angie thought about it, shaking her head.

'He hasn't done anything of note, as far as I can tell. He hangs around with actors and, you know, creative types. They seem to have a lot of projects in the works, but I'm not sure anything ever comes of them.'

'At least he's having fun.'

'Oh yeah, he's having a lot of fun, all right.' Joe took a sip of his wine. 'How about you, Angie? Do you get much work?'

She shrugged. 'Commercials, extras work. It can pay well, but I didn't do this for the money, and it's pretty soulless. I really want to break into theatre.'

'So what's stopping you?'

'You're kidding, aren't you?' said Angie. 'Hasn't your brother complained about this? It's a closed shop. The industry's so small in Australia and the roles so few and far between, that once you get in, you hang on for dear life, taking anything that's going, a line, a walk-on, just to keep your place. I don't blame anyone for doing that, just makes it hard to get your foot in the door. Especially when you don't exactly look like Cate Blanchett.'

It all sounded quite reasonable coming from her, but Joe realised if Will had said the same he'd think he was making excuses. Maybe he was a little hard on his brother. He was beginning to feel as though he didn't belong in his own place, but it wasn't all Will's fault. Truth was, Joe wasn't sure where he belonged. Even Leura didn't feel like a sanctuary any more, huddled under the dark cloud of his father's illness. So he'd found his mind often wandering back to the elevator, circling around the person of Jo Liddell. Okay, she'd been a little spiky at first, maybe a lot spiky, but she had good reason to be, and once she'd calmed down, she was funny and feisty and, he had to admit, bloody attractive. And she smelled good. And he realised he wanted to get to know her, despite the fact that in their couple of encounters it seemed she was hoping the ground would open up and swallow him whole. Which provided something of a challenge.

'You're not saying much, Jo,' said Angie.

She stirred. 'I don't need to, Joe knows everything about me already.'

'That isn't true,' he denied.

'Well, I don't know anything about you,' said Angie to Joe. 'She barely told me a thing, except that you were tall and manly and heroic.'

Jo nearly choked on her wine. 'Angie! I never said that. That was you! You said that!'

'Oh, that's right,' she said wistfully. 'My imagination got carried away with the whole *Officer And A Gentleman* bit, Joe, can you blame me?'

He frowned. 'I'm not following . . .'

'Don't even try,' said Jo. 'It won't get you anywhere that's worth going.'

They smiled at each other then. A genuine, warm smile. Jo realised that it was possibly the first unguarded moment that had passed between them . . . at least one she could remember.

'So how are you settling in at the *Trib*?' asked Angie.

'It's early days yet.' He didn't want to be negative about it in front of Jo. 'I was accosted by that woman today . . . God, I can never remember her name, she does the society pages.'

'Carla Delacqua,' Jo and Angie said in unison.

Joe looked at Angie. 'You know her too?'

'*Her* reputation precedes her.'

'Well, I wish someone had warned me,' he muttered. 'She's a friggin' man-eater. I'm telling you, I feared for my life for a minute there today.'

Jo smiled. 'Oh, come on, a big, strapping war correspondent like yourself, frightened by a flimsy little gossip columnist?'

'You're a war correspondent, Joe?' Angie asked breathlessly.

'Foreign correspondent,' he corrected. 'But I've spent a lot of time in Iraq, last few years almost exclusively.'

Jo could see him growing in stature before Angie's eyes.

'Anyway, you know what she said to me today?' Joe went on.

'Who?'

'Carla. She said war was sexy and I should get out there and lap up all the attention.' He shook his head. 'The woman's an idiot.'

Jo couldn't agree more. Before she could say anything, though, another knock sounded at the door.

'This is getting ridiculous,' said Jo, putting her glass down on the coffee table as she got to her feet. 'This is supposed to be a security block.'

As she crossed to the door Jo was wondering who it was going to be this time, but when she opened it, she should have known.

'Lachlan.'

'This is going to be awkward,' Angie sang under her breath.

Joe glanced at her, frowning. Did she mean Lachlan Barr from the *Trib*? Joe had already identified him as one of the prickly egos he was going to have to contend with. The open door blocked his view, so he couldn't see who it was from where he was sitting.

'How did you get up here?' Jo asked.

'What kind of a welcome is that?'

'It's just that this is supposed to be a security block.'

'Someone was leaving when I arrived. They let me in,' Lachlan explained. 'I have a trustworthy face, what can I say?'

He was smiling but Jo wasn't.

'Okay, I know you don't like surprises,' he went on, as though he was trying to console a child, 'but I come bearing gifts.' He handed her a bunch of flowers and a bottle of wine, but as he leaned forward to kiss her, Jo stepped back, conscious of the onlookers on the sofa.

Lachlan frowned, taking another step towards her, which brought him out of cover and into the room, in plain sight of Joe and Angie. For a moment he resembled the proverbial deer caught in the headlights.

'Hi Lachlan!' Angie greeted him cheerfully. She was enjoying this.

'Angie,' he nodded, vaguely acknowledging her. 'Bannister. What are you doing here?'

'*Lachlan!*'

'What?'

'That was a bit rude,' said Jo in a low voice.

'I'm just surprised,' said Lachlan. 'Didn't you say the place was a mess and you didn't want company?'

Jo leaned back against the door to close it. 'But you came anyway.'

'I wasn't aware you two knew each other so well.' He arranged his face into a smile, but it was really more of a smirk.

'We don't . . .'

'I don't know anyone around here very well,' Joe chimed in, getting to his feet. 'Jo and I got trapped in an elevator the other day, and well, long story, but I owed her a drink,' he added, reaching his hand out to Lachlan.

He was still smirking as he shook Joe's hand. 'You didn't mention,' he said to Jo.

'Yes I did, I told you I got stuck in an elevator.'

'But you didn't mention there was anyone with you.'

'Didn't I?' she said vaguely. 'So, will I open this?' she added, holding up the bottle of bubbly he'd brought.

'Ah, sure,' Lachlan said, glancing at Joe. 'We've worked together for years, old friends, Jo and I. I promised we'd have a drink to her new place after she moved in.'

Joe nodded. He was sleeping with her, obviously.

'I'll get some champagne glasses,' said Jo, 'and put these in water,' she added, backing away.

'I'll give you a hand,' said Angie, jumping up from her seat.

'Sit down, guys, make yourselves comfortable,' said Jo, like that was at all possible. She turned around into the kitchen with Angie hot on her heels.

'How are you going to explain this?'

'There's nothing to explain,' Jo said coolly. At least she was trying to keep her cool. She was furious with Lachlan for showing up uninvited. Bannister hadn't been invited either, but Lachlan had expressly *not* been invited. And he knew she didn't like surprises, whereas Bannister wouldn't know that. How could he be expected to know that? And now she was going to have to explain Lachlan to him. She'd never had to explain Lachlan to anyone before. That's why she didn't want to have to explain him to Bannister. That was the only reason. That was why she was feeling flustered.

Angie was checking out the bottle. 'Told you he was tight.'

Jo turned around with the flutes. 'Why, because he bought me flowers and champagne?'

'I think you'll find it's sparkling wine.'

'Don't be such a snob, that's all you and I ever drink.'

'But I bet it's not what Mrs Barr drinks,' Angie retorted. 'And he wouldn't be giving her any daggy old carnations either.'

Jo handed Angie the glasses. 'Take these out, please,' she said with feigned sweetness. 'And try to keep your opinions to yourself.'

Jo arranged the flowers in a vase – they were carnations, but they weren't so daggy – and carried them out to the living room. She placed the vase on the dining table as Lachlan popped the bottle open. When he had filled their glasses, he raised his own. 'To the mortgagee, congratulations.'

'Thank you.'

Joe and Angie echoed the sentiment and raised their glasses as well. They drank a toast, then after an awkward pause they all sat down again, just in time for another awkward pause.

Someone needed to say something, get the conversation rolling. Jo should probably be the one to do it but she couldn't think of a single thing, her mind had gone completely blank.

'So Joe was just starting to tell us all about his time in Iraq,' said Angie.

Thank God for Angie.

'I was?' he said.

'Well, I was hoping you would. I'd love to hear what's really going on from someone who was actually there.'

'Journalists don't get that close to the action any more though, do they, Bannister?'

Joe turned to look at Lachlan. It always amazed him when people who barely left their desks made grand generalisations like that. But he wasn't in the mood to defend his position. He wasn't in the mood to talk about war. That was part of the reason he'd left Iraq in the first place.

'Close enough,' he said finally.

'You're all holed up in the Green Zone living it pretty cushy, the way I hear it.'

'And exactly where did you hear that, Lachlan?' Joe asked, trying unsuccessfully to keep the brittle edge out of his voice. 'The coalition press office is inside the Green Zone, and they hold briefings there, but journalists don't live there as a rule.'

'Whatever,' Lachlan dismissed. 'Isn't it true that it's just too dangerous now to go out on the street in Baghdad? That all the news services are relying on Iraqi stringers, and there's very little on-the-ground reporting going on?'

'What's a stringer?' Angie frowned.

'A freelance journalist,' said Joe. 'Usually a local, they have the language obviously, and they know the place.'

'But they can't always be trusted,' Lachlan chimed in. 'They're often just doing it for the money, and they don't always double-check their facts.'

'I've worked with some fantastic stringers,' Joe countered. 'Maybe some of them started off doing it for the money, but it's incredibly dangerous for them as well. If the insurgents find out what they're doing, they kill them. Most of them have to hide it from even their closest family.'

'Then why do they do it?' asked Angie.

'Because in the end they want the stories to be told,' said Joe.

'They want the world to know what's going on, at least the guys I knew. I had complete faith in them.'

'So you did have to rely on stringers?' Jo asked him.

'Sure, the streets do get too dangerous at times, though it has settled down a lot since the US troop surge,' he said. 'Some reporters can still get out there because of their background, their appearance, they can pass for Arabic. Even so, if they take out a notepad or a recorder, they can end up with a bullet in the back of their head. But I don't look Arabic, and I had only limited language, so I couldn't risk it during the worst times.'

'You were embedded, weren't you?' Jo had read that when she Googled him. It was the series of articles he wrote while he was an embed that had won him the Walkley.

Joe nodded. 'A few times.'

Angie was biting her lip. 'Okay, at the risk of exposing my ignorance, what happens when you're embedded?'

'It's when they "plant" journalists within a battalion of soldiers.' Lachlan had decided to answer the question. 'It's basically a PR exercise so journalists will write positive stuff about the war effort.'

Joe threw back half a glass of wine. Lachlan was just pissing him off now.

'But travelling around with soldiers in a war zone would be pretty dangerous, wouldn't it?' Angie asked Joe.

'Not really,' Lachlan continued. 'I would imagine it's one of the safest places you could be. The last thing the military want is to have the blood of a journalist on their hands, isn't that right, Bannister?'

Joe clenched his jaw. If he didn't shut up soon . . .

'And of course you're seeing everything from their perspective, to their schedule, it's pretty one-eyed,' Lachlan finished.

'You have to look at things from both sides if you want to do justice to any story,' Joe said plainly. 'An urban war is tough on soldiers, they come in all gung-ho, then reality hits. They see civilians killed in front of them, sometimes from their own fire. A lot of these guys are really screwed up by the time they go home.'

'That's why we should all get the hell out of there,' said Lachlan. 'The sooner the better.'

Joe didn't say anything as he refilled his glass and skolled half of it down.

'You have a problem with that, Bannister?' Lachlan was watching him. 'I wouldn't have had you down as pro-war, the embedding obviously worked on you.'

Joe hadn't wanted to talk about this, but the alternative was to listen to more of Lachlan's bullshit. 'Look, I didn't agree with the war in the first place. But it's not that simple now. The country's shattered, you can't just abandon the people.'

'But doesn't the very presence of the US troops fuel the fire of the insurgents?' said Lachlan.

'Absolutely, but a lot of those insurgents are backed by Iran militia or even al-Qaeda. If the US withdraws too quickly they'll create a vacuum of power and leave the Iraqis extremely vulnerable.'

'Isn't that why we've sent special teams of soldiers and police to train up Iraqi nationals?' Jo asked. 'So they can build their own security forces, right?'

'Yeah, but the problem with that is that individuals still remain loyal to their Sunni or Shiite roots,' Joe explained.

'So we should leave them to it,' Lachlan shrugged, reaching for the bottle. 'It's their own civil war brought about by centuries of pointless ethnic and religious conflict. Isn't it better just to let them split into their various factions and be done with it?'

'Then you end up with a Darfur, or a Rwanda.'

Lachlan refilled his glass and looked at Joe directly. 'So what's the solution, Bannister?'

Joe considered what he was about to say. 'The situation is so complex and so fraught that I wouldn't have the arrogance to suggest I had a solution.'

Everyone was silent. Even Lachlan had nothing to say to that.

Joe drained his glass and put it back on the coffee table. 'I better get going,' he said, standing up.

Jo jumped to her feet. 'Do you have to?'

'Yeah, I do.'

'Then I might head off too,' said Angie, getting up. 'You can escort me to the bus stop, if you don't mind?'

'Sure.' He nodded towards Lachlan. 'See you at the office.'

'No doubt.' Lachlan clasped his hands behind his head and stretched out his legs. He wasn't going anywhere soon by the looks of it.

Jo walked them out to the elevator. Angie pressed the button and the doors opened almost immediately. 'Ha, serendipity,' she said. She gave Jo a quick hug. 'Call me, okay?'

Jo looked up at Bannister; his expression was distant now. Honestly, she could kick Lachlan for showing up tonight, spoiling everything.

'Thanks for coming,' she said with a lame smile, 'and for the wine.'

He nodded, stepping into the elevator. 'See you.'

The doors glided to a close and Angie looked at Joe. 'That was really fascinating tonight, at least when you could get a word in over Lachlan. God, he's an arrogant arse.'

Joe smiled then. 'I take it you don't get on with him?'

'What do you reckon?' she said, glancing sideways at him.

'Doesn't that make things awkward?'

She frowned. 'What do you mean?'

'Well, between you and Jo. You're good friends, aren't you?'

'Absolutely, but I don't have to have much to do with him,' Angie said simply as the doors opened and they stepped out of the lift. They crossed the foyer and walked out onto the street.

'Which way are you headed?' she asked.

'Towards your bus stop, aren't we?'

She smiled. 'You don't have to. I just said that to get out of there. I didn't want to hang around once you were gone.'

'Yeah, it was a little strained,' he agreed as they started up the street. 'Can I ask you something?'

'Sure.'

'Why the charade? Why do they act like they're not together?'

Angie gave him a rueful smile. 'Habit, I guess.'

Joe frowned down at her, not understanding.

'You know he's married, right?' said Angie.

'What?'

'Whoopsy, maybe I wasn't supposed to say,' she said, biting her lip. 'Oh well, too late now. Yep, Lachlan's got a wife, two kids, even a dog, I think. The whole shebang.'

Joe was silent as he processed the information. He'd felt a keen sense of disappointment, he couldn't deny it, when Lachlan showed up and he realised there was something between them. But now . . . well, now he felt like he'd dodged a bullet. She was not the girl he thought she was.

'He's a complete tosser,' said Angie. 'I suppose I don't have to tell you that. Any guy who cheats on his wife . . .'

'It takes two,' Joe muttered grimly.

'This is my stop,' said Angie as they came to a bus shelter. She turned to look at him. 'She's not a bad person, Joe, just a wounded one. And it's made her very, very wary. She's too scared to have a normal relationship, not that she'd ever admit to that.'

Joe shrugged, like it had nothing to do with him. And it didn't. 'Well, it was nice meeting you, Angie,' he said, starting to back away up the street.

'You too, Joe. See you again sometime, I hope,' she said sincerely.

He doubted that was likely. But all he said was 'Bye' as he turned and walked away.

'You lied to me, Jo!'

'I didn't lie, I told you I got stuck in an elevator.'

'You also told me that you'd only met Bannister "briefly" was the word I think you used, at the staff meeting.'

Damn, so she did. Lachlan had pounced on her the moment she'd walked back into the apartment, and he was working himself into a lather.

'You lie about meeting him, you won't answer my calls, you discourage me from coming over, and when I finally get sick of waiting for an invitation, I find him all settled in here like he owns the place.'

'Now you're being ridiculous.'

'And what's with you drinking red wine? You don't even like red wine.'

'Who said I don't like red wine?' said Jo.

'I've never seen you drink it.'

'So? There are a lot of things you haven't seen me do, Lach.'

'Obviously.'

She groaned. 'Yeah, well I've rarely seen you act like such a dickhead as you did tonight,' she said, picking up the glasses and walking to the kitchen.

'Why, what did I do wrong?' he asked, following her.

'I should have just given you a tape measure from the start.'

'What?'

'So you could measure dicks and be done with it.'

'You think that's what was going on?' Lachlan said with a condescending shake of his head. 'Frankly Jo, Bannister didn't seem to know what he was talking about.'

She turned around from the sink to glare at him. 'He's been stationed in Iraq on and off since the war began. He won a friggin' Walkley for his coverage as an embed during the Battle of Fallujah.'

Lachlan regarded her curiously. 'How do you know all that?'

Jo didn't know what to say. 'It's hardly a state secret,' she muttered, brushing past him to go back into the living room.

He watched her, brooding, as she cleared more glasses from the coffee table. 'You've slept with him, haven't you?'

Jo looked incredulously at him. 'I can't believe you're asking me that.'

'Well, have you?'

'Have you slept with Sandra in the last few days?'

'Don't be ridiculous.'

'Then don't you be ridiculous,' she sniped, bustling back into the kitchen. She started to rinse the glasses when she felt him come up behind her, placing his hands on her shoulders.

'Okay, okay, that was out of line.'

She shrugged his hands off of her.

'Come on, Jo-bloh, don't be like that,' he said, nuzzling into her neck.

This time she moved away out of his reach, turning to face him. 'I think you should go, Lachlan.'

'Now you're overreacting. Just like I did, I'll admit. And you want to know why?'

She leaned back against the bench, waiting for his explanation.

'We haven't been *together* in weeks,' he began, taking a step closer. 'And it's creating this tension between us, surely you can feel it,' he said in a low voice. 'It's not healthy, Jo, and there's only one way to fix it.' He leaned his hands on the bench either side of her, effectively hemming her in.

She crossed her arms in front of her. 'Well, you should have thought of that before you started making wild accusations. Because suddenly I find I've got an outrageous headache.' And with that she pushed his arm out of the way and returned to the sink.

He was silent for a moment, but she could feel him watching her. 'You are fucking him, aren't you?'

'Get out, Lachlan.'

Next day

Jo was at her desk early this morning. She hadn't slept well, yet again. And although she blamed the temperature, the full moon, random noises coming from other apartments . . . Lachlan was right. They hadn't had sex in weeks and she was frustrated. Every time she closed her eyes she kept having lurid fantasies involving both him and Bannister, mostly at the same time. She told herself it was only because they had both been there together that night, and she was sexually frustrated, a potent combination. It was like Angie fantasising about Mr Darcy, and about as meaningful.

Finally, as dawn was breaking in the sky, Jo made a decision. Actually, several decisions.

First and foremost she had to remember to buy some batteries for her vibrator.

Secondly, she had to put Lachlan straight. She was not going to allow him to dictate to her; she didn't have to give him explanations about how she spent her time, or who with, or for godsakes, what she drank. He had no rights over her. That was the whole idea of going out with a married man. Jo had discovered a way to have a relationship without becoming just one half of a whole. Without losing herself. She was not going to let him shift the goalposts now.

Which is exactly what he did last night, coming over when she'd expressly told him not to, and planting himself there like he had a stake in the place. If he was a dog he would have pissed on the coffee table.

Well, he wasn't going to get away with that again. She intended to be friends with Bannister, and Lachlan was just going to have to deal with it. Jo had never really fostered close friendships at work, or anywhere for that matter. Even as a girl she had hardly been inclined to have schoolfriends over to her house, given Charlene's shenanigans. So the pattern had been set early on, entwined into her very DNA, much as a vine grows on a trellis or a fence; leave it there long enough without cutting it back and it actually becomes the thing holding the fence up. Angie had managed to graft herself on, and now this man, this Joe Bannister, was giving it a shot as well. Jo found herself intrigued, even a little touched by his persistence. Maybe the elevator episode had forged a bond, or maybe it was the foreign correspondent thing. He was fascinating last night, Jo would have liked to have heard more about his experiences, but she would have had to gag Lachlan first.

Well, no matter, there would be plenty more opportunities. They were going to be working together, closely in fact. Having Bannister as a mentor sanctioned by Leo could only be a positive step in her career. Things were looking up. And she needed be prepared.

So she got up at five and ironed all her shirts, trousers, skirts, T-shirts . . . her entire wardrobe, in fact. After she had finished ironing, Jo proceeded to bathe and shave and pluck various parts of her body, then she trimmed and painted her nails with a clear varnish, while a cool cucumber hydroxy-replenishing mask set on her face. Jo was not altogether sure these things worked, in fact she was highly doubtful that they did, but it was part of a gift pack Belle had given her on some occasion, and she was on a roll. She rinsed the mask off at the allotted time and moisturised as per instructions, then blow-dried her hair and spent ages arranging it into a flawlessly sleek French roll. She applied make-up with the precision of a microsurgeon, and sprayed perfume in the air before walking into the cloud so that she was 'misted' or whatever the expression was.

Jo decided it was safest to eat before she got dressed, she wasn't going to spoil all this hard work with a coffee spill down the front of her blouse. That's when she discovered the pantry was bare, which should not have surprised her as she hadn't done a proper shop since the move. She ate crackers with Vegemite while she wrote a comprehensive shopping list – strictly healthy stuff, no convenience foods, no junk. Of course, that meant she was going to have to cook, but that was okay, she'd do it on the weekends. She would make up big batches of nutritious dishes and freeze them in portions she could eat for dinner or take to work. She added plastic containers and freezer labels to her list. This was good, she was really getting herself organised now. And healthy. She needed to keep her energy levels up if she was going to be putting in the time at work.

As she finally dressed in her best suit, one she usually reserved for interviews with important people, Jo felt a little like Cinderella getting ready for the ball. Everything was perfect. She was going to have a good day, she could feel it. She would start by popping her head into Bannister's office with a friendly hello, thanks for last night, share a joke. That's what friends did.

'Well, look at you, Executive Barbie!' Oliver declared as she approached the counter. 'Who are you interviewing today? The PM?'

'Nope.'

'Who then? Someone gorgeous you're trying to impress?'

'No one, as far as I know,' she said. 'Oh, skim milk, thanks Oliver,' she added as he started making her coffee.

He narrowed his eyes. 'You don't take skim milk, and I'm not ruining one more coffee than I have to with that pale imitation. What's going on, big date after work?'

She shook her head.

'Okay, I give up. What's special about today?'

'You know what they say, Oliver. Today's the first day of the rest of your life.'

He looked at her seriously. 'No, no one says that. At least not since the seventies.'

'Well, that's the way I feel,' she declared. 'I'm taking charge, running my own race, setting my own agenda, blowing my own trumpet –'

'Making me nauseous,' he interrupted, sliding her coffee towards her.

'Oh, and um, I haven't really eaten,' she said, frowning up at the menu board. Her eyes grazed past quiches and bagels and muffins. 'What's something good for me . . . ?'

'All my food is good for you,' he maintained airily.

'Come on, you know what I mean, low-fat good for me?'

Oliver shook his head. 'You're the size of a small forest animal, Josephine, don't go getting weird on me.' He sighed wearily. 'Banana bread, hold the butter, work for you?'

'Thanks, Oliver.'

It was after ten when Jo finally knocked on Bannister's office door. He'd arrived at work about twenty minutes ago, Jo had been looking out for him, but just as she had begun to make her way over to his office, he strode out the door again, not seeing her, and headed towards reception and the lift bay, she assumed. He'd been back now for about ten minutes, with the door closed. Jo figured he was settled in for the morning.

She heard a brusque 'Yep' from inside when she knocked. She opened the door as he glanced up from the computer screen. He did a double-take, only subtle, but she noticed. Then his eyes returned to the computer.

'Hi,' she said.

He grunted a reply.

Jo just stood there, feeling more than a little self-conscious, while Bannister continued to focus on the screen, clicking the mouse intermittently, as though she wasn't even there. He was being quite rude actually.

'Did you want something?' he said eventually, without taking his eyes off the screen.

'Well, um, yes,' said Jo, taking a tentative step into the room. He still didn't look at her. 'I just wanted to say thank you for the wine, and well, you know, the gesture.'

'No problem,' he said, glancing fleetingly in her direction. He certainly did not make eye contact. A moment later he started typing. Jo was perplexed, she felt like an idiot just standing there.

'Was there something else?' he asked offhand. His typing had paused, but his eyes were still glued to the screen in front of him.

'Not really,' Jo said in a small voice.

'Well, I know you think I have – what did you call it? – "carte blanche", but actually I do work and I need to get on with it. All right with you?'

'Sure.' Jo backed out of the office, closing the door quietly. She stood on the other side, breathing hard. What the hell was that? Bugger it, she was going to find out.

She knocked on the door again but this time she walked straight in without waiting for an invitation.

'No it's not all right,' she announced.

'I beg your pardon?' He actually lifted his eyes from the screen this time and fixed them on her.

Jo closed the door. 'I don't understand what's going on. You've made repeated overtures of . . . friendship, and okay, I'll admit, I wasn't very amenable at first. I don't do the friendship thing very well, lots of reasons we don't need to go into now, but last night I think we finally cleared the air and as far as I was concerned we parted friends, so what's with the attitude today?'

He listened attentively as she spoke, and when she had finished he let out a deep sigh and pushed his chair back from the desk. He stood up and walked to the window, propping himself against the ledge. 'The guy's married,' he said bluntly.

'What?'

'Lachlan, he's married, with kids, isn't that right?'

Jo's heart dropped into her stomach with a sickening thump.

'Look at you, you could have anyone you wanted, and you're with someone else's husband? I just don't get it.'

She felt guilty. He was making her feel guilty. What gave him the right to pass judgement on her?

'You know what I don't get?' she returned coolly. 'When this became any of your business.'

He held her gaze for a moment longer, and then he nodded slowly. 'You're absolutely right,' he said. 'It is none of my business. We don't even know each other very well. So let's keep it that way.'

With that he walked back around his desk and sat down, returning his attention to the computer screen. Jo stood for a moment longer, clenching her freshly manicured nails into the palms of her hands. She wanted to leave him with a brilliantly incisive but devastating final blow that would knock him flying off his smug perch of self-righteousness, but she couldn't think of anything, of course. She'd think of something in bed tonight, or in the shower tomorrow, but that didn't do her much good right now.

So instead she left the room in silence, her head held high, not even bothering to close the door in case she slammed it in rage. She didn't want that to be her parting shot. But she was incensed. How dare he? Where the hell did he get off? Bloody arrogant, opinionated, judgemental . . . She should write a column about this. That's how she would have the last word. She sat down at her desk and opened a document on her computer. She typed in *Morality*, and then sat and stared at it for a while, tapping lightly on the space bar as her mind whirred and the cogs creaked into motion. Finally the engine chugged to life and she began to type in earnest.

> Morality. It's a peculiar beast. Some would say it's extinct, or at least endangered. Others would say it's flexible or elastic, slippery and elusive. Most would agree that morality is above all a personal matter, between you and your god, you and your conscience, even you and your accountant. Still others cry it's been abandoned like a baby in a dumpster and it's time we rescued it before all of humanity goes to hell in a handbasket.

But who will reset the moral code for the 21st century? Once upon a time it was written in stone. So who is entitled to cast the first stone in this day and age?

I was watching TV the other night, and the word f@#k was being sprinkled about fairly liberally. Not only that, the c-word followed soon after. Now, as you may have worked out, I'm not allowed to even print those words in full. Yet they can be broadcast uncensored across the airwaves, as long as it's after 9.30 pm.

In 1975 Graham Kennedy was banned from the air after making a crow call that may have sounded like the f-word. Was that a more moral time? A less progressive time? Is anyone really harmed by hearing the f-word or the c-word or any word, except maybe 'Fire!' and only then if you're standing blindfolded in front of a squad armed with rifles.

Should that be the rule of thumb then – first do no harm?

'Jo?'

She looked up. Lachlan was watching her across the half-wall partition that separated the desks of the lowly who didn't merit a whole office to themselves. Or even a whole wall.

'My office?' he said, using his undercover voice. He didn't wait for a response, but simply turned and walked away, assuming he would be obeyed. Jo returned to her column. Damn, she'd lost the flow. She scrolled up to read what she'd written. A few moments passed, and she could see Lachlan approaching again in her peripheral vision.

'Jo,' he said, crouching beside her desk now, his tone bordering on impatient. 'Okay, I get it, you're still upset. So let's talk about it, in *private*.'

'I'm in the middle of something here, Lachlan.'

'Come on, Jo,' he said in a raised whisper. 'We're going to have to talk about it at some point.'

She considered him for a moment. More fool him. He did not want to mess with her today. 'Okay,' she said.

He looked relieved. Jo wondered how long that was going to last as she followed him back to his office. He closed the door and walked around her slowly, coming to perch on the edge of his desk, facing her.

'Jo, I'm sorry if some of the things I said last night upset you.'

So all he could manage was a Clayton's apology. While he had used the word 'sorry', he'd tempered it with that time-honoured qualifier, '*if* I upset you'. He was only sorry if the outcome of his apparently innocuous act had slighted her somehow. It had not been intended. And her reaction was possibly even unreasonable, but he was prepared to apologise even so. That was the kind of guy he was.

'You know I love you, Jo-bloh.'

Ooh, the L-word, he was really pulling out the big guns. It was not the first time Lachlan had professed love to her, but he tended to save it for special occasions when it would have the most impact. No use bandying it about, willy-nilly, diminishing its returns.

As for Jo, she had no idea if she loved Lachlan, she had given up trying to work that one out. There seemed to be a lot of angst spent deciding if you really loved someone, but what difference did it make? People liked to think that love gave an authenticity, a gravity, to their relationships, to their actions. But a lot of harm had been done in the name of love. Whatever that feeling was – call it love, call it infatuation, call it hormones more likely – Jo had decided it was dangerous. It got in the way of thinking straight, or of being able to tell a lie from the truth; it distorted perspective and blocked ordinary commonsense. It interfered with the most basic instinct to protect yourself, or the people closest to you, who depended on you.

'Jo?' Lachlan prompted. 'Aren't you going to say something?'

She took a breath. 'It's none of your business who I spend my time with –'

'Absolutely.'

'Who I'm friends with –'

'Of course.'

'Who I sleep with.'

He opened his mouth but nothing came out.

'Lachlan?'

He winced. 'You would tell me though, wouldn't you, Jo?'

'Why? So you can pull a hissy fit like you did last night?'

'No,' he denied, stretching the word out while he came up with his rationale. 'I'm only thinking about the safe sex aspect,' he said finally. 'If you were sleeping with someone I think you should tell me, so, you know, we can take the appropriate measures.'

Jo rolled her eyes. 'Okay, Lach, here's one for free. I haven't slept with Bannister and I don't intend to sleep with him. You can put that in the bank. It's never going to happen.'

Now he looked relieved. 'He's not really your type, is he?' he said happily.

'That's not the point,' she said. 'If you ever ask me that again, or accuse me, or carry on like you did last night, it's over, Lachlan. I've never spent a Christmas or a New Year's Eve or a birthday with you, I never know when I'm going to see you from one week to the next. I don't believe I've ever made a single demand of you. And I've never complained or given you any grief whatsoever.'

'But you knew what you were getting yourself into,' he reminded her.

'Of course I did, but I didn't realise it would all be on your terms and that I'd be expected to have no life whatsoever. I didn't sign up for that.'

There was a pause. Finally Lachlan straightened up and said, 'Understood.'

He obviously decided that was sufficient and took two deliberate steps to close the gap between them. He cupped her face with his hands, looking intently into her eyes. 'So are we okay?' he asked in a low voice.

He brought his lips close to hers, just brushing them lightly, teasing her. Jo wondered whether to make him suffer a bit longer, but then Bannister came to mind, his judgemental contempt . . . as Lachlan's lips slid down her neck . . . She was not going to let anyone impose their morality on her . . . Jo was in total control . . . His tongue curled behind her ear . . . She was doing exactly what she wanted to do . . . She pressed her body into Lachlan's and looped her arms around his neck. Their lips met and the kiss took on a life of its own, fuelled by the tension still hovering between them, with a little help from the high-octane boost Bannister had added to the fire. Human emotion was a funny thing, it occurred to Jo. Tipped one way and you were barely speaking, tip the other way and you suddenly wanted to tear each other's clothes off.

'So can I *please* come over tonight?' Lachlan murmured, his tone more suggestive than plaintive. 'I'm begging you. I'll do anything.'

'I might hold you to that.'

'Oh, I'm counting on it.'

Jo returned to her desk with a spring in her step. At least she was going to sleep well tonight, eventually. Bannister could take a flying leap. She lived her life the way she wanted, she didn't hurt anyone, and she refused to feel guilty about it.

She reread the last line she'd written – *First do no harm* . . .

> We could do worse than follow that mantra. In fact we do worse every day. The people who think it's fine to send young men and women to war on a lie are often the same ones who decry the erosion of morals in our society. The people who strap bombs to their chests and walk into a crowd and blow themselves and everyone in the vicinity out of existence are the same ones who condemn the infidels for their blatant immorality.
>
> But immorality is not the scourge of our society, it is rather the hasty or biased judgements of those who think they know better. Morality is relative, it changes according to the era you were born in, the

religion you were born into, the society where you live. You simply cannot please everyone.

If you're not hurting anybody, what business is it of anyone else to tell you how to live your life? If someone says 'f@#k' in the forest and nobody is around to hear it, are all the trees going to shrivel up and die?

Two weeks later

Joe dragged his backpack out into the living area as Will walked in through the door of the flat.

'Hey.'

'Hey.'

They hadn't seen much of each other in the last couple of weeks. Joe had always left for work before Will was up in the morning, and Will was out most nights. Occasionally Joe heard him come in late, but he hadn't brought friends home again, not surprisingly.

Will glanced at the backpack. 'Going somewhere?'

'I'm staying up at the house for about a week, there's a summit on climate change I'm covering.'

'Yeah, they've been talking about it on the news,' he nodded. 'Well, just so you know, I'll be moved out by the time you get home.'

Joe sighed, perching on the edge of the table. 'You don't have to do that, Will.'

'Yeah, I do,' he said, walking around into the kitchen. 'We're different, Joe. I hang out with my friends most nights, you want peace and quiet. That's cool, this is your place. You were good enough to let me use it all this time, I appreciate that. Now I'm going to get out of your hair.'

Will opened the fridge door and peered in. This was too polite. They should have thrashed it out, sworn at each other, showed some emotion. But Joe couldn't exactly argue with him, it was right that he moved on and made his own way. He just wished his only brother didn't seem like a distant relative.

'Where will you go?'

'A friend of a friend moved out of a share house in Stanmore. It's a cool place, I can move in next week.'

Joe nodded. 'So why don't you come up and see Dad this weekend?' he suggested.

Will glanced over his shoulder. 'Nah, I don't think so.'

'Why, are you busy?' Joe persisted.

'Not especially,' Will dismissed, closing the fridge door with his elbow as he juggled tomatoes, a jar of mayonnaise, a knob of salami and more, before dumping it all on the bench.

'So you could come if you wanted to?'

Will glanced at him. 'I guess. If I wanted to.'

'What are you saying?' said Joe, crossing to the kitchen bench as Will started to make a sandwich.

He sighed loudly. 'Let's just say I don't think I bring the old man a whole lot of joy.'

'Not when you never visit him,' said Joe. 'Mim said it's been ages.'

'I just upset him. It's easier if I stay away.'

'I think that's what upsets him.'

'You don't know that, Joe. You don't know what it's like between me and Dad, it's not like it is for you.'

'What do you mean?'

'You're the golden child, Joe, you always have been. You followed in his footsteps, did everything right, even scored yourself a matching Walkley. I can't get close to that.'

Joe was listening. 'But you don't want to, right?'

Will looked up. 'Right.'

'So get over it.'

'What?'

'You're always harping on about this, and frankly, Will, it's a little juvenile,' said Joe. 'You're happy with the life choices you've made so far, I assume?'

'Yeah.'

'Then why keep defending them? Just get on with it.'

'That's exactly what I'm doing,' he said, slapping his sandwich onto a plate and walking around into the living area. He sat down on the lounge and began to eat.

Joe went into the kitchen and opened the fridge. 'Wanna beer?'

'Do you need to ask?'

He picked up two bottles and brought one over to Will, before lowering himself into an armchair.

'So,' Joe said, opening his, 'why don't you come up and see Dad this weekend?'

Will sighed, dropping his sandwich back onto the plate. 'Jesus, Joe, give it a rest, will you?'

'What? Like I've just been saying, you don't have to explain yourself to Dad. I'm sure he only wants you to be happy, and if you show him you are, then he'll be happy too.' Joe paused. 'He's not doing well. You really should go and see him, Will.'

'It's not that simple, Joe. You don't understand.'

'Then explain it to me.'

He put his plate on the coffee table and picked up his beer. 'You and Dad are close, you always have been, and no, I'm not going to harp about the other stuff, but you don't know what it was like for the rest of us.'

Joe frowned. 'What are you talking about?'

'He was never there, Joe. Mum may as well have been a single parent, she brought us up on her own.'

'No she didn't, Will. He went away for months, but then he was back again for months.'

'Not after you and Hil left,' he said plainly. 'Things changed.'

'How?'

'You probably saw him as much we did, when you met up overseas. He was hardly ever at home. He'd come back after three months away, and then after a week or two he'd start to get restless. He wasn't interested in coming to the school, watching our sports, nothing. He'd start picking fights with Mum –'

'No,' said Joe. 'That's just what they were like. They always argued about politics and –'

'No, Joe, this wasn't politics. This was Dad picking on her about stupid stuff, the clutter around the house, what she cooked for dinner, for Chrissakes.'

Joe sat there, shaking his head. This was a child's perspective. Will didn't understand the spark between them, the love, the passion.

'After a few weeks, Mum'd get fed up,' Will went on. 'She'd tell him to go. He couldn't get out of there fast enough. And he stayed away longer and longer, often up to six months, once it was eight. He'd come back for a couple of weeks, out of some sense of obligation. I don't know why he bothered.'

Joe was sure now that Will didn't have a clue. 'Maybe it looked that way to you, Will, but they were solid. Mum was just incredibly independent, she did fine without Dad. It's the way they were. It worked for them.'

Will looked at him directly. 'You can be an arrogant tosser, Joe,' he said, but there was no aggression in his tone. 'You weren't even there, and yet you think you know how it was.'

'I was there, some of the time,' he defended, 'a lot of the time. Whenever I came home things were fine. In fact, we always had a great time.'

'That's true, they killed the fatted calf and celebrated the return of the prodigal son.'

Joe rolled his eyes.

'And not just for you, for Hil as well. Crinny was only down in Sydney, so she didn't get quite the same reception, but still, when you all came home, Dad was in his element. He was happy, he was always nicer to Mum, and we'd have a ball. Then you'd all leave, and so would he soon after.'

Joe could only take what Will was saying with a grain of salt, not from arrogance on his part, but from a deep knowing. His parents were tight, he'd never known two people so close, so in sync. Will had been a difficult kid, easily distracted and disruptive at school, always getting into trouble. Joe recalled both his parents sharing their concerns with him at one time or another. Will obviously had a lot of resentment about his father not being around when he was growing up, and that was probably fair enough. But his interpretation of the bigger picture was way off kilter.

'I just felt for Mum, you know,' Will was saying. 'She never got to fulfil her dreams, it was all about him. She was a frustrated journalist her whole life. She used to write angry letters to the paper all the time, you know.'

'What, the local paper?'

'And Sydney ones,' he said. 'The local mob invited her to write articles from time to time. I think she was really starting to get into it when –' He stopped abruptly.

The loss of their mother hung in the space between them, and neither of them spoke for a while. And then it all made sense. Will was still so young when their mum died, he was a teenager. He had never even got to see his parents together through the eyes of an adult. So his grief for his mother had been channelled into anger towards his father. Her lost opportunities were his fault, not the fact that her life had been taken away from her, from all of them, prematurely, inexplicably, without even the chance to say goodbye.

'You know, Will,' said Joe eventually. 'I'm sorry you don't feel close to Dad, but you're going to feel bad when he's gone. And worse, you'll feel guilty if you haven't made an effort to see him, and there's nothing you'll be able to do to change that.'

Will was listening, his head bowed.

'Think about it,' said Joe. 'But don't take too long. There isn't much time.'

Inaugural Australasian Summit on Climate Change

Jo was settling into her room at the hotel. It was worthwhile unpacking properly for three nights. You could live out of a suitcase for a single night, but beyond that it was untenable. At least as far as Jo was concerned. But halfway through she got bored, and flipped the lid of her suitcase closed. She sat back on the bed and sighed heavily.

She had driven up with Matt, a staff photographer, in a work
car, in various degrees of awkwardness. He was a reliable guy
and hardworking, but she didn't know him all that well and
there was a definite Gen X/Y schism between them. Used to
be that you had to be old enough to be someone's mother
to feel a generation gap; not any more. It had been a relief to
finally arrive at the hotel and merge in with everyone else for
welcome drinks. Jo recognised the odd face – colleagues from
other papers, government delegates, business identities – and
she engaged in a few trite conversations while she scanned the
crowd for Bannister. If he was here, he certainly wasn't making
himself known.

So she slipped away after one glass of wine and went to her
room. She felt restless and agitated. There was that word again.
She'd hardly clapped eyes on Bannister in the last two weeks. He
had apparently travelled up to the mountains on the weekend,
but Jo had had no contact with him. And it annoyed her. He was
clearly not prepared to make even the slightest effort to get along,
so how the hell were they supposed to work together?

She should just call him. She took her phone from her bag and
flipped it open, but then she hesitated, tapping it against her lips.
She just wanted to check that he was still coming, that everything
was all right. That was reasonable, surely? He had a sick father,
anything could have happened. She scrolled for his number and
pressed call before she thought about it too much.

'Joe Bannister's phone,' came a woman's voice when it picked
up.

Jo was taken aback momentarily. 'Oh, um, sorry, I didn't,
um . . .'

'You're after Joe? I'll just get him. Can I ask who's calling?'

'It's a –' Jo cleared the crackle from her throat, '– it's Jo Liddell.
From the *Tribune* . . . we, um, we work together.'

'Sure, I'll tell him, just a minute.'

Jo heard footsteps and voices, muffled and indistinct. She paced
back and forth across the carpet at the end of the bed. That was
probably one of his sisters who'd answered. He had three, she
remembered that, three sisters in the Blue Mountains, and the
actor brother. But of course it could have been anyone picking

up his phone. It was certainly none of Jo's business. At least she knew when something was none of her business.

'Yep?' His voice came suddenly and abruptly onto the line, catching her by surprise so she didn't respond straightaway.

'Jo, are you there?'

'Yeah, sorry, um, it's Jo . . . oh, you know that already.'

'What is it?' Now he sounded impatient.

'Well, I just wanted to check that you're still on for tomorrow?'

'For the summit?'

'Yeah.'

'Why wouldn't I be?'

'I don't know, lots of reasons. Something could have happened.'

'I would have let you know if I wasn't going to make it.'

'Okay.'

Silence.

'Was that all?' he asked.

'Yeah, sure, sorry for bothering you.'

And then he hung up. Ouch. Jo had a feeling this could turn out to be the longest four days of her life.

Opening address by the Hon MP, Federal Minister for the Environment, Liv Khouri

Jo deliberately sat on the side of the hall closest to the bank of glass doors that opened out to the courtyard, and from where latecomers would be most likely to slip in unnoticed, or with the least amount of disruption. Bannister was missing in action, or else being very effective at hiding from her. But surely he wouldn't be so petulant? And perhaps she shouldn't be so paranoid. He did say he was coming, maybe he was not a punctual person generally, she had no idea. She also suddenly had no idea what everyone was laughing at. She had to focus, pay attention, there was every chance she was doing this on her own, after all.

Twenty minutes into the opening address, Bannister suddenly and unceremoniously dropped into the seat beside her, giving her a start. Jo turned to look at him. 'You're late,' she whispered.

'Did you miss me?'

She bristled, looking ahead again, but keeping her voice low. 'I'm just saying, you've missed most of the opening. Puts you rather on the back foot.'

He didn't respond so she turned to look at him again. He was smiling, shaking his head.

'Have there been any new policy announcements? Surprise guests? Unexpected budget pledges? Anything?'

Jo sighed, turning her attention back to the speaker as though she was riveted. A moment later she felt him lean into her, his breath on her ear.

'I'll hazard a guess that Ms Khouri has offered a warm welcome,' he said in a low voice, 'appealed to everyone to work cooperatively, outlined what is hoped to be achieved, without being so specific that she can be challenged on it later, and then launched into global warming statistics that I can probably find on Google, but which are included in the press kit anyway.'

Jo turned her head, their faces were close. Bannister smiled a big, fake cheesy smile and then got up from his seat, keeping his head down. 'See you around,' he whispered, and then he was gone.

Day two

Jo saw him around all right. Always on the other side of the room, generally with a gaggle of people surrounding him. Everyone seemed to know him. Women hugged him, men shook his hand and slapped him on the back; government ministers, climatologists, celebrity environmentalists, prominent media hacks. He was getting to talk to everyone who was anyone.

On occasion he happened to walk past Jo, he'd casually ask

'How are you doing?' She'd reply 'Fine', and he'd say 'Good. Let me know if there's anything I can do, won't you?'

He could have introduced her around, he shouldn't have to be told that. Jo wasn't getting to talk to anyone important. She was attending all the presentations, unlike Bannister, and no doubt writing the same copy as everyone else. She had an overwhelming sense that this was turning into a big fat wasted opportunity. And not only that, Leo would see that she'd done nothing more than a workmanlike job, and not be so forthcoming in the future. On the second day she had to choose which sessions to attend; various talks, seminars and workshops were being held concurrently, though most of the seasoned journos had booked individual interviews with all the big names. Jo would have liked to have asked Bannister if he had any contacts, if he was doing any interviews she could sit in on, but she wasn't going to give him the satisfaction. So when she found herself nodding off in a near-empty session with someone calling himself a climate economist, she only had herself to blame.

Jo was attempting to follow a very complex equation linking the degree of global warming per decade to the average GDP across developed nations, when her phone started to vibrate in her pocket. She removed it surreptitiously and flipped it open. It was a message from Bannister.

Where are you?

Jo keyed in the room location, and moments later another message arrived.

Meet me outside asap

She didn't like being ordered, but nonetheless she was glad for the interruption, so she quietly gathered up her things and crept out of the room, closing the door. She looked around to see Bannister marching up the corridor towards her.

'You drove up here in a work car, right?' he snapped as he got closer.

'Yes,' she answered uncertainly.

'Well I need to borrow it. Have you got the keys on you?'

Jo hesitated. 'It's signed out to me, I'm not supposed to –'

'This is an emergency.'

'Okay, but I don't have permission –'

'Fuck, Jo, do you think Leo is going to mind?'

She took a breath. She would not be intimidated. 'Leo doesn't have authority over the insurance company and they're incredibly strict –'

'It's my father,' he said darkly. 'I have to get home.'

'Okay, I'll drive you.'

He dragged his fingers through his hair, hesitating. Too frigging proud just to say yes, or worse, thanks. Something snapped inside Jo.

'Oh for Chrissakes, would you get over this?' She was fed up with his attitude. 'I'm not the devil incarnate. Do you want a lift or would you rather cut off your nose to spite your face, you big baby?'

He looked taken aback, to say the least. 'Okay,' he said. 'I'll take the lift. Thanks.'

Jo stormed off in the direction of the carpark, Bannister following in her wake. As they approached the car, she aimed the remote to unlock the doors. She got in and started the engine as he climbed into the passenger seat.

'Where to?' she asked as she began to reverse out of the space.

They drove along in silence, except for the directions that he muttered at intervals. Jo could feel his anxiety; it filled the closed cabin of the car like a toxic gas, and she drove as fast as was legally allowed through Leura, eventually turning into a pretty tree-lined street.

'Just past that four-wheel drive, pull up at the next house,' said Joe.

As soon as the car came to a halt, he jumped out without another word and ran down to the house, disappearing inside. Jo sat there, clutching the steering wheel, staring after him. What was she supposed to do now? It didn't seem right to drive away. What if they needed a ride somewhere? If it was bad they'd call an ambulance, she supposed. But they didn't let relatives ride in ambulances any more. And if it was that bad, surely an ambulance would have been called already?

Jo turned off the engine. She'd better wait, for a while at least. Bannister would come out soon enough, tell her what was going on. He may even need a lift back to the conference. That seemed unlikely, but how was she supposed to know? She didn't even know what was wrong with his father. Jo had a sudden sensation of dread. Anything could have happened. He could have . . . No, she didn't want to think that way. Jo looked towards the house, wondering what was going on inside, beyond the drawn curtains. Maybe she shouldn't be here. But she couldn't just leave. A friend wouldn't leave. So she stayed.

'I'm so sorry, Joe,' said Mim.

'Don't be sorry,' he said, squeezing her shoulder. 'I'm just glad I wasn't far away.'

'There's always been a nurse here when he's needed the cough-assist machine. I just got scared.'

'Mim, hey, stop it. You have nothing to apologise for,' Joe said gently.

The scene that had confronted him when he first arrived at the house was frankly horrifying. Joe was immediately reminded of an incident in Iraq where he had watched helplessly while a man hit in the chest by mortar had slowly suffocated as his blood filled his lungs. Of course there wasn't any blood today, but the parox-ysms of his father's body as he fought for breath were distressingly similar. Mim was struggling to operate the machine and physically restrain his convulsing figure. Joe took over and managed to keep him still while Mim attached the mask and adjusted the pressures. Eventually his lungs cleared, and he began to breathe at a steady, normal rhythm. He was resting peacefully now.

'How often do you have to do that?'

'It's usually one of the nurses,' said Mim. 'They taught him how to use it, so he can do it himself, but he won't.'

'He couldn't have operated that himself today,' said Joe.

'No, of course not,' she agreed. 'He's supposed to go on the machine regularly, but he doesn't like it, so the nurses run it the days they're here, and once or twice it's been a bit more urgent. Today I kept checking on him, but he assured me that he was fine and he didn't need it. Next thing he was convulsing. I guess I got spooked. If you hadn't been up here, I would have had to handle it myself.'

'I'm glad you didn't have to.'

They looked at each other and a sad knowing passed between them. Joe felt overwhelmed. It wasn't right that this had all been left to Mim. Things were clearly getting too much for her, for anyone on their own. He thought about the options. He could move up here, but even so, the time had probably come for around-the-clock medical care. Joe did not want to think about moving his father out of the house – that would sound the death knell – so he was going to have to look into a full-time nurse, or a team of them.

'It's times like this I wish Mum was here,' Mim was saying. 'She was so good in a crisis, so capable. I remember whenever I had an asthma attack, Dad was hopeless, he'd just walk away, he could never cope. But Mum knew how to calm me down so I could breathe just enough to give the medication time to take effect.'

Joe nodded, listening. 'Do you think she ever got sick of it, though?'

'What do you mean?'

'Always having to be the capable one, the responsible one, with Dad away so much?'

Mim shrugged. 'I don't know.' She pulled her cardigan around her.

'Do you think she was happy, Mim?' he persisted.

'Why are you asking these questions?'

'I'm just wondering.'

'I better get the fire started,' she said, walking out of the kitchen.

'It's spring,' said Joe, following her. 'You still need to put the fire on this early?'

'I will today,' said Mim. 'I don't want to wait for the air to get damp.'

He understood. 'Do you want some help?'

'This I can handle myself,' she smiled, kneeling down at the hearth.

Something caught his eye and Joe glanced out at the street, at the car out front. He moved closer to the window. 'What the . . . ?'

Mim looked over her shoulder. 'What's wrong?'

'The woman who gave me a lift from the conference,' he said, crossing the room, 'she's still waiting out front.'

'Really? All this time?' Mim turned, but Joe was already at the front door. 'Ask her in for a drink,' she called after him.

Jo saw Bannister striding up the path towards her and she got out of the car.

'What are you still doing here?' he asked as he came into earshot.

'Oh, um, I was just worried, in case you needed a lift . . . or anything.'

'My sister has a car, but she couldn't leave Dad to come and get me.' He stopped on the other side of the car, staring at her. Jo didn't think he was annoyed, more curious.

'You didn't have to stay all this time,' he said.

She shrugged. 'So everything's okay?'

'Yeah . . . thanks.'

'I'm glad.' She wasn't sure what else to say. 'Okay, so I guess I'll get going then.'

He didn't respond, so she turned back to get into the car.

'Jo?'

She looked across at him, holding the door open.

'Do you want to come in?' he offered.

'No, that's okay.'

'Come on. Have a drink.'

'I shouldn't . . .'

'Why not?'

She wasn't sure. 'Your dad.'

'He's resting, he's okay, really.' Joe took a breath. 'Come on in, my sister'll scold me if I let you go without a drink.'

He turned around and started back towards the house. Jo watched him for a moment, before closing the door and walking around the car to follow him.

*

'Mim's lovely,' said Jo.

They were sitting out on the steps of the back verandah, having a beer. Mim had begged off, she wanted to stay inside where she could listen out for her father.

'Yeah, she's a sweet kid,' Joe agreed. 'She's taken on all the responsibility for Dad, but I think it's getting too much for her. And I don't know what I'm going to do about it.'

Joe had given her a brief rundown of his father's illness, and what had happened this afternoon, enough so that Jo understood the situation. It appeared to be pretty dire. Although listening to him talk, Jo found his affection for his father, as well as his sister, quite touching. He was softer here in this house. Certainly a lot softer than he'd been towards her lately.

'Thanks for staying,' he said. 'That was really decent of you.'

'It's okay,' she dismissed.

Joe looked at her. 'I owe you an apology,' he said carefully. 'I've been a complete jerk.'

'You were anxious about your dad, I understand.'

'I'm not just talking about this afternoon,' he said.

'Oh.' Jo suddenly felt self-conscious, staring down at her shoes.

'You're right, your business is none of mine. Maybe I was a little too hasty to judge.'

Jo dared to look at him then and he was watching her intently.

'I read your column last week,' he said.

'You did?'

He nodded. 'Point taken.'

'Then apology accepted.'

They sat for a moment in silence, sipping their beers.

'I want you to know,' Joe said after a while, 'I'm really not a judgemental person. I think the world would be a better place if we all minded our own business.' He paused. 'But it just doesn't make sense to me . . .'

Jo wondered what he was talking about.

'I mean, a woman like you . . . I don't understand what you're getting from the relationship, unless he's the love of your life or something?'

She was just staring at him, one eyebrow raised.

'Which is none of my business,' he said sheepishly. 'Okay, the matter is hereby dropped.' He raised his bottle to her. 'Friends?'

She clinked her bottle against his. 'I'd like that.'

Saturday

Jo had filed her final copy in the very early hours of the morning. The sub had decided he wanted her to stay until she was finished, rather than lose valuable working time travelling home in the late afternoon. It was going to be a major spread in the paper and they needed to have it in place so they could work around it. Matt had bummed a lift earlier in the day to get the pictures back, so Jo was free to stay another night and make her way home on Saturday, in her own time.

Bannister had spent most of the remainder of the conference at the house to give Mim a break, but he managed to set up some interviews for Jo and he worked with her to prep questions. He read her drafts and gave her constructive feedback, and Jo gained more than a little insight into why he had been so successful. Her pieces were better for his input, but he refused to share a by-line. When she sent the copy off she included his name anyway; Leo would have dropped it in if she hadn't.

Jo had arranged to pick Bannister up at midday at the house. He had intended to head back to the city sometime over the weekend, now that he'd organised full-time nursing support for his father. So when Jo was delayed until the Saturday, it seemed silly not to travel back together. As she drove into Leura this time, Jo was struck by what a picturesque little village it was. She wondered what it would be like to have grown up and gone to school in the one place, surrounded by a big, loving family. The word idyllic came to mind.

As she stepped out of the car, the scent of eucalyptus tingled in her nostrils. She gazed down at the big rambling house on the big rambling block, which was the way Bannister had described it. But when had he described it to her? It occurred to Jo that it must have been in the elevator, and it pleased her that she remembered. It was a lovely, welcoming, homely house, not a showpiece; in fact it was a little shabby, and that made her smile as she walked down the path. It was the kind of house you read about in stories, where a family has lived for generations. Idyllic indeed.

It was Mim who answered when Jo knocked on the door.

'Hello Jo,' she said, the warmth in her voice tempered only slightly by her inherent shyness.

'Hi Mim. I'm here to give Joe a lift, did he mention?'

'He did. Come inside, he's just in with Dad.'

'Oh . . .' Jo hesitated. 'Maybe I should wait for him in the car?'

'Will it bother you?' asked Mim, watching her.

'Will what bother me?'

'Being around someone who's so sick?'

'No, no, not at all. That's not what I meant.'

'It's okay, some people find it difficult.'

'Not me,' Jo assured her. 'I worked for a while in a nursing home when I was at uni. I'm quite accustomed to it.'

'Then please come in and meet Dad,' said Mim. 'He loves visitors, and he doesn't get so many these days. He'll love that you're a journalist.'

'Are you sure?' She was wary of imposing on the family at such a sensitive time.

'Quite sure. He's having a good day today.'

Jo followed Mim down the wide hall. The door at the end was open but she stopped as Mim walked inside. 'Joe, your friend is here to pick you up. Would you like to meet her, Dad?'

Joe was taken aback, but his father answered before he could say anything. 'Of course, I'd love to meet any friend of Joe's.'

Mim turned around and beckoned for Jo to enter. As she walked in, Joe got to his feet, he didn't know why, he wasn't usually so chivalrous. She came to stand on the opposite side of the bed and met his gaze, giving him a dazzling smile. And he found himself a little dumbstruck for a moment.

'Are you going to introduce us, son?'

He stirred. 'Dad, this is Jo Liddell, the colleague from the *Trib* I was telling you about. She's been up here covering the conference.'

Joe watched her lean in close to his father and take his limp hand in hers. How did she know to do that? Had he told her last night that his father couldn't raise his hand without effort? He didn't think he'd gone into that much detail.

'It's a very great pleasure to meet you, Mr Bannister,' she was saying.

'Call me Joe, please,' he said slowly, 'or you'll make me feel old.'

'Then you have to call me Jo as well,' she replied. 'That should be easy to remember.'

'Jo *Liddell*, did I hear correctly?'

'You did.'

'Been down any rabbit holes lately?'

'Dad,' Joe frowned. 'What are you talking about?'

'She knows what I'm talking about, don't you, Ms Liddell?'

Jo was smiling. 'Alice Liddell was the name of the real girl Lewis Carroll based *Alice in Wonderland* on, apparently.'

'I didn't know that,' said Joe.

'And you don't know your manners either, son. Ms Liddell doesn't have a chair.'

Joe fetched her one and returned to the other side of the bed, where he was pretty much ignored. His father basked in Jo's attention. She said all the right things, laughed at his lame jokes, and managed to ask questions that only required yes or no or short answers, allowing him to maintain his dignity. She admitted she was a big fan of his work, and asked intelligent questions about Vietnam and Cambodia that proved it. His father was enchanted, he could tell. And so was Joe; in fact he could barely take his eyes off her.

He was glad they were friends now, but it had probably been easier when he was keeping his distance. He really was interested to know just how committed she was to Lachlan Barr. How committed can you be to someone who is majorly committed elsewhere? There was no future in it, surely she could see that? Or was Barr one of those dickheads who strung a woman along, letting her believe he'd leave his wife eventually? Jo seemed too savvy to fall for that line.

Joe noticed his father was beginning to tire, he had become attuned to the signs now.

'Sorry to interrupt you two,' he said, 'but we have to get going, Dad.'

'Yes, of course.'

Jo got to her feet. 'It's been such a delight to meet you, Joe.'

'The pleasure was all mine, my dear.' As she took his hand, he added, 'I hope you'll visit again.'

She glanced at Joe. 'I hope so too.'

'You made my father very happy today,' said Joe as they drove out of Leura and onto the freeway.

'It was mutual.'

'You were really good with him. Most people wouldn't cope so well.'

Jo glanced at him. 'I had a stint in a nursing home when I was working my way through uni.'

'Oh, really? What was that like, depressing?'

'No, I loved it,' she insisted. 'After a while, you don't notice the package, you only see the person inside. And that's all they want, you know, to be respected for who they are.'

'That's all any of us wants, isn't it?'

Jo nodded. 'But it must be awful to get to the end of your life, to have accomplished who knows what, to have had status and position, and then to have it all taken away. To be treated like a child again, like you don't have a clue.' She paused, staring ahead. 'Not that that's the case with your father, I should add. It was such a thrill to meet him.'

Joe was listening thoughtfully. 'Where did you come across all his articles, by the way?'

'On the Net.'

'But what were you looking for?'

'Sorry?'

'Well, were you researching Cambodian history for some reason?' he suggested guilelessly. 'The Vietnam War, perhaps?'

'No . . .'

'Then how did you come across articles by a "Joseph Bannister", what could you possibly have been searching for?'

Jo looked sideways at him. 'Okay, so I Googled you. Happy now?'

'Yes I am,' he said expansively, leaning his head back against the seat and gazing at the road ahead.

'Don't get smug, Bannister,' she said.

He smiled. 'Okay, so what will you be taking away from the great talk-fest this week? Apart from the hotel toiletries. What do you know now that you didn't know before?'

She thought about it. 'Well, that Manhattan is the greenest city in the world.'

'How so?'

'Because of the concentration of people, the transportation system, the proximity to everything,' she explained. 'See, if you were to build an entirely green, self-sufficient house out of the city, grow your own food, catch rainwater in a tank, generate your own power, you'd still create more greenhouse gases every time you drove into town than you could ever offset in the house.'

'Well, there you go.'

'You need a fifth of a hectare of trees to offset the greenhouse gases produced by the normal use of a car over one year,' Jo went on, warming up. 'But the real problem is going to be air travel, which is set to increase dramatically over the next few years. It takes a half a hectare of forest, the same as roughly three years of vehicle travel, to offset one return trip to London.'

'You're a regular fountain of greenhouse knowledge,' Joe said dryly.

She glanced at him. 'That's a little like saying I'm full of hot air.'

'You said that, I didn't.'

'Okay then, what did you learn, Bannister?' she asked.

'I learned . . . that cats are mating more because of the shorter winters.'

'So what does that mean for the environment?'

'There's more cats, I guess.'

Jo smiled despite herself. 'I get the feeling that you're not taking this seriously.'

'Oh, I think it's very serious,' he countered. 'But I also think we're fiddling while Rome burns. When a few waterfront properties sink into the ocean, then everyone might start to take global warming seriously.'

Jo glanced up at the cloudless blue sky. 'Weather like this in the middle of September, I don't know how people cannot believe in global warming.' She paused as a troubling thought buzzed around in her brain like an annoying fly.

'Omigod!' she exclaimed. 'It is, isn't it?'

'It is what?' asked Joe, not understanding.

'It is the middle of September,' she said. 'It's the fourteenth today, right?'

'Yeah. So?'

'It's my niece and nephew's birthday,' she explained, hitting the steering wheel with her hand.

'Both on the same day? That's a coincidence.'

'Not when they're twins,' she sighed. 'I remembered, but I figured I just had to get through the conference and then I'd deal with it. But staying on the extra day, I forgot . . . I'm going to be in the bad aunty books now. What's the time?'

'Going on one.'

Jo bit her lip. 'I really should go and see them, but by the time I get back and then make my way out there . . .'

'Where do they live?'

'South, in the Shire.'

'Isn't that on the way?'

'From here?' she frowned. 'Not really.'

'Well, it's kind of on the way; it is between here and the city, if you just veer to the right a little.'

'A little?' She glanced at him. 'Are you suggesting that you drop me there on the way?'

'No, because I'm not allowed to drive the car,' he reminded her. 'But I am suggesting that it's not so far out of the way . . .'

'But what will you do? I can't just dump you at a train station, I wouldn't feel right.'

'So I'll come with you,' he said simply.

Jo turned to look at him. 'You don't want to come with me.'

'I don't mind.'

'You don't want to come with me,' she repeated firmly.
'They're two years old. They're not civilised, they're not even
toilet-trained.'

'I take it they don't live alone?'

'No, but my sister, well, she's great, but she's also a little mad.
And my brother-in-law, well, he's . . . I don't even know how to
describe him.'

Joe sat up in his seat. 'Look, they're not expecting you, we'll
just call in. It's better if I'm with you,' he said. 'Remember how
your parents wouldn't go mad on you when you were late or
whatever, if you had a friend with you?'

'Is that what happens in normal families?' she said wryly.

'Now, you'll have to get them something,' he added, warming
to the plan.

Jo looked at him. 'You're really serious about this, aren't
you?'

'Yeah, why not?' he asked, looking at her.

'You're actually prepared to come with me to visit my sister
and her family, who you've never met?'

Joe shrugged. 'You'd never met my family before . . . until you
met them. That's kind of the way it goes.'

'But you don't have to do this.'

'You didn't have to drive me to my dad's the other day,' he said
simply.

'That was an emergency.'

'So is this, isn't it?'

'Hardly on the same scale.'

'It's all relative,' he dismissed.

Jo bit her lip, hesitating. 'Are you sure?'

'Absolutely. Now what are you going to get them?'

Jo winced. 'I don't know. What do you get a two year old? Two
two year olds?'

'I'd go with colour and movement,' he said. 'We'll stop somewhere on the way, buy them a couple of giant stuffed toys, some
helium balloons, you'll walk in looking like Santa Claus. All will
be forgiven.'

She sighed. 'I don't know, do they really need more stuffed toys?'

'Do two year olds really need anything?' he pointed out.

'I guess, but after that conference, I feel like I shouldn't be filling the planet with more junk.'

'This is an emergency. You can always buy a few hectares of that forest to offset it.'

When they pulled up outside Belle's place an hour and a half later, there were balloons tied to the letterbox and streamers draped around the front door.

'Oh great, they're having a party.' Jo turned to look at Bannister. 'There's still time, you should save yourself, make a run for it while you can.'

'Are you kidding? I bet they'll have those little pies,' he said, opening his door. 'I love them.' He got out and opened the back door to retrieve the garish oversized monstrosities of acrylic fur and foam they had bought. A pink bunny for Cascey and a blue puppy for Carsyn.

Jo sat there for a moment. She couldn't pretend – she felt hurt that her only sister had thrown a party and not invited her only sister. Of course, if she had, Jo probably would have come up with an excuse not to go. She was fully aware of the irony, but it still bothered her.

'Are you coming?' Bannister was standing by her door, holding the toys. She reached for her handbag and reluctantly got out of the car.

He transferred the presents into her arms at the front door, and then she couldn't reach the doorbell, so he pressed it for her, before stepping back to fall in behind her.

'This is fun,' he said.

Jo was beginning to wonder about him, when the door opened and she observed the expression on Belle's face go from welcoming to shocked to guilty. As well it should.

'Jo!' she faltered. 'You're here.'

'Surprise!' Jo sang. 'I hope gatecrashers are allowed?'

'Now Jo,' Belle chided, 'I wanted to invite you –'

'But you managed to restrain yourself.'

'But you wouldn't have come,' she corrected.

'Why do you say that?'

She sighed. 'Because Mum's here.'

Jo nearly dropped her bundle on the doorstep.

'See? There's no way you would have turned up if you'd known Mum was going to be here,' said Belle. 'I didn't know what I was going to do, but when you didn't ring all week, I figured you must have forgotten their birthday.'

'Does it look like I forgot?' Jo declared archly. She had avoided calling because Belle had mentioned Charlene's visit, but that was weeks ago. She didn't think she'd still be here; Belle was right – she wouldn't have come if she'd known. Jo really didn't feel like seeing her, but she could hardly run away now, tempting though the idea was.

'Okay, okay,' said Belle. 'I appreciate the effort, I really do. And I am glad you're here. Only please don't start anything with Mum.'

'Fine, then point me in the direction of the gin bottle.'

'Jo,' she chided, 'it's a children's party, there's no hard liquor.'

'So what's Mum doing? Hiding it in a hipflask?'

Belle would have scolded her for that, except her attention at that moment had been taken by Bannister, who was still waiting patiently in the background. 'Hello?' she said, intrigued.

'He's with me,' said Jo. 'Are you going to let us in?'

'Yeah, sure.' Belle stood back, gaping at Joe as they both walked past her into the house.

'Hi,' he said, offering his hand. 'I'm Joe.'

'Are you her alter ego?'

He laughed. 'That's funny.'

'We work together,' Jo explained. 'We've been up at a conference in the Blue Mountains.'

'Oh right, the climate one,' Belle nodded. 'It was on the news.' She seemed to be having some difficulty taking her eyes off Bannister.

'Can I put these down somewhere?' asked Jo; her arms were beginning to ache.

'Sure, sorry,' said Belle, disentangling her. 'The kids are all outside, everyone is.' She arranged the toys on the sofa, with the balloons twisted around their cartoon paws. 'The twins are going to love them, Jo, they're so cute.' She turned around. 'I really am glad you're here.' She gave Jo a hug. 'But promise you won't start anything with Mum, yeah?' she said in her ear. 'Come on outside and I'll introduce you to everyone.'

As they followed her through the house, Jo felt Bannister's hand come to rest lightly on the small of her back, just for a moment, and she found it strangely reassuring.

Belle slid back the glass doors that opened out to the paved area. 'Look who made it!' she announced.

The children paid no attention. There were dozens of them running around in circles in lopsided party hats, falling over, crying, screaming, dropping food and spilling drinks, while their parents scampered about like hapless kelpies attempting to round up recalcitrant sheep.

Belle's friends were all her neighbours, it was as though she didn't have a life outside these few blocks. Jo wondered how it hadn't suffocated her. The women were all variations on a theme – streaked hair, gym-toned bodies, false fingernails, department-store couture. The men varied only in the extent of their receding hairlines. They were all dressed the same, in long shorts and surf-brand T-shirts, reclaiming their bygone youth and thinking they were getting away with it.

Jo spotted her mother immediately. She was hard to miss, clad in a hot-pink, low-cut dress, dyed platinum hair piled high on her head, make-up visible from half a block away. Mutton done up as hamburger.

Charlene dragged deeply on a cigarette as she fixed her eyes on her eldest daughter. 'Jo, you're here,' she drawled, blowing smoke out as she sashayed over to them. She probably imagined that looked sexy. 'I thought you weren't coming. But I should have remembered you've never been on time in your life.'

Jo swore her mother just made things up for the sake of hearing her own voice. 'What are you talking about, Mum? I'm very punctual.'

'Of course you are, love, if that's the story you're giving out these days.' She swooped closer, thrusting her cheek against Jo's and immediately stepping back again, leaving a lingering haze of cigarettes and perfume. 'It must be some other child of mine who sat stubbornly in utero for a whole two weeks after her due date, till I was fit to burst, in the middle of the hottest summer on record, should I say how many years ago, Jo? It's probably better if I don't at your age, isn't it, love?'

The whole time she spoke she was fluttering her claggy eyelashes madly at Joe. 'And who's this attractive young man?' She extended her arm out to him and he obliged by taking her hand.

'This is Joe Bannister,' Jo sighed. 'Joe, this is my mother, Ms – What surname are you going by these days, Mother?'

'Oh, knock it off, Jo, when have we ever been that formal? Call me Charlene,' she said to Joe.

'Nice to meet you, Charlene.'

'The pleasure's all mine, I assure you, Joe,' she gurgled.

'Hey, look who's here? Aunty JoJo!' It was Darren, holding Carsyn under one arm like a football while the boy struggled to free himself.

'Hi Carsyn, Happy Birthday,' said Jo.

'LET   ME   GO,   DAD-DEEEEE!   I'S   MY BIRFDAAAAAAYYYYYY!'

'Okay, okay, matey,' he said, popping him back on his feet. 'But you're not allowed to bite the other kids just because you're the birthday boy,' he called after him as Carsyn ran back to the fray. 'Hi Jo, this is a surprise. Belle said you had to work and you wouldn't be able to make it.'

Jo glanced at her sister and then back at Darren. 'As if I'd miss their birthday? I got off work early.'

'Unreal,' he nodded, his eyes flickering expectantly from Jo to Bannister.

'Oh, sorry,' said Jo. 'Joe Bannister, my brother-in-law, Darren Grainger.'

'My husband,' Belle piped in as the men shook hands.

'Hey, you two've got the same name,' said Darren. 'That's pretty funny.'

Why did everyone think it was funny? A coincidence, sure, but it was hardly comedy gold.

'I said he was her alter ego,' said Belle, leaning her elbow on Darren's shoulder.

'Good one, hun.'

Perhaps in some circles.

'So don't keep us in suspense,' said Charlene. 'What's the story with you two?'

'There is no story, Mother,' Jo sighed. 'We just work together.'

'I thought it was too good to be true,' she muttered.

Jo bit her tongue, while the knot of rage in her gut twisted another notch. It didn't matter that she was independent with a good career and her own apartment, her mother wouldn't think she'd succeeded till she'd bagged herself a bloke. And then she'd be jealous and bitchy about him. Jo couldn't win a trick with her.

Joe was watching her thoughtfully. 'Oh come on, hun,' he said. 'It's okay to tell family, isn't it?'

'Tell them what?' Did he just call her 'hun'?

'I know you want to keep it a secret at work, but we don't have to keep it from everyone, do we?' He threw his arm around her and planted a firm kiss on the top of her head. Jo hoped she didn't look as stunned as everyone else, though her mother's expression had a tinge of suspicion to it.

'You never mentioned you were seeing anyone, Jo!' Belle exclaimed loudly, drawing the attention of some of the party guests, who began to drift over to the circle. 'How long has this been going on?'

'It's all pretty sudden,' Joe answered for her.

'That's an understatement,' she muttered.

'How did you meet?' Charlene asked, raising an eyebrow.

'That is a good story, actually.' Bannister was smiling down at her like a big galoot. 'Do you want to tell them?'

'No, you go ahead,' said Jo.

'Well, it sounds like something that only happens in the movies, but we actually got trapped in an elevator together.'

'You're elevator guy?' Belle gasped.

He nudged Jo. 'So you did tell her about me.'

'He doesn't look like Viggo Mortensen,' said Belle.

All heads turned towards Joe, and there was a general mutter of consensus that no, he did not look like Viggo Mortensen.

'I never said he did,' Jo reminded Belle. 'You created that little fantasy.'

'Only because you said he was scruffy.'

Dear God, this was turning into a nightmare. Jo dared to glance up at Bannister but he was grinning widely. She'd pay for it later, no doubt.

'That's why I thought of Viggo,' Belle was explaining to the group. 'He was Aragorn in *Lord of the Rings*. You know, scruffy in a totally good way.'

Belle really didn't know when to leave well enough alone.

'So you're a sly horse, Jo!' she declared. 'You didn't tell me anything was cooking between the two of you, you just kept going on and on about your panic attack.'

Charlene cringed. 'You're having panic attacks now? How embarrassing for you, love. Are you getting treatment? You really should see a psychiatrist.'

Jo groaned inwardly.

'I think panic attack is overstating it a bit,' said Bannister. He still had his arm around her, and he gave her shoulder an encouraging rub. 'She had an anxious moment, but she got over it, and then we had to wait about an hour for the technician to get there.'

'And you'd never met each other before that day?' asked a woman in the circle who Jo didn't even know.

Bannister shook his head. 'I've been working overseas for the past couple of years, and I'd just flown into the country that very morning. Probably why I was a bit scruffy,' he added with a grin. 'Anyway, I couldn't believe my luck. There I was, trapped in a lift with this beautiful woman. And not only was she beautiful, she was smart, and funny, and we got on like we'd known each other forever.' He paused. 'I don't usually believe in fate, but when something like that happens, well, you have to wonder.'

Everyone was hanging on his words, not least Jo. Belle leaned in close to her. 'See, that's how you spin a yarn.'

Jo stirred. Yes, exactly. It was just spin.

Bannister turned to Charlene. 'You must be very proud of your daughter.'

'Well, of course,' she said. 'Jo's had opportunities I could only dream about. But then again, you can't have everything. I had to sacrifice any idea of a career for the sake of my little girls, so to see them doing well is all the reward I need.'

Good grief.

'Just look how well Belle's done for herself,' she went on. 'She has a wonderful husband who provides for her, three gorgeous kids, this house. I only worry that Jo's missed that particular boat, you know, the one with the family cabins, children travel for free.' She placed a lingering hand on Bannister's forearm. 'Though maybe I'm speaking too soon. Do you like children, Joe?'

'*Mother!*'

'Well, you can't afford to be coy about these things at your age,' she said to Jo. 'I mean to say, your biological clock is not just ticking away, it's barely keeping time. For heaven's sake, when I was your age, you girls were already teenagers. Of course, I wasn't much more than a girl myself when I had them,' she explained to Joe. 'People can't believe I have two grown-up daughters, and as for grandchildren! You should hear the shrieks. "Charlene, a *grandmother*?" They simply won't have a bar of it. Even when I show them pictures.'

'I need a drink,' Jo said under her breath.

'Come on, I'll get you one,' said Belle, linking her arm through Jo's.

'I thought you said there was no hard liquor?'

'Yeah, but we have fizzy drink for the adults,' she winked.

Thank God.

'Darren, get Joe something to drink, we'll be right back.'

Belle dragged her into the laundry and closed the door. 'JoJo!' she squealed, hugging her. 'Omigod! Why didn't you tell me! He's gorgeous!'

'He's not *gorgeous*,' Jo wrinkled her nose.

'He *so* is! What's wrong with you? You don't have to act all cool, Jo, this is me! I'm so excited, I'm going to burst. Omigod! You have to come over to dinner, this is so great! No, no, I know! Let's go out to dinner, we can have a proper double date, we've never been able to do that!'

Cripes.

'We'll get a babysitter, this is a special occasion after all. You haven't had a proper boyfriend in ages, Jo!'

'He's not my boyfriend!' she cried.

'What do you mean?'

Jo looked at her sister's bewildered face. She didn't want to burst her bubble, and she couldn't make Bannister look like a fool. He'd only done it for her sake.

'I just don't want to call him that,' Jo explained. 'It's too soon, I don't want to jinx it.'

'Aww,' Belle melted, hugging her again. 'I wouldn't worry, the way he was going on about you. My God, Jo, he's so in love. In fact, it sounds to me like he fell in love with you at first sight. This is *so* romantic.' Her eyes were glazing over. 'Can you imagine his wedding speech?'

'*Belle!*'

'Sorry, sorry, I'm jumping the gun.'

'You think?' Jo turned around to the laundry tub that was filled with ice and bottles. 'Is there one opened in here?' She really needed a drink.

'It's pretty funny about the whole name thing,' Belle went on. 'Must be weird, calling out your own name when you have sex?'

The nightmare continued. 'We haven't had sex.'

Belle looked confused.

'Yet, I mean. We haven't had sex yet.'

She gasped. 'Really?' Her eyes had gone all soft and puppy-like. 'He really is special, isn't he?'

Jo wasn't going to be able to take much more of this. 'I thought we came in here to get a drink?'

'Okay, okay,' said Belle, fishing a bottle out of the ice and handing it to her. 'Well, I'll say one thing, I'm just glad you're not seeing that man any more.'

Belle never referred to Lachlan by name. She preferred to keep him anonymous, a shadowy villainous figure who obviously had her sister under some kind of spell. Jo busied herself opening the bottle, ignoring the fact that Belle was watching her, waiting for confirmation.

'You're not still seeing that man, are you?' she persisted.

Jo just shrugged, avoiding eye contact by focusing instead on untwisting the wire cage around the cork.

Belle put her hands on her hips. 'I can't believe it, you're cheating on Joe? *Already?*' she said in an urgent whisper.

'No –'

'He's the nicest boyfriend you've ever had, Jo. Don't mess this up.'

She looked at her sister. 'Belle, he's not my boyfriend, it's not that serious.'

'Maybe not yet,' she persisted. 'You have to give it time. Promise me you're going to give it time.'

'I will give it time,' Jo parroted back at her. 'Now can we please get back out there and rescue him from Mum?'

'Speaking of Mum,' said Belle conspiratorially.

'Do we have to?'

She ignored that. 'I thought you'd want to know that she's been having tests while she's been here.'

'Tests?'

'Medical tests,' said Belle. 'Quite a few, and she's been to all these different specialists.'

'Did she say what for?'

'All she'll tell me is that they're routine, that she's just having a thorough check-up.'

'Good then,' said Jo. 'Can we go now?'

'Jo! You don't believe that, do you?'

'Why shouldn't I? She's hit middle age and she's having her ten thousand kilometre service. So what?'

'I think there's more to it.'

'Okay, she's probably menopausal and she's trying to find a wonder cure,' Jo groaned. 'Look, Belle, she's out there drinking and smoking, I don't think she could be all that worried about her health.'

Belle sighed, conceding the point. 'Okay. But I'll let you know if I find out anything.'

'I don't doubt it for a moment.'

*

Tuesday

'That was a nice little mention,' said Joe in her ear as they filed out of the editorial meeting.

Jo glanced over her shoulder at him.

'You know, nice to hear some praise from Leo for your coverage of the conference.'

'Faint praise,' she sighed.

'Come on, faint praise from Leo is like anyone else shouting it from the rooftops.' He grabbed her elbow and drew her aside. 'So you know how you owe me now?' he said.

She blinked, staring up at him. 'For what? Your input on the feature? You got a by-line, and it was Leo who asked you to mentor me in the first place and anyway –'

'No, no!' he interrupted her. 'I meant for bailing you out with your family.'

Jo frowned. 'Bailing me out?'

'Yeah,' he said guilelessly.

'Oh, you mean for concocting that whole charade that I'm going to have to keep up for an appropriate length of time until I can dump you?'

His face dropped. 'Was it something I said?'

She couldn't help grinning then. 'Belle thinks you're about to propose,' she sighed. 'For the rest of my life I'm going to have to listen to "What happened to that nice man, Joe Bannister? You should never have let that one get away."'

'Did I tell you I thought your sister was very discerning?'

They had stayed about an hour at Belle's, just until the birthday cakes had been cut, because that was about as much as Jo could take. They all seemed like nice people, and very friendly. Relentlessly so. They thought Jo was incredibly interesting. A journalist! How clever! How exciting! How glamorous! No wonder she hadn't settled down yet and had her own family. And they always read her column. At least whenever they got the *Tribune*. They didn't actually read the papers much, they were so full of bad news! They preferred to believe life held no greater conflict than who was going to win this season's *Pop Idol*.

Jo leaned back against the wall. 'So I owe you, you reckon? What do you have in mind?'

'Okay,' he said like he was mounting a pitch, 'my brother, Will, the actor, he's in some kind of "production" Friday night, and he asked me to come, so I was wondering if you'd like to come along too?'

Was he asking her out on a date?

'How is going to the theatre with you payback?' Jo wanted to know, folding her arms.

He looked a little coy. 'Well, I have a feeling it's going to be pretty ordinary. It's "experimental" apparently.'

'So let me get this straight,' said Jo. 'You want to see me suffer to pay you back?'

'No,' he smiled. 'I could use some moral support.'

'Oh, so now you've decided I'm moral?'

He ignored that. 'I'm saying there's safety in numbers . . . I was thinking Angie might like to come along as well? She might actually understand it.'

He wasn't asking her out on a date. You don't invite two women out on a date. Good then, she was glad that was cleared up. Unless . . .

'You're not trying to match your brother up with Angie, are you?' Jo asked.

'No way, I wouldn't do that to her.'

'Well, in that case, I'm sure she'd be up for a night of ordinary theatre. I'll let her know.'

'So you'll come?'

'Sure, why not?' said Jo, trying to sound offhand as she stepped around him to return to her desk, but not before she noticed the glint in his eye. He looked a little too pleased with himself.

*

Friday

Jo was lost. She took a sideways peek at Bannister. Although he was keeping it in check, Jo sensed his bewilderment, but when she turned the other way to look at Angie, her friend was wide-eyed, gripped, literally on the edge of her seat. Jo considered herself reasonably cultured, well read, intelligent, but she didn't know what the hell was happening on that stage. Not that it was a stage as such. They were seated in what had been euphemistically described as a 'performance space', but was actually a vast and rather decrepit former panelbeaters workshop, which smelled vaguely of rubber and urine, tucked away in a back lane in a part of the city Jo had never had the reason or desire to frequent. Bench seating had been placed in rows at right angles to define the 'stage'. Jo's lower back was beginning to feel stiff. Was she just getting too old? Was she out of step with the zeitgeist? Would she soon hear herself making comments like *'That's not music, that's just noise'*?

The end caught her by surprise, happily. She didn't see it coming, but she was certainly glad when it arrived. The troupe all came back into the square and took their bows, to the fairly rapturous applause of the small audience. Jo figured they all must be family and friends, or other out-of-work actors lending their support.

When they were finally able to stand and stretch, Bannister leaned over close to her ear. 'Sorry about that.'

She looked up at him, smiling. 'I think we're even now.'

'Wasn't that awesome?' Angie turned to them, beaming. 'Which one's your brother, Joe?'

'Here he is now,' he said. 'I'll introduce you.'

Will bounded over and slapped Bannister on the back. 'Hey, old man, what did you think?'

'I thought it was . . . awesome.'

'Liar,' Will grinned.

There was a definite family resemblance; the same blue eyes, light brown hair, though Will sported a goatee, and a slightly mischievous glint in those eyes. If they were casting a film Will would easily win the part of his brother, he might even get the role of a younger Joe, though they weren't so alike that it would be a given. He had the height though.

'Will, these are my friends,' Joe was saying. 'Jo Liddell, and Angie . . .'

'I loved the whole production!' Angie blurted, thrusting her hand at Will. 'The metaphor for death, so clever, and the set design, well, it was a metaphor in itself, wasn't it?'

Two chairs on an empty stage was set design? And a metaphor as well?

'Well, you seem to know what you're talking about,' said Will, clearly impressed. 'How do you know my brother?'

'Through Jo,' said Angie.

She smiled on cue, raising her hand.

'Jo works with me,' Joe explained. 'At the *Trib*.'

Will became thoughtful. 'Jo from the *Trib* . . . this wouldn't be Elevator Girl by any chance?'

So now her reputation preceded her. 'I am indeed Elevator Girl,' she confirmed. 'But I need to keep my identity secret, you understand.'

He grinned broadly. 'She *is* cute, bro.'

Jo raised an eyebrow at Bannister.

'It's better than scruffy,' he defended.

She had to give him that.

'So do you work at the *Trib* as well?' Will asked Angie.

'No, I . . . ah . . .'

'Angie's an actor too,' Jo jumped in.

'Oh yeah? Cool. Where'd you train?'

Angie launched into her spiel about how she nearly got into NIDA, which was true, she made it to the third call-back but didn't make the final cut. Her 'qualifications' were a cobbled-together bunch of summer schools and short courses, many run by highly regarded agencies, but it remained a constant source of embarrassment to Angie that she wasn't a fully-fledged drama graduate.

Jo had heard it all before. She glanced at Bannister. 'I hate being "cute".'

'It's not my fault you're cute,' he returned.

'Hey, you might know Mitch,' Will was saying. 'I think he did one of those AFTA courses. Come and see if we can find him.' He glanced at Joe. 'Oh . . . you guys –'

'We'll be right,' said Joe. 'You go ahead.'

'Grab yourselves a drink,' said Will. 'They're putting some wine out up the back.'

He turned to Jo. 'You game?'

'If you are,' she said.

They wandered over to a trestle table where a row of wine casks had been lined up, flanked by two towers of plastic tumblers.

'I can't remember the last time I drank wine out of a box,' Joe remarked.

'I can,' said Jo. 'I just prefer not to.'

He smiled. 'So you don't want a drink?'

'No need to go that far.'

He took a couple of tumblers off the stack. 'What's your poison?'

'I wouldn't call it that, you may be tempting fate.'

'Good point. What vintage would madam prefer?'

Jo considered the casks, all bearing the enthusiastic banner *5 litres for the price of 4!*. 'I think I'll have to go for Classic Dry, whatever that may mean,' she said, 'because I'm not touching Fruity Lexia.'

'Good decision,' said Joe, filling a cup and handing it to her.

He went with the red, and they both moved away from the table as more people made their way over.

Jo looked around the space. If they were going for grunge, they'd certainly achieved it. 'Interesting venue.'

'That's one way of putting it,' he said, taking a sip of his wine and grimacing faintly.

Jo tried hers. It was room temperature. Maybe she should have gone with the red as well.

'So, that stuff Angie was saying . . . did you get that?' Bannister asked her.

She shook her head sadly. 'But just because it doesn't make sense to me doesn't mean anything.'

'Yeah, but sometimes I wonder if this avant-garde stuff only impresses people in the know,' he said. 'They're preaching to the converted, you know what I mean? Shouldn't they be trying to reach a wider audience?'

'And that's how you get reality TV,' Jo pointed out. 'When you only ever appeal to the lowest common denominator, you'll only get the lowest form of entertainment.'

'So you thought that was high art?'

Jo gave him a coy smile. 'What do I know? There were some funny bits, like when the guy was trying to explain black holes.'

'Yeah, that was pretty funny.'

'And then the scene with the old man and his son was really poignant.'

'Okay, I agree with you there, but how did it fit? I thought we were going to find out. But they never came into it again.'

Jo nodded. 'Mm, I think by then I had lost the expectation that it was going to be a linear narrative with any kind of resolution.'

'See that's what I have a problem with,' he said. 'I like a beginning, a middle and an end. They don't all have to make sense or tie up neatly, but I have to feel like I'm on some kind of journey.'

She was listening thoughtfully. 'You're right, that's what it is. Maybe it's because we're journalists? There has to be a conclusion, the story has to wrap up.'

'But isn't that ironic?'

'Is it?'

'Well, in real life, which is what we deal with, how many stories are that neat?'

'Yeah, I guess. But on the other hand, how many real life stories end up with a chorus line of grim reapers singing, "Whoops I did it again"?'

Joe smiled. 'Just as well we're not theatre critics.'

'I'll drink to that,' said Jo, taking a sip from her plastic cup. 'Or maybe not.'

They stood there, surveying the room. Jo mentally compared this mob to the gathering at Belle's. Talk about a study in contrasts. Everyone here was clearly trying very hard not to look like anyone else, but there was definitely a shared aesthetic. Animal prints were big, one guy was wearing a knee-length giraffe-print coat that was so synthetic Jo would have been reluctant to light a match in his vicinity. And dyed hair was de rigueur; she noted blue-black, purple and green, as well as red, the shade of fake movie blood. Nearly all the girls were wearing tightly laced bustieres, a trend that had obviously passed Jo by. Which was just as well, her bosom was not worth showcasing, unfortunately. One woman had completed her outfit with a cheap nylon tutu, torn black fishnet stockings and big black Doc Martens lace-up ankle boots. Jo suddenly felt a little bland in her tasteful black and camel ensemble.

Joe was watching her. 'Look,' he said, 'we can go now if you like. I think I've fulfilled my fraternal duty.'

'But I don't want to drag Angie away.' Jo looked across to where her friend was happily ensconced with a group of the performers. 'She looks like she's having a ball.'

Will turned around, seeing them standing alone. 'Hey, Joe, what's crackin'?' he said as he walked over to join them.

'We're just watching the world go by,' said Joe. 'You know in my day, arty types wore black, head to toe. Didn't anyone tell these guys the dress code?'

Will shook his head. 'Have you got used to his lame jokes yet?' he asked Jo.

She smiled in response. She had the feeling that Will thought they were an item. Not that it mattered terribly. At least he wasn't suggesting a double date. Yet.

'So what happens now?' Joe asked Will. 'Are you guys going to tour?'

'Smart-arse,' said Will. 'For your information, brother, this performance tonight will help our grant application to develop this site. If we can get council support, plus some arts funding, we can spruce up the place, put on more productions, and start charging admission, which will in turn fund us for longer. We want it to become a place where talent gets the chance to develop . . . something like the Pram Factory.'

'Oh,' Joe nodded vaguely.

'You have no idea what the Pram Factory is, do you?'

'Can't say as I do.'

'It was a groundbreaking performing arts space in Melbourne,' Jo explained, 'where David Williamson, amongst others, got his start.'

Will looked impressed. 'Cute *and* smart.'

'You know, Will,' said Jo, 'if you call me cute one more time, I may have to kill you.'

'Loud and clear,' he winked at her as Angie rushed over to them, bright-eyed, her face all flushed.

'This is so great!' she exclaimed. 'I'm meeting all these people, making all these contacts . . . These guys have got a million things going on, my head is spinning . . . Oh,' she said, noticing their cups, 'I might grab a drink. Is that okay, you're not in a hurry?'

Jo opened her mouth to speak but she bit her lip instead. She didn't want to burst Angie's bubble.

'Oh, you do want to get going?' said Angie, reading her expression.

'It's only that I've got an early start tomorrow,' Jo winced. 'You know how Saturdays are crazy at work.'

'That's okay,' said Will. 'You don't have to go, though, do you, Ange?'

'I guess not,' she said.

'Yeah, hang around, you're amongst friends,' he assured her.

Angie actually blushed, but it was with a kind of schoolgirl pride. She'd found her tribe.

'How will you get home though, Angie?' Joe asked.

'Same way I got here. On the bus.'

'Where do you live?' Will asked her.

'Ashfield.'

'No worries, a bunch of us live out that way, we'll share a taxi.' He thrust his hand at his brother. 'Thanks for coming, Joe. I'll call you for a drink soon.'

He suddenly swooped to plant a kiss on Jo's cheek. 'See you again, no doubt.'

Yep, he definitely thought they were together.

They walked outside into the relatively fresher air.

'We'll probably get a taxi easier up on Oxford Street,' Bannister suggested.

But Jo had other ideas. 'Would you mind if we walked for a bit?' she asked. 'It's not really that far, and I'm enjoying this fresh air too much.'

'It's okay with me.'

They turned the corner and headed down a narrow street, past a row of tiny terraces.

'Can I ask you something?' Jo said after a while.

'Sure.'

'What are you doing here?'

He looked a little confused. 'I'm sorry?'

'I mean, what are you doing here, in Sydney, working at the *Trib*?'

He still looked confused. 'Well, you know I came back because of my dad.'

'Yeah, I realise that brought you back to Australia. But why are you working at the *Trib*?' she said. 'You could sell your stuff to any paper, any publication for that matter, and you could work from the Blue Mountains, be with your dad all the time.'

'Well, that's still on the cards,' he admitted. 'But Leo had me committed before I'd really worked out what I wanted to do.'

'Mm, Leo is certainly a force to be reckoned with.'

'I don't mind,' said Joe. 'I figured the pressure would be a lot less at the *Trib*. And I don't really want to write about the war any more.'

'But how can you ignore it when you've been so close to it?'

'I've been so close to it for so long, I needed to get away. And Australia's a good place to do that. You can ignore it, because everyone else is.'

Jo was frowning. 'I don't know how you can stand it. It's like my sister and all her friends – they're so frustrating, living in a bubble out in the suburbs. They don't know what's going on in the world.'

'I think you're being a little hard on them,' said Joe. 'It's the same everywhere you go. When you travel a lot you realise that everyone, wherever they come from, only sees the world from their own limited perspective. We're a lot less of a global village than we think.'

'So that's why we have foreign correspondents,' Jo insisted, 'to open our eyes to what's going on around the world.'

He shrugged. 'Sometimes I wish I didn't know, or at least didn't know so much.'

'How can you say that as a journalist?'

'It's because I'm a journalist that I can say it. The things I know, the things I've seen . . .' He shook his head. 'I'm not convinced it's made my life any better.'

She looked at him. 'What kinds of things specifically?'

Joe thought about it. 'Well, take Iraq . . . the level of mayhem that's going on around you every day, it's hard to describe. The tension is incredible. Everyone's scared, not just the civilians, the soldiers as well, that's why so many civilians end up getting killed. A car speeding down the street, ignoring warning shots, is probably just some guy terrified he's been caught out after curfew, and he ends up getting shot because the soldiers think he's a suicide bomber.'

'You saw stuff like that happen?'

'Sure.' He took a deep breath. 'One of the worst things I ever experienced was in Karbala, back in 2004. It was a holy day for the Shiites, there was something like a million people in the town at the time. We were out on the street this day when a bomb went off, not that far from where we were standing. We started to run towards it . . . that probably sounds stupid, but it's an instinctive reaction, you want to see if you can help. But then another bomb went off, about ten metres in front of us. It wiped out everyone ahead. Everyone . . .' He was staring into space, as if he could see it now. 'We were all splattered with blood and bits of flesh . . . there were parts of bodies lying all around us. It was like standing in the middle of hell.'

Jo listened in stunned silence, her stomach clenched. 'How do you live with something like that? It must affect you . . .'

He nodded. 'Can't stand fireworks.'

'Fireworks?'

'Yeah, close your eyes and listen sometime, they sound like mortar going off. An exhaust backfiring, sirens, a car tearing around a corner too fast . . . they can all scare the crap out of me.' He paused. 'My dad was never able to sit near the front window in a restaurant, he'd seen too many get blown out in Vietnam.'

Jo was confounded. 'I realised it must be hard for the soldiers, coming home, but I thought journalists were more . . . sheltered, I guess – at least from the worst of it.'

'We are,' he said. 'We don't have to be out on the streets, for one thing, if we don't want to be, or when it gets too dangerous.' He paused. 'But in an urban war like Iraq, you can't always avoid it.'

She looked up at him. 'I'm sorry. I didn't know what I was talking about before.'

'It's okay,' he said. 'But maybe now you understand why I don't want to go back?'

'And I'm starting to wonder how you ever managed to stay so long.'

He shrugged. 'You go back and forth, you can't stay longer than a couple of months at a time. I tried once and it did my head in. No, I reckon three months is the limit.'

'I thought you said you hadn't been home for a couple of years?' Jo asked.

'Yeah, but I wasn't in Baghdad the whole time, though I was still working. I based myself mostly in London in between.'

'Why London?'

'I was seeing someone there,' Joe said simply. 'Actually, I was in a relationship.'

'Oh.' She was surprised. 'You never mentioned.'

'Yeah, we were together nearly three years,' he said. 'Sarah was with the BBC, she's English, she came to Baghdad during the fall of Saddam. She was pretty green then, all gung-ho ... So of course she was pretty shaken up by the reality. I helped her acclimatise, we got close. Then after the fall, there was a period of relative peace in Baghdad. You could go out to dinner, walk the streets at night. It was the calm before the storm.'

'What happened to you and Sarah?' asked Jo. She didn't want him veering back on to the war till she got the whole story.

'It petered out,' he said. 'When things got worse again, she wanted to get out of Baghdad so she had herself reassigned back to London. She was always at me to give up, take a post in the UK, settle down, but I wasn't ready.'

'To settle down?'

'Partly,' he said. 'But mostly I wasn't ready to leave Iraq for good right then, and I didn't want to settle down in England, regardless. I always intended to come home.'

'Did she know that?'

'I think so, I think I made it pretty clear. She came home

with me for a holiday once, the first year we were together. She seemed to like it.'

'But not enough?'

He looked at her. 'What do you mean?'

'She didn't want to move here, you didn't want to settle there, is that what ended it?'

He was thoughtful for a moment. 'It's never really just one thing, is it? She ended up on a *60 Minutes*-type program, so she was away on assignment a lot. We'd meet up whenever our schedules permitted, but we were seeing less and less of each other . . . Like I said, it petered out.'

'So it was an amicable split?'

'More or less.'

'Are you still in contact?'

'Nope,' he said bluntly.

He didn't seem inclined to go further than that, so Jo thought she should probably drop it. Her curiosity wasn't quite sated, though; she wished men were better gossips.

They had come to Goulburn Street. 'I guess this is where we part ways,' said Jo.

'Why?' Joe frowned.

'Well, I go further into the city from here, but you should head off up College Street, right?'

He shrugged. 'Nah, I'll see you home.'

She looked at him. 'Joe, I can look after myself.'

'I don't doubt that you can,' he said, touching her elbow lightly to steer her down Goulburn Street. 'So what about you?' he asked.

She frowned. 'What about me?'

'Your marriage, how did it end?'

Jo was perplexed. 'How did you know I used to be married? Don't tell me you found that on Google?'

'No, you told me in the elevator,' he said, watching her. 'You don't remember?'

'No,' she sighed. 'I'd like to know what was in that drug. I've never blabbed so much of my personal business to anyone.'

He smiled. 'It's okay if you don't want to talk about it.'

'There's nothing much to say,' she dismissed. 'I was too

young, it was over before the ink was even dry on the marriage certificate.'

'That's the line you gave me in the elevator.'

She glanced at him. 'It is?'

He nodded. 'Verbatim.'

'At least I'm consistent.'

'Consistently cagey.'

'I just like to maintain a certain level of privacy.'

'Yet you don't mind interrogating me about my personal life,' he pointed out. 'What's good for the goose, Princess.'

'Did you just call me princess?'

'I might have.'

Jo wasn't sure she appreciated the inference. 'Okay, go ahead, what do you want to know about my three-minute marriage from half a lifetime ago?'

'Actually,' he said, 'if I'm getting a free pass, I'd rather ask you something else.'

She frowned. 'What exactly?'

'Promise you'll give me a straight answer?'

'I'm not promising anything of the kind.'

He smiled. 'Okay, I'll try anyway. Why are you having a relationship with a married man?'

'Gee, Bannister, don't beat around the bush, just come right out with it, why don't you?'

'I've only got one question, I don't want to waste it.'

'I thought we decided that was none of your business.'

'Come on, that's not fair, I answered everything you asked me. And we're friends now. You'd tell a friend, wouldn't you? I assume Angie's got an opinion about it all?'

'Which I assume she shared with you.'

'She defended you, actually.'

Jo looked at him. 'She defended my relationship with Lachlan?'

'No, she defended *you*. Said something about you being too afraid to have a normal relationship.'

Jo felt uneasy, the kind of uneasy you felt when you dreamed you were in a public place with no pants on. 'Yeah, well, Angie has theories about everything,' she said, attempting to brush it off. 'To this day, she believes that Diana didn't die in the car crash but that aliens abducted her, and now she's a revered goddess in a galaxy far far away.'

'You ought to write crime novels,' Joe said when she was finished. 'You're very good at red herrings.'

'Well, you ought to write detective novels, you're such a snoop,' she returned. 'Why are you so interested anyway?'

'See, now you're asking me a question and you still haven't answered mine.'

'Okay,' she sighed in defeat. 'What do you want to know?'

'What's the attraction?'

'To Lachlan?'

'To married men.'

She frowned. 'You're making it sound like there's been a procession of them.'

'Has there?'

'Exactly which question do you want me to answer?'

'Well, one would be a start.'

'Fine, there hasn't been a procession of married men in my life.'

'God, you're like a politician,' said Joe, shaking his head. 'You can't answer a straight question.'

'I answered that straight – I said quite plainly there has not been a procession of married men in my life.'

He considered her. 'Has there been more than one?'

Cripes. 'Maybe.'

'So what's the attraction?'

She sighed loudly.

'That's all I want to know,' he said. 'As your friend. So I can understand.'

'So you can judge.'

'I don't want to judge you, that's the thing. I want to understand you.'

'Why?'

They had arrived at a pedestrian crossing and the lights were against them. He stopped to face her. 'Okay, you really want to know? I have a stereotype fixed in my head. The scarlet woman. Which –' he continued as she began to protest '– you clearly are not. You're smart and accomplished and beautiful . . .'

'Stop it.'

'What? You are smart and accomplished –'

'Okay, enough.'

'You don't think you're beautiful?'

'Oh yeah, I think I'm an absolute vision,' she said dryly.

'Good, then we agree,' he said. 'So explain to me why someone like you would choose to be with a married man, with no chance of a future.'

Jo sighed. 'The future is overrated.'

'What does that mean?'

'People get together, and then they start having expectations about forever,' she said. 'Why? Why not just live in the here and now? Why do you have to promise that you'll feel the same way for the rest of your life? It's absurd.'

'Isn't that what the commitment part's about?'

'Yeah, and men are so good at that, aren't they?'

He started to protest but she interrupted. 'Look, I'm not blaming men, it's women who perpetuate the nonsense. They're blinded by the whole wedding fantasy, they get dressed up like a princess for a day and they truly believe they'll live happily ever after. All they're doing is setting themselves up for pain and disappointment.'

The lights turned green and she stepped off the kerb and walked across the street. Joe gazed after her. How had Angie put it? Wounded. She was wounded all right. He roused himself, catching up to her with a few long strides.

'So are you saying there can't be any pain or disappointment with a married man?'

'Not if you go about it the right way,' she said plainly. 'Lachlan and I are two consenting adults who have a very clear understanding of what we're doing. I don't have any expectations of him beyond that, nor he of me.'

He looked a little stunned by her honesty. Well, he'd asked for it.

'But what about his family?'

'What about them?'

'That's a little callous, Jo.'

She bristled. 'Oh, is this you not judging me?'

'I just want to know if you think about the impact this has on his family?'

'Of course I do,' she declared. 'Lachlan would never leave his wife and I'd never ask him to. I don't even want him to. In the meantime she's none the wiser. She has a wonderful lifestyle, a successful husband who isn't constantly nagging her for sex she doesn't want to have, and two beautiful kids. Everyone's okay, everyone's needs are being met.'

He was staring down at her in disbelief. 'Please don't tell me you genuinely believe that, Jo, you're way too smart. Even if Lachlan's family has no inkling of what's going on, they're being affected by this.'

'You don't know that,' she said.

'How can he give a hundred percent of himself to his wife when he's involved with you? And that's what it takes to make a marriage work. A hundred percent.'

Jo had no comeback, and suddenly she felt guilty. He was making her feel guilty, again. 'What the hell makes you the expert on marriage all of a sudden?' she snapped.

'Don't get angry –'

'And why do you care so much?' she went on. 'You don't know Lachlan's family, this has nothing to do with you.'

'I just wonder why you're not giving yourself the chance to be happy,' he said plainly.

Belle had said something like that. 'I'm happy, what makes you think I'm not happy? You don't even know me.' They had arrived at her street, and Jo marched off briskly around the corner towards her building.

He caught up to her as she neared the entrance, grabbing her arm. 'Don't just walk away, Jo.'

'I'm not, I'm going home.' She tried to shrug off his hold, but he kept a firm grip.

'You're upset,' he said.

'I'm not upset.'

'You are, and I'm sorry.' He looked sincere. 'The last thing I'd ever want to do is upset you ... or hurt you, or disappoint you.'

He was gazing down at her, breathing hard. Jo was breathing

hard too, excruciatingly aware of his hand on her arm, his thumb gently beginning to stroke . . .

'I just think you're better than this,' he said.

Jo felt an ache in the back of her throat. This was too intense. 'Yeah, well maybe I'm not. Maybe this is exactly who I am.'

'Jo?'

They both swung around. Lachlan was walking towards them from across the street. Joe released her arm, taking a step away from her.

'What's going on?' said Lachlan.

'Nothing,' Jo said lightly, attempting to recover her composure. 'What are you doing here, Lachlan?'

'I've been trying to call you all evening, but your phone's been turned off,' he said, glancing from her to Joe.

She fumbled in her bag. 'That's right, I had to turn it off, I've been at the theatre.' She retrieved her phone and pretended to be very focused on turning it back on, while in reality she was just taking a moment to compose herself.

'I hope I wasn't interrupting something?' said Lachlan, his voice laden with accusation.

'You weren't,' said Joe. 'I went to see my brother in a play, he's an actor, and Angie and Jo turned up as well. When Angie decided to kick on, I offered to see Jo home. Well, walk with her anyway, we were both going in the same direction.'

Lachlan was listening, clearly dubious.

'Thanks for that,' said Jo. 'I appreciate it.' She glanced towards him, but she couldn't look him in the eye.

'Sure,' he said. 'Anyway, I better keep going.'

'Bannister,' Lachlan nodded grimly.

'Goodnight,' said Jo.

'Night.' He turned up the street and disappeared around the corner.

'What the hell, Lachlan?' Jo said sharply. 'Taken to spying on me now?'

'I didn't realise there was anything to spy on.'

'There isn't,' she said tightly, walking past him to the entrance of her building.

'Look,' he said, coming after her, 'I wasn't spying on you. I told you I was trying to call, and then I decided to drop by on my way home. When you didn't answer the intercom I was headed back to my car when I saw you coming around the corner, and Bannister manhandling you.'

'For Chrissakes, Lachlan, he wasn't manhandling me,' she said, foraging for her keys in her bag.

'Well what was he doing, grabbing your arm like that?'

'Nothing,' she dismissed. She fished out her keys, unlocked the door and walked through into the foyer, with Lachlan on her heels.

'It didn't look like nothing from where I was standing.'

Jo pressed the button for the lift. Her brain was too addled to come up with an excuse. But then it occurred to her, she didn't have to give Lachlan an excuse. She turned around to face him. 'What happened to our agreement that I don't owe you explanations about how I spend my time when I'm not with you?'

'Come on, Jo, I was only worried . . . for your safety.'

'Bullshit, Lachlan. Don't be ridiculous, we were just mucking around, we were having some silly argument about the play.'

The doors of the elevator slid open and she stepped in, turning around. 'So, are you here to fight or are you here to fuck? Because we can't do both.'

Joe walked three, four blocks, so fast he was panting, and sweat had broken out in beads across his forehead. His mind was racing, retracing the conversation, kicking himself for every stupid, negative, judgemental thing he'd said. And more for what he hadn't said. It could have ended so differently. He'd had an almost overwhelming urge to kiss her then, right at the end. It was so powerful, as though every molecule in his body was being magnetically drawn to her, and he had to physically stop himself from pulling her into his arms and slamming his lips down onto hers. And then Lachlan appeared out of the shadows, and Joe realised it couldn't have ended any differently.

As he walked across Hyde Park he thought about what they were probably doing right now . . . his mind involuntarily forming a mental picture . . . and he walked even faster, and he sweated

a little more, and finally he came to a bench and sat down to catch
his breath. He wiped his forehead with the back of his hand.

'Fuck it,' he muttered under his breath as he took his phone
out of his pocket and flicked it open. He scrolled through the
directory until he came to Carla Delacqua, pressing *Call* before he
gave himself too much time to think about what he was doing.

Monday morning

'I thought of Bannister while I was having sex with Lachlan.'

'What was that?' Angie asked loudly over the grinding of the
food processor. It was Jo's day off, but she had to debrief before
her head imploded. She and Lachlan had had pretty amazing sex
the other night. Jo had tried to tell herself that it was because
they hadn't been together in weeks. But it wasn't just that. And
Lachlan knew it too. No sooner had he rolled off her and caught
his breath than he started at her again, interrogating her about
Bannister. Jo just lay there, growing more and more incensed.
How the hell had things got to this? First she was justifying her
relationship with Lachlan to Bannister, and then she was justifying her relationship with Bannister to Lachlan. She didn't have
to answer to either of them. She'd finally told Lachlan to get out.
He'd left messages on her phone the next day, but she ignored
them.

'I said I thought of Bannister, you know, Joe Bannister, while I
was having sex with Lachlan,' Jo tried again, louder this time.

'Oh,' Angie shouted back, nodding, as though she got it at
last.

Jo frowned. 'Why, what did you think I said?'

'I only caught something about a canister and Tex
McLaughlin.'

'What?'

'I said –'

'No, I mean, who's Tex McLaughlin?'

'I don't know, I've never heard of him. That's why I asked.'

Jo's head was beginning to hurt.

'Obviously I couldn't hear you with the blender going,' Angie added.

'Maybe you should turn it off while we're having a conversation.'

'What did you say?'

'I said, maybe you should turn off the blender while we're having a conversation!' Jo was shouting now.

'Oh,' said Angie, turning the blender off. 'I thought you said –'

'Don't worry, I don't need to know,' she said, becoming exasperated. 'So did you hear what I said in the first place?'

'No, I didn't, I told you, because of the blender.'

Jo sighed. 'But you know what I said now, don't you?'

'That you thought of Joe while you were having sex with Lachlan?'

'That's right.'

Angie smiled and nodded as she started to dismantle the food processor.

'Well? Haven't you got anything to say?'

'You didn't call out his name, did you?' Angie asked her. 'Not that Lachlan would notice I suppose, seeing as it's your name too.'

Jo frowned. 'I think Lachlan would notice if I started calling out my own name in the middle of having sex.'

'That's true.'

She watched Angie as she scraped green slime out of the food processor. It looked like pesto. Why did food lose its appeal when it was in catering quantities?

'So that's it?' Jo prompted after a while. 'That's all you're going to say?'

'What do you want me to say?'

'I don't know. I was hoping to get more of a reaction. Help me make sense of it.'

'Make sense of what?'

'Have you been listening at all?' She dropped onto a nearby stool. 'Why would I think of Joe while I was having sex with Lachlan?'

Angie stopped to look at her. 'Are you serious?'

'Absolutely. I don't fantasise, you know that, it's not the way my brain works. I've never had to think of another man while I'm having sex.' She paused. 'And it's not the first time either.'

Now Angie was confused. 'But you just said it's never happened before.'

'No, I meant it's not the first time I've thought about having sex with Bannister. It happened the night after we were trapped in the elevator, and then that night when both he and Lachlan showed up at my place, well, that turned into a threesome in my head. I don't understand why it keeps happening.'

Angie was just staring at her, incredulous. 'Hey, here's a crazy idea – you don't suppose you might be attracted to him?'

Jo pulled a face. 'Okay, of course I'm somewhat attracted to him, but isn't that a bit obvious?'

'What, obvious that you're attracted to him?'

'No, obvious that that would be what it means. Aren't dreams supposed to be symbolic?'

'Oh, for godsakes, Jo, that's only if you dream about something weird, like a purple rabbit that keeps visiting your house and taking away your Easter eggs and leaving little bunny pellets of poo in their place.'

'What are you talking about?'

'Sorry, that was one of my recurring dreams. I used to have it all the time when I was a teenager. I eventually worked out that it had something to do with losing my childhood, or my virginity, or both. Or either. Anyhow, my point is, Joe is not a purple rabbit.'

'Thanks for that startling insight.'

'You're dreaming of having sex every which way with a very attractive man you are well acquainted with. I'm afraid there's only one way to interpret that, girlfriend.'

'Not necessarily,' Jo persisted. 'You know I haven't been getting much lately, and I'm frustrated, and yes, I suppose I find Bannister attractive, and he's someone new for my subconscious to process. So these dreams I've been having are like that pesto, all the ingredients were quite different and distinct before they got shoved together in a bowl and macerated by a spinning blade.'

Angie crossed her arms. 'You're doing that thing you do.'

'What thing?'

'Seeing the trees and not the forest.'

'I don't do that.'

'Oh yes you do. You're doing it now, dissecting this to billy-o rather than looking at the big glaring obvious picture. Yes, you're attracted to Joe. Which means you like him. You may have even found your soul mate.'

'Oh, here we go,' Jo rolled her eyes. 'There's no such thing as soul mates, Ange.'

'Says you.'

'Says commonsense, and a divorce rate that's higher than one in every three marriages. If everyone has a soul mate, why do so many people get it so wrong?'

'Because they settle,' Angie stated plainly. 'They take the person who comes along at around the right time but not necessarily for the right reasons.'

That wasn't a bad point. Jo wondered if there was a column in it.

'I choose to believe I have a soul mate out there somewhere,' Angie continued. 'And some day he's going to walk into my life and I'll know. We'll both know.'

There was her column. Debunking the soul mate myth.

'What if your "soul mate" lives on the other side of the world?' Jo suggested.

'We'll find each other,' Angie said airily. 'Lots of times people meet when they're travelling and they end up together, and it never would have happened in the normal course of events. But you can't escape fate.'

'You can when you don't believe in it.'

'How can you of all people not believe in fate?' Angie exclaimed. 'Look at how you and Joe met, in an elevator that broke down? And he's got the same name as you? You're like yin and yang . . . *Soul mates*,' she added in a perky singsong voice.

'Please don't do that,' Jo said. 'For one thing, I would have met him whether the elevator broke down or not, because he was coming to work at the *Trib*. And we both have the *same* name, so we're like yin and yin, or yang and yang, but not yin and yang. He's not my soul mate.'

'And yet you think about him when you're having sex with

someone else.' Angie dumped the empty food processor bowl into the sink and turned around, wiping her hands on a tea towel. 'What's the problem anyway?' she said. 'Is it because he's not married?'

'That's not fair.'

'It's completely fair, Jo. He's too available for you, you might actually have to have a real relationship with him.'

'This is getting out of hand,' said Jo. 'Now you've got us having a relationship? There's absolutely no evidence that Joe is attracted to me whatsoever. In fact the other night he made it quite clear that he doesn't have much of an opinion of me at all.'

'Why, what'd he say?'

'He had a go at me about my relationship with Lachlan.'

'So, I do that all the time and I still love you,' she said. 'Why do you think he'd be having a go at you about Lachlan if he wasn't interested in you?'

Jo's chest cramped in a slightly uncomfortable way.

'And why do you think he showed up at your place with the wine that night,' she went on, counting off her fingers, 'and offered to go with you to the twins' birthday party – like that wasn't to score brownie points. And then there's the little matter of your date Friday night –'

'It wasn't a date. He asked us both.'

'And then there's the way he looks at you,' she said finally, leaning back against the bench.

Jo was sure her cheeks were going red, she could feel the heat. 'He doesn't "look" at me,' she scoffed.

'Oh he looks at you, all right, with those big brown eyes.'

'Blue,' Jo corrected. 'His eyes are blue. They're very blue.'

Angie raised an eyebrow. 'Are they?'

'Oh, so what if I know the colour of his eyes?' Jo groaned. 'Don't forget I was stuck in a confined space with him for over an hour when we first met.'

'Oh, look at all those trees,' said Angie. 'I wonder if there could be a forest anywhere about?'

Jo pulled a face. 'Yeah, well, you're forgetting one very big tree in that forest.'

'What?'

'Lachlan. I'm not exactly available.'

Angie shook her head. 'So first things first, you need to get that log out of your eye so you can see straight. You're just making excuses and not giving yourself the chance to be happy.'

'What did you say?'

'End it with Lachlan. He's married. You're not unavailable, he is.'

'No, the other bit.'

'That you're making excuses?'

'No, the last bit.'

Angie frowned. 'That you're not giving yourself the chance to be happy?'

Belle and Joe had both said the same thing, almost the same words. This was getting unnerving. Were her friends getting together and comparing notes?

'Don't I seem happy to you?' Jo asked her in a small voice.

'No, you don't, not really,' Angie said squarely.

'Do I seem sour or miserable or something?' Jo had never wanted to be like that. She used to worry she'd become one of those cantankerous old ladies who put the hose on children if they wandered near her front garden.

'No, it's not like that, it's like . . .' Angie thought about it. 'It's like you've covered yourself in bubble-wrap, and we can still see you, though not very clearly. And we certainly can't touch you. Nothing can touch you.' She tore a piece of plastic wrap off the dispenser on the wall and proceeded to seal the container of pesto. 'But then, you thought of Joe while you were having sex with Lachlan. Obviously someone's getting through to you. And he has very blue eyes, apparently.'

Jo felt that cramping sensation in her chest again. She cleared her throat. 'I have to go.'

Angie sighed. 'Of course you do, now that I've hit you right in the home truth.'

'No, really, I have to go, I've got no clean clothes for the week, no food in the fridge,' she said, checking her watch. Her good intentions from a few weeks ago had not converted into habit yet. She picked up her bag and headed for the door.

Angie stood cradling the container in her arms. 'Hey, mind those trees when you step back out into the forest.'

Jo ignored her, pushing through the door and stepping out into the dingy back lane.

When Jo finally got to sleep that night, after an extended period of tossing and turning, she dreamed of a forest. And in the middle of the forest was a clearing, and the moon was shining down onto an enormous four-poster bed, swathed in filmy white curtains, billowing gently in the dreamlike haze. And then Bannister came out from behind the trees and approached the bed, drawing back the curtains. There was a figure lying on the bed. At first Jo got a fright; the figure was wrapped in plastic, like something from a David Lynch movie. But it wasn't just any old plastic, it was bubble-wrap. As he proceeded slowly, lovingly, to peel back the layers of bubble-wrap, Jo was revealed in all her glory, inch by inch, limb by limb . . .

She sat up suddenly in bed, panting, her body clammy with perspiration. Bloody Angie.

Tuesday morning

Joe was pretending to work, but he couldn't concentrate. He hadn't been looking forward to this morning, in fact he'd been dreading it so much he had been tempted to stay up in the mountains another day . . . or three. But he knew that wasn't going to make things any easier.

He'd spotted Jo earlier, when he first arrived. She was across the other side of the news floor. He watched her for a moment, till she looked up, meeting his eyes. He couldn't read her expression . . . was it wistful? Questioning? He wasn't sure. Who knew with women? Then she smiled a faint, Mona Lisa smile. He gave her a tentative smile in return, and she held his gaze for another moment before looking away.

What did that mean? He sighed inwardly. But what did it

matter, anyway. He'd stuffed up monumentally and he didn't know how he was going to put things right again. So he walked into his office, closed the door and pretended to work.

The inevitable knock came maybe half an hour later.

'Yeah,' he said despondently.

The door opened and Carla sidled in. As expected.

'Hey stranger,' she purred.

'Hey.'

She laid the palms of her hands flat on the desk and leaned forward to give him a good eyeful of her cleavage. 'So . . . ?'

'So.' Christ. He'd never been good at this.

'So, you don't answer your phone over the weekend? Is that it?' she asked, but her tone wasn't shrewish, that wouldn't be a woman like Carla's style. She'd keep her cool. At least Joe was counting on that.

'I've been up the mountains, with my dad,' he said, his voice catching a little in his throat. 'Sorry, that's why I had to leave.'

She nodded slowly. 'No problem. I wasn't expecting a cosy breakfast, Joe, I'm not that kind of girl.' She came around to where he was sitting and perched on the desk facing him. 'It's okay, I realise you probably don't want to make a thing of this at work. I get it. It'll just be between you and me.' She leaned forward and planted a lingering kiss on his lips.

Say something, you gutless wonder.

His phone rang. Saved by the bell, coward. He gave her a weak, apologetic smile as he picked up the receiver.

'Joe Bannister.'

'Good morning, Joe, Judith here. Leo would like to see you.'

'Sure, I'll be right there.' He hung up. 'Sorry,' he said, getting to his feet. 'Leo wants to see me.'

'Well, we can't keep the boss waiting,' said Carla, standing up. But she didn't move out of his way. What did she want? A goodbye kiss? He couldn't deal with this now. He circled around the desk the other way, but she intercepted him at the door, blocking his path.

'Listen, Joe, I meant what I said, you don't have to be wary of me. I like clandestine. I find it exciting. Stimulating even.'

Christ. 'Okay . . . well, Leo's waiting.'

He had to reach his arm around her to open the door, and as he did she sidled in closer to him, making sure her body came into as much contact with his as was physically possible. This was hardly what he would call clandestine. She lifted her hand and kissed the tips of her fingers, before grazing them against his lips. 'Call me,' she breathed, and slithered off.

He looked up and Jo was standing by her desk, staring directly at him. No Mona Lisa smile this time. *Fuck*.

There was nothing he could do about it right now, he had to see Leo. Maybe lunch, he would ask Jo to lunch, to explain. Explain what? And why? He already knew how she'd react. She'd get all uppity and distant again, insist it was none of her business, that they just worked together. But they didn't just work together. There was something else, something more, and he wanted to bring it out into the open and deal with it, once and for all.

So why'd you sleep with another woman working in the same office, you bloody idiot?

Jo headed for the ladies room; she needed a minute to collect herself before the editorial meeting. She felt agitated again. She'd felt agitated almost constantly since the day she'd had the misfortune to be trapped in an elevator with Joe Bannister. Soul mate? He was more like a thorn in her side.

At least he wouldn't be at the meeting. He never came to editorial meetings, obviously considering himself above the rest of the staff, whose attendance was more or less mandatory. Jo walked into the ladies and straight into a cubicle. She lowered the lid of the toilet and sat, propping her elbows on her knees and her chin on her hands.

Bloody Ange and her bloody romantic ideas. Why had she paid her the slightest bit of attention? But the real mistake Jo had made was in thinking she and Bannister could be friends. Men and women could never be friends. Men didn't even like women. They tolerated them so they could get them into bed. That was all Bannister had been angling for all along, and when he missed his chance the other night, he obviously found someone more willing. Jo was glad she hadn't kidded herself that it was anything more than that. Maybe her heart was wrapped in bubble-wrap, but that was not such a bad thing, it had stopped it from getting broken.

Someone walked into the toilets, but didn't proceed to a stall; the clacking of high heels came to a halt at the basins. Jo waited to hear the taps running, but nothing happened. Whoever it was, they were having a good gawk at themselves in front of the mirror. She had better make some noise to announce herself. She rustled the toilet paper and then stood up, pressing the button to flush. When she opened the door, Carla was pouting at the mirror, applying lipstick. Jo gave her a cursory smile as she crossed to a basin and turned on the tap.

'Hi Jo,' Carla said with weary indifference. She was much more interested in her own reflection, as she proceeded to fluff and primp and buff. Jo noticed a rather hefty cosmetics bag propped on the edge of the basin. It was nine-thirty in the morning, how could she already need to touch up her make-up? Jo walked to the dispenser and pulled out a paper towel, wiping her hands as she surreptitiously watched Carla's reflection in the mirror. She thought about her and Bannister together, she could see him coming up behind her, kissing her neck, his hand sliding across her shoulder and down . . .

'Are you right there, Jo?' said Carla, raising an eyebrow as she looked straight at her.

'Sorry,' she jumped, 'in another world.' She turned on her heel and hurried out of the room, feeling like an idiot.

She stopped by her desk to grab a pad and a pen, and then made her way to the conference room. Hugh Moncrieff was already there, contemplating a series of food photographs he had spread out before him with the kind of relish another bloke might reserve for porn. Jo skirted around to the other side of the table and pulled out a chair.

He looked up. 'Hello there, Jo. Been for a run?'

'Sorry?' she said, sitting down.

'You're looking rather flushed, pink, like the outside rim of the centre of a lovely piece of rare sirloin.'

'I'll take that as a compliment.'

'As well you should.'

Others began to drift in, with nods and hellos, engaging in polite but meaningless chatter, as per usual. Jo didn't consider any of these people close friends, and that had always worked fine for her. She should never have messed with the system.

Then Lachlan arrived. He fixed his gaze on her as he took a seat almost opposite. 'Jo,' he said with a faint nod.

'Hi Lachlan,' she said lightly. He had a strange, tortured look in his eyes that was quite off-putting. Jo picked up her pen and started to scribble in her notepad . . . the date, a heading – all completely superfluous, but it made her appear occupied.

Leo swept into the room, talking over his shoulder to Bannister, as it turned out, who followed him a moment later. What was he doing here?

'Morning everyone,' Leo croaked, making his way to the head of the assembly where he slapped a wad of papers down on the table. Jo kept her eyes focused on him, but was unnervingly aware that Bannister had taken a seat across from her, one down from Lachlan. If she were to draw a line to connect the three of them, it would form a perfect triangle.

Then Carla sauntered in, took a quick inventory of the seating, and deposited herself in the vacant chair between Lachlan and Bannister. Jo watched out of the corner of her eye as Carla turned to give Bannister a seductive wink. Yeesh.

'Okay, let's get on with it,' Leo was saying as he shuffled the papers in front of him. 'We've got a lot to cover today, with an important announcement upfront. We've been allocated a place as part of a special envoy of journalists travelling to Iraq under the direct auspices of the Minister for Foreign Affairs and the Deputy Commander of Australian forces in Iraq, to report on our current commitment to Operation Catalyst.' He began to read from a press release. '"The envoy will tour the Joint Task Force Headquarters and meet members of the Australian Security Detachment as well as representatives from the Australian Army Training Team. They will also travel to the southern Iraqi province of Dhi Qar to inspect the headquarters of Overwatch Battle Group–West at Tallil Air Base."'

Leo looked up from the paper. 'I'm pleased to say that after consultation with our senior journalists, Lachlan Barr has accepted the assignment. Because of his already high profile, Lachlan is well placed to bring a lot of kudos to the paper. He deserves congratulations.'

Jo was staring wide-eyed at him, but he was modestly accepting the sprinkle of applause that rippled through the room. Then his gaze returned to Jo, giving her that same vaguely tortured look.

Leo went on in more detail, mostly about how the paper would capitalise on the opportunity, but Jo didn't listen to much after that. Everyone's voices seemed to echo incomprehensibly in her ears. Why was Lachlan doing this? He was the *Trib*'s poster boy, he didn't need to get his hands dirty. This was something Don would have taken part in happily. Though Jo remembered that his wife had been unwell recently. Had Lachlan been given little choice? Is that what the tortured looks were about? She could feel someone's eyes on her now and she glanced up, but it was Bannister staring at her from across the table. He looked away immediately. Why the hell wasn't he going? All right, his father was sick, but it was only for a few weeks, and he was the one with all the experience, the big famous war correspondent . . . Lachlan was the suit and tie man who went to premiers' conferences. He was so not the guy for this.

Eventually the meeting returned to business as normal, but Jo's head was still spinning. When it was her turn, she spoke on autopilot. She would do her column on Paris/Britney/Lindsay's latest escapades, something about bad girls becoming role models, link it with increasing rates of drug and alcohol abuse in young women . . . Jo didn't even know if she was making sense, and it all seemed so painfully trite. But Leo must have been satisfied, because he moved on when she had finished her spiel, without any comment except 'Next'.

As soon as he wrapped up the meeting, Jo sprang from her seat and sidled past everyone and out the door. She went directly to her desk and took up watch. When Lachlan appeared she was going to follow him into his office and find out what the hell was going through his head. But he was taking longer than expected. Some of the staff had probably hung back to talk to him about it. Jo started to scroll through her emails to fill in time, but they were a blur. Her phone rang and she picked it up.

'Jo Liddell.'

'Hi Jo, it's me.'

'Oh, hi Belle, what's up?' She sincerely hoped this was not going to be some conspiracy theory about the state of Charlene's health.

'Well, I've got some dates for you ... I know how busy you are, so I thought if I offered you four alternatives, we should be able to find something that suits.'

'What are you talking about?'

'Our double date!' she chirped.

Oh, for ...

'You know, even Darren's excited about it,' she went on eagerly. 'And I've lined up little Tegan from around the corner to babysit. Well, she's not so little any more, she's fifteen now and she's started doing babysitting around the neighbourhood. Her mum or dad always make sure they're home so she's got back-up. You met them I'm pretty sure ... Bill and Tracey, they were at the twins' party? Tracey has the blonde flick cut, and I think she was wearing a blue tank top that day, and a nice pair of cuffed shorts, she's got the legs ...'

Jo had stopped listening back at 'Tegan from around the corner'. Lachlan finally appeared, heading for his office.

'Belle,' she interrupted, 'I have to go, I'm in the middle of something.'

'Sure, sure,' said Belle. 'Let me just give you these dates, and you can get back to me later.'

Jo sighed. 'Look, it's not going to happen, Belle,' she said bluntly.

'Why, what do you mean?'

She could hear the hurt in her sister's voice. She had to put an end to this, once and for all.

'We broke up.'

'No!' she cried. 'Jo, you promised you'd give it a chance. He's so lovely, he's the nicest boyfriend you've ever —'

'Yeah, well he cheated on me, Belle.'

Finally there was silence down the line.

'Are you sure?' Belle said after a while, her voice small and hushed.

'What do you mean, am I sure?' said Jo. Lachlan went into his office and closed the door. 'I really have to go.'

'Are you all right?'

'Of course I am.'

'Jo . . .'

'I *really* have to go, Belle. I'll talk to you later.' She hung up the phone and walked briskly over to Lachlan's office, knocking on the door.

'Come in,' he said wearily.

Jo slipped inside, closing the door behind her. Lachlan was reclined back in his chair, facing the window, his feet crossed, propped up on the edge of the desk. He was tossing something – paperclips? – into a wastepaper basket that he'd positioned on top of the filing cabinet.

'Lachlan,' she began, 'why are you doing this?'

'To see how many I can get in without missing. So far, fifteen.'

Jo dragged a chair around to the other end of the desk where she could see his face, and sat down. 'Why are you going to Iraq? You've got kids, Leo would never make you go if you said you didn't want to.'

'I volunteered,' he said simply.

'What? Why?'

'Why do you think?' he said, meeting her eyes for the first time.

'I have no idea.'

'You don't, huh? Well, let's just say I wanted a challenge.' He tossed another paperclip. 'Score,' he said, making a victory fist.

'What does Sandra have to say about it?'

'She doesn't know yet.'

'You volunteered for something like this without discussing it with your wife?'

'She won't have a problem with it, she never does.'

'You've never gone into a war zone before.'

He was aiming another paperclip. 'No . . . I . . . haven't,' he said, as he lobbed it into the basket.

'Lachlan . . .'

He glanced at her.

'Talk to me?'

'Sorry, hun, I want to beat my previous record, twenty-seven not out, and you're putting me off my game a little.'

Jo sighed. She got up and moved the chair back before crossing to the door, where she paused as another paperclip sailed into the bin. She opened the door and stepped out, straight into Bannister's path as he went to walk by.

'Sorry,' he muttered, manoeuvring awkwardly around her.

'Can I talk to you?' she said tightly.

'Sure.' He stopped, but he couldn't look at her.

'Your office, perhaps?' she suggested.

He indicated for her to go ahead, and Jo proceeded around the perimeter of the news floor till she got to his office. The door was open, so she just walked straight in. He followed her, closing the door behind him.

'Do you want to sit down?' he asked as he moved around his desk to his chair.

'He's going because of you, you know,' Jo blurted.

'I'm sorry? Did you start the conversation without me?'

She sighed. 'Lachlan is going to Iraq,' she began, saying each word distinctly, 'because of you.'

He frowned, dropping down into his chair. 'I don't get the impression that Lachlan would try to emulate me in any way at all.'

'He's going to prove some kind of a point.'

Joe shrugged. 'That's his issue then, it has nothing to do with me.'

She bristled. 'Well, can't you speak to Leo? You're friends.'

'And just what do you expect me to say, Jo?'

'Tell him it's dangerous, tell him some of the stuff you told me, tell him that someone without experience shouldn't be going there.'

Joe sat back in his chair, considering her. 'I don't think it's any of my business.'

'Well, that hasn't stopped you butting your nose in before.'

He sighed. 'I don't think either Leo or Lachlan would care about what I had to say,' he said levelly.

'Why didn't you offer to go?' she snapped.

'What?'

'You know the place, this'd be a picnic for you.'

'What did you say?'

He looked shocked, angry even. What did she say? A picnic? She just compared going to Iraq with going on a *picnic*? After what he'd told her the other night?

'Um, sorry, bad choice of words,' she muttered. 'I didn't mean . . . it's only . . . look, you know the place, I was just thinking it wouldn't be that big a deal, a couple of weeks . . .'

'I can't help you, Jo, sorry,' he said brusquely.

Well, she'd botched that. She turned to walk out, flustered and frustrated. But he had no right to get on his high horse. She paused at the door and turned her head, but she didn't look at him.

'Honestly, Bannister,' Jo said. 'Carla Delacqua?'

'At least she's not married.'

He probably shouldn't have said that. She left the room without another word.

He'd stuffed up monumentally, and he still didn't know how he was going to put it right.

That afternoon

'So how's the little woman?' Will asked Joe.

They were sitting at a table by the window in an Irish pub down in Haymarket, the peak-hour traffic clogging the road outside. Joe had been calling him for days, and leaving messages, but Will was notoriously difficult to track down, mostly because of his exasperating habit of forgetting to turn on his phone, or keep it charged, or even to keep it on him. But now that they were out from under each other's feet, Joe didn't want the relationship, such as it was, to fade away. So when Will chose today to finally reply to his latest message, Joe jumped at the opportunity to leave work early and meet him for a drink. He had been feeling claustrophobic in the office. He'd had to stay low to avoid Carla, and though he'd barely laid eyes on Jo, he could feel the tension between them permeating the atmosphere, making it hard for him to breathe, or at least breathe easy.

'Little woman?' he frowned.

'Little Jo.'

'Don't ever let her hear you call her that.'

Will smiled, sipping his beer. 'So . . . you two seemed to be hitting it off.'

'What?' Joe blinked. 'There's nothing going on between me and Jo.'

'There isn't?' He appeared surprised. 'I thought I picked up on a bit of chemistry happening there. A spark, if you will.'

Joe looked at him. 'You think?'

'I do.' Will considered his brother. 'You like her, don't you?'

He shrugged. 'Doesn't much matter, she can't stand me.'

'Didn't look that way the other night.'

'Yeah well, things went downhill from there.'

'It's your sense of humour, Joe, I've told you before. Don't try to be funny, you can't pull it off.'

Joe shook his head, gazing out the window.

'So what happened?' Will prompted him.

He sighed. 'She's seeing someone, he's married, and well, I had an opinion about that, which she didn't exactly appreciate.'

Will was nodding slowly. 'Smooth, Joe. Women love being told they're in the wrong. That kind of sweet-talk reels them in.'

Joe didn't say anything, just took another long drink from his glass.

'So how are you going to fix it?' said Will.

'There's nothing to fix. Nothing's actually happened between us.'

'And it's not going to if you keep that attitude up.'

'What am I supposed to do?' he protested. 'She's with some-one else.'

'Does she think he's going to leave his wife? 'Cause she didn't look that stupid to me.'

'She doesn't want him to leave his wife,' said Joe. 'She made out it was more of a convenience, sex with no strings attached.'

'Wow,' Will said thoughtfully. 'There are women who want that too?'

'Apparently.'

Silence fell between them as Joe contemplated the lay of the land. It was pretty obvious that he needed to put Jo Liddell out of his head and move on. He didn't know why he'd got so stuck on her, maybe it was the whole experience of being trapped in the elevator together. She had mentioned something about not developing a siege mentality, he remembered, that they shouldn't pretend there was some kind of bond that would hold them together. She'd hardly led him on. In fact you could say she'd made her position crystal clear from the start. But then she'd sat outside his house for hours, and she'd charmed his dad . . . And there was the little problem of wanting to kiss her every time he so much as looked at her.

'You need a grand gesture,' Will declared suddenly.

'Huh?'

'You've got to sweep her off her feet.'

Joe shook his head, smiling. 'You're such a tragic. If only life were a musical, eh, Will?'

'Piss off,' he said. 'Your problem is you've spent too long around sweaty blokes with crew cuts and big guns. You've got to start courting her, Joe.'

'Jesus, now I really do feel like I'm in a musical. Who says courting any more?'

Will was shaking his head. 'I'm telling you, that attitude is not going to get you anywhere,' he insisted. 'Have you even asked her out?'

'I asked her to your play.'

'But that wasn't like a *date* date, was it?'

'I don't know. What makes it a *date* date?'

'Did you ask Angie or did she? Because if she did, she was letting you know that it wasn't a date. But if you did, you were sending her the same message.'

'I invited Angie along,' Joe admitted, staring down at the table.

Will dropped his head in his hands with a groan. He looked up again, leaning forward. 'You know, I used to think you were the

coolest guy out. I wanted to be you when I grew up. You always
had gorgeous women hanging off you, jetting around the world,
you were like James Bond. What happened?'

Joe was laughing, shaking his head. 'I guess your alarm clock
went off.'

'Come on, I wasn't dreaming, and it wasn't my imagination.
You can't pretend that you haven't got a certain level of experience with women, Joe.'

No, he supposed he couldn't pretend that.

'So what happened? Did that simpering Brit break your
heart?'

'Who, Sarah?' he frowned. 'She wasn't simpering.'

'You reckon?' Will frowned. 'I don't know how you put up
with her. She complained about everything, the heat, the flies,
even the food, for Chrissakes, and she was from England! Hardly
the culinary capital of the world. You'd never have known she
just blew in from a war zone, she was so fucking precious about
everything.' He paused. 'I can't believe you let her break your
heart.'

'I didn't. She didn't.'

'So what happened?'

'Nothing, we just drifted apart.'

'Good. I couldn't understand what you saw in her in the first
place. Or she in you, for that matter.'

Joe glanced sideways at him. 'Thanks.'

'No, I just mean you weren't suited. But you and Elevator
Girl . . . like I said, there's chemistry there.'

He felt an unexpected warm rush across his chest.

Will was watching him. 'You've got it bad, haven't you? That's
why you're fart-arsing around like an overgrown adolescent.'

Joe laughed, shaking his head at the irony of Will calling
him an overgrown adolescent. Though perhaps he did have a
point. 'Aren't I supposed to be the one giving you big brotherly
advice?'

'Not if you suck at it,' he declared. 'Did you lose your mojo
over there or something?'

Joe shrugged. 'It's never been this hard before. I've never really
had to pursue a girl, I've never had to put in any effort, anyway.

You meet someone, you hit it off, things . . . develop. But this, it's up and down like a friggin' roller-coaster.'

Will grinned. 'Ain't love grand? Mark my words, brother, you need to do something dramatic.'

'I guess I could challenge her lover to a duel. Pistols or swords, do you reckon?'

'I reckon you're a pistol,' he said wryly. 'I'm telling you, grand gesture. And then once you've got her attention, ask her out on a real date.'

'Are you forgetting she's taken?'

'Bullshit. She's hanging around with someone who's taken. All's fair, buddy.'

Joe drained his beer. 'Is it my shout?'

'Do you have to ask?'

5:30 pm

It was warm outside the airconditioned building as Jo trudged home. The atmosphere had that stuffy feeling, like someone needed to open a window and let some air in. It was the cloud cover, it trapped all the heat and pollution and grime as effectively as if it was plastic wrap stretched taut across the sky. The strap of her handbag dangled from her fingers so it was almost scraping on the pavement as Jo passed noisy, dusty building sites, weaved her way around snarling traffic, being shoved and jostled by equally snarling commuters.

Needless to say, Jo had not had a good day. In fact she'd had a crap day. The crappiest. She'd handled everyone and everything with about as much aplomb as a brash schoolgirl, but with less maturity.

She had tried to speak to Lachlan again, but he was still in that weird cryptic mood. She had even invited him over tonight, but he had declined. He did have to talk to Sandra, and Jo had at least summoned enough commonsense to defer to that.

She had also managed to avoid Bannister for the rest of the day, not that it had been difficult, she'd barely laid eyes on him. He'd obviously decided to keep a low profile. She knew she hadn't handled that particular encounter well either, suggesting that he was somehow more expendable than Lachlan. She hadn't meant that, only that he was more experienced. But she was still kicking herself for that 'picnic' remark, it was completely out of line, considering what he'd told her the other night. It was just that she was genuinely worried about Lachlan. He was doing something totally out of character, and for dubious reasons. And she didn't think that was the best mindset to take into a potentially dangerous situation. He needed to be focused and clear about his intentions, yet it was quite evident to Jo that his intentions were anything but clear. Was he trying to prove something to her, or to himself?

Jo groaned out loud, no one would hear her anyway. She hated days like this; days where not only did everything go wrong, everything seemed wrong, bleak, tedious, or just too hard. It was impossible to see the good in anything, and her whole life looked like a series of bad decisions and wrong turns, compounding exponentially towards the ultimate futility of her eventual demise.

You really knew you were having a bad day when your thoughts turned to death.

As she walked into the quiet of her apartment she didn't feel that comforting sense of home. She felt lonely. God, she had to snap herself out of this mood or it was going to be a long night. She dumped her bag and keys on the table, kicked off her shoes and slipped out of her jacket, hanging it over the back of a dining chair. She was on her way to the bathroom when the intercom buzzed. Had Lachlan decided to come after all? Or maybe Bannister wanted to have it out with her? That was a ludicrous notion. It was probably only Angie; she hoped so anyway, she could use the company.

She picked up the receiver. 'Hello?'

'Hi, Jo, it's me.'

'Belle? Is that you?'

'I just said it was, didn't I?'

'But what are you doing here?' Jo said anxiously. 'What's happened?'

'You broke up with the nicest boyfriend you've ever had. Where do you think I'd be?' she said, her voice almost breaking.

'But it's a week night, Belle . . .' Jo was speechless, overwhelmed that her sister had actually left her sorority in the suburbs to be with her. 'I don't know what to say.'

'"Come on in" would be a start.'

Jo immediately pressed the button to release the door, and hurried out to wait by the elevator, just as the ping sounded and the doors began to glide open.

As their eyes connected Belle squealed and lurched at Jo, hugging her tight.

'I don't believe I'm here, I don't believe I actually did it!' Belle bubbled over excitedly. 'I couldn't stop thinking about you all day,' she went on, stepping back to look at her, 'and all the times you've been there for me. And I was telling Darren when he rang at lunchtime, and he said he'd take the day off tomorrow. Just like that. Apparently there's not much work on at the moment, so he said if I wanted to visit you . . . and you know what, I said yes! Without even thinking about it! And then I was running around like a chook without a head just to organise myself, I didn't even have time to get something ready for their dinner, so they're really on their own. God only knows what Darren's going to feed them tonight. But you know what? I don't want to know. I don't care. I mean, of course I care, it's just that coming in on the train, I had this overwhelming sensation of freedom. And it didn't feel bad, at all!'

Jo eyed the sizeable overnight bag slung over her sister's shoulder. 'How long are you planning to stay?'

'Oh, don't worry,' Belle laughed, 'just the night. But I had to bring supplies. You weren't expecting me and I didn't think your cupboards would be all that well stocked anyway.'

'Belle, I'm not out in the sticks,' Jo reminded her as she led her down the corridor to the apartment. 'We're in the middle of the city, you can get anything you want around here.'

'Yeah, for twice as much as I can get it at my local shops.'

She had a point. Jo opened the door and stood back for Belle to go through. She dumped her bag on the floor and gazed around the room. 'It's still very . . . stark, isn't it?'

'That's because I haven't unpacked all my bits and pieces.'

'Well, good, we can do that later,' she said, crouching down. 'But first things first.' She unzipped the bag and drew out a bottle in a paper bag, passing it up to Jo. 'I brought gin, of course. And . . .' She pulled out a cooler bag and opened it. 'Tonic . . .' She passed up a four-pack of mixer bottles, chilled. '. . . and lemons!' she said finally, holding one in each hand as she stood up again.

'What? No ice?' Jo remarked.

'Ha ha.'

Jo regarded her sister with a mix of incredulity and amusement.

'What?' said Belle.

'I can't believe you're here,' she said. 'But I'm really glad you are. I had such a crap day.'

'I know, that's *why* I'm here.' Belle smiled. 'And it's why God made gin. So let's get on with it.'

Ten minutes later they were sitting cross-legged at the coffee table, halfway through a couple of very potent G&Ts. Belle had insisted on doubles to get them started.

'It's like when the doctor puts you on antibiotics,' she explained authoritatively. 'He always says to start with a double dose so the effect kicks in sooner.'

There was enough food spread out on the table to keep them going for most of the night. Chips and dips and olives and cheese and gorgeous bread. Jo decided Belle's local shops were all right, and after another gulp of her drink, she decided her sister was more than all right. And then she felt a little weepy. Bloody gin.

'So come on, spill, tell me the whole story,' said Belle. 'Get it off your chest.'

Oh God. She felt awful about the whole bloody charade, but it was the first thing that had actually motivated Belle to visit her in the city in years. So that made it okay, kind of, didn't it? Besides, it wasn't her idea in the first place. Bannister got her into this pickle, and then he'd gone and poked his pickle elsewhere, leaving her with . . . chutney? This gin was strong.

She felt Belle's hand covering hers on the coffee table. 'Oh, poor thing, you can't even bring yourself to talk about it. But you'll feel better if you do.'

Jo gave her a lame smile. 'I just don't know what to say.'

'Okay,' said Belle, 'I'll start you off. Personally, I don't understand how he could have cheated on you. He was *besotted* at our place. My friends noticed too. It was the hot topic at Tuesday morning coffee after Spin class. Everyone was swooning over him. We were trying to work out who he was like, and the consensus in the end was that he was a cross between Denny from *Grey's Anatomy*, do you remember him? He was the one who died after Izzy cut his lifeline, well, not directly because she cut his lifeline, I mean, he would have died anyway.' Belle gave her head a little shake as though to clear her thoughts. 'It's a long story and it doesn't matter, the point is we all agreed that Joe is a cross between Denny, with a smattering of Mark Ruffalo, just the rumpled part. Then Nicole nailed it in the end, she said he had something of the Jake Gyllenhaal's about him, but of course, he's a bit younger than your Joe, so we decided maybe he was like Jake Gyllenhaal's dad, well, not actually, because none of us knows what Jake Gyllenhaal's dad even looks like, for all we know he may have taken after his mother, and besides his dad is probably a little too old for Joe, so if you can imagine what his father would look like at Joe's age, or better still what Jake Gyllenhaal would look like at Joe's age . . . crossed with Denny from *Grey's* and Mark Ruffalo.'

Jo was beginning to lose the will to live when she realised Belle had come to an end, of that avenue at least.

'Anyhoo, he was just *so* lovely,' she was saying. 'I mean, really genuinely likeable. Didn't you find him just so likeable, Jo? Well, of course you did, what am I saying? So I just can't believe that he would have cheated on you. Did he actually cheat? As in *cheat* cheat?'

'What do you mean?'

'Well,' Belle hesitated. She took a long drink from her glass then set it back on the table, gazing solemnly at Jo. 'Did he actually *sleep* with another woman?'

Jo pictured the scene in his office doorway, the way Carla was pressed up against him. And more telling, the look on his face when he realised Jo was watching. Besides, he more or less admitted culpability with his 'at least she's not married' remark. He *cheat* cheated all right.

What the hell was she thinking? Bannister didn't cheat on her. He was a single, unattached man who hooked up with a single, unattached woman at work. This whole charade was messing with her head. But she couldn't tell Belle the truth now, she'd dug the hole too deep already. Maybe she could still play the game without telling more lies.

'Yes,' Jo said finally, 'he actually slept with another woman.'

Belle winced. 'Okay. Now, I want to say something, Jo, and I hope you're not going to take it the wrong way. But didn't you say you were still seeing that man? So doesn't that mean that technically you were cheating too, right?'

This was getting murky.

'Did he know? Did Joe know you were seeing that man?'

Jo nodded sheepishly.

'Then why is he in the wrong?'

'I didn't say he was in the wrong, I just said that he slept with someone else and we broke up.'

Belle frowned, considering her. 'Who broke it off?'

Murkier and murkier.

Jo hesitated, anything she said would be an outright lie.

'You did, didn't you, Jo?' She didn't wait for an answer. 'That pride of yours. I mean, the guy knows you're seeing someone else, you're insisting on taking it slow, what's he going to do? He has his pride as well. I mean, maybe he was trying to get a reaction out of you, see how you would feel, if you were jealous. There are so many possibilities. You two really need to get together and talk it out and see if you want to try again, for real this time.' She paused, watching Jo. 'Have you even talked about it?'

'Not really.'

Belle sighed. 'I just think you've got a real chance with this guy, Jo. I mean, let's face it, you haven't exactly given yourself much of a chance with anyone else, considering they're always married. Which I've never been able to understand, Jo, much as I try. I mean,

I know why you do it, or why you think you have to, but I've never understood it. And I knew you'd just think I was a prude if I said I disapproved, and well, I don't have a right to disapprove anyway, it's not my life, and you're a grown woman, and let's face it, after the example Mum gave us, maybe you couldn't help it or something.'

Eew. Jo didn't like the idea that somehow she had been conditioned by Charlene, much less that she was following in her footsteps.

'Anyway, can you imagine how happy I was when you showed up with someone you could actually have a future with?' Belle gushed. 'I've been on a high, that's why I was so devastated when you told me what he did. And so worried about you. I just can't understand why this had to happen to you, when it's taken you so long to trust again. It seems so unfair. And I wouldn't want this to set you back.'

Set her back? Where to? Did everyone think she had a disability she was heroically learning to overcome?

The intercom buzzed again. Jo had no idea who it could be, but she was grateful for the interruption. She had to get Belle onto a different track.

'Are you expecting someone?' asked Belle, her eyes wide. 'Maybe it's Joe, come to apologise, beg you to give him another chance . . .'

What if it was Bannister? That could get awkward.

Jo roused herself. Of course it wouldn't be Bannister. She was allowing herself to get sucked into this little fantasy scenario of Belle's. She had to find a way to close the book. She walked over to the intercom and picked up the receiver. 'Hello?'

'Hi Jo, it's me, and I have a bottle of bubbly in my hand.'

Jo smiled, relieved. 'Come on up, Ange.' She pressed the button to release the door downstairs and hung up the receiver.

'It's Angie?' Belle said brightly. 'This is really turning into a girls' night.'

'You don't mind?'

'Of course not, it'll be fun.' Then her face dropped. 'Oh, sorry, that was a bit insensitive.'

It took Jo a second to twig what she was getting at. 'Don't be silly, I don't want to sit around moping all night.'

'Does Angie know . . . you know, the latest?'

Bugger. When worlds collide. How was she going to stage manage this? She was trying to fabricate a reason to ask Belle not to talk about it when there was a knock on the door. Too late now.

Jo hurried over to open it. 'Hiya,' she said, receiving Angie's hug. 'Just go along with whatever I say, okay?' she whispered in her ear. 'Look who showed up a little while ago,' she announced, stepping back to let Angie through.

'Hi Belle!' she said crossing over to her. 'Wow, footloose and baby-free. How did you manage that?'

'The twins are two years old now. I figure Darren can handle it.'

'Too right.'

'Besides, I wanted to be here for my sister. You heard about her and Joe?'

'No, has something happened?' She turned to Jo expectantly.

'He slept with Carla,' Jo said quickly.

Angie pulled a face. '*Carla?*'

'Yeah, so much for being my soul mate, eh?' She might just be able to swing this after all.

'Bugger,' said Angie, plonking herself in an armchair. '*Carla?* I would have thought he had better taste.'

'Well, that's hardly the point,' said Belle primly. 'Who's Carla anyway?'

'Trampy McTramp-Tramp from the *Trib*,' Angie told her. 'She does the social pages. And I mean, *does* them.'

'Okay, so now that we're all up to speed, can we talk about something else?' Jo asked hopefully.

'No way, I want to hear *everything*.'

'They broke up,' Belle said sadly.

'Who?'

'Jo and Joe, of course.'

Angie looked confused, not surprisingly. But she quickly recovered. Jo knew she could count on her to improvise, but she'd have some explaining to do later.

'So . . . you broke up?' Angie said, raising an eyebrow at Jo. 'Because he slept with Carla?'

'That's right,' Jo said plainly. 'What choice did I have?'

'Well, things have certainly moved ahead at a cracking pace. Last I heard, you were thinking of Joe while you were having sex with Lachlan, so –'

'Jo!' Belle exclaimed. 'This is exactly what I was trying to say to you. Angie, I said that Joe was probably confused –'

'What's she confused about?'

'No, no, I mean Joe, guy Joe.'

'Oh,' Angie murmured. 'So what's he confused about?'

'About whether she was really committed to him,' said Belle, 'because she was still seeing that man.'

'That man?'

'Lachlan,' Jo informed Angie.

'So,' Belle resumed, 'Joe – guy Joe – maybe he slept with Ms McTrampy to get a reaction out of Jo – our Jo. Don't you think that's possible? So I reckon Jo – our Jo – needs to decide once and for all what she really wants. And she should start by getting rid of that man, don't you think, Angie?'

'Couldn't agree more.'

'And then she should have it all out with Joe,' Belle went on. 'They should both lay their cards on the table.'

'I, for one, would certainly like to see all the cards laid on the table,' Angie nodded. 'Face up.'

Jo rolled her eyes. 'Who needs a drink?' she asked, she hoped divertingly, when the intercom buzzed again.

And Jo had thought she was going to be lonely tonight.

She walked over to the intercom. This time it had to be Lachlan. He would have told Sandra by now, and he was probably ducking for cover. But she couldn't let him come up here, it'd be like feeding him to the lions. She picked up the receiver. 'Hello?'

'Hi . . . Jo?'

It wasn't Lachlan. Jo held her breath.

'It's Joe Bannister.'

She turned into the wall. 'Look, this is not a good time.'

'Is Lachlan there?'

'No, Belle and Angie are.'

'Who is it?' they whispered loudly in unison.

'I just need to talk to you for a minute,' Bannister was saying. 'It won't take long.'

Jo was startled by Belle's sudden materialisation at her side. 'Is it Joe? Ask him up.'

'Hold on a sec.' She covered the receiver with her hand and turned to look at her sister's expectant face. 'Yes, it's Joe. But I'm hardly going to ask him up here now.'

'We'll disappear into the bedroom, won't we, Angie?'

Angie had stepped into the kitchen to make herself a drink. 'Sure,' she called. 'We'll still be able to hear everything from there, won't we?'

'Which is exactly why I'm not going to ask him up,' Jo stated firmly.

'But he must want to make things right,' Belle pleaded. 'Why else would he be here? You have to hear him out at least.'

Angie came out of the kitchen holding a glass. 'You really should hear him out,' she agreed with a mischievous glint in her eye. 'What are you afraid of?'

Jo glared at her. 'Fine, but there's no way he's coming up here.' She put the receiver back to her ear, elbowing Belle out of the way.

'Joe,' she said, 'give me a minute, I'll come down.'

'Okay, I'll be waiting.'

She hung up the receiver. 'Happy?'

Belle clapped her hands together. 'Yes! As long as you're going to be honest and open with him, and accept your part of the blame.'

Jo sighed, crossing to the coffee table and skolling the rest of her drink. She passed the glass to Angie. 'Fill her up. I'll be back in a minute.'

She walked out to the lifts and pressed the button for down. She didn't like leaving the two of them alone, but she was pretty sure Angie had it covered, she was enjoying herself too much. The doors slid open and she stepped in, pressing G. As the lift descended, it occurred to Jo that maybe she could use this to her advantage. It could actually give her an out. Whatever happened, and she really had no idea what Bannister wanted to talk about, she would be able to tell Belle that she had ended it. Finito. Over and out.

Jo stepped out of the elevator when it reached the ground floor. As she crossed the foyer to the glass entrance doors, she couldn't see Bannister, but when she pushed them open, she spotted him leaning against a lamppost. He shoved his hands in his pockets and ambled over towards her.

'Thanks for coming down,' he said.

She stood there, folding her arms. 'What did you want to see me about?'

He took a breath. 'I spoke to Leo about the Iraq trip.'

'You did?' She wasn't expecting that.

He nodded. 'You shouldn't worry, it's just a press junket. They hand-pick high-profile journos and take them around to show them all the reconstruction projects, the training of Iraqi nationals, the good stuff, so they'll go home and write positive pieces.'

'I seem to remember Lachlan suggesting something like that about what you were doing over there,' Jo said, 'and you didn't take it too well.'

'Because it's not the same thing,' he maintained. 'Look, it's dangerous going into Baghdad now, I'm not going to lie to you, but it's in the best interests of the military to protect this group. They'll be heavily guarded, travelling around in armoured Land-cruisers. You should see these things, they're like tanks. It's a Joint Task Force responsibility to provide protection for diplomats and government personnel working at the Australian Embassy. It's what they do. And there's the Military Police Detachment as well who primarily function as bodyguards for visiting VIPs. They will be under tight protection at all times by people who know the situation and know what they're doing.'

Jo bit her lip, thinking. 'What about the other place they're going to, in the south, wasn't it?'

He nodded. 'The OBG-W has a security overwatch role as part of the larger coalition force. But they'll be kept well away from any hotspots. They'll only visit the headquarters at Tallil. I guarantee you, they won't be taking any risks with this group. The whole point is to prove that violence is down since the surge, so they're not going to take them anywhere that has even the potential for violence.'

He looked very earnest about it all, like it really mattered to him.

But it couldn't matter to him.

'Why do you care?' Jo asked.

'I don't particularly. But you do, so . . .' He shrugged, staring down at the footpath.

She felt self-conscious, and a host of other feelings she did not care to name. 'Look . . . Joe . . . I owe you an apology for the way I behaved today, the things I said to you. It was inexcusable.'

'It's okay,' he said. 'You were upset.'

Why was he doing this? Guilty conscience over Carla? He didn't need to feel guilty, he was a free man, he could sleep with whomever he wanted. So why was he here, and what did he want from her?

'So you came here just to tell me this?' said Jo.

'There was one other thing . . .' He hesitated. He seemed nervous. 'Um . . . I just wanted you to know that Carla was a mistake. A knee-jerk reaction.'

Jo frowned. 'A knee-jerk reaction to what?'

He shook his head. 'It doesn't matter. I'm just saying, it's not going to happen again. With Carla.'

Though her heart was doing strange palpitations, Jo tried to appear nonchalant. 'Well, that has nothing to do with me.'

'Yes, it does.'

She looked up at him and he was gazing unblinking back at her.

'We both know that it does, or if you don't know that it does by now, then I guess I'm trying to make it clear that it does. For me.' Christ, was he even making any sense? 'Anyway, it's on the record now.'

Jo didn't respond. She wasn't sure she wanted whatever she said to go on the record.

'So, I'll let you get back to it . . .' he said, backing away from her. She still hadn't said anything, but she did look a little rattled. That was probably a good sign, he decided. And she was watching him, her eyes were locked on him, in fact. He'd had that urge to kiss her again, which is why he'd backed away. If they were in a movie he would have pulled her into his arms and held her just so, and she might have resisted, for a moment, and then their lips would have met and their noses wouldn't bump or their teeth knock against each other . . . But this wasn't the movies and he had to bide his time, play this right. And he wasn't going to become entangled in some kind of weird inter-locking triangle with Mr and Mrs Lachlan Barr. He'd made his position clear, and Jo knew where he stood. Now it was up to her.

She was still watching him. 'See you at work,' he said, raising his hand in a wave, and then he turned and walked away up the street.

'So, what happened?' said Belle breathlessly as Jo walked through the door a few minutes later.

She had been trying to make sense of it on the way up in the elevator, but she wasn't any the wiser before the lift doors opened on her floor. What just happened? Had Bannister actually 'declared his intentions'? Or had Jo got the wrong idea, having missed some vital piece of information, some crucial scene in a film. She hated when that happened, when she drifted off in the middle of a movie and was never quite sure after that if she was supposed to be confused or whether she had missed some essen-tial plot point. That's what this felt like. Nothing had happened between them, they'd been trapped in an elevator, after which they were not exactly friendly, then they were friendly, then not friendly, and then all of a sudden he's telling her he's not going to sleep with Carla again and it has everything to do with her. What exactly did he expect her to do with that?

Angie and Belle were still waiting for an answer.

'Um, well, we . . . talked,' she said, attempting to sound off-hand. But Belle was not going to leave it at that. Nor was Angie, by the look on her face.

'What did you talk about?' Angie prompted her.

Jo dropped into the vacant armchair and leaned across to pick up her drink. 'Um, Iraq mostly,' she said, before downing half the contents of the glass.

Belle's face dropped. 'What?'

'He came to tell me about the envoy of journalists that's going to Iraq.'

'Is he going back?' asked Angie.

'No, Lachlan's going. They made an announcement about it at work today.'

Belle frowned. 'I don't get it, what's that got to do with Joe?'

'Nothing. I was upset about Lachlan going, and he wanted to reassure me that he'll be safe . . .'

'That's a little weird,' said Angie.

'But sweet,' Belle added. 'Is that all he said?'

Jo hesitated. Close the book. Do it, stop it here, now. This is your chance.

'He wanted me to know that it didn't mean anything with Carla and that it won't be happening again,' she blurted, then immediately covered her mouth with her hand, closing the gate once the horse had bolted.

Belle squealed with delight.

'Is that really what he said?' Angie asked, looking meaningfully at Jo.

'It really is,' Jo nodded, meeting her gaze directly. Poor Ange didn't know what was real and what was made up any more. Jo was beginning to feel the same way, except she wasn't making this up.

'So how do you feel about that?' Angie went on.

Jo thought for a moment. 'Unprepared.'

'What did you say to him?' asked Belle.

'That it had nothing to do with me.'

'Well, of course it does!' Belle scolded. 'That's why he was telling you.'

Jo nodded faintly. 'That's what he said.'

Angie leaned closer to her. 'So how do you feel about him?'

'I don't know,' she said, bewildered.

'Of course you do,' Belle tut-tutted. 'You wouldn't have gone out with him in the first place if you didn't like him.'

Jo sighed inwardly.

'And you wouldn't have been thinking about him while you were having sex with Lachlan,' Angie added, bringing truth back into the equation.

'Which brings us neatly back to the fact that you have to break it off with that man,' Belle stated firmly.

'Hear, hear.'

Jo sighed. 'I can't break it off with Lachlan just before he goes to Iraq.'

'Why not?' they chorused.

'It wouldn't be right. What if something happened to him? I'd never forgive myself.'

'He's not going over to fight,' Angie reminded her.

'That doesn't mean the trip doesn't involve risks.'

'What about Joe?' said Belle. 'You can't just leave him hanging. He's swallowed his pride and made the first move, and if you don't give him some kind of response, what's he going to think? I'll tell you, he'll think you're not interested, what else could he think? You drag your chain now, waiting till that man's back safe and sound, and Joe will have moved on. And who could blame him? He's an attractive man, and a very eligible one, and from what I hear they're pretty thin on the ground. I bet you there are plenty of women with their eye on him, waiting for the opportunity, and some of them may not be as dithery as you, Jo. She who hesitates . . .'

Jo sagged back in her chair. 'Cripes, this is all getting too complicated.'

'More complicated than going out with a married man?' Belle asked in a rhetorical tone.

'Yes, actually, if you want to know the truth.'

'Well, I don't understand that.'

'I know where I stand with Lachlan. I don't have any expectations of him beyond that, so I don't have any of the angst that comes from having all your expectations resting on someone who's probably going to let you down in the end.'

Belle was shaking her head sadly. 'What about the good stuff?'

'What good stuff?'

'I know they let you down,' she said. 'Darren gives me the shits on a daily basis. But I'm still glad he's there at the end of the day. Even if we've been at each other all night, he still lets me stick my cold feet up against him in bed. And I know sometimes it feels like the footy-tipping comp is more important to him, but the fact is, if anything happened to me, he'd be the first one there.'

'You're certainly not going to get any of that from Lachlan,' said Angie.

Jo shrugged. 'I can always wear bedsocks.'

Angie and Belle both shook their heads in unison, like a Greek chorus of pity.

'Does he actually make you happy?' Angie asked.

'He doesn't make me unhappy.' Most of the time.

'Don't you want more than that?'

It didn't really matter what she wanted. Jo had learned early on that you don't always get what you want. In fact, you hardly ever do.

'You know what I do want?' said Jo, slapping her hands on her thighs. 'I want to change the subject. I reckon we've exhausted this topic, and I'm going to pass the baton. How's, um, Gourmet Sandwich Man?' she asked Angie; she'd given up trying to remember his moniker from whim to whim.

'Who's that?' Belle asked.

As Angie launched into to the latest instalment of the Amazing Adventures of Gourmet Sandwich Man, Jo tuned out, retreating to the privacy of her own thoughts. Belle and Angie just complicated things, with their talk of happily-ever-afters, as if that was even on the cards.

But it was clear she had a choice to make, between the relatively safe, if somewhat rudderless, pleasure cruise with Lachlan, and the unchartered waters of an actual regular relationship with Joe. What Belle and Angie were not taking into account in all their excitement was that there were no lifejackets on such a voyage, and Jo had never been a very strong swimmer.

The following week

Lachlan rolled off her and lay flat on his back on the bed beside her, catching his breath. Like he always did. It annoyed Jo actually, not that she'd ever told him so. But the way he sprang off her after climaxing had always made her feel cheap somehow. It was a little too 'wham bam, thank you ma'am'.

Jo didn't know why she was having thoughts like this tonight, when it was the last time they would be together before he left for Iraq. But in the past week she'd found that a lot of what Lachlan did got on her nerves. Things she hadn't noticed before, like the way he frequently cut her off mid-sentence, either because he felt what he had to say was more important, or because he clearly wasn't listening in the first place. And when he did speak, he often sounded as though he was reading aloud from one of his own op-ed pieces. He was completely oblivious to criticism, it barely even registered. It was as though Lachlan was coated in Teflon, everything just slid off, leaving no mark, no stain, no impression at all. And then there were his other quirks, like this post-coital indifference, which Jo had always been aware of but largely ignored. After all, he wasn't her partner for life, she didn't have to 'work' on the relationship, or else she might have told him that a bit of affection after sex was not too much to expect. But Jo had no expectations, that was the deal, that was her mantra. No expectations, no disappointment.

So why was it all beginning to seem cold and empty? Was this the person she'd become? Had she built up a Teflon coating as well? The idea sent a shiver through her. She didn't want to be a cold person, she didn't feel as though she was a cold person. In fact, whenever she'd laid eyes on Bannister this week she'd felt quite the opposite. She could see him now, smiling at her across the news floor, passing her in the corridor with a wink, and the day they found themselves once again in an elevator together. Jo had been waiting for the lift when the doors opened and Bannister was standing there. His face broke into a broad smile as soon as he saw her, and her heart had missed a beat; she felt it again now just thinking about it.

'Going down?' he'd asked.

Jo had nodded as she stepped in. 'You too?'

'Yeah,' he said, as though he'd just decided that was a good idea.

Jo pressed the button for the ground floor, and leaned back against the wall, surveying the interior. 'I wonder if this is the –'

'No,' he interrupted. 'Our elevator is the second from the end on the left-hand side of the bay, facing reception.'

Jo met his eyes then, with a faint lift of her eyebrow. *Our* elevator?

'I was thinking of having a plaque installed,' he added.

They smiled at each other as the lift stopped on a lower floor. The doors slid open and Lachlan was standing there. He took in the scene, his eyes darting suspiciously from Jo to Bannister and back again.

'Hello you two,' he said in a smarmy tone as he stepped inside the lift. The doors closed and the three of them formed a triangle, facing each other. To call the moment awkward would be like calling Mount Everest a grassy knoll.

'So when do you head out, Lachlan?' Bannister was first to break the silence.

'Monday,' he replied curtly.

'Looking forward to it?'

Lachlan sniggered. 'As much as one can look forward to travelling into a war zone, with the attendant risk to life and limb.'

Jo watched as Bannister cast his eyes downward, rubbed his hand across his forehead, then around his jaw, all in an attempt, she suspected, to stop himself from laughing in Lachlan's face.

'I think you'll make it out alive, Lachlan,' he said finally when he'd composed himself. 'After all, journalists don't get too close to the action these days, isn't that right?'

Lachlan regarded him with a smug sneer.

'It's all just a cushy PR exercise, the way I hear it,' Joe had gone on. 'And you'll be under military protection the whole time, probably one of the safest places you could be, as a matter of fact.'

'I'll pay the penny . . .' said Lachlan, running his fingers across her abdomen.

Jo jumped, startled. He was propped on his side, looking down at her. She was miles away, she'd almost forgotten Lachlan was there in the bed beside her.

'What did you just say?' she murmured, feeling disoriented.

'I was offering you a penny for your thoughts,' he explained. 'You were a long way away then.'

She shrugged. 'I was just dozing off. I'm pretty tired.'

He smoothed his hand across her midriff and up to cover her breast as he leaned in to kiss her. Jo could feel his urgency building, and she recoiled inside. She really wasn't in the mood, she'd had to force it the first time around. Lachlan must have sensed it now, because he stopped abruptly, looking down at her.

'What's up?'

'Nothing, why?'

He hesitated. 'You don't seem to be into it tonight.'

'I told you I'm just tired.'

'Okay then,' he said, his hand slipping away from her breast.

'Lach, it's fine if you want to . . . go ahead.'

He gave her a wounded look, before turning away to lie on his back again, staring up at the ceiling.

Jo sighed loudly. 'What's wrong?'

'I didn't realise it was such a hardship for you to have sex with me. Especially as I'm going to be out of your hair for a couple of weeks.'

It was the Saturday night before he was to leave. They had slipped away from work early, Leo would have frowned upon that had he known, but there was no late breaking news, and this was their last chance to be together before he went to Iraq. Every night this week Jo had put him off, for one reason or another, but she'd finally run out of excuses. She'd relented tonight when he told her he wouldn't be able to stay long because his wife had planned a family dinner at home.

Jo propped herself up on one elbow to look at him. 'It's not a hardship, Lachlan. I just thought you didn't have much time. But I don't mind, if you want to.'

He frowned at her. 'Such enthusiasm.'

'Look, I told you I was tired. I can't help the way I feel.'

'No, you can't, can you?' He held her gaze for several moments. 'There's something I want to ask you, but I think you'll get annoyed if I do.'

Jo lowered her eyes. 'Well, you shouldn't ask a question if you're not prepared to hear the answer.'

He sighed deeply. 'Something's changed, it feels like you've lost interest.'

'I'm just tired, Lach, how many times do I have to say it?'

'I'm not only talking about tonight,' he said. 'It's been happening for a while now.' He seemed hesitant. 'Ever since Bannister came on the scene.'

'Christ, Lachlan!' she exclaimed, lying back flat on the bed.

'See, I said you'd get annoyed.'

'Well, you were right about that at least.'

He shifted onto his side, looking down at her. 'So I'm not right about . . .'

'What?' she prompted, arching her eyebrow.

'You know what I'm trying to say.'

'And you're not normally so reticent.'

'Or you, defensive,' he countered.

'Why are you doing this tonight, Lachlan?' she pleaded. 'I don't want to fight with you before you go away.'

'Okay, you're right.' He reached over to stroke her arm. 'Are we still . . . Do you . . . What's going to happen when I get back?'

'I can't do this now,' said Jo, throwing off the covers as she got up out of bed.

'Are you talking about us?' he said accusingly, sitting up.

She pulled on a robe. 'This is all because someone else paid me a bit of attention, and he happens to be male, and you can't stand it. Lachlan, are you forgetting you have a wife, who I've never bitched about, or been jealous of, because I came into this with my eyes open. What we have is here, right now, when we're together. Beyond that, there is no "us".'

Lachlan was listening intently. 'What if that's not enough any more?'

Jo's heart was racing. 'What are you saying?'

He scratched his head. 'I don't know, I don't know what I'm saying.'

'Do you want to break up?' she asked tentatively.

'No!' he insisted. 'Is that what you want?'

Bloody hell. Why did this have to come up now?

'Lachlan, I don't even understand what you're talking about, you brought this up.'

He leaned back against the bedhead. 'Never mind, I'm just feeling a little antsy, I guess.'

Jo softened. 'About Monday?'

He nodded, giving her a plaintive look. She walked around his side of the bed and sat facing him. 'You're not going to try and be a hero or do anything crazy, are you, Lach?'

He gave a half-hearted laugh, stroking her arm. 'Who, me? You know me better than that.'

He drew closer to kiss her, and Jo realised she was forcing it again. Lachlan was a good kisser, it was one of his better attributes, but her heart wasn't in it any more. Maybe he sensed it, she didn't know for sure, but he drew back first.

'I better get going,' he said huskily. 'Sandra will be waiting.'

'Yes, she will.'

J O   L I D D E L L

B I T C H

Something has gone awry in the world. Perhaps you already knew that, but I have the figures to prove it.

At the height of the Iraq war, the US was spending $2 billion a week, to achieve what exactly? The displacement of 4 million Iraqis? 30,000 US casualties? Collateral damage running into billions of dollars?

While all this was happening, Americans spent over $38 billion per year on their pets, with specialty pet spas and hotels experiencing a major boom.

Before you get smug, Australians are just as good at spending up big on unnecessary crap, like almost $1 billion on unwanted Christmas gifts each year. Yes, you

read that right. A population of just over 20 million people manages to spend one billion dollars, most of it over the space of a few weeks in December, on stuff no one wants. Little wonder we share in over $30 billion of credit card debt in this country, paying interest on stuff that someone will put on eBay, so someone else can go into further debt to buy it.

Yet, before we were shamed into doing more, Australia initially pledged a paltry $7.5 million to the voluntary fund set up under the Kyoto Protocol to assist poor nations, which is actually the amount we spend on airconditioners and desk fans every two days. Every two days.

We spend $13 billion on

gambling a year in Australia, where a full one-fifth of the poker machines in the world can be found, because after all, it's a lucrative source of revenue for the government. As are cigarettes, which net the government in excess of $5 billion a year in taxes. So although smoking is the leading cause of death, it more than pays for itself, particularly when you take into account – and they do – that fewer smokers are around to burden the health system into advanced old age.

I could go on, and that's the really tragic part, I could go on, and on.

bitch@thetribune.com

Sunday

Jo realised she had just read the same line over again for the third time and she still didn't know what it said. The article was about Renee Zellweger and whether she was going to sign up for a third instalment of Bridget Jones, for which she would have to gain the usual amount of weight, and then lose it on camera as Bridget prepares for her wedding, only to put all of it back on again after she's left at the altar.

Why was she even reading this?

Because she was bored. Clearly. It was Sunday and she had nothing to do. All of Angie's spare time lately had been taken up with her new best friends in the drama group she'd met through Will Bannister. She was currently helping them clean up what they liked to euphemistically call their performance space. Angie had invited her to join them when Jo had phoned earlier to suggest a movie. Or something. Anything but cleaning that smelly old condemned shack. She was not that desperate.

Visiting Belle was out, she was at some neighbour's kid's christening. And Lachlan was still away, not that she would have seen him on a Sunday anyway. That was a fairly sacrosanct family day, as it should be.

Jo had flirted with the idea of calling Bannister, but it seemed too forward. Because flirting was about all that was going on between them at this juncture, despite the fact that the mouse was away. Jo was a bit stumped by it all. She had expected him to make his move once Lachlan was out of the picture, or at least out of the office, but nothing had changed. Still lots of smiles and winks, little jokey, flirty exchanges here and there, and that was about it. He hadn't even asked her out for coffee. Nothing. Was he waiting for her to make the first move? Well Jo wasn't so sure that she wanted to. Belle was right, she hadn't had a regular boyfriend for a long time, and there was a reason for that. In fact many reasons. Her brain would go into instant replay mode and start compiling a long list every time she thought about it. So while this thing with Bannister seemed to have a life of its own, Jo was happy to go along for the ride and see where it went, but to take over the wheel was way too daunting.

And so here she was, alone on a Sunday afternoon with nothing to do except lounge around and read the papers. Which always sounded good in theory, particularly on days when she was run off her feet, but was boring as all get-out in reality. She sighed loudly, gazing down at her feet where they were propped on the coffee table. Maybe she could paint her toenails. Was she really that bored? Yes, she really was, but still, there had to be something better to do than paint one's toenails.

Jo yawned, stretched and sighed loudly again. Then silence. This place really was quiet. She couldn't even hear footsteps in other apartments, doors banging, water running. She supposed everyone was out. It was a beautiful spring day after all. Why would anyone hang around in their apartment?

Her mobile rang into the silence. Hallelujah! She jumped up and ran around in circles for a minute before she realised it was in her handbag. She retrieved it finally, holding it to her ear.

'Hello?'

'Hi Jo.'

It was Bannister. Her heart dropped down into her stomach and then shot back up and lodged in her throat when she tried to speak. Which was really quite a ridiculous overreaction.

'It's Joe . . .'

She swallowed. 'Yeah, I realise. How's it going?'

'It's going okay,' he said. 'I just read your column.'

'Oh?'

'It was very good.'

'I'm glad you think so,' she said. 'I had to fight for it.'

'What do you mean?'

'Leo thought it was much too heavy for my flimsy little column.'

'But you won out in the end?'

'Yes, I did.'

'Well, good for you,' he said. 'We should celebrate.'

'Pardon?' Her heart jumped again.

'What are you up to today?'

Don't sound pathetic. Or desperate. 'Oh, well, I've finally scored one of those days where I have absolutely nothing to do but read the papers and veg out. I'm hovering somewhere between heaven and nirvana.'

'Oh,' he said, like he hadn't expected that. 'So I wouldn't be able to talk you into getting off your couch and out into the sunshine?'

Of course you could. 'Depends on what you're suggesting,' she said demurely.

'How does rollerblading sound?'

'Like something from a lame eighties movie starring a guy called Corey with a mullet and a bad attitude.'

He laughed. 'Okay, but seriously –'

'Oh but you can't be serious if you're talking about rollerblading.'

'Oh but I am.'

Jo paused. Was he pulling her leg or was he actually suggesting rollerblading for real?

'I think we might be a little past rollerblading, Joe,' she said carefully.

'Speak for yourself. I do it regularly.'

'You do not,' she scoffed.

'Do too. I got into it a few years back in the US. It's good exercise, especially for skiing.'

Jo had always been bemused by the term 'good exercise'. Surely that was an oxymoron? And good exercise that got you ready for even more exercise was plain overkill.

'I was going to do the Bridge,' he was saying, 'but it's such a beautiful day, I thought Manly instead. We could ride over on the ferry. What do you think?'

'Are you still talking about rollerblading?'

'Absolutely, Manly's a great spot for rollerblading.'

God, he really was serious.

'So how about it?' he prompted.

'Thanks, but I don't think so.'

'You don't sound very sure about that.'

'Oh no, I'm quite sure,' she insisted. 'I'd only hold you back, I'm hopeless at that sort of thing.'

'Have you ever rollerbladed before?'

'No.'

'So how do you know you're hopeless?'

'I just know. I'm all thumbs, or toes, or whatever it is.'

'I could teach you.'

'Thanks, but no, I'm good.'

'You might even have fun?'

That was unlikely. A walk might have been nice. Along the boardwalk, by the water . . .

'Come on,' he cajoled, 'you know you want to.'

'I know I don't.'

'Last chance.'

She took a deep breath. 'Thank you, Joe, but I have news-papers to read, a navel to contemplate, that kind of thing. You know how it is.'

'Well, I'm not going to beg.'

'I'm glad to hear it.'

'I'll be off then.'

'Have fun.'

Jo felt a sinking sensation in her chest. She looked down at the newspaper and Ms Zellweger squinted back at her. She really didn't feel like doing nothing, here on her own, all day. But rollerblading?

'Bye Jo.'

'Bye,' she said quietly, hanging up.

Her heart sank all the way down to her feet. Rollerblading of all things.

Yeah, because she was having such a ball right now. And Bannister had finally done something, made an overture. She could hear Belle's voice in her head ... *You can't leave him hanging, you have to give him some kind of response ... he'll move on.*

But why did it have to be *rollerblading*?

She dialled his number and he answered on the first ring.

'I knew you'd change your mind,' he said.

'Ow! Not so tight!'

'Stop whining,' said Joe. He was down on his knees in front of her, fastening the clips on her rollerblades. 'Your boots have to be secure,' he insisted, 'or else your feet will move around too much inside and you could injure yourself.'

'Well, I have no feeling in my feet now, so I suppose they won't be moving around any.' She frowned down at the lurid purple apparatuses encasing her feet, then at the hard plastic lime-green domes strapped to her knees, that matched the smaller versions on her elbows, which were the same colour as the dinky helmet Joe insisted she hire. Of course, he sported no such unsightly accoutrements. He didn't need them, he maintained. Yeah, well he didn't need to be so smug about it either.

'Is it too late to change my mind back?' Jo asked.

'Yes it is,' he said, standing up. 'Don't be a spoilsport.'

'But I feel self-conscious,' she said. 'I'm not seeing a whole lot of rollerblading going on.'

'You will,' he assured her. 'Come on, this'll be fun.'

She considered him dubiously as he held his hands out to help her up. She grabbed both hands firmly, but as soon as she lifted her bottom off the bench, her feet gave way underneath her and she shrieked as her legs shot forward between Joe's. He managed to grab her before she fell flat on her back, but he was laughing so hard he couldn't lift her upright again. She was forced to just hang there, Joe straddling her while he held her round her waist and she clung to him around his neck. It was a compromising position, to say the least.

'Will you stop laughing and help me up?' she gasped.

He took a deep breath before he straightened himself, hoisting her up so that her feet actually left the ground. Then he settled her back down gently, gradually letting her take her own weight, but not releasing her. His arms were fastened securely around her like a harness. There may have been method in his madness choosing this rollerblading caper after all.

'You can let go of me now,' she insisted.

'No I can't, you'll fall down.'

He was right; she couldn't seem to keep her legs steady, the boots kept sliding away from her on the smooth pavement.

'Well how am I supposed to do this?' she shrilled.

'You just have to relax, Jo.'

'Easy for you to say.'

'You have to get used to the feel of the boots and the way they move.'

'They seem to be moving any old way they want. It's like I've got a pair of shopping trolleys strapped to my feet.'

'That's because you're reacting to every slight movement,' said Joe. 'You have to move with them, not against them; use just the right amount of control so that you can find your own natural rhythm.'

She groaned. 'I have no idea what you're talking about.'

'Okay,' he said. Their faces were so close his forehead was resting against her helmet. 'I'm going to let go of you now, but not altogether,' he assured her. She felt his hands move to take hold of her hips. 'I won't let you fall,' he promised as he carefully shifted away from her so there was space between them, though her own hands were still firmly clenched together around his neck. 'Now, put your hands on my shoulders and let your arms rest along my arms. And relax,' he added.

Jo moved her hands to his shoulders, consciously relaxing the muscles in her arms. She hadn't realised how tense she had become. He talked her through releasing the tension in her shoulders, her back, her legs, until she felt more at ease. 'Look, see, you're not shaking any more,' he pointed out.

Jo realised she was standing squarely on her own feet, he was only supporting her lightly.

'Now bend your knees a little, and lean towards me.'

He instructed her to do scissor movements with her legs, slowly sliding one foot back and one forward to get used to the roller action of the boots. When she could manage that, he got her to transfer her weight from one foot to the other and back again in a steady rhythm, allowing the boot to roll forward a little each time.

'And we have lift-off,' Joe said after a while.

She realised they were actually moving along. Which made her wobble violently and clench his shoulders.

'A-ah,' he admonished. 'Relax, you were doing great.'

'Until you told me I was moving,' said Jo. 'You're doing this, aren't you?'

'We both are,' said Joe. 'I'm doing exactly the same as you, only backwards. Now, can you slide your hands down so you're holding onto my forearms?'

'I don't know,' she said warily. 'I'm okay like this.'

'You'll be fine.'

'Are you going to let go of me?'

'Jo,' he said, bringing them to a halt, 'I won't let go, not until you're ready. You have to trust me.'

He didn't realise what a big ask that was. She took a breath. 'Okay.' She moved her hands from his shoulders to his forearms and held on.

'Not quite so tight, Jo.'

'Sorry', she said, loosening her grip. They started to move again, with Bannister chanting in a quiet voice, 'Weight on one foot, now the other . . . one foot . . . the other . . .' He kept it up, like a mantra, interspersed occasionally with 'Lean forward', or 'Bend your knees', or, her least favourite, 'Don't stick your backside out so far'. After a while, Jo realised they were proceeding at quite a respectable pace. She was, in fact, rollerblading. She let out an excited little laugh.

'You're doing great,' Joe said, smiling at her. 'Are you ready for the next step?'

'I don't want to let go.'

'You don't have to let go. Just hold my hands instead.'

She looked up at him uncertainly.

'You can do it,' he reassured her.

She took a breath and released her grip on his forearms, sliding her hands down to clasp his.

'Now relax your arms,' he reminded her. 'You're tensing up again. And don't forget to breathe.'

'Don't go too fast,' she warned.

'I won't, I promise.'

They continued along at a steady pace, with Bannister reminding her to relax and lean forward every so often when she got a little wobbly. Soon Jo felt she had a good rhythm going, she was even enjoying herself.

'So are you ready?' Joe asked.

'What next?' she looked alarmed. 'I told you I don't want you to let go.'

'I won't let go,' he assured her. 'But I think you're ready for one hand.'

'You do?'

'I do,' he nodded.

Jo took a deep breath in and out. 'Okay.'

'So I'm just going to let go of your right hand and swing around out of your way till I'm beside you. You don't have to do a thing,' said Joe, 'and I'll have hold of your left hand the whole time. Okay?'

'Okay,' said Jo, frowning with concentration. 'What do I do with my free hand once you let go?'

He smiled. 'Nothing special. Whatever feels natural.'

'Okay.'

'Ready?'

'Ready.'

Joe loosened his grip till he was barely touching her fingers. Then he let go, falling back in step beside her. 'How was that?'

She glanced sideways, not ready to turn her head to look at him. 'Okay, so far.'

He kept a firm hold of her hand and stayed in step with her, gradually encouraging her to pick up the pace. Jo looked out at the water to her right and breathed in deeply. She felt the breeze lifting her hair, and she felt oddly happy. Free. Unfettered. And then she heard her own voice cry out, 'Whoo!' She never 'whooed' or anything like it. She glanced at Joe, who was grinning broadly at her.

'Having a good time?' he asked.

'I am,' she called back. 'I really am.'

'I knew you would.'

She smiled happily, looking forward again just as a whole group on rollerblades rounded a bend ahead and came hurtling towards them.

Jo shrieked. 'What do I do?'

'Don't panic, they'll go around you.'

'But I can't let go.' Her focus disintegrated, along with her bravado. Her legs started wobbling furiously and she felt herself losing balance. She was going to fall and end up sprawled out in front of the advancing troops bearing down upon her. Along with her own life flashing before her eyes, Jo saw the rollerbladers falling like tenpins, limbs flailing about in every direction, bones snapping, skin scraping on pavement. The only thing she could do, the only recourse left to her, was to close her eyes and squeal like a girl.

At that moment she was suddenly scooped up and over to one side, becoming momentarily airborne before falling to the ground with a thud. Jo opened her eyes and she was looking at the sky. She was lying on top of a body, Bannister's she assumed. She hoped.

'Are you all right?'

'I will be when you get off me.'

'Oh, sure,' she said, shifting onto the grass beside him. 'Sorry about that. I guess I just froze.'

'They would have gone around you.'

'They didn't look like they were going to go round me. They looked like they were going to mow me down where I stood.'

He shook his head. 'Everyone's not out to get you, Jo.'

She was not so sure of that. She began to undo her helmet, but she couldn't work out the clasp. He leaned over, hooking his fingers under the strap around her chin and releasing it. 'Thanks,' she said.

They lay back against the grassy bank edging the boardwalk while Jo caught her breath. After a while she turned her head to peer at him. 'Are you really okay? It felt like we landed pretty heavily.'

He shrugged. 'I'm tough, I can take it. How about you, are you all right?'

'I'm fine,' she said, a giggle escaping from her throat. 'You broke my fall.' For some reason that amused her and she started to laugh, a joyous, unadulterated belly laugh. And pretty soon Bannister started to laugh too. Jo gazed up at the sky, laughing till tears trickled from the corners of her eyes, till her stomach ached, till she couldn't laugh any more. She sighed a vast, contented sigh, and threw her hands back over her head.

'Ready for another go?' he asked.

'Soon,' she replied. 'I just want to lie here for a while.'

Jo would never have imagined in a million years she'd be spending the day learning to rollerblade. Wait till Ange got wind of it. She hadn't done anything like this since . . . she couldn't remember when. She'd forgotten the exhilaration of doing something just because it was fun. Everything always had to have a higher purpose, an important objective. It was the way of the world. Wasting time had become the cardinal sin of the new millennium. But how could this be wasting time when she hadn't felt so good in ages?

'I'm glad you talked me into this,' she said eventually.

'Me too.'

'I never do stuff like this.'

'You don't say?'

She elbowed him. 'Not just rollerblading, obviously, I mean . . . playing, I guess. Having fun just for the sake of it.' When she thought about it, she realised that perhaps she'd never learned how in the first place. Her childhood had not exactly been a time of carefree fun and games. When she did create games with Belle, they were often to protect or distract her little sister. It occurred to Jo she'd been a grown-up for a very long time.

'Come on,' said Joe after a while, interrupting her reverie. 'You're going have to start all over again if we don't get you moving again soon.'

Forty minutes later, Jo finally declared her thigh muscles could take no more. Bannister suggested they find somewhere to eat, but Jo worried that if she sat down for any length of time she was likely to seize up and he would be forced to carry her home in a sitting position.

'Best keep you moving then,' he agreed.

They returned the gear to the hire shop and stopped to buy salad wraps at a place on the Corso, before crossing back over to the beach and down onto the sand.

'Can I ask you something?' she said after a while.

'Sure.'

'It might be a little nosy,' she warned.

'I said you can ask, I didn't say I'd answer.'

'Fair enough.' She paused, thinking of the right way to put it. 'It's about Sarah, your ex . . .'

'What about her?'

'Well, you were a bit cagey about the details.'

He laughed. 'I was a bit cagey? That's rich, coming from you.'

'It's also a little rich to criticise me for being cagey if you're going to persist in being cagey yourself.'

'Touché.' He shook his head with a smile. 'What do you want to know?'

'You said it was an amicable break, that you just drifted apart?'

'That's right.'

'But then you said you don't have any contact with her any more. Why is that?'

He shrugged. 'I don't have any reason to. We're on opposite sides of the world, we don't have anything to do with each other.'

Jo thought about it. 'Do you keep in touch with anyone else you knew overseas?'

'Sure, I was a correspondent for a long time, I made a lot of friends over the years in different places. I try to keep up with them.'

'But not Sarah, even though you had a lengthy relationship and it ended amicably?'

Joe looked at her sideways. 'Okay,' he admitted. 'It probably didn't end all that amicably, but that wasn't my fault. We'd been drifting apart for a while –'

'So you keep saying.'

'Because it's the truth. We hadn't spent much time together for months. I really had the feeling that we both knew it had to end but we were waiting for the other one to actually pull the plug. So when the first Australian troops started to withdraw, and my dad was getting worse, I told her it was time for me to go home. She started to freak out, saying where did that leave her, what if she didn't want to live in Australia, had I even considered that? I told her I had, and that I didn't think she'd want to come, and then she really blew up.'

'And you weren't expecting that reaction?'

'No way, I was completely thrown. She acted like we were perfectly happy and had planned our whole future together, and I was some kind of bastard dumping her out of the blue.'

It seemed a bit odd to Jo that they could have been so out of kilter. Bannister sounded genuine, but what if he was just as myopic as the next bloke, only able to see things from his own narrow perspective, and completely clueless about what his part-ner may or may not have expected?

'Why do you think she acted that way?' Jo asked.

'It was all about having a baby in the end. She said I'd led her on to believe that we'd settle down and have kids together. She said I was a typical commitment-phobe, and she'd wasted the best years of her life on me, by which she meant her childbearing years.'

'And you had no idea this was what she was feeling?'

Joe looked at her. 'You keep asking the same question in dif-ferent ways,' he said. 'You're on her side, aren't you?'

'I don't even know her,' Jo protested. 'It just sounds like an extreme reaction if you'd never even talked about those things.'

'We had talked, pretty vaguely though, there were never any set plans.' He sighed. 'You know, guys get a raw deal in this debate. I would like to have kids, I do want to "settle down", whatever that means. But in the end, I didn't want to with Sarah. Does that make me a bad person? Does it mean I can't commit? No, I just couldn't commit to *her* in the end. I didn't love her, or love her enough. Surely you can relate to that?'

Jo blinked. 'What's that supposed to mean?'

'You have a very brief marriage behind you,' he said. 'I assume you wish it hadn't happened, that you hadn't jumped into it so quickly?'

'I guess.' She stared out at the ocean, hugging her arms to herself. 'That breeze is starting to pick up.'

'You're being cagey again.'

She didn't look at him. 'And you're being snoopy again.'

He laughed. 'You are the biggest snoop I know, Jo Liddell. You've been angling to find out about Sarah since I first mentioned her, and now you've got the whole story. So why won't you tell me about your ex?'

She shrugged. 'There's nothing to tell. It's just so far in the past, I don't even think about him any more.' They had come to the rocky outcrop at the end of the sweep of beach, and Jo picked her way briskly across to where the waves were breaking. Truth was, she didn't like to talk about Richard because that involved thinking about Richard, and she didn't like to think about Richard.

She stood at the edge of the rock platform, gazing out at the ocean, the waves tossing up a fine spray from time to time. Bannister came to stand beside her. 'Okay, I get the hint, I'll drop it.' He paused, before adding, 'I just can't help wondering what he did to you.'

Jo looked up abruptly. 'Who says he did anything?'

'Angie said you were wounded –'

'Angie thinks life is a soapie.'

Joe shook his head. 'Well, that's it, I'm beat,' he said, raising his hands in defeat. 'You wouldn't want to interview you, you know.'

'That's right, I wouldn't want to interview me, because it would be incredibly boring.'

He regarded her thoughtfully. 'Your mother used to tell you your father left because you didn't behave, and then she would leave you for days at a time to look after your sister when you were only a child yourself. But you survived and eventually graduated from university with first-class honours, and you worked hard and got yourself a position on a metropolitan newspaper, and eventually your own column. But still you always think the worst is going to happen. You only go out with married men so you won't get hurt, supposedly. You put this wall up around yourself so no one can get close, yet you'll sit waiting in a car for hours outside a friend's house just in case he needs you.' He paused. 'You're anything but boring, Jo Liddell.'

Jo's chest tightened, then her throat. And if she wasn't mistaken, tears would come next. She turned abruptly and walked back towards the beach, swiftly negotiating the rocks. She could hear Bannister calling her above the roar of the waves.

'Jo, wait.' He caught up with her, blocking her path. 'I didn't mean to upset you.'

'I'm not upset,' she said, but she couldn't look at him.

'Are you angry with me?' he asked.

She shook her head. It seemed she'd managed to contain the tears, so she lifted her head to look at him. 'Just, no one's ever held a mirror up to me like that before.'

'Well, you should be proud of what you see.'

He met her gaze openly, he wasn't having a dig. She sighed, dropping down onto the sand to sit cross-legged. Joe lowered himself tentatively to sit beside her at a right angle. They sat there in silence for a while, maybe five minutes, maybe longer. He glanced at her from time to time, but she remained staring out to sea, lost in thought.

'I met Richard when I was working in a hotel when I first started uni,' she said eventually.

'Richard?'

'My ex-husband.'

'Jo, you don't have to tell me any of this –'

'Oh, so now you don't want to know?' she said, raising an eyebrow. 'Just let me go on before I change my mind,' she said. 'Richard was the hotel manager and I was waitressing and working the bar part-time. I was only nineteen, he was thirty-eight.'

Joe let out a low whistle. 'A little father fixation there?'

'You hardly have to be Freud to work that out,' Jo said wryly. 'I think I even realised it at the time; after all, I'd been waiting for my father to rescue me all my life. Richard seemed so worldly and confident and strong, and I'd come from so much chaos, I appreciated having someone to lean on, to rely on . . . to make the decisions. I was supporting Belle, we were sharing this tiny flat; she was straight out of school, doing a secretarial course, I was at uni. Charlene had hooked up with a bloke she said was the "one", for probably the one hundredth time, and she kicked us out, told us we were old enough to fend for ourselves.'

Joe just shook his head.

'Anyway Richard invited Belle to live with us when we·got married, but she didn't want to impose; so he paid her rent so she could stay in the same place. I moved into his duplex, but he encouraged me to pick out new furniture, whatever I needed to feel at home.'

'He sounds pretty decent.'

'Doesn't he though?' said Jo, shaking her head. 'I should have picked the signs, I should have been more wary.'

'You were only nineteen.'

'Old enough to realise I was too young and not jumped into marrying him so quickly,' she sighed. 'The first thing I remember that unsettled me was one time when I had my hair dyed. I'd always kept it fairly short, but he encouraged me to grow it a little, just to my shoulders. He made such a fuss about how much he loved my hair, I figured it was a small sacrifice on my part. But I was bored with blonde and decided to get it dyed a kind of auburn colour.' She paused, looking off at nothing. 'When I came home, he freaked, I'd never seen him so angry. He said he'd married a blonde and if I wanted to stay married to him, I had to stay blonde. He insisted I go back to the hairdressers the next day, it's a wonder my hair didn't fall out altogether from all the chemicals. The hairdresser didn't want to do it, but I insisted. I realised I was scared to go home if I wasn't blonde, I was scared.' She crossed her arms in front of herself.

'That was just the start of it. He made me give up my job, because no wife of his was going to work in a bar. I didn't mind, it wasn't my career and it meant I could focus on my study. But then he decided he didn't so much like me studying either. I wasn't around during the day when he was more likely to be home, he worked most nights. So I enrolled in night classes, but then he decided he wanted me available to hostess functions, or to come in and have dinner with him, whenever he clicked his fingers basically. I started to get tired of it, to question him some-times. We started fighting more, I saw an aggressive streak in him that I'd never really noticed before. And finally one day he hit me.'

Joe looked across at her, like he hadn't heard right. 'What did you say?'

'He hit me,' she repeated plainly, 'so hard I fell over. And then he walked out. He didn't even wait to see if I was all right. He just walked out.'

'Were you all right?'

'More or less,' she shrugged. 'I packed up what I could and went to Belle's. Richard arrived on the doorstep the next day. At first he did this whole "I'm sorry, I'll never do it again" spiel, and when that didn't work he got angry. That's when I knew. I'd watched my mother, my whole life, letting men push her around . . .'

Jo paused, taking a deep tremulous breath. 'She'd have them back, again and again. But nothing would ever change, until it'd get so bad we'd be forced to move town. So that's the only way I knew how to deal with it. I told Belle we had to pack up and leave that very night. I knew Richard would make her life hell if I left her behind; besides, he was partially supporting her. She wasn't keen to leave everything, but she knew the drill. And she trusted me. So we came down to Sydney, we didn't even tell Mum where we were till I was sure he'd given up. We both found work; I couldn't go back to uni full-time, though I did a couple of semesters by correspondence over the next few years. Then Belle met Darren, and eventually they moved in together, so that gave me the freedom to go up to Bathurst to finish my degree, finally. We never looked back, but I never trusted myself with men again.'

'Why?' said Joe. 'It wasn't your fault. And you had the sense to get out.'

'But I chose him in the first place,' said Jo, 'and that spooked me. I've read all about abused women who are drawn to violent men, victims of incest who end up with paedophiles, children of alcoholics who marry alcoholics. It's like some kind of self-destructive genetic programming. I didn't trust myself to be able to choose someone who wouldn't hurt me. I didn't trust my instincts. I still don't.'

'Except with married men?'

Jo glanced at him. 'It's not that calculated, Joe,' she said. 'I don't hunt out guys with wedding rings, you know. In fact I didn't go out with anyone for a long time, so long I was like a nun. But you know what they say, a girl has needs.' She smiled faintly. 'There was this guy at the first paper I went to, down in the Riverina. He was nothing like Richard, the polar opposite in fact. He was sweet and very easygoing. Things developed slowly between us, till one day he broke it to me he was married. At first I freaked out and refused to see him any more. He gave me all the usual lines – he and his wife had grown apart, he was staying for the sake of the kids, one day he would leave her . . . and that's when I realised I didn't want him to. I didn't want ownership of his life, and I certainly didn't want to give him ownership over mine. So after a while we picked up again, and then six months later I got a better job offer in a bigger town, and though he was sad to see me leave, he knew he had no say in it. I liked that, having that independence, that kind of autonomy. I realised that I didn't have to put up with being told what to do ever again, at least not in my personal life.'

Joe was listening. 'But I don't get what makes a married man a safer option?' he asked. 'Surely they're just as likely to be abusive or aggressive?'

'Yeah, I guess,' said Jo. 'But the married men I've been with – and just to get the record straight, there was one other since the Riverina and before Lachlan, and that was only for a few months,' she added. 'Anyway, they've been easier, I guess, less demanding. They don't try to control my life because they're trying to keep cover themselves. And it's easier to break it off and walk away.'

She glanced at Bannister. He was staring out at the ocean, a pursed expression on his face. 'You're judging me again, aren't you?' said Jo.

'No,' he shook his head, turning to look at her. 'I was just thinking,' he said carefully, 'how do you know you can't get all that with someone who's not married?'

Jo dropped her eyes. 'I told you, I don't trust my instincts.'

'Maybe your instincts aren't as bad as you think,' he suggested.

'Oh, they are,' she assured him. 'When I left Richard, I shoved everything I owned into a few bags, I didn't have time to sort through it. When we were settled down here, I finally got to go through all my stuff, and I came across love letters we'd written early in the relationship, Valentine cards, that kind of thing. I was so embarrassed at how gullible and stupid I'd been. I had no perspective whatsoever, I was a hopeless, giddy, lovesick fool.'

'You were nineteen and you were in love,' said Joe. 'You're too hard on yourself.'

She shook her head, remembering. 'I sat there that night and ripped the lot to shreds and threw them away.'

'You shouldn't have done that.'

'Why not?' Jo asked, looking at him.

'You should never get rid of old love letters,' he said. 'They're part of who you are. Even your mistakes are part of who you are.'

'Is that how you feel about Sarah?'

'I don't have any ill will towards her. Besides, she's got enough for the both of us.'

They smiled at each other then. They sat in a comfortable silence, watching tiny children playing on the shoreline, running in as the waves withdrew, and squealing and running away as they rushed forward again. The slightly bigger kids ventured a little further, where the water lapped against their thighs or higher as the swell came in. Then there were the sulphur-crested surfers out the back, straddling their boards, their feet dangling in the dark water. Jo wondered how they could sit there so relaxed, only looking for the next wave, not worried about what might be lurking just under the surface.

She rarely ever revisited her life with Richard, even Angie had learned that it was off limits. But today she had talked about it, and she was still standing. Maybe picking at scabs was not advisable, but exposing a wound to fresh air occasionally might just be healing.

'I guess we should think about heading back,' said Joe after a while. 'The ferries run every half an hour, but they'll be packed on a Sunday afternoon.'

The ferry they boarded was certainly packed, but they

managed to squeeze onto a seat outside, facing the water. As they approached the Heads, Jo could feel that the swell had come up considerably since that morning and she immediately tensed up.

'I hate this part,' she muttered, closing her eyes and clutching her arms around herself.

'What? Going past the Heads?' Joe asked, watching her. 'It's only the ocean swell, Jo. Nothing's going to happen, you're perfectly safe.'

'You don't know that. If the swell got big enough, surely it could tip a ferry over.'

He shook his head. 'There's never been a recorded incident of a ferry capsizing because of the swell coming through the Heads.'

Jo opened her eyes and peered at him. 'Is that true?'

'Look it up for yourself.'

Just then the ferry lurched as it hit a particularly large set, and Jo gasped, closing her eyes again.

'Here.' He took her hand and tucked her arm securely under his. 'If it goes down, we'll go together.'

'How does that make it any better?'

'Well, at least you won't be alone,' he said. 'And besides, I'm a strong swimmer.'

Jo opened her eyes, staring at him as he gazed out to sea. The ferry ploughed through the set, then on past South Head and into calmer waters. She felt his grip on her hand relax, and she took that as a signal to disengage herself. But he gave her a wistful smile as she did.

'I'm going to break it off with Lachlan,' Jo said suddenly.

'Pardon?'

'I'm going to break it off with Lachlan,' she repeated. 'I decided before he left. I just wanted to wait till he got back from Iraq.'

Joe nodded faintly, taking it in. 'Why are you telling me?'

'Because,' she hesitated, 'I guess I wanted to put it on the record.'

They looked at each other for a long moment. Jo held his gaze, she didn't waver.

'Thanks for letting me know,' he said finally.

She nodded, looking back out over the water. They were sitting very close, she could feel where his body came into contact with hers. She could feel the sun on her face. And she felt content.

'You don't know for sure that no ferries have ever capsized, do you?' she asked after a while.

'No,' he admitted. 'But I'm pretty sure. You can Google it, find out.'

She smiled. 'Maybe it's better if I don't.'

It was a long slow queue off the ferry when they eventually docked at Circular Quay. But Jo wasn't bothered. As they walked up out of the terminal, she saw flowers blooming in planter boxes along the Quay. She'd never noticed them before. Or the gardens over in front of the MCA. There were new leaves on the trees out the front of Customs House; young girls were wearing flimsy dresses and strappy shoes, their legs bare. Spring always held that sense of promise, that things had a chance to start all over again, fresh. Something had definitely shifted since Jo was lying on her couch this morning. A butterfly had flapped its wings somewhere and now everything was subtly transformed. And clearer, so much clearer. She wanted to be with Bannister . . . with Joe. Preferably as soon as humanly possible.

'You know what?' she said, looking up at him. 'I don't think I can face walking any further. My legs have had it. Do you want to share a taxi?'

'Sure.'

It would only take a few minutes to get to her place, the traffic was relatively light in the city at this time of the afternoon on a weekend. Jo spent the short trip rehearsing how to say 'Would you like to come up?' so that it didn't sound rehearsed, so that it sounded casual, even if she was feeling anything but casual. She really wanted him to come up. She really wanted him. What was she so worried about? She doubted she was going to have to talk him into it, he was a man, after all. They pulled up at traffic lights, a block away from her street. Maybe she should say it now.

'I had a really good time today,' said Joe before she had the chance. 'I'm glad you decided to come.'

That threw her. The only reply she could think of was 'It doesn't have to end yet', which was too clichéd for words.

She nodded lamely. 'Have you got plans later?'

'Yeah, I do actually,' he said, watching her. 'I'm going home, up to the mountains.'

She looked . . . thrown. Oh crap. She was going to ask him up when they got to her place, he just realised. Crap. He'd had no idea this morning that this was how things were going to turn out, or he would have . . . what? All week he'd been working himself up to ask her out, even just for coffee, but every time he tried to approach her there was someone hanging around, or else he couldn't find her in the first place. Truth was, he kept freezing up, she had this effect on him . . . As the week flew by, he knew he had to do something before he went up to the mountains, because by the time he got back, his not-so-grand gesture of the week before was going to be barely more than a distant memory. *Crap.*

He had to give her some kind of explanation. 'I finally talked Mim into going away for a few days,' he said. 'She's barely left that house in years –'

'Just up there on the left,' Jo instructed the taxi driver.

'Anyway,' he continued, 'she's off to some poetry symposium in Melbourne. I have to get up there tonight because she's leaving at the crack of dawn tomorrow, you know, it's a long way back down to the airport, and her flight's at, like, ten or something.' Jesus, he was just babbling now. But she wasn't saying anything. Why wasn't she saying anything? She was upset. And it was his fault. He'd stuffed up again.

Jo opened the door even before the taxi had fully come to a stop. She had to get out of here. She felt like crying. Screw him.

'Jo, wait –'

'Oh, sorry,' she shook her head, rummaging for her wallet in her bag. 'I'll give you some money for the taxi.'

'Don't be silly, I've got it.'

'Okay then.' She leapt out and swung around to look at him. 'See you,' she said, slamming the door.

'Where to, sir?'

Joe watched her skitter over to the entrance of her building and then disappear inside.

'Sir?'

He looked at the taxi driver

'Where to?'

'You know what,' he said, reaching for his wallet, 'I think I'll get out here too.'

Joe didn't fail to notice the knowing smile on the face of the driver as he paid him, before he dashed out of the taxi and over to the door. He could see Jo in the foyer still, waiting for the elevator. He banged on the glass and she looked around. She seemed to hesitate for a moment, before she walked slowly over to the door and opened it, stepping outside to stand in front of him. She didn't say anything, she just stared up at him expectantly.

'I have to go, Jo.'

He saw her shoulders drop. 'You already said that. Why would you come back to say it again?'

He took a breath. 'Because every time I've walked away from you lately, there's been something I've wanted to do, and I haven't because I wasn't sure how you'd take it. And every time I've regretted it.'

'What are you talking about?'

Okay, this was it. The grand romantic gesture. Will had better be right.

'This.' He pulled her into his arms, and although he heard a mild gasp, she didn't resist him. Their mouths met with fluky precision, there was no colliding of teeth or noses. Her body was a little tense, but then he felt her relax in his arms, melting into him. And then he became conscious of her lips, and tasted her mouth, and it was as good as he'd always imagined it would be. Better.

He wanted her so badly . . . okay, he had to stop. This couldn't go anywhere now. He had to stop. He felt her hands slide around him, her body pressing against his. In a sec. Just a little longer. Her tongue slipped into his mouth and entwined around his . . . Oh God, he really had to stop.

He started to draw back from her lips, reluctantly, gradually breaking away. He opened his eyes to look down at her. Her head was resting in the crook of his arm, her beautiful, beautiful eyes were glassy as she gazed up at him. He smoothed his hand around her face, his thumb across her lips.

'I'm sorry I have to go,' he said huskily.

'It's okay,' she breathed.

'I really wish I didn't.' He couldn't resist her. One more kiss. But this time he kept it short and sweet, definitely no tongue. Then he held her close, pressing his cheek against hers. He could feel her heart beating hard. This was going to be a long week.

He finally released her, taking hold of her hands. 'So, I'll see you . . . end of the week . . . I'll call . . .' He brought her hand up to his lips and kissed her palm. She was smiling at him, like she'd never smiled at him before.

He stepped backwards, till he had to let go. 'Bye.'

'Bye Joe.' He liked it when she called him Joe. She leaned against the door, watching him. He backed away slowly, till finally he turned and walked up the street. He could feel her eyes tracking him. When he got to the corner, he turned to look at her again. She was still leaning against the door, still watching him. She raised her hand in a wave. He smiled and waved back, as he walked around the corner and out of sight.

J O   L I D D E L L

BITCH

Have you noticed the gardens around Circular Quay? Have you ever once lifted your head as you've swarmed with the rest of the hive off the ferry through the turnstiles before being swallowed up into the cavernous corridors of the CBD?

Well, stop and take a look tomorrow. In fact, take five minutes to detour over towards the MCA perhaps, or to linger in the forecourt of Customs House. It'll put a spring in your step, I guarantee you.

Or better still, take fifteen minutes to walk through the Botanic Gardens. It's springtime, people! What time is that, you say? Time to stop and smell the roses!

Aren't you sick of scurrying about like a rat in a sewer? Why are we all working so hard? Who are we trying to impress? What are we trying to prove? Is this how you thought life was going to be?

What are we here for anyway? Jerry Seinfeld expressed it well when he was asked to address a graduation ceremony some time ago. He came up with three rules for life. First, he said, "Bust your ass." Okay, putting aside the American vernacular, we get it, and we're all pretty much doing that already. Just make sure you're doing it because it's what you want to do, because it brings you joy and satisfaction, not because you help line the pockets of some faceless corporation, where you're barely more than a cog in the wheel.

But what's the alternative, I hear you ask? Get a life. A real life. Have fun, stop being so serious. Waste time. Play. That's right, play. It shouldn't be just kids who have all the fun. What's the point of growing up if all we get to do is work and have all the responsibility?

Secondly, Mr Seinfeld said, "Pay attention." Check out those flowers tomorrow. Smile at the people who pass you, look them in the eye and give them a real shock, say hello.

And thirdly, says Seinfeld, "Fall in love." Couldn't agree more.

bitch@thetribune.com

'What the hell is this?'

'I gather it's my column, Leo,' Jo said calmly.

He had summoned her to his office, and he was standing on the other side of his desk, waving a piece of paper with obvious disdain. Jo had emailed her column to him after she'd written it on Sunday evening, after Joe had left her standing outside her building. After he'd kissed her. She'd been a bundle of nervous energy and it had just come pouring out.

'The column's called "Bitch", Jo, not "Barf",' Leo was saying.

'I am aware of the name of my column, Leo.'

'So how is this piece of motivational tripe a bitch?'

'It's a bitch about being stuck on the treadmill, and an exhortation to get off it occasionally —'

'And smell the roses?' he said, the sarcasm dripping from his voice. 'You've been reading too many of those little books with the nature photographs and the saccharine slogans.'

Jo sighed. 'What do you want me to do, Leo?' she said in a level voice.

'I want you to rewrite it,' he said plainly. 'Make it ... I don't know ... make it a piece about the time and money the city council spends maintaining those gardens. And the water, yeah, make it about the water. While the rest of us have to suffer under draconian water restrictions and plant drab natives in our gardens, council gaily abandons such restrictions themselves, planting water-hungry annuals that will be dug up and discarded in a few weeks. There you go, there's your bitch.'

Though that would have normally made her blood boil, Jo was serenely unaffected. Not even Leo could drag her down today. Nothing could drag her down.

It was all because of that kiss. Jo had not been kissed like that in a long time, if ever. She hadn't seen it coming, she was too busy feeling frustrated and annoyed with herself that she'd built her hopes up like that. See, if Lachlan had been unable to come up, she couldn't have given a flying fig, such was life with a married man. But pin your hopes on someone who's available and they're bound to get dashed. She shouldn't have risked it, she told herself as she stood waiting for the lift, feeling sick in the stomach and sore in the hamstrings and disappointed on a level she'd never experienced with Lachlan. It wasn't worth it.

Then he was banging on the glass. Jo had frozen momentarily, before forcing herself to put one foot in front of the other and walk out to meet him. It was all a bit of a blur, like when someone has an accident and their brain wipes out the events leading up to it. Not that Jo had suffered any trauma. Hardly. And she could remember the kiss perfectly. The way he caught her in his arms and held her just right, and their lips met as though they'd rehearsed it, like a scene in a movie or something. It was the most romantic kiss Jo had ever experienced, and she had thought she was immune to romance.

'It literally took my breath away,' she told Angie, still with a measure of dreamy disbelief, when they'd met for breakfast at Oliver's that morning.

'I've never heard you talk like this,' said Angie, 'and it's beginning to freak me out.'

Jo suddenly felt self-conscious. 'I sound lame, don't I?'

'No! Not a bit,' she insisted. 'I was only joking.'

'No, this is really schoolgirlie, isn't it?' Angie tried to protest but Jo forged ahead. 'I'm building it up too much. So he kissed

me, and he's a good kisser, a really good kisser. Doesn't mean anything. We're adults, not teenagers, it was just a kiss –'

'Oh shut up, would you, Jo?' Angie groaned.

Jo blinked at her.

'I mean, come on, sometimes things just aren't that difficult to
read. Joe kissed you, no one forced him, you didn't even expect
it, so I think that means he probably wanted to kiss you, which
means he probably likes you. It's not rocket science, Jo.'

Just vaguely terrifying.

'In fact, some people might actually think it was a good thing,'
she went on. 'I for one – if I was to be gathered up into the arms
of a gorgeous bloke and kissed into the middle of next week,
well, I think I'd probably enjoy that.'

'Sorry, you're right,' Jo sighed. 'I sound like a prat. I'm sorry.'

'Oh, don't listen to me,' Angie dismissed. 'I'm happy for you, I
really am.' She paused. 'It's just that every now and then it hits me
that I'm alone, and will most likely remain alone, and when your
best friend falls in love, well, that's one of those times.'

Jo was about to refute the falling in love part, but this was
about Angie now. 'You're not going to be alone forever, Ange.'

'Mm, I guess only time will tell. We'll see who's right on our
ninetieth birthdays, shall we?'

Jo decided to avoid the detour into self-pity and take her on
a more pleasant route. 'Enough about that, it's your turn. Tell me
about Sandwich Man.'

'There's nothing to tell,' she shrugged. 'And we both know
there never has been.'

Jo frowned.

'I actually finally struck up a conversation with him the other
day,' said Angie, 'and he was just plain rude, like I was bothering
him. I've made that man's lunch several times a week for the past
year. And you know what I realised? He's never even seen me.'
She paused, staring into space. 'You know that saying, "Boys don't
make passes at girls who wear glasses"? Well, they don't even see
fat girls. Ironic, isn't it, when we're actually pretty hard to miss.'

'Angie, you're not fat!' Jo insisted. 'You're . . . voluptuous and
luscious and –'

'I think the particular "ou" word you're searching for is *round*.'

'An-*gie!*'

'Jo-o!' she mimicked. 'I love my female friends, I really do, you all tell me I've got a pretty face and lovely hair and my weight is no obstacle, but get real!' She slapped the side of her thigh. 'This is a bloody big obstacle in the course of true love.'

'Only if you allow it to be,' Jo said.

Angie shook her head. 'That's bullshit, Jo. And not only that, it's insulting,' she said seriously. 'You think it's our attitude that's the problem, that fat girls don't want love the same as everyone else? You're going to blame us for that as well? Everyone has their insecurities, their secret shame, their guilty pleasures. But when you're overweight, yours are out there for all the world to see. You can't hide in the closet because you can't fit in the closet. And so everyone has an opinion about you on the basis of your dress size. In the world we inhabit,' she slapped her thigh again, 'this means I must be lazy, I have no self-control and, worst of all, if I have a thick waist I probably have a thick head as well.'

'But none of that is true.'

'When did truth ever have anything to do with anything?' she declared. 'Do you think there'd be a market for gossip rags if people cared about the truth?'

Jo was staring across the table, her mind ticking over. 'I'm going to write a column about this.'

'Great,' Angie said wryly. 'That'll change everything.'

Jo blinked at her.

'No offence, sweetie, write your column,' said Angie, 'and some of us will feel momentarily better about ourselves, while a few bigots might think twice, for a week or so. But nothing's really going to change, not in my lifetime.' She smiled blithely, picking up her coffee cup.

Jo watched her, frowning. This wasn't like Angie. Something was wrong. 'What's happened, Ange?'

'Nothing, ignore me,' she dismissed. 'I'm just bitter and twisted.'

'But you're not, you never are, no matter what happens,' said Jo. 'What's the matter?'

Angie sighed, putting her cup down on the table again. 'I missed another audition, which, as we all know, is the story of my life. But I really wanted this part. It was only a small one, but it was ongoing, in a six-part series commissioned for SBS.' She smiled ruefully. 'Probably no one will even see it, but I didn't care if this was going to be my break, or what it would lead to, I just wanted to do it so bad. I wanted to play that character, I knew I could do it, and that I could do it well. I felt like the part had been written for me, so did my agent.'

'So what happened?'

'The producers gave it to a slim little whippet,' she said. 'You'd probably recognise her, she does a lot of tampon ads. But the part didn't require good looks, or any particular body type, it could have been played by anyone. So why did the skinny girl have to get it, she can go for so many parts that I can't.' Angie groaned. 'God, I sound like a child. It's not fair, miss, I haven't had a turn yet!'

'You don't sound like that,' Jo reassured her. 'It sucks, it completely sucks, Ange.'

She sat there, staring at her cup. 'You know, the thing is, that part made me remember why I went into acting in the first place. Because I love it, I love getting lost inside a character.' She sighed. 'But instead I do dog-food commercials and walk-ins as a waitress and spend most of my time making sandwiches for stuck-up nobs who think I'm beneath them.'

'Oh, Ange.'

'Now look what I've done,' she said, and Jo could almost see the bubbles rising to the surface as her humour returned. 'I've been a big fat downer raining on your parade.'

'No,' Jo said seriously. 'I'm worried about you.'

'Oh stop,' she scoffed. 'I'm just having a whinge. And I've got it off my chest now, so let's go back to that kiss.'

'No, we've done that kiss to death, it's not such a big deal.'

'Oh, yes it is!' she exclaimed. 'It was a wonderful breathtaking kiss, and that should be celebrated.'

'What should be celebrated?' said Oliver, swooping down on them. 'Am I going to have to get the apricot tux out of mothballs? Has Roasted-Goat's-Cheese finally come to the party?'

Angie grinned. 'He hasn't been Roasted-Goat's-Cheese for ages, Oliver.'

'He'll always be Roasted-Goat's-Cheese to me,' he said. 'So, come on, what's the goss?'

'The goss is all about Jo.'

His eyes lit up. 'Budge, petal,' he said, sliding into the booth next to Angie, opposite Jo, looking at her expectantly. 'Come on, out with it, I haven't got all day.'

'There's not a lot to say,' said Jo. 'Nothing's really happened.'

'With whom?'

Jo hesitated. 'If I tell you, you have to promise me you won't breathe a word, Oliver, he works at the *Trib*.'

Oliver pulled a face. 'Oh, not another married one?'

'No!' She was really getting a reputation. 'It's only because, like I said, nothing's really happened –'

'What about the kiss?' Angie pointed out.

'There was a kiss?'

'Such a kiss,' said Angie, 'it took her breath away. Her words.'

Oliver was beaming. 'So who's the lucky man?'

'You promise you won't say anything?'

He mimed locking his lips and throwing away the key. He was so gay.

Jo glanced surreptitiously around the room, then leaned in closer, her voice low. 'His name's Joe Bannister.'

'Excellent choice!' Oliver declared, slapping his hand on the table.

Jo was wide-eyed. 'You know him?'

'Of course, big bear of a man, very cuddlesome, but as straight as the day is long, I'm afraid. Though lucky for you! You have done well for yourself, Josephine.'

'How do you know him?' she asked.

'I know everyone,' he dismissed. 'He works in the building, he's polite, he introduced himself after he'd been in a couple of times . . . quite the gentleman. So I approve. You have my blessing, but I still want you home by eleven on a school night.'

'You won't say anything to him, will you, Oliver?'

'Why the secrecy? Doesn't he know about it yet either?'

'It's just at a very early stage.' She felt like a broken record. 'And nothing's really happened –'

'There was a kiss,' Angie chimed in.

'That took your breath away,' Oliver added.

Jo winced. She was beginning to think she should never have mentioned the kiss. 'Look, I might be pinning way too much on that kiss. In fact, all he said was that it was something that he'd always wanted to do, that he regretted not doing it before, and then he kissed me, and he walked away. It might have been some kind of closure for him.'

Oliver was frowning. 'Closure for what? You said nothing's really happened. The kiss was an entrée, not an after-dinner mint, darling heart.'

Jo shrugged.

'Have you heard from him since?'

'No,' she said in a vaguely troubled voice.

'Because he's visiting his sick father,' Angie reminded her.

'Well there you go,' said Oliver. 'He can hardly sit there at his father's bedside chatting up his new girlfriend on the phone.'

'Oliver, I'm not his girlfriend!'

'No, you are a bit old to get away with being called a girl, aren't you?' he said, pretending to duck for cover as he slid out of the seat. 'Back to the coalface, that coffee's not going to make itself!' He leaned across the table and gave her hand a squeeze. 'I am happy for you, Josephine, you deserve to have something nice happen. Enjoy it.'

Leura

Joe hadn't spoken to his father the night he arrived at the house, or even seen him. It was late and he was already asleep. Mim was bubbling over with excitement and nerves, and Joe was happy he was able to do this for her. Correct that, he wasn't doing this for Mim, he was doing it for their father. He should never have become Mim's sole responsibility. At least Joe was around more now, and he would continue to be, as long as was needed.

But the next day he was confronted with the grim reality of his father's deterioration. Joe sat with him for a while in the morning, but the old man didn't even have the energy for a conversation, and he mostly drifted in and out of sleep the whole time.

'His lungs are becoming so weak,' Janice explained to him later. 'He has to be on oxygen for longer periods during the day, and overnight. It's all very well to get the oxygen into him, but the problem we're encountering now is that he can't dispel the carbon dioxide effectively. It's particularly bad when there's a lot of moisture in the air, so these damp days haven't helped.'

'So what's the next step,' Joe asked, 'when he needs help to breathe both in and out?'

Janice lowered her eyes. 'Well, there are machines . . .'

'What, like a ventilator?'

'Let's not think about all that at this point,' she said briskly. 'He still has lots of good days.'

They had nurses round the clock now, so Joe took off for a long walk in the bush behind their place. He was sweating when he reached the top of the ridge, but felt immediate relief from the cooler air at this level. He sat on a flat sandstone ledge looking out across the next valley, breathing in the fresh air. Joe knew what a ventilator meant, but he hadn't thought things would get to that. He couldn't imagine his dad would want to be hooked up to a machine to stay alive, but he would suffer needlessly if he didn't have some kind of intervention as his condition deteriorated. Joe would have to arrange a meeting with the specialist, find out just what their options were. And he was going to have to call Hil, make her aware of what was going on. She was already talking about coming out for Christmas. Joe was beginning to think that was a good idea.

He heard the plaintive cry of a black cockatoo and turned to see a pair of them swoop out of a nearby stand of gums and fly across the sky as though they were in slow motion.

He thought about Jo. He hadn't phoned her yet. He was worried that if he called just to talk it might break the spell of the kiss, and he had to wring as much magic as he could out of that moment. He'd toyed with the idea of inviting her up here, till he realised that was really not appropriate under the circumstances. But he missed her. More than he imagined he would.

He had wondered if he oughtn't write to her instead, an email, maybe even just a text message. But that might seem impersonal, unless he said what he really wanted to say, and then that might freak her out. No, he had to see her face when he eventually said what he really wanted to say, if he had any hope of reading what was going through her mind.

But that was going to have to wait. The black cockatoos were flecks in the distance, and for now he needed to get back to his dad.

Wednesday

Joe was sitting out on the back verandah reading the paper when Janice appeared at the screen door.

'Excuse me, Joe?'

He turned to look at her.

'Your dad's asking for you.'

'He is?' he said, standing up and folding the paper.

'The air is dryer, can't you feel it?' she said, smiling. 'He's going to have a good day.'

Joe followed her inside. He hadn't spent much time with his father at all in the last couple of days, and it was beginning to get him down. He felt as though he was witnessing his dad's life ebb away. Mim called every night, but Joe didn't let on. He kept the chat positive, assured her that Dad was resting comfortably, having a quiet week, nothing to report.

As he walked into the room and over to his bedside, Joe was relieved to see his father's eyes were bright and alert.

'Hello son,' he said.

Joe smiled. 'Hi Dad,' he said, taking a seat by the bed. 'How are you feeling?'

'Better today.'

'I can see that.'

'But I'm going to type, Joe,' he said slowly, in his now familiar, halting speech. 'Talking . . . it gets too hard . . . and I have a lot to say . . . my head's clearer today.'

'Okay.' Janice must have already attached the keyboard to his arm for him, so Joe drew the monitor closer on its wheeled base, positioning it so they could both see the screen.

How's that pretty girlfriend?

That was his first burning question? And who did he mean – surely not Sarah?

'I don't have a girlfriend right now, Dad.'

So there's nothing between you and that lovely young woman Jo who came to the house?

'Well, there might be something,' Joe admitted, 'but I wouldn't call her my girlfriend. It's early days yet.'

Then get on with it. You're too old to be mucking around.

Joe grinned. 'Don't worry about me, Dad.'

But I do worry, I want to see you all settled and I don't have much time.

He frowned. 'Don't talk like that, Dad.'

I am going to die, Joe, and it's not far off.

Joe went to interrupt but his father kept on typing.

I'm tired, son. I've had a full, busy, rich life, but this is no life now. I dream a lot, about the places and the people, the things I've seen. I've been so privileged. Some people spend their whole lives in the one place, their imaginations going no further than what they see on the television. But I've been to so many places, I've done so much. I've had my share, my fill. It's time.

Joe's heart ached for him. He could express himself so eloquently in writing. No wonder Joe had never guessed the severity of his condition before he saw it for himself.

I'm at peace, son. You should be as well.

'We don't have to talk about this now.' Joe felt uneasy.

We have to talk about it sometime. Your problem is you're too sentimental.

'I'm not sentimental.'

Of course you are, you're sentimental like your mother, passionate people usually are. All your talk about settling up here in the mountains, you'd probably go nuts if you did.

'You don't like it here, Dad?'

Sure I do, now. But while I could still get around I wanted to be any-where else. I wasn't suited to settling down, I'd never stayed put in the one place before.

'How did Mum feel about that?'

I'm sure it must have been very frustrating for her at times, but she loved you kids so much, she was content. I could have been a better hus-band, a better father to the younger two especially. I was away so much. No wonder Will doesn't have much time for me now.

'That's not it, Dad. Will doesn't have much time for anyone but himself.'

He's young, that's okay. I would like to see him though. There are things I'd like to say to him, things he should hear from his dad.

'I'm sure he'll come soon,' said Joe, vowing silently to drag Will up here if he had to.

And I worry about Mim. She's had to look after me all this time, she hasn't built a life for herself.

'She's got plenty of time, Dad, and she wouldn't want to be anywhere else right now.'

She should though, she should want to be somewhere else. She should be out there making her own life. I'm glad she went to the symposium.

He paused for a while. Joe didn't know if he was getting tired. Then he began to type again.

So where to next for you, son?

'I think I've had enough, Dad, enough travelling, certainly enough war. I like the idea of settling down in the one place.'

You won't know until you do it. But I warrant you'll get restless after a while.

Joe shrugged. 'I don't know if I could do that, leave my family behind.'

You have to get yourself a family before you start worrying about leav-ing them behind.

He smiled then. 'Point taken.'

Is this girl the one?

'I don't know, Dad. How do you know for sure?'

There are no guarantees.

'I'd be happy if I had what you and Mum had together.'

You're too idealistic, son. You put your mother and me on a pedestal,

*and we didn't belong there. Or at least I didn't. You don't know how
many times I thought of not coming back.*

'So why did you?'

There was a pause before he began to type again.

*Because I missed her. I wanted to see her face. She's the reason I kept
coming back.*

The Tribune

Jo got back to her desk after lunch and checked her messages, her
current obsession. Unfortunately it had been a slow week, news-
wise, everything-wise. She hadn't heard from Joe, and she didn't
know what she was supposed to make of that. She'd thought of
calling him, but that might seem a bit desperate. Besides, he was
with his father, she didn't want to impose. He'd said the end of
the week, he'd call her at the end of the week. She was pretty
sure anyway, some of the specifics after that kiss were a bit hazy.
But she didn't like that she'd been put in the position of waiting
for him to call, she had thought she'd become immune to such
preoccupations.

Although she'd similarly had no contact with Lachlan, Jo was
aware of his every move. The news floor had been tracking his
progress with daily updates from the government press office, but
he was unable to make direct contact while he was in Iraq. That
suited Jo: she knew he was safe but she didn't have to deal with
him. However, he was due back any day, and she would have liked
some confirmation of where things stood with Bannister before
she had to face Lachlan again.

But there was still no message from him, instead there was a
voicemail from Belle, asking Jo to call her back. She hadn't told
Belle about the kiss, thank God, she didn't want to jinx it any
further than she possibly had already. She picked up her phone
and dialled. Belle answered.

'Hi, it's me,' said Jo.

'Oh, hi Jo, thanks for getting back to me.'

'What's up?'

'It's Mum.'

Jo groaned inwardly.

'She rang me late last night,' Belle went on. 'She sounded drunk.'

'So, nothing out of the ordinary.'

'She said she has to come down to Sydney again. She was babbling on about more tests, or treatment, I couldn't follow her, she wasn't making much sense.'

'You said she was drunk.'

'Don't be flippant about this, Jo. I think something's really wrong with her this time.'

'I'm not being flippant,' Jo said levelly. 'But I don't think it helps to start jumping to conclusions.'

'Well it has to be something serious!' Belle exclaimed. 'She's already had a whole battery of tests, and now she's coming back for more? And possible treatment?'

'You don't know that,' said Jo. 'You said she wasn't making much sense. You need to talk to her when she's sober. Do you know when she's planning to come down?'

'No, she said she had to organise it.'

'Think about it, Belle, if it was an emergency she'd be arriving at your place now. Or she'd be having the treatment up there in Queensland. Come to think about it, why isn't she having the treatment up there? And the tests?'

'Maybe she wants to be close to her family.' Belle's voice was breaking.

Cripes. 'If you're that worried, Belle, then give her a call, now, during the day, when you have a chance of catching her sober.'

'Don't you think I've already tried that?' she said. 'There was no answer.'

'So she's out buying new clothes for the trip.'

'Jo, you're being flippant again.'

'I'm not. Look, when you find out something, let me know. I'll come to the airport with you to pick her up if you like.'

'You will?'

'Sure,' she faltered. Why did she say that? 'If I can get away. If not, I'll come to your place and we'll have it out with her, find out exactly what's going on.'

'Oh, that'd be so great, Jo. I don't think I can handle this on my own.'

'Well, you won't have to.'

Leura

'Hey Joe.'

'Will, is that you?'

'Last time I checked.'

'What's up?'

'I need a lift from the station.'

'I'm up home, Will. At Leura, I told you.'

'And I'm at Leura station, so you won't have far to go.'

'You're at the station? Now?'

'Yeah.'

'What are you doing here?'

'You asked me to come, Joe.'

'I've been asking you to come and visit Dad since I got back in the country. Why now all of a sudden?'

'You want me to justify why I'm here?' Will sounded a little frustrated. 'Is this a bad time or something?'

'No, sorry, Will,' Joe said quickly. 'It's perfect timing, Dad's been asking after you. He's going to be so happy to see you.'

Joe was pacing around in the kitchen, staring down at the timber floor, the worn patches in front of the sink, the stove, in the doorway. Will had gone straight in to see their father when they arrived back from the station. He'd seemed resolved, he wanted to get it done with, the sooner the better. Joe had only stayed long enough to see the tears well in his dad's eyes, then he'd left them alone. There was a nurse in the room, tactfully sitting reading a book in a corner. She'd make sure Will didn't tire his dad out.

He came out after about twenty minutes, looking shaken.

'I'll get you a beer,' said Joe.

'Thanks.'

They sat out on the verandah, drinking their beers. Joe waited for Will to speak first.

'He hasn't got long, has he?' he said finally.

'I don't know. Not long, no.'

Will sighed heavily. 'I should have come sooner.'

'You're here now. That's all that matters.'

'I've been so angry with him for so long, thinking I didn't care if he lived or . . . then you see him like that.' Will took another long swig, draining the bottle. 'Silly old bugger.'

'What did he say to you?'

'Not much. He mostly just cried.' Will's voice caught in his throat with the last word, and he bowed his head.

'I'll get you another beer,' said Joe, standing up. Will didn't move, didn't lift his head. Joe walked into the kitchen and stood for a moment leaning against the sink, staring out the window. He took deep breaths as his throat tightened uncomfortably. Then it passed. He wiped his eyes with the heel of his hands and went to the fridge. He picked up another two beers and walked over to the back door. Will was standing now, leaning against a verandah post. It was coming on dusk, the insistent chirp of cicadas filled the air. Joe pushed open the wire door and walked out to join him.

He passed him a beer and Will clinked his bottle against Joe's.

'Cheers,' he said. 'I've just been thinking about when we used to go down to the creek to catch yabbies, but I don't remember if I ever went with you. Crinny used to take me down. Mim came a couple of times, but she just sat on the bank. She was probably making up poems in her head.' He smiled then, glancing at Joe.

'I think I might have taken you down to the creek, but you were only little. I carried you on my shoulders. I don't think we fished for yabbies.'

'We have different memories, you and I,' said Will.

Joe nodded. 'I think I owe you an apology.'

'What for?'

'Dad's said some things.'

'Such as?'

'Just stuff,' he shrugged. 'We do have different memories, you and I.'

Will turned to face him. 'You were a good brother, Joe.'

'I was hardly even around while you were growing up.'

'But I could idolise you from afar, boast about you to my friends.'

'I don't know what good that would have done you around high-schoolers.'

'Helped me pull some chicks, I reckon.'

Joe grinned then, shaking his head. 'I don't think you needed me for that.'

'That's true,' said Will, his voice finally lifting. 'I got all the looks, brother, you were just an early prototype.'

'And then they broke the mould,' said Joe, stepping back to sit down.

Will turned around to face him, still propped against the post. 'Speaking of women. How's it going with Jo?'

'Well, you'll be pleased to know I took your advice, little brother.'

'The grand romantic gesture?'

He nodded, smiling now as he thought of it.

'So,' Will urged him, 'what did you do?'

'I kissed her.'

Will regarded him curiously. 'Okay, that's romantic, sure, don't know that it could be considered all that grand.'

'Ah, but it's all in the context,' Joe explained. 'She wasn't expecting it, in fact she was a bit annoyed with me because I'd just told her that I was coming up to stay here for the week –'

'So this just happened?'

'Last Sunday,' Joe nodded. 'We spent the day together, it was a date, you could say. A *date* date,' he added, glancing at Will. 'And things were going well, and I was pretty sure she was going to ask me up to her place when we got back, but I couldn't because I had to come up here. When I told her, she walked off in a huff into her building. So I followed her, and then I did this little speech about how I'd always regretted not doing something, then I just took her in my arms and kissed her.'

Will was smiling, nodding his head slowly. 'Nice. So it worked?'

'I think so. I haven't seen her since.'

'But you've called her?'

Joe hesitated. 'No.'

'Why not?'

He shrugged. 'I don't know what to say.'

'Are you shitting me?' said Will, pushing himself off the post. 'You have to call, Joe, women want to be called. She'll be reading all kinds of things into why you haven't called, that's what they do. They invent these scenarios in their heads and it makes them crazy. You *have* to call.'

Joe sighed, contemplating his beer.

Will was shaking his head. 'Honestly, Joe, how the hell did you ever get any women in the past?'

'This is different.'

'How?'

'I dunno,' he said, thinking about it. 'I get nervous about approaching her, or calling her, but then when I'm with her, I'm more at ease than I am with anyone. How does that make any sense?'

'It doesn't, but I don't think falling in love is exactly rational,' said Will. 'Call her, you big tool. If you don't know what to say, tell her you've been thinking about her – they like that.'

He nodded vaguely. 'Okay. I'll call her.'

'When?'

'Tomorrow. I'll call her tomorrow.'

Tomorrow

Jo had just checked her messages again, on her landline, her mobile, her computer. Still nothing from Bannister. She had, however, received an email from Lachlan; he'd touched down at the RAAF base at Richmond only late last night and he'd managed to email already. It was Friday, what did Bannister mean by the end of the week? Did he think it was not until Saturday because that was still a work day for them? Nothing like leaving it till the last minute.

She tried to think of reasonable excuses as to why he hadn't called. Worst-case scenario was that his dad wasn't doing well. To be honest, for Jo, the worst-case scenario was that he was avoiding her and he had no intention of taking that kiss any further. But selfish concerns aside, his father's condition was the most important factor, and the most valid reason for him not calling. If not, what else could it be? He'd been snowed under with visitors? Catching up on odd jobs around the house? An old school friend had knocked on the door one day . . . she'd had braces and knock-knees when he'd last seen her, he hardly recognised her now. She was tall and lithe and brunette, no – she had red hair, flaming tresses of gorgeous auburn hair cascading over her shoulders. And she played cello for the Sydney Symphony Orchestra. She spoke two or three languages, fluently, from her time living in Europe. They clicked immediately, spent their days walking along tree-lined avenues, dropping into cafes, bookshops, antique stores, their nights in intimate restaurants, talking about old times . . . till one evening, when she least expected it, he took her in his arms . . .

Oh, Christ! Why was she doing this to herself? But why hadn't he called? Why did men do this? Why couldn't they simply communicate? Bannister was a communicator by profession, yet he still couldn't manage it in his personal life. It was going to drive her nuts. She could see problems already. This was a bad idea. Really, when he was back in the office, Jo was just going to have to tell him that it wasn't going to work, that they should cut their losses now.

But then she'd remember that kiss, and dwell on that kiss, and picture him every time she closed her eyes. And it was not just that she pictured him, it was the way she pictured him. It was like her imagination had crossed over some arbitrary line in the sand, and now it was running free, frolicking in the surf, rolling in . . .

No, stop! Don't go there!

But it was too late. Now all she could see was her and Joe writhing around on the shoreline, like in that old black and white movie, Angie would know which one she meant, where the couple kissed as the surf frothed over them, ravaging, hungry, animalistic –

'Penny for your thoughts.'

Jo screamed and lurched back, butting her head fair square into the head behind her.

'Ow, Jo.' She swivelled around in her chair. Lachlan was standing there, cupping his nose with his hands.

'Lachlan, what are you doing here?'

'I wanted to surprise you,' he winced, rubbing the bridge of his nose. 'I didn't think you'd get such a fright. You must have been a million miles away.'

'I'm so sorry.' She stood up. 'Are you all right? Can I get you anything?'

He shook his head, perching himself on the edge of the desk.

'But really, what are you doing here?' Jo repeated. 'You only got back last night. No one expected you in till next week.'

'I came to see you,' he said, gingerly feeling around his nose.

Jo brushed over that, coming closer to check out the damage. 'Take your hand away, let me see.' She gently prodded his nose; it was a little red, but she didn't seem to have done any serious damage. Lachlan was staring at her, she could feel his eyes, and now she could feel his hand slipping under her skirt and creeping around her thigh. She jumped. 'Lachlan!'

'You're very skittish today,' he murmured, leaning in close to her neck, so close she could feel his breath on her skin.

'What are you doing?' she whispered frantically. 'Have you forgotten where we are?'

'There's no one around,' he said. 'Everyone's gone home.' Now both hands had found their way underneath her skirt to grasp her backside and pull her up against him.

'Not everyone's gone, someone could walk past any minute.'

He brushed his lips fleetingly against hers. 'So, I'm getting used to living dangerously,' he murmured.

He had hardly been living dangerously. From all reports, he

hadn't come anywhere near live combat, they'd been heavily guarded, whisked in and out of safe locations, and kept well clear of any hotspots. But still, he was acting weird, this wasn't like him at all, showing his hand in public.

'Lachlan,' Jo demurred, gently but determinedly easing his arms away and drawing back from him. He released her, looking a little forlorn, which was not like him either.

'Let's go back to your place,' he suggested. 'I can stay a couple of hours. Sandra thinks I've come into the office to catch up on some work.'

'Uhmm . . .' Jo backed away from him to lean against the filing cabinet. She wasn't prepared for this. She thought she wouldn't see him till next week, till after Joe was back, till she knew where things stood. She was going to break it off anyway, but that was how she'd figured it in her head. And this was throwing her off course.

Lachlan was frowning curiously at her. 'Are you all right, Jo?'

'I'm fine,' she dismissed. 'What about you, how's the nose?'

He touched it again. 'I'll survive.' He stood up, coming over to her and propping his elbow on the cabinet beside her, hemming her in. 'So what do you say?'

'About what?' she swallowed.

'Going to your place.'

'What will you tell Sandra?' Jo didn't know where that came from. She never asked him those kinds of questions. She didn't want to know.

He was clearly puzzled. 'I told you, she doesn't expect me back for a few hours, she thinks I'm working.'

So he lied. Of course, what else did she think he did? She knew the deal perfectly well. It was a bit late to play the innocent. She really needed to end it, but she couldn't do it now, here, like this. But she couldn't sleep with him again either.

'Tonight's no good, actually, Lach,' she said. 'I've still got work to do.'

'Really?' he frowned.

'Uhuh, what do you think I'm doing here so late?' Filling in time actually, but he didn't need to know that. She got antsy at home, waiting for Bannister to call; it was better to keep busy.

'What are you working on?'

'Sorry?'

'You're working late, it must be important.'

'It's just been a busy week and I have a whole lot of loose ends to tie up. Haven't even finished my column yet,' she lied.

He sighed deeply, stroking her arm as she shrank further back against the filing cabinet. 'I don't know when we're going to get any time alone, there's the auction tomorrow night.'

'That's right,' she nodded. 'Of course, the auction's tomorrow night.'

'You're going?' He sounded surprised.

She shrugged. 'I don't have much of a choice.'

'You usually manage to get out of it,' he said. 'It's not really your thing, is it?'

No, swanning about with people who seemed to have little else to do with their time than dress up in designer labels and 'be seen' was not Jo's idea of a good time. Tomorrow's folly was for charity of course, that made it noble. Auctioning off worthless bits of junk that suddenly had value because they had been signed, worn or somehow touched by a celebrity. The *Trib* was one of the major sponsors and employees were encouraged, if not expected to attend. Jo usually managed to have a passable excuse, and she was barely missed in the rush of wannabes and gonnabes and Queen bees that thronged to these events.

However, she wasn't going to sit at home on a Saturday night waiting for Bannister to call.

'I think I've used up my nine lives on that one,' said Jo. 'You and Sandra will be there, I assume?'

Lachlan nodded, nuzzling in closer to her. Even the mention of his wife's name wasn't cooling him off.

'Then you should spend some time with your kids tonight,' said Jo. 'They must have missed you.'

He sighed. 'You're determined to throw a bucket of cold water on me, aren't you?'

'Look,' she said as she slipped out of the arc of his arms and went to stand by her desk, 'it's just that I really do have work to do, Lach.'

He was staring at her, his eyes wandering down the length of her body and back up to her face again. He sighed regretfully.

'See you tomorrow night,' he said.

She nodded. Out in public with his wife in tow. Safest place to be.

Leura

'Of course it's okay.'

'Are you sure, Joe?' said Mim down the phone line from Melbourne.

He smiled. 'Why don't you tell me how many times I have to say okay before you're convinced?'

She was having a ball, clearly, and Joe was happy to hear the animation in her voice. After the symposium, Corinne had talked her into staying on a couple of extra days with her. Mim hadn't had a break in so long, he wasn't going to be the one to drag her back. But he couldn't deny his heart had sunk with the news. He had planned to call Jo, ask her out Sunday, but now he wasn't likely to be back until early next week, when she would be back at work. He had to rethink his approach.

'You won't be missed at work?' Mim was asking.

'Leo wasn't expecting me this week anyway, and things don't start up again till Tuesday,' he told her. 'And it wouldn't matter anyway, Mim. I can work from here if I have to. Just forget about it and have a good time.'

After more assurances that their dad was fine, Joe eventually hung up. He had to call Jo now, right away, he'd put it off long enough. But he wasn't sure what kind of reception he was going to get.

He grabbed his mobile and walked out to the back verandah as he scrolled for her number. He hesitated, thinking about what to say. It all depended on the tone of her voice. Would she be frosty, or pleased to hear from him? And what was the best way to avoid the former, and ensure the latter? Bugger it, he was just going to have to wing it. He pressed call and held the phone to his ear.

'Jo Liddell.' His heart skipped a beat just hearing her voice.

'Hi,' he croaked. He cleared his throat. 'Jo, it's me, Joe . . . Bannister.'

There was a slight pause before she answered. 'Oh, hi.'

'How are you?'

'Fine.' Definitely frosty. Or at least curt. 'How are things with you?'

'Okay. Dad's been up and down.'

'Uhuh.'

'Will, my brother, you know Will, he came up a couple of days ago.'

She didn't respond.

'So that's been good.'

'Uhuh.'

'So . . . how are things going there?'

'Fine. Busy, you know, it's Saturday.'

'Okay, so I won't keep you.'

He thought he heard a sigh.

'Anyway, the thing is, my sister . . . you've met Mim, well, Mim's coming back a little later than planned.'

'I see.'

'She probably won't be home till Monday. So . . .'

'Okay then. Well, you have a nice weekend.'

'You too.' Shit, she was going to hang up. 'Jo?'

'Yes?'

He didn't know what to say. 'So what are you doing?'

'I'm at work, I said.'

'I meant for the weekend?' Why was he asking pointless questions? Winging it was not turning out to be the best strategy.

'I'm busy actually. I'm going to the auction tonight.'

'Auction?'

'The charity thing, the *Trib*'s a major sponsor. You must have got an email about it.'

'Oh, sure, I think I remember.' He'd ignored it, it didn't interest him. He didn't imagine it'd be Jo's kind of thing either.

'So, I better go,' she went on. 'We're trying to get the paper to bed early, they'll only have a skeleton staff on tonight, everyone'll be at the auction. It's a big deal around here.'

'Okay, I'll let you go then. Have a good night.'

'I intend to.'

'See you next week, Tuesday probably.'

'Whatever.'

And she hung up. *Whatever?* Frosty was putting it mildly.

'Hey.'

Joe turned around as Will came through the screen door.

'Who was that?'

He sighed. 'It was Jo.'

'You finally called.'

'Yeah.'

'How'd it go? Did you tell her you've been thinking about her?'

He shook his head. 'Didn't really get the chance. She was at work.'

Will looked at him. 'So what did you say?'

'Not much. I had to tell her I wouldn't be getting back till next week.'

'Why not?' he said, dropping into a nearby chair.

Joe leaned back against the verandah post. 'Mim called before, she's staying a few extra days. She's having such a good time.'

'Okay. So I'm here.'

Joe looked at him with a frown.

'What? There's nurses with him constantly, it's not like I have to do anything responsible.'

'It's not that.'

'Then what is it?' said Will.

Joe shrugged 'You must have things to do.'

'Nuh. I can stay. Me and the old man are getting on like old mates.'

It was true. Will had sat with his dad for a while most days. He said they hadn't talked this much in years. He was a captive audience, and Will was making the most of it.

'I've told her I won't be back now. She's not expecting me.'

'So go surprise her. They love that.'

'She's at work today.'

'So surprise her after work. Show up at her place with flowers and a bottle of champagne, you'll be a shoo-in.'

Joe smiled at that. 'But she's going out, some big charity function.'

Will thought about it. 'Have you got a tux?'

'Yeah, hanging in the back of my wardrobe somewhere. Unless you nicked it.'

Will pulled a face. 'What would I do with a tux? Seriously, go put on the penguin suit and show up at this shindig and sweep her off her feet. She'll –'

'– like that,' Joe finished for him.

'You're getting the hang, finally.'

'Yeah, but I don't know,' he winced. 'She seemed a bit pissed off on the phone.'

'For Chrissakes, Joe!' Will exclaimed, getting to his feet. 'For someone who's spent half his life in war zones, you're such a wuss. Just get the hell out of here, would you? Before I change my mind.'

Saturday night

The auction was being held in one of the swankier hotels in the city, naturally. That irritated Jo as well. Arriving late, she was unsurprised to find the usual suspects all present and accounted for, dressed to the nines in the requisite frippery. If every woman in the room simply donated what she'd spent on her frock, they'd probably raise the same amount of money and all this nonsense could be dispensed with. But of course they loved the nonsense, it's what drew them here, like mindless moths to an artificial flame. She passed by Carla, who gave Jo one of her signature diffident smiles. Glen was fawning over a couple of what Jo assumed were footballers, judging by the larger than average circumference of their necks. Leo was huddled in a corner with a bunch of other media players, talking newspaper business probably – he rarely talked about anything else – while his hapless wife stood by, staring around the room with a glazed expression.

Jo had the sensation she was being watched, and she turned to see Lachlan gazing at her from across the room. And he was being quite open about it too, which was so incredibly unlike him it was beginning to freak her out. She wondered if he'd got hold of some kind of mind-altering substances during his sojourn in the Middle East. He was standing where he belonged, in the midst of a clutch of beautiful people, though none more beautiful than his very own wife, dutifully taking her place beside him. Tall, mannequin-slim, stunning Sandra, with a mane of rich brunette hair so sleek and glossy she could have been on a Pantene ad. Sandra was a premium accessory, like one of those designer-label handbags you have to go on a waiting list to get. Jo watched as Sandra glanced up at her husband, before turning her head to look directly at her. It was too late to look away, at least discreetly, so Jo just smiled a friendly smile, and Sandra, who had never been anything but pleasant to her, smiled a friendly smile back. Though it seemed a little strained. Her eyes looked sad, or wistful, something.

Okay, Jo accepted her paranoia was hitting new heights. She needed a drink. She was making her way to the bar when she felt a hand on her elbow.

'Hey, slow down.'

Jo swung around. 'Lachlan, what are you doing?'

'Saying hello to a colleague,' he replied. 'A particularly beautiful colleague, I might add. When I saw you walk into the room just now –'

'Lachlan, will you cut it out?' Jo hissed, trying to be outraged while keeping her voice down. 'Have you forgotten you came with somebody tonight, somebody you happen to be married to?'

'Sandra?'

'Who do you think I'm talking about?'

'Sandra's fine,' he dismissed. 'She wouldn't think anything of it even if she did notice. You and I work together.'

'She looked at me funny, Lachlan.'

He smiled indulgently. 'What do you mean "funny"? You're the one being funny.'

'I'm not funny!' she snapped. 'I've never been funny.'

'Okay,' he agreed, a little startled.

Jo sighed. 'I need a drink.'

'I'll get it for you.'

'No, Lach, go back to Sandra.'

'I don't want to. I want to be with you.'

Jo looked squarely at him. 'Lachlan, would you stop being weird. What's gotten into you?'

'You have,' he said seriously. 'You've gotten under my skin and I can't stop thinking about you.'

'Okay, that's enough, Lachlan. I want you to stop. This is not what we do.' She turned away but he stuck right behind her.

'Can I come over later?' He stooped to say in her ear.

'No.'

'Why not?'

She turned to face him. 'Because you're out for the evening with your wife and I'm not going to let you ditch her to meet up with me later.'

'Why not?'

'Because it's not going to happen,' she said plainly. 'You're making me cross, Lachlan. Stop following me around and go back and be with Sandra.'

He glanced around. 'Look, she's not even there any more. She knows tons of people here. She'll have a ball, she wouldn't even notice if I left, just for a while –'

'What? You're not suggesting what I think you're suggesting?'

'We could slip out . . .'

Jo was shaking her head in disbelief. 'I don't get what's going on with you, Lachlan. But I don't like it, and I'm going to have to insist you don't come anywhere near me for the rest of the night.'

'Can't do that.'

'I'm walking away now.'

'And I'm following you.'

'To the ladies'?'

His face dropped. Jo couldn't take this any more. She turned around and swiftly weaved her way through the crowd till she made it out to the hall where the rest rooms were located. She pushed through the outer door, and the inner door, and came face to face with Mrs Sandra Barr.

Wipe that look of shock and guilt off your face, Jo. Quickly, before she notices.

'Hi Jo,' Sandra said warmly. Warmly was how she said it, there was no other way to describe it.

'Hello Sandra.' Jo hoped she achieved a similar tone, despite the strangled quality in her voice.

'That's a lovely dress.'

'Oh, thank you,' Jo said, glancing down at herself. It was a simple dress, but it was well cut. She'd paid a lot of money for it, but she'd had it for years and she'd certainly got her wear out of it. 'This is just my standard, all-occasion formal outfit. I don't exactly have a wardrobe bulging with couture.' God, did that sound bitchy? She didn't mean it to sound bitchy.

'Well, it's a good choice, it suits you,' Sandra said kindly. 'They call that periwinkle blue, don't they? It matches your eyes.'

I've fucked your husband, lately while thinking of another man. Don't be nice to me.

'Anyway,' said Jo by way of ending the conversation so she could go hide in a cubicle.

'Can I ask you something, Jo?' said Sandra.

No, don't ask me anything. I don't want to talk to you. I want to get out of here.

'Sure.'

Sandra leaned back against the polished slab of black granite that housed the bank of handbasins. She swept her hair forward, just like they do in the Pantene ads, draping it over one shoulder. Jo could see the detail at the back of Sandra's dress reflected in the mirror. Maybe twenty fine strings of pearls weaved in an intricate web across her creamy olive skin. The effect was spectacular. She was spectacular.

'Before Lachlan went away,' Sandra began, her voice even and steady, 'he was very distracted, moody, agitated I suppose you'd say. Even though it could have been dangerous, I thought it would be good for him to get away, to have a break, from . . . everything here.'

Jo wanted to ask her why she was telling her this. But her powers of speech had fled for the coast, leaving no forwarding address.

'Since he's been back,' Sandra continued, 'he's only been worse. He's like a caged lion.' She took a deep breath, as though she needed to compose herself for what was coming.

Shit. Jo was beginning to feel like a trapped animal as well.

'The thing is, Jo, if you don't want to be with Lachlan any more, it might be kinder to break it off cleanly.'

Jo pictured a bucket above her head, *Carrie*-style, dumping the blood of Sandra and her two small, innocent children all over her. She thought she might pass out.

'Don't be alarmed, I've known the whole time.' Sandra's voice was very calm, she wasn't being histrionic. Why wasn't she being histrionic? Why didn't she slap Jo? Really hard. That would be so much easier to take than this.

'He's done it before,' she was saying. 'I'm sure I'm not telling you anything you don't already know. You strike me as a very savvy person, Jo. And as for me, well, I've always accepted that this is just who Lachlan is. It was going on even before we were married, I went in with my eyes open. I love him, and the way I look at it is that if Lachlan needs it, and he stays with me and the children, well, I can . . . accommodate it.'

Jo wanted to cry out, No! Don't accommodate any of it. You deserve so much better. But her role as an advocate for her lover's wife was somewhat compromised.

'So, anyway, think about it,' said Sandra. 'He's really not having a good time of it lately. So if you care at all, for Lachlan . . .'

She said it with no malice, or judgement, or moral superiority. If anything there was only polite respect. She didn't know whether Sandra Barr was an amazing woman, or just plain mad.

Jo decided she was probably an amazing woman with a proportionately amazing deficit of self-esteem.

Sandra smiled at her. It wasn't forced this time, though her eyes still had that poignant expression. Now Jo understood why.

'Anyway, I better go back to the party. If you'll excuse me?'

Jo nodded, and moved aside as she passed. She couldn't say anything. Quite aside from having no voice, what could she say?

Sandra hesitated at the door. 'Oh, and it's entirely up to you, but I'd appreciate it if you didn't say anything to Lachlan. He doesn't realise I know, I'd rather keep it that way.'

Jo nodded again, mouthing, 'Okay.'

Sandra left the room. No one else came in. Sand flowed through an hourglass somewhere on the planet, and Jo remained rooted to the spot. She had to get out of here, but her limbs didn't seem to be functioning.

Her phone rang. Jo fumbled in her bag and drew it out. She realised her hands were trembling as she flipped it open and held it to her ear. 'Hello?' she said, fear rising in her chest. God, she wasn't going to have another panic attack, was she?

'Hi Jo?'

'Hello?' she said again, confused. It sounded like Bannister.

'It's me, Joe.'

'Oh.'

'Did you end up going to the auction tonight?' he asked.

'Yes,' she said in a tiny voice, as though she didn't want anyone to know.

'So where are you?'

She didn't understand what he was getting at. 'Where are you?'

'I'm here, I've been looking all over for you.'

'You're here? In Sydney?'

'I'm here, at the hotel.'

'I don't understand.'

'Will took over my watch. I thought I'd surprise you.'

'Oh.'

'So where are you, Jo?'

'Um, I'm in the bathroom.'

'Oh, you're still getting ready?'

'No, no, I'm here, at the hotel. I'm in the ladies'.'

'Okay.' Joe paused. 'Are you coming out any time soon?'

'I don't think I can.'

'Why not?'

She was trembling. She didn't know what to say.

'Jo, are you okay?'

'No. I'm not okay. I'm a bad person, a very bad person,' she stammered.

'What are you talking about?'

She was really trembling now. Shaking even. She could feel

tears welling in the back of her throat. Oh God, she was frightened, she didn't want to have a panic attack in here, on her own.

'I'm a bitch, aren't I? That's why I have that column. I'm a cold, heartless bitch.' No, if she didn't have a heart she wouldn't be feeling like this right now. The tin man should count himself lucky.

'Jo, what happened?'

Now the tears. 'Sandra Barr just told me – no,' Jo blubbered, 'she just *asked* me, nicely, if I would consider not fucking her husband any more. Only she didn't say fuck, she wouldn't, because she's too nice. She's not a slut like me,' she sobbed loudly.

'Jo,' he chided. 'I'm outside the ladies', the one on the ground floor? Up the hall from the ballroom?'

'Go away, don't come near me,' she wailed. 'I'm a bad person. I'll drag you down to hell with me, and I don't even believe in hell.'

'Have you been drinking?' he asked, not unkindly.

'I haven't had a single drink, not even one.'

'We might have to do something about that then. Is there anyone in there with you?'

Jo glanced around. 'No.'

'Are you sure?'

'Yes, why?'

She heard the outer door, and then the door in front of her swung open and Joe strode in, pocketing his phone as he did. She froze, staring at him. Was she hallucinating now? Where did he come from?

'What's all this about?' he said in the kindest voice she had ever heard as he removed the phone from her hand and closed it.

'I want to go home,' she whimpered.

'Okay,' he said, bringing his arms around her and holding her close. She leant against his chest as he stroked her hair. 'It's okay, I'll take you home.'

Jo looked up at him plaintively. 'You will? You don't mind being seen with me?'

He smiled down at her. 'Of course not. But you may not want to be seen out there looking the way you do.'

'Why?' Jo sniffed, staring down at her dress. Periwinkle blue. 'Do I look like a slut? Does it show?'

'No,' he assured her. 'You look beautiful, it's just your make-up's a little worse for wear.' He held her shoulders and turned her around to face the mirrors.

'Oh my God,' she winced, rubbing under her panda eyes.

'Hold on,' he said, turning her around to face him. 'You're going to make it worse.' He snatched a paper towel from the dispenser and wet it under the tap. Then he held her face, and dabbed under her eyes, ever so gently.

Jo gazed up at him. His eyes, they were so blue, and his brow was all furrowed from concentration. Why was he being so nice? She didn't deserve it. She was a home-wrecker.

'There, that's better,' he said after a while. He turned her around to look in the mirror again. Her eyes were still smudged, but less obviously. And her nose was a bit red, but she couldn't do much about that.

'Okay, we better get out of here before someone comes in,' said Joe.

They heard the swish of the outer door.

'Too late,' he added.

The door opened and two women appeared engrossed in conversation. They stopped in their tracks when they saw Joe.

'Sorry, ladies, safety pin emergency, out of reach, you know how it is,' he said, sweeping past them. 'I'll wait for you outside, Jo.'

They turned to look at her.

'Are you all right?' one of them asked. 'Was he bothering you?'

Jo sniffed. 'No, no, not at all.' She took a deep breath. 'He was helping me. Really.'

'Here,' said the other woman, opening her clutch purse. 'You better borrow my powder, it'll take away the redness.'

Jo felt more composed as she walked out into the hall a few moments later. Joe was leaning against the wall opposite, and he straightened when she appeared. She hadn't even had a good look at him. He was wearing a tux . . . what was it about men in suits?

'Wow,' she sighed. 'You really know how to wear one of those.'

He smiled as he walked over to her. 'Ready to go?'

'You don't have to do this, Joe.'

'I want to.'

'But you're all dressed up for the party. And you only just got here.'

He shook his head. 'Why do you think I'm here, Jo?'

'I don't know,' she said. 'Why are you here anyway?'

'I wanted to surprise you,' he said plainly. 'I wanted to come back, I did, but when Mim said she was staying on . . . Anyway, Will offered to stay with Dad, so, here I am.'

'Here you are.'

'At your disposal,' he said. 'So what do you want to do?'

She hesitated. 'I want to get out of here.'

'Then let's go,' he said, offering her his arm.

Jo accepted it gratefully. 'Stay close?' she asked.

He patted her hand reassuringly. 'Don't worry, I will.'

They walked down the hall and back into the main auditorium. The noise level had risen substantially, music was playing, and a few people had started to dance. The actual auction would not be held until later in the evening after enough alcohol had been consumed to ensure impulsive spending.

Speaking of which, Jo veered to the left when she spotted a waiter with a tray of champagne. She picked up a glass. 'Thanks.'

'Didn't you want to get out of here?' Joe asked her.

'I'll drink fast. Uh-oh,' she pulled a face. 'Steel yourself.'

Lachlan was coming towards them and Jo could almost see the steam coming out of his ears. She proceeded to skol down the rest of her champagne.

'Hi there, Lachlan,' Joe greeted him first.

'Bannister,' he nodded, his mouth set in a grim line. 'Can I talk to you for a minute, Jo? In private,' he added, casting a rabid glare in Joe's direction.

'We were just leaving,' she said. 'Joe's going to take me home.'

'You could have asked me to take you home.'

'No, I couldn't have. Or at least, I wouldn't have.'

'Can I take your glass, ma'am?' asked a different waiter, appearing at her side.

'Sure you can,' she drawled. 'As long as you give me a full one in return.'

He smiled, passing her a glass of champagne as Jo set the empty one down on the tray. 'Thank you,' she said, taking a slurp.

'Jo,' said Lachlan, grabbing her arm, 'a word, please?'

The band started to play 'R.E.S.P.E.C.T', right on cue, as though they were in a movie and that was the soundtrack for the auction scene. Jo looked at Lachlan's hand clenched around her arm and then back up at him. He released her arm.

'Go dance with your wife, Lachlan. Let's get out of here,' she said to Joe.

They made their way across the room, Lachlan didn't follow them. On their way out, Jo noticed another waiter by the door. She drained her glass and swapped it again for a full one as they walked through into the foyer.

Joe was watching her. 'Do you really want that?'

'I really do,' she replied, taking another sip. Well, more of a gulp.

'It's your third in as many minutes.'

'But who's counting?'

He sighed a quasi-parental sigh. 'Come on then, let's get you home.' He led her towards the front entrance as she scoffed down the third glass and promptly burped. Joe looked faintly appalled.

'Sorry, but I had to finish it, I can't take the glass with me,' she shrugged, leaving it on a stand near the doorway. As they walked out into the fresh air, the champagne made its way to the appropriate sector of her cerebral cortex and Jo suddenly felt a little woozy. She grasped Joe's arm with both hands as they crossed to the kerb.

'Are you right?' he asked.

'Uhuh,' she nodded, making a mental note not to move her head so quickly.

He raised his arm as a taxi pulled over.

'You know what, let's walk a while,' said Jo as he opened the passenger door.

He considered her doubtfully. 'You want to walk in those shoes?'

'Come on, it's a beautiful night.'

He sighed, leaning down to talk to the driver. 'Sorry, the lady has decided she'd prefer to walk.'

'Yeah? Well, next time the lady ought to make up her mind before she makes you hail a taxi.'

'Hey,' Jo objected, leaning down to look inside. 'I didn't make him, and don't you talk to my friend like that.'

'Have you ever thought you should keep your mouth shut occasionally, lady?'

Right. 'Hey! You're not talking to your wife now, buddy!'

Joe promptly hoicked her clear and closed the door, and the taxi took off, screeching away from the kerb.

'Wow,' Jo called after him, 'that showed us.'

'He can't hear you, you realise.'

She shrugged, taking his arm again as they started down the street. She winced, these were probably not the most appropriate shoes for an evening stroll. Jo had always marvelled at women who could run for a bus in shoes like this; the girl with the triple barrel name from that *Sex in New York City* show was clearly a freak of nature. Jo felt as though she was teetering along on a pair of romper-stompers, and about as ungainly.

'So what exactly happened in there?' Joe said after a while. 'I couldn't really understand what you were saying over the phone.'

Jo had been able to forget about all that for a few moments, distracted by champagne and taxi drivers and shoes, but now the bathroom scene reared its ugly head again, making her queasy.

'Jo?' he prompted again.

She took a breath. 'I bumped into Lachlan's wife in the ladies'. She knows, she's always known.'

When he didn't respond, Jo nudged him with her elbow. 'Did you hear what I said?'

'I heard, I'm just not exactly surprised,' he said. 'I told you this could happen.'

Jo stopped, taking her hand from his arm and perching it on her hip. 'You told me Lachlan's wife would corner me in the ladies' room and ask me to lay off her husband?'

'Is that what she said?'

'Yes, only she was very polite about it. She just said that he's been agitated and unhappy lately, and that if I was thinking of breaking it off with him, perhaps I should make it a clean break.'

'So what's the problem?'

'Huh?'

'Well, did you tell her you have broken it off with him?'

'No,' she declared, walking off again.

'Why not?' he asked, falling in beside her.

'Why not what?'

'Why didn't you just tell her you've broken off with him?'

'Because I haven't, as such.'

'What does that mean?' Joe stopped walking this time.

She turned around to look at him. 'I haven't had the chance, he only got back the other day.'

'So you haven't seen him until tonight?' he frowned.

'I saw him yesterday. Briefly.'

'And?'

'It wasn't the right time.'

'Oh, and it wasn't the right time before he left either. Just when will it be the right time, do you think?'

'What's with the tone?'

'Nothing,' he muttered, starting off up the street again.

Jo trotted after him. 'What's your problem?'

'I don't have a problem.'

'You could have fooled me.'

'No,' he swung around to look at her. 'I'm not the one with the problem here, Jo.'

'Hoh!' she exclaimed indignantly. 'What do you mean by that?'

He glared at her. 'You know exactly what I mean,' he said, marching off again.

'No, I don't,' she persisted, catching up to him and grabbing his arm. 'Spit it out, Joe.'

He turned to look at her. 'I'm beginning to wonder if you have any intention of ever breaking it off with Lachlan.'

Jo shook her head, frowning. 'That's ridiculous, I just haven't had the chance,' she repeated slowly and distinctly.

'Yeah, well, I'm not going to play the hysterical mistress and start begging.'

'That is so sexist,' Jo declared.

'Oh great, let's have an argument about sexism now, waste half an hour on that.'

'Oh, you think that would be a waste?'

'Fuck this,' he said, striding off ahead.

She couldn't keep up with him. 'Joe!' she called sharply.

He turned around.

'So you're just going to walk away?'

He sighed loudly. 'I never wanted this, Jo, I tried to back off when I found out you were with him. But you kept leading me on.'

'Excuse me?' she shrilled. 'I wasn't the one showing up at your place with bottles of wine and asking you rollerblading and saying this is "on the record", and then kissing you!' she cried. 'You're the one who's been . . . courting me.'

He frowned. 'What did you say?'

'Courting,' she repeated airily. 'Okay? That's what you've been doing, and you can't deny it, but it never goes anywhere.'

'Because you are seeing someone else!' he cried, lifting his arms. 'You're right, I've made my intentions crystal clear the whole time, while you've been having a bet each way.'

Jo rolled her eyes, planting her hands on her hips. 'Well aren't you the virtuous one, Mr Holier-Than-Thou with your perfect happy family, and your awards and . . . somehow you can even spin dumping your girlfriend to make it sound like you were the one wronged. Get off your fucking high horse, you're tall enough without it.'

'Now you're just being infantile,' he said, shaking his head.

Jo took a couple of steps towards him. 'I'm sick of you judging me, thinking you're better than I am. Well, I don't need your contempt.' She saw a taxi out of the corner of her eye and raised her arm. 'Stay out of my life!'

'Oh don't worry, I intend to.'

'Good!'

'Great!'

'Fan-fucking-tastic!' Jo finished as the taxi pulled over and she jumped in.

'Where to?'

'Just drive,' she gasped.

He took off. After a couple of blocks they stopped at traffic lights. 'Are we going in the right direction?' the driver asked her.

'Yes, sorry, it's actually just another block, you can drop me off at the next corner.'

Jo was fuming. This was the whole reason she stayed out of 'normal' relationships; men thought they could tell you what to do, grow your hair, dye your hair, get your cute arse down here, come rollerblading . . . Well Joe could go back to the fucking red-headed cello player for all she cared. Fuck him.

Not that that was on the cards any more.

She got out of the taxi and walked up the street to her building. Bloody Lachlan wasn't any better, following her around like a sick puppy. She didn't know what had gotten into him, except that he didn't want anyone else getting into her. He'd marked his territory and he was not prepared to give up any ground. Well, he wasn't going to get a choice, she was breaking it off with him regardless. She was going to wipe the slate clean and fly solo and stop mixing so many metaphors. She had a vibrator, what did she need a man for? All they did was give her grief.

She stepped into the elevator and pressed the button for her floor, backing into a corner. She gazed around, feeling a tightness in her chest as her eyes began to sting. Must be the fluorescent lighting.

The doors opened and she marched up the hall to her apartment. She needed a drink. Bugger, she should have got the taxi to take her past a liquor shop. Maybe there was something left over in the fridge . . .

But first she had to get out of this dress. She struggled for a while with the zip, contorting to get a hold of it, till she gave up, pulling the whole thing up and over her head and tossing it across the couch. She kicked the ridiculous shoes off and staggered over to the fridge, opening the door and peering in. There was an open bottle. She picked it up, holding it up to the light. Half empty. No, screw it, it was half full, which was a damn sight better than nothing at all. She pulled out the cork and took a swig.

There was a knock on the door, startling her, and a little wine escaped down her chin. She stepped quietly out of the kitchen, wiping her mouth. The knock sounded again.

'Jo?' she heard a muffled cry. 'It's me.'

Her heart caught in her throat. 'How did you get up here?'

'The security door was ajar.'

Bugger, she was probably the last person through and she didn't check to make sure the door had closed behind her. She wondered how many people did that.

'Jo!'

'What?' she said.

'Let me in,' his voice more plaintive now.

She took another swig out of the bottle before setting it down on the dining table. 'How did you get here so fast?'

'I ran.'

Her heart was pounding in her chest as her legs carried her inexorably across the room.

'Please let me in.'

She was standing in front of the door now. 'I'm not dressed.'

There was a pause before he answered. 'So?'

Jo's throat went dry. Her hand trembled as she reached for the handle, turning it slowly until it released. She drew the door back till he came into full view. He was leaning against the architrave, panting for breath, his face damp with sweat.

He thought he was going to have a heart attack coming up in the lift. But he had to come after her. He was sick of the games, of going one step forward and two back. He wanted to find out once and for all if they had something here, or if he should just give up trying.

And now she was standing there right in front of him, in her underwear, for Chrissakes. She was so beautiful. In one stride he caught her in his arms and brought his mouth down onto hers. And she responded, thank God, drawing her arms up around his neck. Joe ran his hands over her bare skin. He had to have her. He lifted her so her feet left the floor, as he stepped further into the room.

'The door,' she gasped.

He swung his arm back and his hand connected with the door as he gave it a good shove. He heard it slam as her legs drew up and wrapped around his hips.

'Where's the bedroom?' he breathed against her lips.

She pointed to the left and he careered across the room, hold-ing her up, kissing her mouth, her face, her neck. He made it through the doorway, then lurched towards the bed and they fell on it together. He shifted, propping himself above her, as she slid her hands under his jacket to ease it over his shoulders. He had to get out of this stupid penguin suit. He leaned on one arm as he wrestled with the jacket before he reefed it off and then swapped, lifting his other arm out of it. She began to unravel his bow tie as he bent to kiss her open mouth again. He felt her hands moving down, unbuttoning his shirt, and then she was peeling it over his shoulders. He lowered his bare chest against her. Jesus, her skin was so soft. His tongue tracked down her neck to her chest, as he pulled aside the flimsy fabric of her bra and covered her breast with his mouth. She moaned, her fingers raking his hair as he slid his hands underneath her, tugging at the contraption at the back of her bra. Why did they make it so complicated? It suddenly released, and he untangled the straps away from her arms, flinging it aside. He paused to look down at her, smoothing his hand across her breasts. Her legs were open around him, her pelvis nudging against him. He had to get inside her.

'Joe ... Joe ...' She brought her hands up against his chest as he went to lower himself. 'You have to wear something.'

'Aren't you on the pill?'

'And haven't you heard of safe sex?' she chided.

'He only sleeps with his wife, doesn't he?' he asked.

She held his face with both hands and glared at him. 'Yeah, but you slept with Carla Delacqua and I don't know where the hell she's been!'

'Sorry, sorry,' he said smoothing her hair back off her forehead. He leaned down to kiss her and she responded. He hadn't screwed it up again.

'Hold on,' she said, breaking away. She slithered out from under him, turning over to reach for the drawer in her bedside table. He ran his hand down her back, hooking his fingers over her pants and easing them down, as he kissed the soft skin on her hip.

'Hold your horses,' she muttered, thrusting a condom packet into his hand.

He rolled over onto his back with a heavy sigh.

'You do know how to use one of those, don't you?' she teased.

'I'll work it out.'

When he was ready he propped himself on one elbow looking down at her. 'Jo . . .' he said.

'Hmm?'

She was gazing up at him, her eyes glassy and beautiful. He wanted to say . . . I love you. That's what he wanted to say to her. He was sure, he didn't have the slightest doubt. He was in love with her. So why not just tell her? He hesitated . . . she was too unpredictable. It was one of the things he loved about her, but it was what made it impossible to tell her that right now. She was likely have one of her crazies, spoil the moment altogether.

'Joe?' she prompted, skating her fingers across his chest.

He wasn't going to risk it. 'You know,' he said, 'I only slept with Carla once, and I did use protection. It was that night after the play, when Lachlan showed up at your place. I was walking home and I couldn't stop thinking about you . . . with him. So I called her.'

She screwed up her nose. 'So Carla was my proxy?'

He smiled sheepishly. 'Kind of. I was thinking of you the whole time.'

She smiled back at him. 'I thought of you that night as well, when I was with Lachlan.' She brought her hand up to his face and stroked his cheek. 'So I guess this is the real thing?'

He gazed down at her; this was the real thing all right. He bent to kiss her again, sliding his knee between her legs as he centred himself above her.

And then he was inside her, and that was the end of all rational thought.

Jo was losing it. She arched back, holding her breath as she gripped his shoulders. She cried out. He was still thrusting into her, but she was gone already, past that exquisite peak, tumbling down now until her whole body went limp. Finally he collapsed into her. But after barely a moment, he rolled off her to lie flat on his back, catching his breath.

No, she cried inwardly, not you too.

But then his arms were encircling her, drawing her close to him. Jo's eyes filled with tears, spontaneously, she hadn't felt them coming. This had never happened to her before. Crying after sex?

That was so lame. She'd never cried after sex, except for the first time, and that was out of disappointment. She buried her face in his chest, steeling herself. She felt his hands stroking her hair, her shoulder, she felt his heart pounding against her cheek, and a sob escaped from her throat.

'Hey,' he said, lifting her chin so he could see her face. 'Are you okay?'

She couldn't speak, she just nodded her head, before another strangled sob burst forth.

'Honey,' he soothed. 'What's the matter?'

She tried to laugh it off, but her throat went into spasms, releasing more sobs. This was really embarrassing. But he just drew her closer, pressing his lips to her forehead and holding her tight. Jo took deep breaths, consciously calming herself, regaining control. There was nothing to be so . . . emotional about. Eventually she felt herself relax into him. This was nice, lying so close like this, skin to skin. She'd dreamed it often enough, but in her imagination she couldn't hear the rhythm of his heart beating, feel the rise and fall of his chest, smell the muskiness of his skin. She'd forgotten how good a man could smell when he wasn't doused in expensive cologne.

'You okay?'

She felt the reverberation in his chest as he spoke. 'Uhuh.'

He shifted, turning onto his side, bringing himself level with her face. 'I want to tell you something, Jo, but I don't want to freak you out.'

Her heart revved warily. 'What is it?' she frowned.

Joe smiled at her, bringing one hand up to cup her face. 'It's nothing bad. I'm just not sure how you're going to take it.' He paused, gazing intently at her. 'So I'll just say it, okay? I think I may have fallen in love with you. In fact I think I have . . . I know I have.'

'Oh.' Jo breathed, her heart thumping in her chest.

'You don't have to say anything back,' he said. 'I just wanted you to know.' He kissed her tenderly and then nuzzled his face into her neck, wrapping his arms and legs around her so she felt cocooned almost. Jo lay there, stroking her fingers through his hair. So he was in love with her. She waited for the cynic in her to come to the surface, but nothing happened. And she didn't feel like reasoning her way out of it either. Whatever this was, it was pretty wonderful.

Joe lifted his head to look at her. 'What are you thinking about?'

She gave him a coy smile. 'Nothing.'

'Oh yes you are,' he said, propping himself on one elbow.

'I was just trying to come up with a word . . .'

'A word for what?'

'For this, us being together . . .'

'That's easy, perfect.'

She giggled lazily. 'No, I mean . . . physically . . . the sex . . . how would you describe it?'

'Perfect still works for me.' He shifted so he was above her. 'Perfect,' he said, kissing her, 'and passionate,' he said with another kiss, 'and . . .'

'Fervent?' she suggested.

'Okay, a little religious maybe . . . how about erotic?'

'A little obvious . . . I'm thinking more . . . euphoric . . .'

'Exhilarating.'

'Electrifying,' she grinned.

He paused, gazing down at her. 'How about "long time coming"?'

She made a tiny 'mm' noise in her throat.

'How about . . . best ever?' he said in a low voice.

She nodded faintly as he bent to give her a soft kiss, his lips lingering gently against hers.

'Joe,' she breathed.

'Hmm.'

'I think . . . I know . . . well, maybe I've fallen in love with you too.'

He drew back to look at her, his heart full. 'Okay then.'

He kissed her forehead, her cheek and then he closed his mouth over hers, and they kissed passionately, and made love again, fervently, euphorically and long into the night. And as Jo fell asleep in his arms, she felt safe. She dreamed they were in the elevator again, and no one knew where they were, and no one could get to them.

*

Morning

Joe drifted into consciousness, slowly surfacing from a deep sleep. He opened his eyes. He was lying on his back, staring at the ceiling. But it wasn't his ceiling. It was Jo's ceiling. He smiled, remembering, as he turned to look at her.

But she wasn't there.

'Jo?' He sat up, rubbing his face. 'Jo, are you in the bathroom?'

No answer. He swung his legs off the side of the bed, leaning down to grab his pants off the floor. He pulled them on, standing up and walking over to the bathroom door. 'Jo?' he said, pushing back the door. The room was empty.

He walked out into the living room. 'Jo?'

No answer. The place was empty. She'd fled the scene.

But that was ridiculous. This was her apartment.

Jo was walking briskly up the street when her phone rang. It would be Joe, it had to be Joe. She was hoping she'd be further away by the time he discovered she was gone. She'd been lying there this morning, for how long she didn't know, wondering how she should handle this. She hadn't woken up with someone for such a long time, which was freaky enough, but what the hell happened last night? He said he loved her and she said maybe she did too. She did only say 'maybe', didn't she? But why did she say anything at all? He'd have all sorts of expectations now.

Initially she'd thought of hiding. But there was nowhere to hide in a one-bedroom apartment. So she decided to flee. She went on automatic pilot, grabbing clothes, shoes, and slipping quietly out of the room. She quickly dressed out in the living area, leaving the apartment in a matter of minutes. She'd just started up the street when her phone rang. Maybe he'd heard her. She glanced at the screen. It was Joe. Of course it was Joe.

'Hi,' she said.

'Where are you?' She could hear the pique in his voice.

'Oh sorry, I had to go, I have an appointment.'

'Bullshit. Don't lie to me, Jo. At least don't lie to me.'

She was silent.

'Where are you?' he repeated.

She cleared her throat. 'Um . . . up the road.'

'Are you heading north or south?'

'I . . . I don't know.'

'Are you near the café on the corner?'

'Yes.'

'Okay, get us a table and order me a long black. I'll be there in a minute.'

'Joe –' but he'd already hung up. She shoved the phone back in her pocket and stood there, considering her options. She could make a run for it. No, that was stupid. What was wrong with her? She was hopeless at this, that was the problem, that's what she had to tell him. It wasn't going to work, because . . . well, there was a whole raft of reasons. And she had a much better chance of explaining them sitting in a café with lots of people around than waking up next to him naked. They would be able to talk rationally, without being distracted by the nakedness . . . and the proximity . . . Jo was getting a little flushed just thinking about that.

She took a couple of deep, calming breaths as she walked the last few metres to the café. Outside was better. Definitely. Noisier, less private . . . which in a weird kind of way made it more private. She took a seat at a small table on the periphery and a waiter immediately approached to take her order. When he had left again, she looked up and saw Joe striding up the street towards her, in his suit trousers and white shirt, open at the neck and untucked. He'd dressed in a hurry, obviously. His expression was on the grim side, if she had to describe it. She supposed he had no reason to smile happily and wave at her. He should have, that would be the normal response after spending a night with someone. As long as the someone hadn't sneaked out of the apartment while you were sleeping.

He dropped heavily into the chair opposite her.

'What the hell, Jo?' he began. 'What the *hell*?'

Nothing like getting straight to the point.

'You're angry.'

'Are you surprised?' he exclaimed. 'You walked out on me. Out of your own apartment. That's weird, Jo.'

It was weird. She knew it. But she'd panicked. He should know better than anyone that she was a panicker. 'I'm not used to waking up with someone.'

'Well you better start getting used to it.'

She blinked at him.

'Are you going to pretend you don't remember what we said to each other last night?' he demanded.

'No,' she said in a faint voice.

They were interrupted by the arrival of the waiter with their coffees, which he set down on the table in front of them. It was a wonder the poor man could wade through the tension it was so thick.

'So what is it?' Joe resumed when they were alone again. 'Are you going to tell me you didn't mean it? That you were drunk –'

'I wasn't drunk.'

'Then what? You've changed your mind? You want to take it back?'

'No . . . it's . . . it's just . . .'

'What?' he snapped.

Jo swallowed. 'I don't think it's a good idea.'

He looked at her. 'You don't think what's a good idea?'

'You know what I mean.'

'No, I don't have any fucking idea what you mean.'

Okay, he was obviously very agitated, so Jo had to be the one to stay calm. 'I mean . . . this, you and me, it's not going to work.'

'Why not?'

'Lots of reasons.'

He paused, watching her. 'Well, go ahead. I'm listening.'

She groaned. 'Joe –'

'No,' he said firmly. 'I mean it, Jo. You're not going to get away with that, a vague "it's not going to work". Not after last night. We're going to have this out.'

'Well, you see, there's one straight up,' she said. 'We're always arguing. We fight all the time.'

'No we don't.'

'Yes we do.'

'I disagree.'

She sighed, noticing the glint in his eye. 'You're not taking me seriously.'

'I am,' he maintained. 'But I think arguing is normal, I grew up with it, my parents argued all the time,' he said. 'You see, Jo, people can have an argument –' His voice dropped a little, '– and they don't have to get violent, and they don't have to walk out on each other, and everything doesn't have to fall apart.'

She was listening, her heart pounding.

'So,' he said, 'you're going to have to come up with something better than that. What else have you got?'

Jo took a sip of her coffee and set it back in the saucer. 'We work together,' she said finally.

'So? You work with Lachlan.'

'But we're not having a relationship, as such.'

'Oh,' he nodded. 'So there's a difference between having a relationship and just having relations?'

'Don't be cute.'

'I'm not trying to be cute,' said Joe. 'I'm trying to work out the coordinates on your moral compass here. Sex with a co-worker is fine if he's married –'

'Joe . . .'

'Well, it's true, isn't it? You've had no problem carrying on an affair with a married man you work with. It won't lead to anything, you can keep it hidden, or pretend to, because everybody knows. But try having an open, honest, real relationship with someone you work with, and well, that's just fraught with problems, isn't it? There's no easy escape route when the going gets tough.'

'Now you're just being mean.'

'Because I'm pissed off, Jo, that after last night you wouldn't at least give me the benefit of the doubt, talk to me, tell me what's bothering you, instead of walking out like that.' He paused, leaning forward on the table. 'You see, I think if you love someone, you don't walk out, and it doesn't matter if you work together, if you live in different cities, different sides of the world . . .'

'But you left Sarah.'

'Because I didn't love Sarah.'

'And one day you won't love me.'

His expression softened. 'Is that what you think?'

'That's what I know.'

'You don't know that for sure.'

'You don't know for sure that you will.'

'Yes I do.'

She sighed. 'Joe, you don't know how you're going to feel about me in a few weeks, let alone a few years. You don't even know me.'

'Oh I know you, Jo Liddell, maybe even better than you know yourself,' he said, sitting back in his chair and stretching his legs out in front of him.

'Oh, do you?' she raised an eyebrow. 'Please, share your insight.'

'Okay, for example, ever since I met you, you've insisted that you're punctual, but you're hardly ever on time; and you like to put across that you're highly organised, but you're all over the place. Don't get me wrong, you get the job done, in fact you excel, but that's despite, not because of, your organisational skills. And you give off this whole thing of being in control, but one slight tip off centre and you freak out or run away. You're a bundle of contradictions. You're not claustrophobic, you just panic in enclosed spaces. You're full of all this outward bravado, but you're too afraid to go off and see the world, or even fall in love ...'

Jo felt a twisting sensation in her chest. She crossed her arms in front of herself. 'Well, I could give you a few home truths too, you know, Joe Bannister.'

'Go right ahead.'

She thought about it. 'You told me once that you're not usually a judgemental person, but you are the most judgemental person I've ever met. And when things don't go your way, you throw tantrums.'

'I don't throw tantrums,' he scoffed.

'You do so,' Jo insisted. 'You get all huffy and self-righteous ... you do it all the time. And you're a hopeless communicator. You couldn't even pick up the phone for a whole week while you were away, how do you think that made me feel?'

A smile was forming on his lips.

'And you're too tall for me,' she finished.

'But you love me anyway.'

Her eyes flew up to meet his, gazing steadily back at her.

'And you're smug,' she added.

'And you're beautiful.'

'Don't try and flatter your way out of this.'

'I don't flatter,' he said, leaning forward again. 'Jo, all those things I said before, I love you despite them, or actually because of them. You're trying all the time to be something you're not, because you don't realise how wonderful you are. But I do. That's why you should be with me.'

Her heart was racing. 'You're so sure of yourself,' she said in a small voice.

'Yes I am.' He dragged his chair around the table closer to her, so they were facing. 'Because I've looked for a long time, Jo,' he said, taking her hand in his. 'All over the world, in fact. And I've finally met the person I can actually picture spending the rest of my life with.'

She snatched her hand away. 'That's crazy talk.'

'No,' he shook his head, 'it's not crazy, I just have to find a way to convince you, because I want to get on with the rest of my life.'

Her eyes were wide, staring at him, as he brought his hands up to her face and kissed her with so much tenderness that Jo was a little overcome as he drew back to look at her.

'What are you thinking?' he asked her.

'I don't know. I don't know if I can keep up.'

'Well, I'm not going anywhere,' he said, taking both her hands in his. 'We don't have to rush this, Jo. We can take it as slow as you like. You know, aside from all my faults, I'm a very patient man.'

She smiled shyly then.

'So what do you say?' he asked gently. 'You want to stop all this mucking around and get on with it?'

She paused for a moment, looking into his eyes, those lovely blue eyes, and she knew that's exactly what she wanted to do. 'Okay,' she breathed.

'Okay?' he said. 'You're saying okay?'

She smiled. 'I'm saying okay.'

He glanced around. 'Do you think if I jumped up on this chair and yelled, "She said okay!" that would draw attention?'

'I think if you chucked a Tom Cruise in the middle of a busy city street I might run away again.'

'No, uh-uh,' he said, drawing her hands close and kissing them. 'No more running away. Okay?'

She nodded. 'Okay.'

'There is one thing,' he said, sitting back a little, though not releasing her hands. 'I don't want to tell you what to do, Jo, and I won't ever try to run your life, I promise you that. I only want to be part of it. But I need you to do something for me.'

She held her breath, waiting.

'I need you to finish it with Lachlan.'

Jo breathed out. 'Of course,' she said. 'But I'm doing that for me.'

'Well, that's good, but I need you to do it before we go any further,' said Joe. 'I can't be with you again until I know it's over with him. Really over.' He paused. 'I'm not judging you, Jo, I just can't bear to think of you with him. That's all it's ever been, you know.'

She nodded faintly.

'Okay,' he said. He leaned forward and kissed her again, a nice, soft, lingering kiss. Then he stood up, taking out his wallet and leaving a ten-dollar note on the table.

'You're leaving?'

He looked at her. 'I want to start fresh, Jo. I don't want anything, or anyone, coming between us ever again.'

'He won't,' Jo assured him. 'I'm going to break it off.'

'So, give me a call when it's done, and we'll take it from there.'

'It's Sunday,' she said. 'I'm not sure I'll be able to get on to him today.'

'That's okay,' said Joe. 'I'm not going anywhere,' he smiled reassuringly. 'Talk to you soon, I hope.'

She nodded. 'You will.'

Jo went back to her apartment in a daze. After she let herself in, she stood leaning against the back of the door, gazing around the room. She was alone. That had never bothered her before, barely even occurred to her. But now she felt alone without Joe.

She walked across to her bedroom and stared at the bed, thinking about last night, and her heart beat a little faster. She noticed Joe's jacket on the floor and she walked over and picked it up as she sat down on the bed. She held it up by the shoulders, and folded it in half down the back seam, holding it against her as she smoothed it out. Then she buried her face in the lapel. It smelled of him. She dropped back to lie on the bed, hugging the jacket to her as tears welled in her eyes. But she wasn't sad. This was something else. It was exhilarating, and exciting, and a little frightening, she had to admit, but she didn't want it to stop. Ever.

Jo wished she could talk to Angie. But she couldn't, not after the other day. She knew Angie loved her, knew she would listen to her, knew she would probably get cross with her when she found out what had happened and that Jo hadn't called her.

But still, she wouldn't call. She already knew what Angie would say.

There was one person she would call, though. She had to call. She wanted to get on with the rest of her life as well. She reached into her pocket and pulled out her mobile, scrolling for Lachlan's name. She pressed call and waited.

It took him a while to answer. She imagined him checking his phone there at home with the family, seeing her name come up on the screen, walking out of earshot somewhere. She didn't know where, she'd never been to his house. Didn't even know what it looked like.

'Jo,' he said in a low voice. 'What are you doing calling me here, on a Sunday?'

'I have to see you.'

'Well it's about time.' He paused. 'Look, it might take me a little while to get away, maybe not till later this afternoon?'

'That's okay.'

'Great, well, I'll buzz you when I'm on my way.'

'Don't come here.'

'What?'

'Let's meet at the Botanic Gardens.'

'Why?' he said, his tone suspicious. 'What's going on?'

'I'll explain when I see you.'

There was a weighted pause. 'I don't know if I can get away . . .'

'When you thought you were getting sex you could manage it,' she said plainly. 'I really need you to do this for me, Lachlan. It's important.'

He sighed heavily. 'Fine.'

'I'll see you along the path that leads out to Mrs Macquarie's Chair, say about four?'

'Can you at least tell me what this is about?'

'Yeah, I will, around four, at the Gardens.'

Joe wandered restlessly around the flat. He was beginning to think he shouldn't have left her like that. It possibly wasn't the best move to tell her he'd always be there for her one minute, and then walk away the next. It was just the sort of thing that would send her head spinning off on all kinds of tangents. But she said okay. So this was it, make or break time.

'You gave her an ultimatum?' said Will, when Joe rang to check on their dad. 'I don't know whether they like that.'

'Well, that's the way it has to be.'

'Woohoo, trying a bit of tough love. You think that's the best strategy?'

'You know what, Will, I think I've got it from here.'

'Okay, if you say so.'

Will reported that his dad had had a quiet, uneventful night and was in good spirits today. Mim would be back in the morning, and Will was going to stay on another day or two to catch up with her. So there was really nothing for Joe to worry about.

He hung up the phone and looked around the flat. Jo had never been here, it occurred to him. That was obviously going to change. The whole place was coated in a film of grime and dust and neglect. He usually got a cleaner in when he was back for an extended stay, but he hadn't got around to organising one yet. He wondered if he even had cleaning stuff in the place.

Three hours later Joe was taking a shower in his squeaky-clean, if over-bleached, bathroom. You could perform surgery in here it was so spotless. He had found the cleaning stuff and gone into military mode, scrubbing the place from top to bottom. He'd taken three large garbage bags full of rubbish down to the skip. Magazines and newspapers went into the recycling, and he filled another bag with old clothes to take to a charity bin. He stripped the beds and washed the sheets and hung the quilts out on the balcony to air. He vacuumed every square inch of the place, moved furniture, lifted rugs, and collected a record $18.35 in change from the back of the couch and the armchairs. Some small reimbursement from Will and his entourage.

He finished up in the bathroom, nuking it with so much bleach he had to walk out after a while so he could breathe. The smell was still hanging in the air when he turned the taps off in the shower, despite the fact the exhaust fan was running full bore and every window in the place was flung wide open.

While the frenzy of activity had kept him occupied, it hadn't exactly taken his mind off Jo. He kept wondering what she was doing, if she'd decided to call Lachlan today, if she was getting cold feet. But then he'd think of last night, and remember that she had said she loved him, and the look on her face today. He had to be patient, he told her he was patient; he had to keep to his word if he expected her to do the same.

He was drying off when he thought he heard a knock at the door. He switched off the exhaust fan and walked out into the bedroom. There it was again.

'Just a minute,' he called. He rubbed his head with the towel and tossed it back into the bathroom. It couldn't be Jo, could it? Did she even know where he lived? She'd dropped him off that time after the climate summit, but she wouldn't know which flat was his. It was probably just a charity collector, he decided as he pulled on a pair of jeans. But his heart was racing anyway as he grabbed a T-shirt off its hanger, yanking it over his head as he hurried out to the door to open it.

If he'd had to nominate the last person he thought he'd see standing on the other side, he still wouldn't have come up with her name.

'Sarah.'

*

4 pm

Jo had been sitting on the stone wall, looking across the harbour, for probably quarter of an hour now. She'd been too restless at home, and finally, around three, she'd decided she'd walk it, try to burn off some of this nervous energy. It was a beautiful day; she could actually smell summer in the air. She remembered the last time she was down at the harbour, and that was Sunday, only a week ago, she realised. When she'd told Joe she was going to break it off with Lachlan. And he'd kissed her. Her lips tingled just thinking about it. That was their first kiss, she could mark it on the calendar.

God, when had she gotten so lame and sentimental? But she couldn't help it. She finally understood all the sap, all the hearts and flowers stuff. When you were really in love the sky actually did seem bluer, so did the water. The air was clearer. Everything was clearer. Of course she knew rationally that it had more to do with the time of year and the angle of the sun and a whole lot of other meteorological conditions, but love wasn't exactly rational, or so she'd heard. And she did love Joe. She knew it for sure. She wasn't going to pretend she didn't have some niggles, but they were good niggles, healthy niggles . . . healthy fear. In fact, it wasn't even fear, it was anticipation, like when you lined up to go on a scary ride and your heart was pounding and you were breathing quickly, but you could hardly wait till it was your turn.

'Jo . . .'

She swung around to see Lachlan leaning against the wall, a few metres away. He looked guarded. He had to know what was coming, had to have some idea at least.

Jo eased herself off the wall and took a step towards him. 'Hi Lachlan,' she said in a calm, level voice. She was calm, and resolved. This was the right thing to do. The only thing to do. 'Thanks for meeting me.'

His expression was dour at best. 'So what's all this about? I don't have much time.'

Oh, he had more than an idea. And he was pissed.

'Why don't we walk for a bit?' she suggested.

He sighed loudly. 'Fine.'

Jo turned along the path, heading away from the Quay.

'You made it home all right last night, I trust?' Lachlan spoke first.

'Thank you, I did.' Wow, it occurred to Jo, that was just last night. Her whole life had changed in the space of twenty-four hours. Less than.

'So did you make it home, or did you go to his place?'

'That isn't any of your business, Lachlan.'

'I think it is when you're about to dump me for the guy.'

She stopped walking and turned to face him. 'It's not like that. We have to end this, Lachlan, because it's not right.'

He narrowed his eyes, considering her. 'When did you get a conscience all of a sudden?'

'It's not that sudden,' said Jo.

'Yeah, it is,' he maintained. 'Ever since Bannister came on the scene. I've been right all along. You have been sleeping with him.'

Jo could feel her hackles rising, but she wasn't going to let him get the better of her.

'Lachlan, this isn't about Joe,' she said levelly. 'Maybe it is a belated bout of conscience, I don't know, but I just don't want to do this any more. I keep thinking about your kids, and Sandra —'

'This doesn't affect them.'

'You have to stop kidding yourself on that one, Lach,' said Jo, stopping to look at him. 'We both do.'

He turned away, leaning his hands on the wall and gazing out at the harbour. Jo came to stand beside him.

'I don't get it,' she said. 'Sandra's beautiful. When I saw her again last night ... I mean, she's stunning. And she seems like such a lovely person. Is she dull? Or is she a real shrew behind closed doors? What is it?'

He was shaking his head. 'It's me. I get bored easily. I put it down to being hyperactive as a child,' he added ruefully.

'That would have bode well for us then.'

'No, Jo,' he said, turning to look at her, 'it's different with you and me.'

'Oh please, Lachlan, do I look that naive?'

'But it's true.'

'Lachlan –'

'I was even beginning to think Sandra and I should have a break.'

'No you weren't,' Jo said plainly. 'Your problem is that you want the unattainable. Sandra should make you work harder.'

'Is that what you're doing?'

'No.'

'You've been flaunting Bannister in my face to test me –'

'No I haven't,' she said firmly. 'God, Lach, while you had me all to yourself you were never this interested.'

He went to protest but she continued. 'Don't get me wrong, I'm not complaining, I never expected more from you. But as soon as Joe came on the scene you couldn't stand it. You had to win.'

'It's not about winning,' he insisted, 'it's about not losing you.' He paused for effect. 'Maybe I did need a jolt to realise how much I wanted to be with you –'

'Stop it, Lachlan,' Jo said. 'You are married, and I have never, and will never, break up a marriage. I've said that all along.'

He shook his head. 'You think that makes you the moral superior?'

She looked at him.

'Happy to fuck another woman's husband, but you draw the line at following through.'

'Lachlan, don't be like that.'

'Like what? Honest? You're a user, Jo. I just never realised how calculating you were about it. I was useful for a time – a good fuck, high enough up the ladder that I could put in a good word for you with the boss.'

When the hell did he ever put in a good word for her?

'Then you get stuck in an elevator with an award-winning foreign correspondent.' He wasn't finished yet. 'You must have been salivating, especially when you found out he was old friends with Leo.'

'You sound ridiculous, Lachlan,' said Jo. 'Can't we be grown-up about this? We've known each other a long time. We have to work together, I was hoping we could still be friends.'

He had a sneer on his face. 'I wouldn't count on it.'

And then he turned and walked away. Without another word. Jo felt a little rattled, but only for a moment. She realised he had to drag her down so he could feel okay about being dumped. That was Lachlan, Teflon man – he couldn't let anything sully his own image of himself.

But she didn't feel any bitterness as she watched him disappear into the distance. Truth was, she felt unburdened, lighter somehow. She was free. Free to be with Joe.

And she could be with him, right now, it suddenly occurred to her. She took off through the gardens, almost running up the path, up stairs, till she arrived at the side of the art gallery. She looked across the conglomeration of freeways towards East Sydney. Joe lived over there somewhere. She was trying to remember the best way to go, she'd only been to his place once, when she'd dropped him off after the climate summit. His street ran off Hyde Park, she'd probably recall it when she got to it. But even if she recognised his building, she didn't know which apartment was his. So she'd call him. He said to call, didn't he, when it was done, so they could take it from there.

She took out her phone and called him. He was taking a long time to answer, she wondered why – his place couldn't be all that big.

'Hey,' he answered finally.

'Hi . . . it's me, Jo.'

'I know, your name came up.'

His voice sounded a little strained. Of course, he was waiting to hear what she had to say.

'Joe, I wanted to let you know straightaway. I've just talked to Lachlan, it's over.'

She heard him sigh. 'Are you sure you're okay with that?'

That was not the reaction she was expecting. 'Yes, absolutely, I feel great. He was a little . . . testy, but I guess that's to be expected. Anyway, it's over, it's done.'

There was a pause. 'That's good, I'm glad, really,' he said, but his voice was strangely flat.

'So, anyway,' said Jo, 'I met him at the Botanic Gardens and right now I'm walking home. I'm just passing the Domain carpark, and it occurred to me, why don't I just come right on over, but I'm not sure which –'

'Jo, you can't,' he interrupted. 'Um . . . this is not a good time.'

Her stomach started churning. 'Is everything all right? Is it your dad?'

'No . . . no, it's not my dad,' he said. 'I can't explain now. I'll call you tomorrow.'

'Oh.' Not till tomorrow? Her heart sank. 'Are you okay?' she asked.

She heard him breathe out heavily. 'I'm fine, don't worry about me. I'll call you, I'll explain everything tomorrow. I'm sorry, Jo, I'm really sorry about this.'

'It's okay, really,' she said, recovering. He sounded genuine.

'I do love you, Jo.'

She smiled as tears sprang into her eyes. 'I love you too,' she said. 'Talk to you tomorrow.'

He hung up. God, now she had to call Angie. She dialled her number and she picked up straightaway.

'Hi Jo, wassup?'

'You're not going to believe this. I wasn't going to call you, I didn't think it was fair, after the other day –'

'The other day?'

'– I didn't want you to think I was insensitive and only think-ing about myself,' Jo blathered on over the top of her. 'But last night I slept with Joe, we slept together, and he told me he loved me and I said it back, and then I broke it off with Lachlan, but then I just called Joe to tell him and he said it wasn't a good time and he'd call me tomorrow, and I do trust him, I do, or at least I'm trying so hard to trust him, but I'm going to go nuts tonight thinking the worst, you know what I'm like, better than anyone, and so I had to call you, even though I didn't want it to be about me next time we talked, so we can talk about you, if you like, anything to stop my head spinning –'

'Jo!' Angie interrupted loudly. 'For godsakes, I have my bian-nual meltdown and you tar me as bitter and twisted forever? Give me a break! You had sex with Joe. You told him you loved him. You broke it off with Lachlan. I'm so coming over.'

*

Next day

Jo had not woken alone for the second morning in a row, but this time it was Angie lying alongside her in the bed. They had drunk their combined body weight in alcohol last night, and in the wee hours of the morning they had both collapsed, not before Angie had remembered that she had to work the next day and had somehow had the foresight, not to mention the fine motor skills, to set the alarm. Jo had heard her staggering out of bed, cursing and stumbling about. She had rolled off the bed and offered assistance but Angie had assured her she wouldn't be much help in her condition, and Jo had had to agree as she climbed back into bed and promptly passed out.

The next time she woke it was ten to eleven. She lay there for a while, staring at the ceiling, assessing her condition. The difference between an intolerable hangover and a tolerable one was often just a few hours sleep, and Jo decided that she wasn't feeling too bad. Poor Ange, she was standing in that sandwich shop, surrounded by food, possibly mixing up that gross green slime right this very minute. The thought of it turned Jo's stomach, but it passed. She sat up carefully, giving herself a moment to get accustomed to being upright. All good so far. She made her way to the bathroom, brushed her teeth, stood under the shower for ten minutes, and emerged feeling tentatively human.

Her stomach started to rumble and she tottered out to the kitchen to see what the fridge had to offer. Not a lot, unless she fancied limp vegetables and week-old bread. Jo wasn't sure how old the eggs were, so she wouldn't risk it. She picked up a bottle of water and closed the door. There was an overripe banana and a shrivelled orange sitting forlornly in the fruit bowl on the bench. Why did she even buy oranges? It must be from some underlying fear of contracting scurvy, even though she never ate them. Her kitchen bin would certainly never get scurvy, she thought, as she dropped it in. She grabbed the banana and walked into the living room, plonking down on the couch. Potassium and a little sugar would help. And hydration. She opened the bottle of water and guzzled down half of it, then peeled the banana, taking a cautious bite. It dissolved in her mouth and she swallowed. Okay. Good. It was staying down.

She squinted over at the clock on her DVD player. Quarter past eleven. Joe hadn't called yet. Or maybe he had, she hadn't thought to check. She got up and walked over to the phone. The light wasn't flashing on her machine, but she pressed the button anyway, to hear the halted voice announce, 'No new messages.' Didn't hurt to double-check. She peered more closely at the screen. There were two messages stored; she pressed the button to recall them.

'Hello Jo, it's me. You told me to let you know when Mum was coming and she's flying in today, and I know you said you'd come with me to meet her, but honestly, I kind of forgot, because you never do that, and anyway, it's Sunday so it doesn't matter. Darren's going to drive me to the airport and then we won't have to park, he'll drive around with the kids while I go in and get her. Though I'll probably bring Caelen in with me because you know how he loves planes. Anyhow, I was thinking that because you have Mondays off you could come over tomorrow so we can talk to Mum, like you promised. Caelen will be at preschool and I know I can get Nicole, you remember Nicole, from two doors up? She has Brianna, who's Caelen's age, and an older boy, Jayden. I know she won't mind watching the twins for an hour or two. Then we'll have —'

The machine cut out, probably out of sheer boredom. Jo vaguely remembered checking the messages yesterday when she got back to the apartment, but she pressed skip when she realised it was only Belle.

'Oh, hi, it's me again.' The next message started to play. 'I always do that!' Belle laughed at herself. 'They should make the message space longer.'

No, they definitely should not do that.

'Anyway, I'll keep it short and sweet. Give me a call when you get this and we'll organise what time to pick you up from the station tomorrow. Thanks so much for doing this, Jo, I really appreciate it.'

Tomorrow was today. Jo groaned. There was no way she was up to an intervention with Charlene today. Besides, she had to wait for Joe to call. He said he would, and she trusted him. Angie had convinced her that she had every reason to. That whatever was going on was nothing she had to be anxious about.

'It'll be a family thing,' Angie had assured her. 'You said he's close to his family.'

'Yeah, but I asked him if it was his dad and he said no.'

'But he has a brother and sisters, and who knows what other family,' said Angie. 'Think about it logically, Jo, there's nothing else it could be. Or maybe there is something else it could be, it could be anything really, but it doesn't have to be something bad. He said he loved you, remember.'

Jo had recounted the phone call, verbatim, several times as the night progressed, and Angie was right, she had no reason to think the worst. He'd assured her he'd call today, he'd said he was sorry, and that he loved her. He wanted her to know that.

The phone rang, which made her jump since she was standing almost right on top of it. She snatched it up without looking at the caller ID.

'Hello?' she gasped, hoping she didn't sound too desperate.

'Jo, it's me, did you get my message?'

Her heart sank. 'Sorry, yes, Belle, just now, I've been . . . out, and . . . tied up.'

'So, you haven't left yet? Obviously, if you're answering your landline . . .'

Jo took a breath. 'I can't make it today, Belle.'

'Jo-o,' she whined.

'Listen to me, Belle. It's not as though you gave me much notice,' she said firmly. 'And I have something really important I have to be here for today.'

'Are you waiting on a delivery?'

'What?' Jo said, confused.

'I just thought you might be waiting on a delivery to your flat. A new washing machine or something.'

Jo's head was hurting. 'I don't need a new washing machine.'

'No, it's just you said you have to be there for something important, like you can't leave the flat.'

'It is important, and I can't leave the flat, but it's not for a washing machine,' Jo sighed, collecting her thoughts. 'I can't explain right now, but when I do, you will completely understand.'

'Why so mysterious?' Belle asked, and then she gasped. 'Omigod, does it have to do with Joe?'

'Yes, it does actually.' Bugger. Why did she say that?

'Well you have to tell me now!' she insisted.

'No, I can't.'

'Come on, I'll die of suspense otherwise.'

'What flowers do you want at your funeral?'

Belle groaned. 'Well how long is this going to go on for?' she pleaded. 'Mum's seeing some specialist on Wednesday and she won't tell me anything. And I'm really worried –'

Jo wasn't going to get into this now. 'I'll come tomorrow,' she blurted.

'Tomorrow? Won't you be at work?'

'Oh, yeah,' Jo said, remembering. 'But that's okay, it's only Tuesday, I can leave early, I'll come down in the afternoon. I can probably get there around four . . .'

'So you'll stay for dinner?'

'I suppose,' she said weakly.

'That'll be so great, Jo,' Belle gushed. 'And you'll tell me all about this mystery then?'

'Sure.'

'So give me a call, or an SMS will do, with what time your train's coming in. But I'll expect you sometime around four.'

'Okay,' she sighed. 'I'll let you know.'

Jo hung up the phone and gazed around the room. She had to do something. And she had to eat something more substantial than a soggy banana.

She went to the fridge and took out the stale bread; it'd be okay toasted. As she waited for it to toast, she set about cleaning out the fridge, tossing out all the old vegetables and yoghurt, along with her resolutions of eating healthy and being organised. Joe was right, she was all talk. But maybe she had to stop trying to be something she wasn't, like he said. Because apparently, she was pretty wonderful. She smiled.

Jo had discovered over the years that one of the most effective cures for a tolerable hangover was housework, but it had to be vigorous housework. She quaffed down a couple of slices of Vegemite toast as she attacked the rest of the cupboards, chucking out out-of-date food and empty containers and broken crockery and smelly dishcloths. She put on a load of washing, and set about scrubbing the kitchen sink until it gleamed. Then she got down on the floor on her hands and knees and scrubbed it as well. Forty minutes later she was exhausted. She wouldn't be doing that again in a hurry. Not that she'd need to, you could eat off this floor now. Why that was ever considered an achievement Jo had no idea, because the kind of person who had a kitchen floor clean enough to eat off was not the kind of person who would ever consider actually doing that.

She looked around the flat, at the layers of dust, the unvacuumed carpet . . . but Jo had had enough. Instead she walked into the bathroom and turned the taps on in the tub. The one thing, more than any other feature that had drawn her to this place, was the bathtub, something rarely ever found in a one-bedder in the city. And she couldn't have been more appreciative of it than today. She squirted in some bubble concoction – 'Patchouli', according to the label – that someone had given her, probably Belle. Jo sank down into the bubbles and made a conscious effort to unwind. But though her frenzied bout of house-cleaning had occupied her physically, it hadn't succeeded in taking her mind off Joe. In fact she hadn't been able to get her mind off him all day. What was he doing? Where was he? What the hell was going on?

She sighed a big loud sigh, sinking further into the suds. She had to be patient, she'd find out what this was all about soon enough, and then she'd probably feel silly for having even the slightest worry, Angie had suggested. It was like when Mr Darcy was waylaid rescuing Lizzie's wayward sister from certain ruin. Jo tried to remind Angie that Belle didn't need rescuing from anything, and more to the point, life wasn't like a BBC miniseries. Angie in turn reminded her that the BBC miniseries was based on a Jane Austen novel, and that Jane Austen was in fact a brilliant chronicler of what life was like, if you took away the mansions and the women sitting around all day doing needlework and going for turns about the shrubbery.

Jo was drifting off in the rapidly cooling patchouli bubbles when she heard a buzzing sound. She started, rising up and grabbing the phone.

'Hello?'

There was no reply. The buzzing continued. Bugger, it was the intercom. She launched herself out of the tub, creating a mini tsunami as she grabbed a towel and hurried out to the living room.

She snatched up the receiver. 'Hello?' she said breathlessly.

'Hi Jo, it's me.'

It was him, finally.

'Oh, I thought you were going to call first?'

'Sorry, is this a bad time?'

'No, no, not at all,' she assured him. 'Come on up.' She pressed the button to release the door downstairs and dashed back into her bedroom. She stood in front of the wardrobe for a second, catching her breath. She really would have liked enough time to pull herself together. Her hair was damp and bedraggled, her skin all ruddy, and she was still coated in patchouli froth. She quickly towelled herself off, and grabbed a sundress, pulling it over her head. She flicked her fingers through her hair as she raced out to the door, arriving as a knock sounded from the other side. She paused, taking a deep breath and straightening her dress, before she grasped the handle and opened the door.

Joe melted inside as soon as he laid eyes on her. She looked beautiful, all pink and dewy, in a flimsy white dress and bare feet, smiling up at him. His heart ached; he didn't know how he was going to get through this.

'Hi,' she said, her eyes shining expectantly at him.

'Hello.' He stepped forward, taking her into his arms. She smelled so good. He held her close for a long time, holding onto the moment, making it last.

She lifted her face to his, angling for a kiss, and he couldn't resist her. He met her lips in a heartfelt kiss, somehow trying to let her know that whatever happened, he loved her, and that he never intended to hurt her.

She broke away after a while, smiling up at him. 'So, weirdly, I missed you,' she said, almost embarrassed to admit to it.

'Me too. You don't know how much.'

'Well, you better tell me all about it then,' she said.

She slipped out of his arms and ducked behind him to close

the door. 'Can I get you something?' she asked sweetly. 'Actually, I think I can only offer you coffee or tea, or water, of course. Angie was here last night and we drank anything alcoholic that wasn't nailed down,' she grinned. 'I think we may have tried cough medicine towards the end.'

He nodded, smiling faintly. 'Water's fine, thanks.'

'Okay, have a seat,' she chirped as she skipped off to the kitchen.

He sat down heavily on the couch. He'd been wanting to get here all day; the jet lag had finally caught up with Sarah and she'd taken herself off to bed. He'd written her a note, in case she didn't sleep right through. *Had to go out for a while. Don't know when I'll be back. J*

Jo was walking over with two tall glasses of water. She set them down on the coffee table and planted herself beside him, one leg underneath her as she turned sideways to face him.

'So,' she said expectantly, 'what's been going on with you?'

He took a deep breath, reaching for her hand. 'Jo, I want you to know I meant everything I said yesterday.'

She frowned, slipping her hand out of his.

'Don't,' he said, reaching for her face instead and leaning forward to kiss her. Their lips touched but she pulled back.

'Joe,' she said warily, 'what's going on?'

He grabbed her hand this time and held it firmly. His heart was thumping sickeningly in his chest, reverberating right down into his stomach. 'Sarah showed up on my doorstep yesterday.'

'Sarah?' she said, frowning. 'Sarah-from-England Sarah?'

He nodded.

She looked uneasy. 'Should I be worried?'

'About Sarah, per se, no. Absolutely not.'

'What does that mean?'

'Everything I told you about her was the truth, Jo. It was over between us, at least it was for me. Very definitely over. I had no reason to expect I'd even see her again, except incidentally, if our paths ever crossed, you know . . .'

She looked perplexed, as well she might. He was still perplexed and he had the whole story.

'The thing is . . .' He just had to say it. 'She's pregnant.'

Jo recoiled from him, pulling her hand away. 'What does that have to do with you?' she asked, but her voice was full of dread.

'She's nearly seven months along.'

Jo sprang to her feet, taking a few steps back. 'What are you saying exactly?' she cried. 'Because you should just say it, Joe, stop dancing around it.'

He stood up to face her, his heart heavy. 'It's mine, Jo. Sarah was pregnant before I left England.'

Her eyes grew wide. 'You knew?'

'No, no, of course I didn't,' he assured her. 'She didn't find out till just before I came home.'

Jo was confused. 'So she knew before you left?'

He nodded.

'Why didn't she tell you then?'

'She was about to, when I said I was leaving. That's why she freaked out the way she did, took it so badly. She thought if she came out with it then it might sound like she was trying to trap me, and she didn't want it to be the only reason I stayed when I was making it pretty clear that I wanted to go.'

'So why is she telling you now?'

'Her conscience got the better of her,' he explained. 'She felt I had a right to know, that the baby should know its father.'

Jo was rubbing her temples, obviously struggling to make sense of what he was telling her. 'So what does this mean?' she asked him.

'I don't know,' he said weakly.

'Surely she didn't come all this way just to tell you? What does she expect from you?'

He sighed as he sank back onto the couch, holding his head in his hands.

'Joe,' she prompted. 'What is it?'

He lifted his head but he didn't look at her. 'All of Sarah's family,' he began slowly, 'her friends, her whole life is in England. She has no one here in Australia . . . except me.'

Jo was staring at him, her stomach churning.

'She knows I always wanted to settle down here, so she came out in a gesture of goodwill, to prove that she's prepared to give it a go . . .'

He watched Jo's expression change as the full ramifications gradually dawned on her.

'If there isn't any hope,' he went on quietly, 'for us to be a family, then she'll go home again.'

'She's threatening you?' Jo snapped. 'She'll take your child away if you don't marry her? It's not the frigging 1950s, Joe, she can't do that. You can't blackmail someone into loving you.'

'She's not blackmailing me or making threats, Jo,' he said, trying to maintain some semblance of calm. 'It's just the facts. If it's not going to work out then of course she'll go back to England, to her family, where she has support. I couldn't expect her to stay here. And she'd never stop me from seeing the baby as often as I want.'

'So, okay then . . .' said Jo.

He took a breath. 'I don't know how that would work, Jo, being a father from halfway across the world, seeing the child a couple of times a year. I just don't know if I can do that.'

Jo nodded faintly. She hugged her arms to herself as she started to pace the floor again. 'So it's not that complicated after all,' she said. 'She's having your baby, you want to be with her –'

'No, I want to be with you, Jo. I love you.'

'Well, I don't even know if I want kids, but you obviously do.' She kept talking, kept pacing. 'Really, this is for the best –'

'Jo –'

'I told you it was never going to work between us,' she went on, a hint of hysteria creeping into her voice. 'I'm not the girl who gets the guy, I'm the girl who gets a bit on the side. But I got greedy, didn't I, thinking I could have a happy ending. But girls like me don't get happy endings –'

'Stop it, Jo!' he cried, standing up.

She turned to look at him.

'You think this is a happy ending for me?' He was almost shouting. 'Until yesterday I had my happy ending. That's when it was simple, now it's complicated. I didn't sleep all night, trying to work out how I can be with you and still do the right thing by this child, who didn't choose to come into the world, who didn't choose to have a father who'd stopped loving his mother, who doesn't deserve not to have a father because of that. So if you have a solution, then tell me, please Jo, I'd give anything. Because this is breaking my heart too.'

She was breathing hard, staring helplessly across at him, her eyes filling with tears. He started to come towards her, but she shook her head, turning to run into her bedroom.

Jo threw herself on the bed, burying her face in a pillow to stifle her sobs. She was not going to cry. There was no point. What good would tears do anyway? They'd only muddy the issue with emotion.

She heard him come into the room. She clenched the pillow tighter as she felt him climb onto the bed behind her, then sidle over to spoon her, his arms closing around her. Her heart was aching. For a brief, tantalising moment, she indulged in the feel of his body wrapped around hers, the comfort, the security . . .

But everything had changed. He was going to be a father. His baby had come into existence before they had even met. He was never hers to have, it had all been an illusion.

'No, Joe,' she said firmly, arching away from him. 'You should go, go back to her. You shouldn't even be here.'

'But this is where I want to be,' he insisted, drawing her close again.

She shoved him with her elbow. 'We don't always get what we want.'

He held her tight as she thrashed against him, trying to wrench him off her. 'What is it, Joe?' she cried. 'You want me to be your mistress? Is that it? I suppose you think I wouldn't have a problem with that, it's what I do, after all.'

He released her then. 'Jo, don't talk like that. This is different, I love you.'

She turned over to look at him. 'Lachlan said he loved me too, how is it different?'

Joe's heart flinched painfully. 'You don't think this is different?'

'Not any more,' she said. 'There's a woman who has a prior claim on you, there's a child involved. That's where I draw the line, Joe. I've never broken up a family, and I never will.'

'We're not a family,' he said plainly.

She looked at him. 'Yes, you are. And I've seen what family

means to you, Joe. You're not going to be able to let her go back to England with your child.'

He sighed heavily, lying back to stare up at the ceiling. She was right. He'd have to follow Sarah if she took the baby back home. He wondered if Jo would consider going with him ... that was probably a bit much to ask. He didn't even want to go and live in England, so how could he expect her to give up everything and go with him so he could be close to the child he shared with another woman? But if he stayed here with Jo, how was that going to work with his child on the other side of the world?

Jo turned on her side again, gazing out the window. She knew she was right. If Sarah went back home and Joe stayed here because of her, he'd resent it, she was certain. He'd want to be close to his child, he'd have to go to England. She supposed she could go too ... but surely it was way too early in their relationship to be pulling up stakes and following him across the other side of the world, to stand in the background while he played co-parent with his former lover, who, by all accounts, was still holding a torch for him?

It was all too tenuous, too unpredictable. There was every chance the bond between them would grow deeper when the baby was born, that was to be expected. Jo felt a chill in her heart, imagining herself in a flat on her own in London, while Joe was off spending time with Sarah and the baby ...

She rolled onto her back, scattering the image from her mind. She needn't worry. He hadn't even suggested her going with him as a possibility, even though apparently he hadn't slept all night trying to think of a solution.

Jo glanced at him. 'Did you tell her about me?' she asked in a small voice.

'I told her there was someone,' he said, 'but she didn't really take it in, she was too focused on what she had to say.'

Of course, the baby trumped everything. 'I have to ask ... you're sure it's yours?'

He sighed, nodding slowly. 'I'm sure.' He was still staring up at the ceiling. 'I keep thinking about my parents. You know my mother fell pregnant with me when they were both working in Vietnam. They weren't married, they hadn't even been together that long. She could have gone back to the US, Dad would never have known . . .'

'But they loved each other.'

'They did,' he admitted. 'So they came to Australia, made a life. We had a mother and a father and I had a happy childhood.'

Will didn't have it quite so good, though. Joe imagined a lifetime of trying to make up for never being there; he saw a polite eight year old who thought of him as a distant uncle, a sullen sixteen year old full of resentment, a young adult who didn't want to know him.

A happy childhood sounded like an impossible dream to Jo. Her childhood was spent pining for an absent father, littered with all the broken dreams of an abandoned mother.

She imagined Joe walking into the flat in London. *We have to talk.* A sob caught in her throat.

'Jo?' He turned to look at her, propping himself on one elbow. Her face crumpled as the tears finally broke. He drew her into his arms and held her close.

'You have to go and be with her, Joe,' she sobbed into his chest. 'It's the right thing. She shouldn't have to do this on her own, and your baby needs a father.'

Joe didn't want to hear that right now, he didn't want to think about that. He just wanted to stop her crying, stop her pain somehow. He rocked her in his arms, soothing her, saying he was sorry, over and over. He smoothed the hair away from her face, wiping her tears away, kissing her cheeks, her forehead, her lips.

She pulled back. 'We can't, Joe. You should go.'

'I don't want to leave you now,' he said plaintively. 'Not tonight, can't we just have tonight?'

Jo sniffed, staring up at him. 'But what will you tell her?'

'I don't know, I don't care,' he said. 'I just want to be with you now. I love you so much, Jo.'

'I love you too.'

And then, because it was just the two of them, alone in the room together, and they were never going to have this chance again, they made love. And it was sad, and heartwrenching, and poignant, and tender. And they eventually fell asleep wrapped in each other's arms.

And Jo dreamed they were in the elevator again, and no one knew where they were, and no one could get to them.

Morning

'Joe ... Joe ...'

He stirred sleepily, resisting her.

'Joe, wake up.'

He blinked, opening his eyes a little. The room was still dark.

'You fell asleep, it's nearly morning, you have to go.'

'No, not now,' he murmured, nestling his head into her shoulder.

'Yes, now,' she said plainly. 'Believe me, I know the drill.'

He lifted his head to look at her. 'Jo, I wish you'd stop talking like that. We haven't been having an affair.'

'Not until last night,' she said. 'I can't do it, Joe. Not with you.'

He sighed, propping his head up with his hand. 'I don't even know what's going to happen yet, nothing's settled,' he insisted. 'I didn't make any kind of commitment to her.'

'And you're not going to while you keep me on the side. Joe, you were the one who told me you have to give a hundred per-cent of yourself in a relationship,' she reminded him. 'You don't know how you're going to feel when that baby's born – you think it's fair to keep us both in circulation so you can decide then?'

He breathed out, dropping his head onto her chest, and Jo brought her hand up to stroke his hair.

He lifted his head after a while. 'You really don't think there's any other way?'

Jo looked at him steadily. 'Do you?'

They gazed at each other a long moment, before he lowered his lips to meet hers, and they kissed with a sad, desperate long-ing. The pain rose to the surface again, and suddenly Jo couldn't bear it, couldn't bear that she was losing him. She wrapped her arms around his neck, holding him tight and kissing him frantically as she straddled him with her legs. She pushed him onto his back and rolled over on top of him, rocking her pelvis against him. She felt him becoming aroused, heard his faint moan as she reached down to take hold of him. He grabbed her face, bringing her mouth hard against his, kissing her hungrily as she pushed and pounded and bore herself down onto him, as though she was trying to meld their bodies into one, so she could keep him with her always, They climaxed together with such intensity it was almost unbearable, and Jo collapsed onto him, sobbing freely. She didn't try to hold it back, she didn't care any more, she wept freely as he held her close, burying his face in her hair. And she realised he was crying too.

Jo didn't know how long they stayed like that, entwined, clinging to each other. Finally she broke away, someone had to. She unravelled her limbs from his. 'You have to go.'

'Jo –'

'Just go, please. Don't make it any harder.'

Reluctantly he got up out of the bed, and put on his clothes, and Jo lay on her side, watching him. He was going to be a father, she had to keep telling herself; his baby had come into existence before they had even met. He was never hers to have . . .

He sat back on the bed when he was dressed, gazing down at her, stroking her arm. They didn't say anything, there was nothing else to say. He leaned down and pressed his lips to her shoulder, pausing for a moment, his eyes closed. Then he slowly got to his feet and walked out of the room.

Jo remembered she still had his jacket from the other night. She threw the covers off and grabbed her robe. 'Joe, wait,' she called as she pulled it on.

He was standing by the door when she hurried out.

'Your jacket,' she said. 'You better not leave this behind.'

As he took it from her, he drew her into his arms again, holding her close. He felt as though he was leaving his whole heart behind. He was empty; he had nothing for Sarah, and worse, nothing for the baby.

She pulled back first, looking up at him. 'Goodbye, Joe.'

His eyes lingered on her for a long moment, before he touched his hand to her cheek and turned away, walking up the corridor. Jo didn't quite close the door, she watched him through the narrow chink as he pressed the button for the elevator. She saw him wipe his eyes with the back of his hand, then he stepped into the lift, and he was out of sight.

Jo went back to bed, but she lay there awake, for hours, not moving, not crying, not even feeling much. She watched the clock tick over. When it made it to eight-thirty, she reached across and picked up the phone. She rang the office and told the receptionist she wasn't well, she wouldn't be coming in today. She didn't have to put on an act, she sounded dreadful, and the girl, Jo didn't catch her name, was very sympathetic, assuring her she would pass the message on, and that Jo should just concentrate on feeling better.

But she wasn't going to feel better any time soon. She hung up and rolled over onto her side. Sometime later she drifted off to sleep.

8:40 am

Sarah was still asleep, or at least she hadn't emerged from the spare bedroom when Joe had let himself into the flat earlier. He'd gone directly to his room and fallen onto the bed. He didn't sleep, he just lay there for hours, thinking about Jo, and the fucking awful hand fate had dealt them.

He found himself wishing he didn't know about the baby, at the same time hating himself for even thinking that. He wanted to feel excited about becoming a father, but right now he couldn't muster up the least bit of enthusiasm. He hoped that would come in time; it had to or else life would be unbearable.

But what bothered him more than anything was that he'd hurt Jo so badly. If Sarah had showed up sooner it wouldn't have come to this. He wouldn't have said all those things to Jo, wouldn't have tried to convince her that he was the guy she could trust, who wasn't going to leave her, who was never going to let her down. And he wouldn't have fallen in love with her so completely and know that he couldn't love anyone else the way he loved her.

'Joe?' He heard Sarah's voice outside his door.

'Yeah,' he said.

She pushed the door open and peered in.

'You came in late. I didn't hear you.'

He had to get over this disdain he felt for her. When he'd opened the door yesterday to be confronted with her obviously pregnant girth, he had gone into a kind of shock. He knew it had to be his, but he had proceeded to interrogate her for most of the night, trying to make sense of it, trying to dodge the inevitability of what it meant.

Sarah had finally interrupted him. 'Is this so terrible, Joe? I know things had cooled between us before you left, but that was only because we'd been apart so much. I don't blame you, we were both distracted, we weren't making an effort. But before that it was good, wasn't it? Can't we salvage that, build on it, for the sake of the baby?'

'You don't understand, Sarah. I've met someone.'

She'd barely registered a reaction. 'Well, unless you met her the first day you arrived home, it can't have been going on long, Joe. We had three years together, and now we're having a child together. You think I'm not making sacrifices?'

He had let his mind drift, imagining instead that it was Jo who was pregnant. It would have caused no end of drama, he knew what she was like. She'd have protested that they hadn't known each other long enough, that she wasn't even sure she wanted a baby, what this would do to her career – she'd have come up with a whole raft of reasons against it, that was her specialty. But just the thought of it, the idea of it, gave Joe such an overwhelming sense of joy. That's what he should be feeling now. Maybe he had to wait for the birth. Surely he'd fall in love with his own child then, and that would be enough.

'I was going to make a pot of tea,' Sarah was saying. 'Would you like a cup?'

He swallowed down the ache in his throat. 'Sure, I'll be out in a minute.'

'Okay,' she said, slipping away again.

So now this was his life. Who the hell ever said you got to choose your own destiny?

3 pm

Jo was sitting on the train to Sutherland, her head lolling against the window as she stared out at the passing scenery, but it was all a blur. Belle had sent a text message around the middle of the day, prompting Jo to give her an idea of when she'd be arriving. Her immediate impulse was to message straight back and say she couldn't make it. But she knew Belle would argue the toss, and demand a good excuse, and Jo would have to tell her what had happened, and she couldn't face that. Besides, she had to get out of the apartment. Jo had a sickening feeling that if she didn't drag herself up out of that bed today, she might never get out of it. She had to put one foot in the front of the other and get on with her life.

She saw Belle's monster truck parked on the side of the road as she walked down from the station.

'Hi, you made it.' Belle chirped as Jo opened the passenger door. Then she frowned. 'God, you look terrible.'

'Thanks Belle,' she said, clambering up onto the front seat. While she'd made the effort to get out of bed, she hadn't made much of an effort beyond that. It wasn't until she'd seen her reflection in the polished doors of the apartment elevator that she realised how drab she looked, in a grey mottled T-shirt, brown cardigan and old jeans. Her hair was pulled back roughly into an elastic and she hadn't bothered with make-up, though she probably should have, given the dark circles under her eyes.

'No, really,' Belle persisted, 'are you all right, Jo?'

'I'm fine.' She clicked her seatbelt into place, but Belle was still staring at her.

'What happened? Is it Joe?'

She sighed. 'Not now, Belle, can we just get going? You better fill me in on what you know about Mum so I'm up to speed.'

Belle hesitated for a moment, then she started up the engine and pulled out from the kerb without looking. A car beeped its horn behind them. 'What's your problem? I used my blinker,' she said to the rear-vision mirror. 'So, about Mum. I haven't got much out of her, that's the whole problem.'

The conversation remained on Charlene for the drive back to Belle's house. Not that it was a conversation as such. Belle blathered on the whole way: Charlene was being typically cagey, only admitting she had to have some more tests, and that she may have to have a minor 'procedure' which was nothing for Belle to concern herself with, but she'd probably have to stay around for a few weeks, and if Belle had some kind of problem with that she'd book herself into a cheap hotel somewhere, not that she could afford it, but if she had no choice, if her daughter wasn't prepared to support her . . .

'So what am I supposed to do?' Belle was saying as they pulled into her street.

'Don't worry,' said Jo. 'We'll get to the bottom of it.'

Belle swung the car into the driveway and yanked on the handbrake. She turned to look at her sister. 'I really appreciate you coming, Jo, even though I know you don't want to be here.'

Jo unbuckled her seatbelt. 'I do want to be here, Belle, for you. And let's not forget, she's my mother too.'

Belle launched over and pecked her on the cheek. 'What would I do without you?'

Jo felt tears spring into her eyes. God, she had to keep her emotions in check. She sniffed. 'Let's do this.'

Belle let them into the house and sang out, 'Hey Mum, we're back.'

'Whoop-de-do,' came a call from the family room. She sounded like she'd been drinking, which was hardly a surprise.

They walked through the house into the kitchen. Charlene was reclined on the lounge wearing a leopard-skin print wrap dress and full make-up, her feet propped on the coffee table, and a martini glass in her hand. She was such a cliché.

'Isn't it a bit early for cocktail hour, Mother?' said Jo, plonking her handbag on the breakfast bar.

'Well, you know what they say, it's five o'clock somewhere in the world.'

Such a cliché.

'So,' Jo began, walking over to an armchair and sitting down, 'what's the story?'

Charlene sat forward. 'My God, you look shocking, Jo. What have you been doing with yourself?'

Jo sighed, crossing her legs. 'Oh, you know, working hard, making a living. Some of us have to.'

'You need a good beauty therapist, Jo. I don't know Sydney, up in Surfers I could give you the name of several.'

'I find that hard to believe.'

'Well, you two,' Belle said with a nervous laugh. 'How about a drink? I see you're right at the moment, Mum, can I interest you in a G&T, Jo?'

She thought it was probably best to steer clear of gin. 'No, just water, thanks Belle.'

She frowned. 'Are you sure?'

'Yes I'm sure,' she nodded, looking meaningfully at Belle.

'Okay,' she chirped, turning around to the fridge.

Jo looked back at Charlene. 'So how are you, Mum?'

'I'm fine, love, how are you?'

'Well, I'm fine too, but I'm not booked in for tests at the hospital tomorrow.'

Charlene sighed loudly as Belle walked over with a tall glass of ice water for Jo. She handed it to her and went to sit in the other armchair. Charlene raised an eyebrow, glancing from one daughter to the other.

'What is this, an inquisition?'

'No, Mum,' Belle said carefully. 'I asked Jo to come because I'm worried about you, and you won't tell me what's going on.'

'I told you all you need to know, Belle darling,' said Charlene. 'You're such a stress-bunny,' she shook her head. 'My sweet little Tinkerbell. Always fussing, even when there's nothing to fuss about.'

Jo sighed. She could see this wasn't going to work as a three-some. 'Can you come here for a minute, Belle?' she said, getting to her feet and marching back through the kitchen to the front room, Belle scampering along behind her.

Jo turned around to face her once they were out of earshot. 'You should go pick up Caelen.'

'But Darren's picking him up.'

'Okay, where are the twins?'

'With Nicole –'

'– two doors up,' Jo nodded.

'That's right!' Belle exclaimed, clearly pleased that she remembered.

'Go to Nicole's, and stay there,' Jo instructed. 'I think it's better if I talk to Mum alone. She'll only play us off each other, and we won't get anywhere.'

Belle nodded. 'She can be so . . . so intractable.'

Jo blinked, that was unexpected. 'Yes, she can, Belle, that's exactly what she is. Intractable. Good word.'

Belle smiled proudly.

'All right, so you go to Nicole's,' said Jo. 'And I'll take it from here.'

'Are you sure?' she winced.

'Absolutely.'

'Thanks,' she mouthed before throwing her arms around Jo's neck. 'I'm so glad you're here. I love you so much.'

Jo's throat tightened again, or maybe it was just because Belle was almost choking her in her enthusiasm. Jo removed her arms and propelled her towards the door. 'Take your mobile, I'll buzz you when it's safe to come back.'

She turned down the hall. 'So, Mum,' Jo said as she walked into the kitchen, 'now that it's just you and me, let's cut the crap.'

Charlene was at the kitchen bench, making herself another drink.

'Well, I'm sure I don't know what you mean,' she drawled, doing a pretty good impression of Blanche what's-her-face from that Tennessee Williams play. God, Angie was beginning to rub off on her.

'You know exactly what I mean, Mother,' Jo said firmly.

'I'm going out for a smoke,' said Charlene, picking up her drink and heading for the sliding doors.

Jo followed her. Charlene put her drink down on the outdoor table and picked up her cigarette packet. Jo had the sudden urge for a cigarette herself, though she hadn't had so much as a puff in ten years. And she certainly wasn't going to give her mother the satisfaction of asking for one.

Charlene lit her cigarette and drew back on it deeply as she settled herself in one of the sun-loungers. 'Pass me my drink, would you, Jo?'

Jo picked up the glass and handed it to her. Then she dragged a garden chair over and sat down, facing her.

'So what's going on, Mum?' she said. 'What are these tests about?'

Charlene blew out smoke. 'That's my business.'

'Well, you see, it becomes our business when you land on Belle's doorstep expecting her to put you up, care for you, run you around, when she's got enough on her plate as it is, with three kids to look after. She doesn't need another one.'

'Honestly, you're so melodramatic, Jo. You always have been.'

'Then I know who I get it from.'

Charlene shook her head. 'No, you must have got that from your father, because I'm actually trying to avoid a drama, in case you haven't noticed.'

'But you're not succeeding,' said Jo. 'Belle is beside herself, she's really upset. Don't you give a bugger about anyone but yourself, Mum?'

'Of course I do, that's why I don't want to bother her with this.'

'But she is bothered, can't you see that? You've always been so damn self-absorbed, you never saw how what you did affected us.'

Charlene dragged on her cigarette. 'You know, Jo, you're a successful journalist with your own apartment in the city. Belle has a wonderful husband, beautiful children and a fabulous home. You two seem to have done all right out of the supposed "difficult childhood" you're always harping on about.'

Jo couldn't believe what she was hearing. 'Are you seriously going to sit there and suggest that you are in any way responsible for the fact that we turned out okay? That we even made it to adulthood?'

'There you go again with the melodrama.' Charlene was unmoved. 'You love to blame it all on me, don't you, Jo? But you forget that the reason we had it so hard was because your father walked out on us. Things were different then, Jo. They didn't throw money at single mothers the way they do now, giving them bonuses just for having a baby to begin with. I could have used a handout like that. There was barely even any childcare back then.'

'Well, you didn't need childcare, you had me, Mum.'

'Thank God for you, Jo,' her words oily with sarcasm. 'How would we ever have gotten by without you? You have no idea what I went through.'

'Over a hundred blokes at last count,' said Jo.

Now she just looked miffed. 'You don't seem to realise that I had to rely on the kindness of strangers, I had no choice.'

For crying out loud, she was Blanche de ... whatever her name was.

'I don't remember any "kind strangers", Mum, only a lot of drunken no-hopers who made our lives a misery.'

'You can be so smug, Jo. You've had one decent boyfriend in the last decade, that big bear of a man you brought here, and how long did he last? It obviously didn't take him long to get your measure.'

Jo got to her feet, rage bubbling up inside her. She wasn't going to discuss Joe with Charlene and she wasn't going to let her get the better of her. 'Okay, here's how we're going to do this. Either you tell me what these tests are about, what's going on, right here, right now, or I'm personally escorting you to the airport tonight, buying you a ticket and putting you on a plane back to Queensland, where you can do whatever the hell it is you're doing without any interference from us. I guarantee that. But you can't have it both ways, Mum. If you want to stay here with Belle, you're going to give me an explanation right now, or we're off to the airport. And if you don't think Belle will back me up on this, then go ahead, put it to the test.'

Charlene glared at her but Jo held her gaze. Finally she breathed out loudly. 'Fine, I have a lump in my breast, are you happy?'

'So what's the prognosis?' Jo asked levelly.

'It's malignant,' said Charlene, stubbing out her cigarette.

'And?'

'What do you mean "And?",' she asked haughtily. '"And" I'm going to cark it, is that what you want to hear?'

'Who's being melodramatic now?' Jo returned, unfazed. 'What I meant was, what treatment are they recommending? A lumpectomy, a partial mastectomy, a full mastectomy, ray treatment, chemotherapy . . .'

'When did you become the expert?'

'I'm a journalist, Mum. I know stuff.'

'Always the know-it-all, and always rubbing our noses in it,' Charlene murmured, shaking her head.

'I'm not rubbing your nose in anything,' Jo retorted. 'I just want to know where things stand.'

'That's what I'm going to find out tomorrow.'

Jo crossed her arms, looking down at her. 'Belle's taking you to your appointment?'

'She said she would. Do you have a problem with that?'

'Fine,' said Jo. 'I'll get the details from her and meet you there.'

Charlene glared at her. 'Why are you doing this?'

'I'm doing it for Belle. I'm going to see to it that she doesn't have to put up with any more of your nonsense, same as I always have.'

Jo would have preferred to have left then, but she'd promised to stay for dinner, and Belle was more than a little frazzled after she got her aside and filled her in. Somehow they got through the meal, mostly because Belle and Darren's constant stream of bickering, blended with endless and exhausting interruptions from the kids, did not require or even allow input from anyone else. Jo barely ate, she took a bite here and there, and moved her food around on the plate, but Belle didn't seem to notice, she was too preoccupied with what her children were eating, or not eating, or smearing over themselves or dropping on the floor. When Jo announced she should get going, Charlene promptly said goodbye and walked outside to smoke. Belle insisted she would drive Jo to the station, despite Darren's protestations.

'No way, mister, you can have crazy hour tonight,' she said, picking up the car keys. 'I expect the kids to be all tucked in bed by the time I get back, and you can make a start on the dishes as well.'

Belle pulled out of the driveway and turned up the street. 'I knew it had to be something like this,' she said gloomily. 'I just didn't want to think the worst.'

'It's not the worst, Belle,' said Jo. 'Breast cancer is the most common cancer in women, but it still lags behind lung and bowel and prostate cancer mortality rates, and well behind heart disease.'

'You're not just saying that?'

Jo shook her head. 'Every pink ribbon day we do saturated coverage on breast cancer, I know the stats almost by heart. It has one of the highest survival rates of all cancers, especially if it's treated early.'

'But we can't be sure how early she's caught it.'

'We'll have a better idea tomorrow.'

Belle glanced at her as she careered through a roundabout. 'You're sure you want to come?'

'Of course.' She wasn't. Jo didn't know why she'd insisted on it, but she just couldn't leave it all to Belle. It was the right thing to do, to look after a sick parent. It just bugged her that Charlene had not fulfilled her part of the bargain and looked after them a little better when it was her turn.

They drove on mostly in silence, which was unusual for Belle, but Jo supposed she needed to process all this. When they arrived at Sutherland station, Belle pulled the car into the kerb with a scrape of the tyres, and Jo made ready to jump out.

'Hold on, Jo,' said Belle, turning off the engine. 'You haven't told me about the big mystery.'

Jo glanced at her. Damn. 'It doesn't matter.'

'Yes it does. You looked terrible today, and don't say it was just because you had to see Mum. You were so quiet at dinner and you hardly ate a thing.'

So she did notice.

'Besides,' Belle went on, 'you promised, and I'm not letting you out of the car till you tell me.'

Jo was not so sure that she had actually promised, and it wasn't as though Belle could physically stop her from getting out of the car. But she knew she had to tell her. It was just going to be really hard to say it out loud.

'Joe and I,' she began, 'we're really over this time.'

'Oh, you two,' Belle dismissed. 'You have more ups and downs than a seesaw. It'll be on again next week, mark my words, Jo . . . Jo?'

She had dropped her head to hide her face and attempt to hold back the tidal wave rising up in her gut.

'Jo?'

But she couldn't do it. She covered her face as she burst into tears. Really burst, like a dam. Jo had seen films of dams bursting, their huge concrete walls cracking as the water broke through. That's how she felt right now, like she was cracking up.

'Jo!' Belle exclaimed, obviously startled.

But she couldn't stop. She kept on crying, wailing even, as huge sobs lurched from deep inside her. Belle undid her seatbelt and sidled closer. She wrapped her arms around her and held her tight, rocking her and shushing her as she would one of the children, rubbing her back in a circular motion. It was strangely mesmerising, and comforting, and after a while Jo wasn't shaking any more; her tears subsided and she was calm again.

'Oh my God, Jo,' Belle sighed. 'I've never seen you cry like that, I've barely ever seen you cry! What happened? What on earth did he do to you?'

Jo sat up straight, wiping her eyes. 'Joe didn't do anything. His old girlfriend from England arrived on his doorstep, pregnant, with his child.'

'Oh bugger!' she gasped.

That was putting it mildly.

Belle looked at her. 'You really fell hard for him in the end, didn't you?'

Jo nodded.

'So what's going to happen?'

She shrugged. 'He's going to do the right thing by her, and the baby, of course.'

'Of course,' Belle sighed. 'You wouldn't love him if he didn't.'

'What?' Jo frowned.

'You could never have fallen this hard for someone unless he was a really decent man, who you could trust with your whole heart. But you never thought you'd find anyone like that, I reckon you didn't even think anyone like that existed. And then you met a guy in an elevator.... and you had no time to put up all the defences ...'

'Oh, but I tried.'

'I know you did, but it didn't work, did it?' said Belle. 'And you know what that means. Your earthly powers were no match for him. Because he really was the one ...'

Jo frowned at her. 'Is this supposed to make me feel better?'

'Oh, sorry,' Belle smiled lamely. 'I'm just saying that you wouldn't have fallen in love with Joe if he wasn't the kind of guy who has to leave you to do the right thing. That's ironic, isn't it?'

She stared in front of her. 'Yeah, I believe it might be.'

Belle was watching her. 'Jo, I can't let you go home like this. Come back with me and stay the night. We can get drunk.'

But Jo was already shaking her head. 'This isn't the kind of thing to get drunk about. It's bigger than that.'

Belle nodded, understanding. 'Then come back and we'll drink hot chocolate, whatever. I don't want you to be alone.'

'No, I'll be okay. I feel a lot better after that cry, I really do. And you're probably the only person I could cry like that to.' Except for Joe, she sighed inwardly. 'I just want to go home now, sleep in my own bed.'

Belle reluctantly agreed, and they hugged again before Jo climbed out of the car.

'See you tomorrow,' she said, closing the car door. And then she put one foot in front of the other, and walked down onto the platform to catch her train.

*

Friday

Joe had finally got to sleep sometime in the early hours of this morning. He hadn't slept well all week, he was worried about Jo. He hadn't seen her since he left her apartment on Tuesday morning; she hadn't shown up at work since. He wanted to call her, but he'd resisted so far, he knew she'd want some space. He finally sent her an email yesterday, only brief, just asking after her, but she hadn't replied yet. If she wasn't at work today, he was going to call her regardless; he had to make sure she was all right.

When he had eventually drifted off to sleep, Jo had filled his dreams, as she had every other night. Mostly they were disturbing, nonsensical dreams, but sometimes he dreamed she was lying there in the bed beside him, and he could hold her and kiss her and make love to her. Sometimes they were so vivid, like right now, he knew he was only dreaming, but he could actually feel her hands smoothing across his chest, one hand moving down, slipping under his boxers. He reached for her wrist. 'Jo.'

'*Joe?*'

He opened his eyes to find Sarah was leaning above him. 'What are you doing?' He rolled away from her and sat up on the opposite edge of the bed.

'Hoping to get reacquainted,' she said. 'You always used to like it in the morning.'

'But, but . . . you're pregnant.'

'It's okay, Joe, it's not against the rules,' she said, clearly flustered. 'I had to do something, I feel so distant from you. If I waited for you to make a move . . .'

Christ, what was he supposed to say to that? He reached down to the floor and grabbed a T-shirt, pulling it over his head. He didn't feel comfortable sitting here across the bed from her in his underwear.

'You know you called out your own name then?' said Sarah. 'What's that about?'

Joe rubbed his eyes. 'The woman I was seeing, her name is Jo.'

'Oh, I see,' she said, her expression hardening. 'Well, that must have been funny, you both having the same name.'

'Everyone seemed to think so,' he muttered. It was time he gave her the whole story. 'The thing is, Sarah, I actually did meet Jo the first day I got back home, and I think I even fell in love with her the same day, at least a little. I know that doesn't amount to three years, but you're going to have to give me some time to get over her.'

She looked a little vexed. 'You didn't say it was that serious.'

'You didn't ask. You kind of skipped right over it.' He paused. 'But I can't.'

'Are you saying you can't give her up?'

'I'm saying it's going to take time.'

'Are you still seeing her?'

'No.'

Sarah pulled her robe around her, crossing her arms. 'So how long do you think it's going to take?' she said curtly.

He honestly didn't know how he was ever going to get over Jo. Or how he could ever be with Sarah again. He couldn't think about that. The only thing he could do right now was focus on the baby.

'I suppose . . .' he hesitated. 'Well, I guess when the baby comes, we'll take it from there.' That was the best he could do.

He could see the pique in her expression. 'Fine,' she said. 'I'll stay out of your room until I'm invited. Only I was hoping to start fixing up somewhere for the baby, seeing as I don't have much else to do, and there is only one other bedroom . . . I just thought . . .'

He knew what she was getting at, and he didn't know what to say. He wasn't ready to share a flat with her, let alone a bed.

'Never mind,' Sarah went on, 'I'm sure we can fit a crib in the room with me, a change table. Maybe you could come shopping with me?'

He looked up. 'What's the rush? There's still a couple of months.'

'Because this is what you do, Joe,' she said, slightly exasperated. 'You prepare yourself, you start . . . nesting, that's what all the books say. It might help you to come to terms with the fact that there's going to be a baby actually living here.'

He nodded thoughtfully.

'So can we go shopping?' she persisted.

'Sure . . .'

'Today?'

'I have to work today, Sarah.'

'Tomorrow then?'

'I have to work tomorrow too.'

'But it's a Saturday.'

'And it's a Sunday paper.'

'I don't understand,' she said. 'I thought you were only writing features and op-eds, it's not like you have to be there all the time.'

'I just had a whole week up with Dad, I told you that. I have to make up some time.' And he had to make up any excuse to get out of here as much as possible. At least until he got used to this.

She was watching him. 'I'm nagging, aren't I?'

'Little bit.'

'Okay,' she said, as though something was resolved. 'I'll leave you to get ready. Do you want a cup of tea?' she asked on her way to the door.

He looked at her. 'You don't make coffee, do you?'

'You buy coffee at a café,' she said archly. 'You make tea at home.'

'Whatever you say.'

The Tribune

It was easy to wander around a newspaper office without looking obvious or bothering anyone. Everyone wandered around in various levels of chaos, vacillating from mild to frenetic, depending on the day or even the time of day. So although Joe had probably done ten laps of the news floor throughout the morning, no one would have noticed or thought anything of it if they had.

He hadn't seen Jo yet; he kept walking by her desk, but her computer hadn't been turned on; there was still no sign she had been here for days, nothing in the wastepaper basket, nothing had been disturbed on the desk, her chair hadn't even shifted. Joe leaned against the half-wall staring into the cubicle. He was really beginning to worry about her. Surely she'd understand if he rang her.

He spotted Leo walking around the other side of the news floor, his head bent over a wad of papers. Joe quickly manouevred through the maze of desks to head him off at the pass.

'Leo?'

He glanced up briefly. 'Joe,' he acknowledged, returning his attention to the papers as he continued on his way.

Joe fell in beside him. 'Listen, you haven't heard from Jo Liddell, have you? She hasn't been in for a few days as far as I can tell.'

'She's taking some personal leave,' he muttered without looking up.

'Do you know why?'

'There's a reason it's called "personal" leave, Joe.' They arrived at the elevator bay and Leo pressed the button to go up. 'Do you know anything about this Libyan-based militia group that has suspected ties to al-Qaeda?' he asked.

'A little,' Joe shrugged.

'What do you know?'

'That there's a Libyan-based militia group that has suspected ties to al-Qaeda.'

'You want to look into it?' Leo said, holding up a manila folder.

'Sure,' Joe said, taking the file from him as the elevator doors opened.

'Illness in the family,' said Leo, walking into the lift.

'What was that?'

'Jo's taking leave because of an illness in the family.'

'Oh, not her sister, I hope?'

Leo pressed the button for his floor. 'You'll have to ask her.'

'I intend to.'

Leo nodded as the doors began to glide to a close. 'Apparently it's her mother.'

'Thanks.'

He walked quickly back to his office and closed the door,

tossing the folder onto his desk. He picked up the phone and dialled for an outside line, then he took his mobile out of his pocket and scrolled down to find Jo's mobile number. The *Trib*'s number was blocked so she wouldn't know it was him calling. Maybe he was being paranoid, but he wasn't sure whether she'd pick up if she did. He didn't know what their relationship was now. As he waited for the call to connect, he wondered if her mother really was sick. They weren't very close, it was possibly just an excuse.

'Hello?'

Joe was taken aback for a moment at the sound of her voice. 'Hi, Jo, it's me.'

'Oh . . . hello.'

She sounded guarded.

'I'm calling, well, I just wanted to see if you were all right.'

'I'm all right, Joe.'

'Leo said you're taking some personal leave?'

He heard her sigh. 'Yeah, it's my mother.'

He moved around to sit down at his desk. 'Is she okay?'

'Well, no, not exactly. She has breast cancer.'

'God, Jo, how bad is it?'

'Bad enough. Not that she seems to get that.'

'What do you mean?'

'She's refusing to take the doctor's advice, she's worked out her own treatment plan instead.'

'Based on what?'

'Her vast medical knowledge and experience, I suppose.'

'Jo, what's going on?'

She sighed again. 'I wish I knew, Joe,' she said, her defences dropping finally, he could hear it in her voice.

'Talk to me.'

'She agreed to have the lump removed, which they did Wednesday, and she'll start ray treatment next Tuesday, despite the fact that the doctor preferred a partial mastectomy to be safe, and possibly a course of chemo depending on the pathology results after surgery.'

'I don't understand,' said Joe. 'Why wouldn't she listen to the doctor?'

'I have no idea, she won't discuss it at the moment. I might have a better chance of getting it out of her once she moves in here.'

'She's moving in with you?' He was surprised to hear that, given their relationship.

'Well she can't stay out at Belle's, she has to go to the hospital five days a week for the next seven weeks. It's a short ride by taxi from my place, so this was the best solution.'

'How do you feel about that?'

'It doesn't matter how I feel,' she said. 'I'm doing it for Belle mostly. And because it's the right thing to do. Sometimes you have to do the right thing even if you don't feel like it.'

He wished he could see her, touch her. Be there for her.

'I miss you,' he said.

'Joe, you can't say that. Do you think it helps me to hear you say that?'

'I'm sorry, it's just the way I feel.'

'Like I said, how we feel doesn't matter.'

'Yes it does.'

'Joe –'

'I'm just saying, it matters.'

'But it doesn't change anything.'

'No,' he said quietly. 'It just makes it hard.'

'I can't listen to this, Joe,' she said. 'I'm going to have to hang up if you keep talking like that.'

'Don't, please,' he said. 'I'm only trying to work out where we go from here. Can't we be friends at least, Jo?'

'Not if I have to listen to you talking about how hard it is.'

'Fair enough,' he sighed. 'When am I going to see you?'

'I'll be back at work next week,' she told him. 'I'm sure we'll bump into each other from time to time, Joe. But I have to be honest, I'm probably going to try to avoid that.'

'I understand.' But it hurt to hear her say it anyway.

'I hope you do,' said Jo. 'And I hope you will respect that.'

'I will,' he said. 'But Jo, I want you to know that I'm here if you need me. Always remember that.'

*

Tuesday

Jo heard her phone ring twice and then stop. That would be Belle; she was dropping off Charlene and Jo had warned her there was no way she would get a park in the middle of the afternoon on a week day. She said to prank her phone, and she'd come down and meet them on the street. Jo grabbed her keys and headed out the door. She didn't know if she was prepared for this, but now she had no more time to think about it. The arrangement eventually agreed upon was that Belle would take Charlene for her first session of ray treatment, and then bring her back to Jo's place, to stay. Charlene had obviously wanted to delay the inevitable for as long as she possibly could. But Belle had stood firm with Jo, so she'd had no choice in the end. It had taken some convincing on Jo's part, Belle was weak where her mother was concerned, but it was Darren who'd put his foot down finally. Belle could not be expected to run Charlene back and forth to the hospital every day, he insisted, there were the children to consider, and it was too much to expect of her anyway. Jo was impressed by his show of force, and for maybe the first time she got a glimpse of what Belle saw in him.

When Jo stepped out of her building she spotted Belle unloading Charlene's bags from the back of her car, just a little way up the street, and walked up to meet her.

'Hi Belle.'

She turned around, looking harried. 'How are you going to manage all of these?'

'Mum can help.'

Belle winced. 'I'm not sure, she seems a bit down after the treatment.'

Maybe it was the treatment, but Jo knew it was more likely she was just having a sulk because she had been usurped from the little principality where she lorded it over Belle. For the first time in her life she had to do what suited her daughters, and she didn't like it. Despite the fact that this was all for her sake anyway.

Jo walked to the passenger door and opened it. 'Hi Mum,' she said matter-of-factly. 'You have to hop out, Belle can't stay parked here for long or she'll get booked.'

Charlene just gave her a withering look.

'Do you need a hand getting out of the car?' Jo added, unfazed.

'I'll manage,' she grunted.

'Good then,' said Jo, turning around to consider the bags lined up on the footpath. 'I might just take a couple of these into the foyer,' she said to Belle.

When she returned, Charlene was hanging onto Belle's arm, talking emphatically. She stopped abruptly when she saw Jo approaching.

'Okay, Mum, say goodbye to Belle,' said Jo. 'She has to get going.'

Belle gave her mother a hug. 'I'll call you later, see how you're doing.'

'Don't pretend you care,' Charlene retorted. 'I'm sure you'll be too busy living it up tonight, glad you've got rid of me.'

'Mum –'

'Come on, Belle,' said Jo firmly, taking her by the arm. 'You have to get back for the kids.'

She led her around to the driver's side and turned to look at her. 'She's going to be okay, she's just trying to make you feel guilty.'

'Yeah, well, she's succeeding.'

'Belle,' Jo shook her head, 'you've done enough for her. More than enough.'

'But are you sure this isn't going to be too much for you?' she asked. 'Where are you going to sleep?'

'We've been through all this,' said Jo. 'I'll sleep on the pull-out lounge, it's perfectly comfortable. I'll be fine.'

Belle looked unconvinced.

'Go home to your family,' said Jo. 'I've got it from here.' She almost had to push Belle into the car. 'Say hi to the kids. And Darren,' she added.

Jo went back to the kerb and stood with Charlene, waving as Belle pulled away with a toot of her horn.

She passed a small overnight bag to her mother. 'Here, you take this. I'll get the rest.'

'This doesn't look like everything,' said Charlene, frowning at
the remaining bags.

'Yeah, I took two of your suitcases into the foyer already.'

'What?' she looked alarmed. 'And you left them there?'

'It's a security block, Mother, no one can get in from the
street.'

'But what about the people who live there?'

Jo ignored the inference. 'Let's go in, shall we?'

The bags were still sitting undisturbed in the foyer, so Jo got
Charlene to hold the door while she transferred the extra bags
into the lift, repeating the process when they arrived at her floor.
She walked down the corridor to her apartment and opened the
door, standing back for Charlene to go through first.

'Well,' she said, looking around, 'not exactly homely, is it?'

Jo wouldn't even credit that with a response.

'Come on through to the bedroom, Mum, and you can get settled.' She walked ahead, carrying what she could of the luggage.
'I've cleared some space in the wardrobe for you,' she said, dropping the bags and sliding the door open as Charlene appeared in
the doorway.

'Hmm, I don't know how I'll fit all my things.'

Jo didn't know why she had so much stuff, but she wasn't
going to bite. 'You can always rotate, leave what you don't need
in suitcases.'

'I need everything.'

'I'll help you put your things away later, when you're up to
it,' Jo said briskly. 'Bathroom's just through there.' She had spent
the weekend scrubbing the place from top to bottom; she was
not going to let her mother find any grounds for complaint.
Not that Charlene would ever have earned prizes for house-
cleaning, but she would have won a championship trophy for
fault-finding.

'Where can I smoke?' Charlene asked bluntly.

'Down on the street,' Jo returned, just as bluntly.

She looked at her daughter in horror.

'And not just outside the door,' Jo went on, 'you have to be
three metres away from the entrance. Body corporate rules.'

'So I'm going to have to schlep down the elevator every

time I want a cigarette, and stand out on the street with all that pollution?'

'You do have cancer, Mum, maybe this would be a good time to think about cutting down.'

She grunted. 'I'm tired,' she said curtly. 'I'm going to have a lie-down for a while.'

'Okay,' said Jo. 'Call me if you need anything.' She backed out again, closing the door as she did.

It was going to be a long seven weeks.

The Tribune

'Leo, you have got to give me something to do.'

Jo had made an appointment to see Leo in his office the day she got back to work. He finally fitted her in two days later.

'You've got plenty to do,' he said, scrolling down his computer screen, not looking at her.

She shook her head. 'No, I mean you've got to give me something substantial.'

Jo knew that if she had an assignment she could really sink her teeth into she could kill a whole flock of birds with one stone. It would keep her occupied, keep her mind off her own troubles; and she wouldn't have to be at the office so much, therefore avoiding both Lachlan and Joe. She could ignore Lachlan's sneering contempt, but it was harder to ignore Joe. She could sense when he was watching her across the news floor, and she had to steel herself not to look up. She really wished she didn't have to see him at all, it would be so much easier.

If she had an independent assignment she could work from home a lot of the time. That way she'd be close at hand for Charlene, and when that got too much, she could be out and about, meeting with contacts, gathering information.

Leo regarded her over the top of his glasses. 'I don't "got" to give you anything, Joanne. You want to write a big story, go write a big story.'

'Yeah, and any time I've tried to do that, Leo, you take my research and give it to Lachlan or Don, and I get screwed.'

He narrowed his eyes, considering her. Oops, that might have been a bit strong. She didn't know if he was annoyed or intrigued.

'I gave you the climate summit,' he reminded her.

'Yeah, and I did well, didn't I?' she said, holding onto what was left of her bravado.

'I said you did . . . didn't I?'

She folded her arms. 'You vaguely acknowledged it during an editorial meeting.'

'Jo, it's your job,' he sighed, sitting back in his chair. 'If I'm supposed to go around kissing the feet of my journalists because they do their job . . .'

'I'm not asking you to kiss my feet, Leo,' she said firmly, 'I'd just like you to give me the opportunity to do my job to the best of my abilities. You did give me the climate summit, you obviously thought I could handle it. So now what? Do I have to wait another three years before I get to do anything that big again?'

He seemed to be giving it some thought. 'What about the tollway story?' he said finally.

'I thought there was no story,' said Jo. 'Lachlan couldn't find anything.'

He shrugged. 'You want to prove yourself.'

'Leo, it isn't exactly fair to give me something from the too-hard basket that your senior journalists haven't been able to crack.'

'Hear me out,' he said, leaning forward on his desk. 'I met this guy at a function just last night. He was wondering why none of the papers had persisted with investigating the rumours. I told him we kept running into dead ends. He said he'd be happy to talk to someone, even go on the record.'

Jo was intrigued. 'Who is he?'

'He used to work for one of the major contractors.'

She sighed. 'Leo, disgruntled past employees don't generally make reliable informants.'

'He wasn't digging ditches, Jo. He's a senior project manager, and he walked out after he became, let us say, disillusioned with the tender process. And he still has some of the paperwork to support his suspicions.'

Now she was really intrigued. 'Who else knows about this?'

'I was about to hand it to Lachlan,' said Leo. 'But I'll give you a couple of days headstart before I pass it on.'

That was all the motivation she needed.

Two weeks later

Jo stepped into the elevator of her apartment block and pressed the button for her floor. It was only three-thirty, but she tried to get home early most afternoons since Charlene had come to stay. She didn't like to leave her alone into the evening. Not that they spent a great deal of time together, mostly they kept to themselves. Charlene either napped or watched TV or went out for cigarette breaks.

Jo had met with Leo's contact the following day, and he had given her more than enough to go on. She made some calls to verify his credentials, and started to piece together an outline. Leo gave her the go-ahead, and after that, he was content for her to work on it away from the office.

Jo let herself into the apartment and traipsed over to her desk, kicking off her shoes and dumping her briefcase on the chair. She wondered if Charlene was sleeping, she couldn't hear the television. The first week it had driven her mad; the TV was going almost constantly and there was nothing that put Jo more on edge than daytime television. It reminded her of coming home from school when she was a kid. If she could hear the TV as she walked down the front path she knew her mother was either recovering from a hangover, or in the process of getting one, but she would be insufferable in either case. Sure enough, Jo would find Charlene lying on the couch in a haze of smoke, a gin bottle within easy reach, or else coffee mugs and dirty plates and junk food wrappers were strewn across the coffee table and spilling onto the floor. The voiceovers for those tacky afternoon game shows could actually make Jo's palms sweat.

Charlene had the weekends off from treatment, so she spent them at Belle's place. The first time Darren brought her back on the Sunday afternoon, he arrived with a portable TV and set it up in the bedroom for her, much to Jo's eternal gratitude.

She went to check on her mother. She was lying on her side under the covers. Jo couldn't tell if she was awake or asleep until she walked right around the bed. Her eyes were open, staring blankly out the window.

'Hi,' Jo said tentatively. 'Have you been asleep?'

'Mm,' she grunted. 'Till a siren woke me. It's so noisy around here, Jo. What possessed you to live in the middle of the city?'

'It's close to work, I love living in the centre of everything.'

'What, traffic and pollution and noise, and drug addicts down on the street?'

'Yeah, all that,' said Jo, perching herself on the end of the bed. 'How are you feeling?'

'Like you could care less.'

'Okay, you're going to have to give that a rest, Mum,' said Jo. 'It's getting old.'

Charlene sighed. 'I'm tired, okay? I'm constantly tired now. And I'm sore from the radiation.'

'Is that cream helping?' asked Jo.

She rolled over onto her back. 'I don't know, I suppose it's not making it worse,' she said, propping herself up to sit.

Jo considered her. 'I really don't understand why you're doing this, Mum.'

'Because I have cancer, or did you think I was doing it for fun?'

She ignored that. 'I don't know why you're putting yourself through this much discomfort for a course of treatment the doctor said is unlikely to be all that effective.'

'It has to do something,' she dismissed. 'Keep it at bay, at least.'

'Mum, that's not how it works. Cancer's like a weed – if you don't get rid of it, roots and all, if you only part-treat it, then it could come back worse than before,' she said. 'If you'd just had the partial mastectomy, the doctor said you might even have avoided the need for any follow-up treatment.'

'Well I wasn't going to have half my breast hacked off,' she said grumpily.

'So why not have the chemo – that would have had a greater chance of killing off anything that was left.'

'Then I'd lose my hair.'

'But you'd save your life,' Jo said, frustrated.

She snorted. 'What kind of a life would that be, with no hair and a deformed breast?'

'It would be a life,' said Jo, 'whereas you're risking an early death. Besides, your hair will grow back soon enough, and you can have breast augmentation surgery.'

'You have to go on a waiting list for that,' she said curtly. 'Unless you have money, or fancy private medical cover, and I don't have either. So I'd have to put up with looking like a freak for a couple of years or more. I'm not prepared to do that.'

'You wouldn't have to look like a freak, Mum, you could wear a wig, a prosthesis.'

'Oh, and that's not freaky?'

Jo shook her head. 'I just don't get it.'

'What's new?' Charlene said bitterly. 'You never did get me, Jo.'

'Well, you have my undivided attention now, Mum. Help me understand.'

'You don't want to understand, you want to judge.'

Jo felt a pang in her chest. 'Maybe I need to understand so I don't judge you.'

Charlene sighed, turning her head to gaze out the window again. 'All I've ever had is my looks. You think that's trivial, Jo, because you've got other things to fall back on, but I never did. I had you when I was eighteen. By the time I was twenty-two I was on my own with two girls to look after. What was I supposed to do?'

'You had choices, Mum; even if it was harder than it is today, you still had options.'

Charlene shook her head. 'You've never been in the situation, Jo, you couldn't possibly know what it was like for me.'

'I walked out on a man when I was twenty-one, Mum,' she said flatly. 'I have a bit of an idea.'

'You didn't have children to worry about,' she reminded her. 'You had looks, and a brain. And you were so bloody independent from the day you were born, you never even needed a mother, let alone anyone else to look after you.'

'I needed a mother,' said Jo, 'I just had to learn to get by without one I could count on.'

Charlene looked at her. 'This is you not judging me?'

Jo held her hands up in surrender. 'I'm sorry, you're right. Go on, please.'

'I did the best I could,' she continued. 'I was a teenager when I got pregnant, I was clueless, the only thing I was really good at was attracting men.'

'You weren't all that good at it, you kept attracting the wrong ones.'

'They don't wear a warning label, you know, Jo,' she retorted. 'Look, maybe I made some mistakes, but am I going to have to pay for them forever? I'm getting past my prime and I'm not going to be able to attract any sort of man for much longer. I have to think of my future. Do you know what happens to women on their own when they get old? They don't have super, they don't have any security. They're on the bottom rung, reduced to eating dog food on toast –'

'Mum,' Jo interrupted, cutting through the melodrama. 'You know we'd never let that happen.'

'Yeah, well, the thing is, I did meet someone, earlier this year,' she said. 'He's got some money, he's secure, anyway. He likes a drink, but he doesn't have a temper. Things were going well between us, and then this happens.'

'Well, if he was any good, he would have supported you through this,' Jo maintained.

She shook her head. 'For all your brains, you are so naive, Jo. Why do you think I came down here for the treatment? I haven't told him, I don't want him to see me like this. And I'm not going back there bald and deformed.'

Jo frowned. 'So what does he think you're doing here all this time?'

'I told him my daughter was starting work and I was going to look after the kids while she settled into a routine.'

Boy, she really had him fooled. 'He won't want to come and see you?' asked Jo. 'Even for Christmas?'

'He runs his own boat charter company,' said Charlene. 'Summer is his busiest time, it's impossible for him to get away. That's why I waited till now.'

'You waited?' said Jo. 'How long have you known about the lump?'

'I found it months ago, just after I met him, actually,' she said. 'I thought it was hormonal, but then it didn't go away. I went to my GP just before the twins' birthday, and she said I had to do something right away, so I told her I'd have all the tests in Sydney. That way no one needed to know.'

Jo was listening in disbelief. 'What about your friends?' she said. 'Don't you have friends that you told?'

'No, no one knows,' said Charlene.

'Why wouldn't you tell your friends?'

'Because cancer smells like death, Jo,' she said bluntly. 'People are afraid of it, especially at my age. We're all going around pretending we're not getting old – fifty is the new forty, everyone keeps saying. Then someone gets sick and no one wants to know. I've seen it happen. I wasn't going to let it happen to me.'

The next day

Jo felt a heavy sadness permeating everything she did. She decided to go into the office; she had to get out of the oppressive atmosphere in the apartment, and she didn't have the wherewithal to investigate her story today. She could barely string words together into sentences; her writing was clunky and stale, everything seemed like an effort. She had slept fitfully, her dreams disturbing, flashes of her childhood, her mother all dressed up, overdone, but secretly Jo had always thought she was beautiful. And then there were the men – leering, loud, obnoxious, touching her mother, putting their hands all over her. Jo would lie awake in her bed after Belle had gone off to sleep, listening, confused, afraid. She wanted them to leave, to stop touching her mother, to stop what they were doing in her bedroom, making her cry out like that, she sounded like she was in pain. But the men kept coming, they never stopped coming.

Now Charlene was refusing life-saving treatment in order to hold onto a man who, for all she knew, might stand by her anyway. But she was prepared to risk her life rather than risk that he wouldn't. Jo couldn't imagine her desperation, her desolation.

She was scrolling through her emails, disinterestedly, when Joe appeared, leaning over the half-wall of her cubicle.

'Hi,' he said.

She glanced up at him briefly, before returning her gaze to the computer screen. She didn't want to linger on those eyes.

'Hello,' she replied.

'I haven't seen you around much lately. How are you?'

'Okay,' she said, staring at the screen but seeing nothing.

'You don't look okay.'

She shrugged.

'Jo?' His tone was expectant, he was waiting for her to look up, but she couldn't. 'Jo, can you come to my office for a minute?'

'I don't think that's a good idea.'

She heard him sigh. 'Just for a minute.' He dropped his voice. 'Please?'

Maybe she should, so she could tell him that she couldn't come to his office any more, and that he couldn't hang around her cubicle any more, because she couldn't take it any more.

'All right. For a minute.'

She got to her feet, and he waited for her to pass. She walked directly to the door of his office and let herself in. He followed her, closing the door behind him.

'What do you want, Joe?' she said abruptly, turning to face him, but still not looking him in the eye.

'I just want to know if you're all right,' he said, in that gentle, concerned voice he did so well. 'I'm worried about you.'

'You can't keep doing this, Joe.'

'I don't know how I can stop caring about you.'

'Well, you're going to have to. I'm not your concern any more.'

'Jo, can't you even look at me?' he pleaded.

She slowly raised her eyes to meet his. It felt like touching him, looking into his eyes. It was too hard. She turned away and crossed to the window, leaning against the frame as she gazed out at the street below.

'How's your mother?' Joe asked.

'She's okay. The treatment makes her tired. I just try and keep out of her way, mostly.'

He nodded. 'I can relate to that.'

She turned to look at him. 'Do you want me to ask how it's going for you, Joe? Because I can't. Because no matter how hard it is for you — and if you feel anything like I do, then I imagine it must be very hard — I can't have that conversation with you.'

'I'm sorry,' he said, defeated.

He looked so sad, and it was breaking her heart. 'Joe, you have to promise me something,' she said.

'Anything.' That made him look hopeful.

'Well, that's the thing, you can't promise me anything,' she said plainly. She took a breath. 'So you have to promise me this — that you're going to try to be happy.'

'Jo, I can't —'

'No, I mean it,' she said. 'What's the point of all this if you're just going to be miserable, Joe? You have to go and be a wonderful father to that little baby. And it can't just be about the baby, you have to be good to Sarah, so she can be a good mother to your child. You have to make them both feel loved and secure, build a life together. Stay together.'

He was shaking his head slowly. 'I don't know how I'm going to be able to do that, Jo.'

'You have to find a way. You can't be half-hearted about it. Or else nobody wins.'

Joe sighed, rubbing his forehead. 'What about you?'

'I'll get by, I always have,' she dismissed.

He was gazing at her with so much love in his eyes, she had to look away again. It took all the will she possessed not to close the gap between them and put her arms around him and hold him tight, even for a moment. But what good would that do? It would only make it that much harder to walk away.

'You have to forget about me, Joe,' she said finally, as she walked past him, opened the door and left the room.

Sydney Airport

Joe was waiting for Hilary at the arrivals gate at the international terminal. He could hardly wait to see her, and they had the whole drive to Leura together to catch up. Sarah had stayed back at the flat. She wasn't exactly keen about coming up to the mountains for Christmas, though all his family was going to be there and they were planning a major celebration, despite Joe Senior's rapidly deteriorating health. Or rather because of it. They knew this would be their last Christmas with him, and they wanted to cherish it. They were all too aware that they had not had that chance with their mother. Corinne and Alex and the kids were driving up from Melbourne and were due to arrive sometime today, and Will had promised he was making his way up today as well. Joe would have a night with them all, and tomorrow, or perhaps the next day, he'd travel back down to pick up Sarah.

Hilary finally appeared through the automatic doors, pushing a trolley laden with luggage undoubtedly weighed down with too many gifts for them all. She was an exceptional woman, his sister, and Joe was desperately proud of her. She'd never married, but she had a long-time partner, Gregory, an academic at Harvard. They'd been together more than a decade, and although they maintained separate houses ten minutes apart, by all accounts it was a happy arrangement. She'd never had children of her own; she had adopted a tiny, sickly orphaned boy from Serbia who, despite all the best medical care, and Hilary's boundless love and nurturing, had died two years later. She admitted she didn't have it in her to go through that again, and so she had become wedded to her career.

Her face lit up when she spotted Joe. She was a striking woman; she and Corinne were tall like the boys, only Mim had inherited the smaller frame of their mother. Hilary was slender and statuesque, but she had a smile just like their mum's, warm and dazzling.

Joe came forward to meet her as she wheeled her trolley down the walkway, releasing it as she got to him to throw her arms around him.

'Joseph, Joseph,' she exclaimed. She was the only one who called him that. She leaned back to inspect him. 'Oh, what are you doing looking older? You're dragging me along right behind you, you realise.'

'Steady on, you only saw me a few months ago,' he said. 'I can't have aged that much.'

'Maybe it's the light here?'

Joe sighed. 'You know, I'd like it if just one of my siblings could be a little complimentary, or I'm going to end up with a complex.'

'Oh, that's Corinne's job,' Hilary dismissed. 'She'll tell you you're gorgeous and you haven't changed a bit, you wait.'

He pushed her trolley through the terminal out to the carpark while they got the small talk out of the way – how was her flight, had she managed to get any sleep, the weather she'd left compared to what she'd arrived in. Joe opened the car door for Hilary, and tossed her heavy overcoat over the back seat, before stowing her bags into the boot of the car. He'd bought the medium-sized family sedan at Sarah's behest, but he supposed she was right. They would need a car once the baby arrived, as she had pointed out, and lots more besides, apparently. His flat now resembled some kind of baby goods storeroom, every other day more gear jostled for the available space. Joe wondered if one little baby needed so much stuff, but it kept Sarah happy and off his back. He went to the doctor's visits with her, took the hospital tour with her, and had experienced one small glimmer of hope when he'd accompanied her for an ultrasound and caught the first shadowy glimpses of the baby. His baby. He was still waiting for the love to hit, but it was a start.

Once they had negotiated their way out of the carpark, and

paid the ransom at the gates to be released, Hilary turned to him.

'So, Joseph, you're going to make me an aunt again?'

'That I am,' he replied, focusing on manoeuvring the car across two lanes of traffic to get onto the freeway that would eventually take them home.

'How is that sitting with you?'

He glanced at her. 'I'm getting used to it.'

'Hmm,' she murmured thoughtfully. 'I'm sorry, Joseph, I have to say this. I just can't forget the conversation we had in Boston before you flew home.'

'Which conversation was that?'

'The one where you were relieved things had come to a head and it was over with Sarah.'

He shrugged. 'What can I say? I spoke too soon.'

'What about the woman you mentioned in your emails? Her name was Jo, wasn't it? I thought it was kind of sweet, you having the same name.'

That made him smile.

'I'm not quite sure of the chronology,' she went on, 'did that end before the baby, or after?'

'Well, the baby came first, but I didn't know about it. So then the thing with Jo had to end.'

'That's what I thought.'

He didn't say anything.

'Joseph, are you sure you're doing the right thing?' Hilary asked.

He shook his head with a half laugh. 'That's the only thing I am sure of,' he said. 'It might not be what I want, but it is the right thing.'

She reached across and squeezed his arm. 'You're a good guy, Joseph, that's your tragic flaw, you know. Good guys always come last.'

He shrugged. 'I don't know about that, Hil.'

'What do you mean?'

'I mean I don't think I'm such a good guy,' he said. 'I wasn't paying attention towards the end, with me and Sarah. I switched off. She had a completely different idea about where our relationship was at – she thought we were going to settle down together, I thought we were coming to an end.'

'So are you saying she got pregnant because she thought that's what you wanted?'

'No, no, it wasn't planned,' he said. 'It's just, if I'd spoken up sooner, if I'd said something, maybe we would have settled things earlier, and the pregnancy wouldn't have happened. But I just cruised along, avoiding confrontation, till I thought we were done. I didn't have the balls to be honest with her, and now I'm paying the price.'

'That's a pretty huge price to pay, Joseph.'

'But I have no one to blame but myself. It's not Sarah's fault and she shouldn't be left holding the baby – literally.' He glanced across at his sister. 'I need you guys to understand that, to accept her, if I'm going to make this work. It's hard enough as it is.'

Hilary frowned, watching him. 'Were you in love with the other woman?'

'She wasn't the other woman,' Joe said quietly. 'And yeah, I was. I still am.' Even though they barely had anything to do with each other any more, he was still deeply, inconsolably in love with Jo. True to her word, she avoided him at work, and true to his word, he respected that. So he didn't go to editorial meetings, though he would have done anything just to sit in the same room with her. And he never approached her; he even tried not to look at her across the news floor. But sometimes he couldn't help himself.

'If you're in love with someone else,' Hilary was asking, 'how can you do this, Joseph?'

'I have to try, Hil,' said Joe. 'Sarah followed me across the world, she left everything for me. And she's having my baby. There's enough there to build on. It's what Mum did for Dad, Hil.'

'But Joseph, he loved her, he adored her, and he would have gone anywhere for her as well.'

'Yeah, but in the end he left her to fend for herself with five kids a lot of the time.'

Hilary frowned. 'What's your point?'

'I'm just saying, things don't always turn out the way you plan, but people manage with the circumstances thrust upon them, if they're doing it for the right reasons.'

'Yes, they do,' she agreed. 'But I think it helps if they feel loved and supported.'

'You think Mum did?'

'I'm quite sure she did. Look, I realise Dad was difficult –'

'I never saw that, you know.'

'Because you idolised him,' said Hilary. 'So did Mum. They just wanted different things. She was happy to settle down and have kids, but it was hard for him. He was a bachelor at thirty, which was getting on in those days. He was a bit of a loner before he met Mum. That's where you two are different, you're like Dad intellectually, but you're a lot more like Mum emotionally. He didn't need people; he liked the isolation of being a correspondent, the life on the road, no ties. It suited him.'

'I always thought he was happy when we were all around.'

'Of course he was, Joseph, he loved us, he's our dad. But he could only take us in small doses. Mum understood that. That's why they worked ultimately.'

'Do you think she was happy?'

'I don't think she was unhappy. I don't know that she was always fulfilled, she was constantly in my ear about having a career, not giving it up for anything.'

'So she had regrets?'

'You know, I don't think she did,' said Hilary. 'She fell in love with Dad, so she accepted everything that went with that. And she loved her children, and she wanted to be with us. She was no more conflicted than any woman of her time.' She paused. 'Come to think of it, times haven't changed all that much.'

'Well, Sarah says she loves me,' said Joe. 'And she's having my baby, so the least I can do is to stand by her.'

'I just think you're really up against it if you're not sure how you feel about her, and worse, if you're in love with someone else.'

Joe sighed, rubbing his forehead. 'You've made your point, Hil.'

'I'm sorry Joseph, I'll support whatever you do, you know that.'

'Thanks. I appreciate it.'

'So when am I going to meet her?' asked Hilary. 'I thought she'd be with you today?'

'No, she wanted to give us all time together first, given the circumstances,' added Joe. 'She'll come for Christmas.'

Hilary nodded. 'So, how's Dad? You'd better prepare me.'

So he did. The pattern had continued, of good days and bad, though the good were fewer and the bad more frequent and more intense. Joe had wanted to spend more time with him, but Sarah was strangely reluctant. She hadn't visited once, and she complained if Joe wanted to go up on the weekends in the little time they had together, as she put it. So he went during the week, just staying a few hours and coming back the same day.

'The doctor said the most serious threat at this point is infection, namely pneumonia, due to respiratory weakness,' Joe explained. 'He's on non-invasive ventilatory support for extended periods, but we may have to consider invasive options.'

'Why are you talking to me like a doctor, Joseph?' asked Hilary.

'Sorry,' he shook his head. Somehow it was easier to say when he made it less personal. 'If Dad goes onto a permanent ventilator when his lungs get too weak to function on their own, he won't be able to speak, or eat or drink. He'll lose any quality of life. He could have a tracheostomy, where they put a tube directly into his throat, but that's a surgical procedure, and it takes quite a bit of getting used to, to adjust to eating and drinking, so really it would be a bit much on him at that stage.'

Hilary was thoughtful. 'How does Dad feel about going on a ventilator?'

'He's not going to like it,' said Joe.

'You haven't spoken to him?'

He shook his head. 'The medical staff have. I wanted to wait till we were all here before we ask him what he wants to do.'

'Am I right in assuming that the ventilator would basically become life support as he deteriorates?'

Joe nodded.

'So then we have to decide when to turn it off?' she said quietly.

'That's right. But if there's no intervention, he'll die slowly, struggling for breath, like a drowning man. Except it could take days. Or longer. We can't let him go through that.'

*

When they eventually pulled up at the house, Corinne and Alex were in the drive, unloading bags from the boot. Corinne looked up, beaming, and virtually ran to meet them as Joe cut the engine. She grabbed at the passenger door before Hilary could even get out, and they were hugging as Joe walked around the car to join them.

'Joe,' Corinne cried, lurching at him. 'Well, you only get more handsome with the years,' she said, throwing her arms around him.

Hilary caught his eye across Corinne's shoulder. 'What did I tell you?' she said with a grin.

Corinne had completed an honours degree in comparative literature and begun her career as an editorial assistant in a large publishing house. But her natural effervescence was constrained by the hours she was forced to spend alone poring over manuscripts, and it was soon decided she was better suited to publicity, where she excelled. She had risen to the rank of head publicist for nonfiction before she left to have her babies and, like her mother, she'd have happily stayed at home if not for the publisher luring her back with an attractive offer to work part-time on projects of her own choosing.

Alex walked up to shake Joe's hand. 'Good to see you, Joe,' he smiled. 'It's been too long.'

'Yeah, it has.'

Alex had been a foreign correspondent, like Joe and their dad, when he became one of Corinne's early charges; she was the publicist assigned to his book which recounted his experiences reporting on the massacre in Rwanda. He was a quiet, self-effacing man, and everyone was well aware Corinne had married a version of their father. But unlike their father, he quit roaming once the children arrived, and now split his time between teaching and writing.

'Where are the kids?' Joe asked.

'They're inside with Pop,' said Corinne, a shadow passing across her eyes though she continued to smile bravely. 'He couldn't wait to see them.'

'Neither can I,' said Hilary.

There was a moment's pause, weighted by the underlying

sadness that no one was prepared to express just yet.

'Well,' said Corinne brightly. 'Let's go inside and get this shindig underway. I just know this is going to be the best Christmas ever.'

Three days before Christmas

'I'm determined to make this the best Christmas ever,' Belle announced, waving a gaudy piece of red and green tinsel like it was a cheerleader's pompom.

'Why are you setting yourself up for failure?' Jo said dryly.

Belle had called to suggest meeting in the city for lunch, which was something she never did. Jo assumed it was a thinly disguised ruse to visit Charlene, who had probably been in her ear, making her feel guilty for abandoning her. But it turned out to be a ruse of a different kind. No sooner had they met on the corner of Market and Elizabeth than Belle was dragging her by the arm inside David Jones to search out the Christmas-trim shop.

'This is a chance to put this horrible year behind us and focus on the good things,' Belle persisted cheerfully.

'You sound like a bad greeting card.'

'And you sound like Scrooge!'

'Guilty as charged. I don't even like Christmas, Belle.'

'Of course you like Christmas.'

Jo was often amused by Belle's myopic insistence about the way things were, regardless of all evidence to the contrary. But it was hard to be amused by anything much at the moment. The overwhelming, glittering juggernaut of Christmas was getting Jo down like never before. No other season made you so intensely aware of your loneliness. And despite the presence of her mother in the apartment, Jo had never felt so alone.

She missed Joe with such a painful longing, she wondered if it was ever going to get easier. Time passing certainly hadn't helped. She avoided him at work; the odd glimpses of him across the news floor hit her like a direct blow to the chest. She tried not to think about him, but he was there, in her head, in her heart, all the time. Especially as she toiled away on her investigation. As the trail got murkier, and the implications more and more serious, Jo sometimes had the feeling she was in over her head. She didn't want to admit that to Leo, and she couldn't talk to Lachlan any more, not that she'd want to. But she would have loved to sound out Joe, get his feedback, his calm, solid reassurance, his support. But that was no longer possible. And what was worse, a picture kept forming in her head, of him and Sarah in the flat Jo had never even stepped foot in, decorating a tree, setting up things for the baby. Babies and Christmas, it was all so unbearably perfect.

'You always made Christmas wonderful,' Belle was prattling on, picking her way through a buffet of sparkly paraphernalia. 'I knew it wasn't Mum, and I wasn't all that old when I knew it wasn't Santa either. It was you, Jo.'

Christmas had always required a major covert operation. Jo had to build up funds for months so that Charlene wouldn't notice. And then she'd usually pick a fight with her daughters just before Christmas, berating them for the state of the house, their rooms, their clothes, whatever she could seize upon. Then she would inevitably make the pronouncement that there would be no Christmas that year, because they were selfish girls who didn't deserve it. Poor Belle would always get so despondent – she was such a Christmas tragic. She watched every Christmas movie that aired on TV, and actually enjoyed listening to Christmas music, and she spent the weekends and afternoons after school leading up to the big day making elaborate decorations for the tree and the house. Jo realised it was the fantasy Belle was embracing, the chance to dress up the house and pretend they were like everyone else. 'Don't worry, we will have Christmas,' Jo would always assure her. 'Mum's just . . . going through a hard time, she doesn't mean it.' Usually Charlene managed to pull together a few cheap trinkets and they would be sitting forlornly under the tree when Jo crept out in the early hours of the morning with her more substantial stash. She often wondered if her mother actually did believe in Santa; she never spoke to Jo about the gifts, never asked where they came from.

'I only did it for you, Belle,' Jo was saying.

'So I want to do this for you.'

Jo sighed. 'I don't even know if I'm going to come.'

Belle was genuinely shocked by the idea. 'What are you talk-ing about? You have to come for Christmas!' Her voice increased in pitch with each exclamation. 'What are you going to do, spend it in that stark little flat on your own?'

Charlene was staying with Belle over Christmas, so having the place to herself for a couple of days actually sounded appealing to Jo. She could hide out, pretend it wasn't even Christmas maybe, wait till it was over.

'Well, I won't hear of it,' Belle was saying. 'I know you've had a hard time of it, Jo. You don't talk about him, and I don't ask. But I understand, I do. And I just think, if you let it, Christmas could be a time to bring some joy into your heart, put all this unhappiness behind you, and look on the new year as a fresh start.'

She sounded like a character in one of those syrupy movies she used to watch, all about Christmas miracles. Jo wasn't expecting a miracle, and she wasn't going to get a miracle, she just wanted to get through it. She looked at Belle; her sister's eyes were almost pleading. She'd do it for her. She'd show up, put on a brave face, get through it.

'Of course I'm coming,' she dismissed. 'But what on earth are we doing here, Belle?' she added, looking around. 'Your house already looks like a Christmas-trim shop.'

Belle smiled widely. 'You can never have too much Christmas bling.'

The next day

Joe was driving back from the mountains. He'd spent two idyllic days with his family, with Sarah's blessing. When he phoned her yesterday she encouraged him to stay another night; she was fine, she assured him. He didn't argue. He relished being with all his sisters and Will for the first time in years. Even his dad had rallied with everyone around him, though he could only cope with short bursts of their company. He was growing weaker by the day, but the mood remained resolutely positive. No one wanted to talk about what was going to happen. Not yet. They could pretend for now that they were just another family preparing for Christmas together, not facing imminent loss.

It would be different once Sarah joined them, and Joe knew that would largely be his fault. He was still uncomfortable around her, still reticent. The last two days had only made it worse. He found himself dwelling on how things might have been had he been introducing them to Jo, and he knew in his heart she would have fitted in perfectly. She and Hilary had the same spunky intelligence, and Corinne got on with everyone, she would have loved Jo. They would have been so happy for him, because they would have seen how happy he was. He wasn't going to be able to pull that off so convincingly with Sarah.

So he had been in no particular hurry to leave today. But Hilary had eventually suggested he should get going so he'd get back all the sooner. Will had walked him out to the car.

'How's it going?' he asked tentatively.

Joe shrugged. 'Inevitably.'

Will cocked an eyebrow. 'Cryptic.'

Joe smiled faintly.

'Do you see Jo at all?' Will asked.

'A little, at work.'

He nodded. 'It sucks the big one, brother.'

'I'm not going to argue with you.'

It was nearly two o'clock when Joe turned into the driveway of his block and pulled the car into one of the visitor's spaces. He wouldn't be here long; as Hil said, he wanted to get back to them all as soon as possible. He climbed the three flights of stairs to his flat, two steps at a time, so he was a little breathless when he got to the door. He was about to knock, but that seemed a weird thing to do at his own front door. He put the key in the lock and turned it, calling out 'Hi' as he pushed the door open.

Sarah was on the couch and there was a man sitting beside her, a man who looked vaguely familiar. She struggled to get up as he came through the door. She couldn't move so quickly these days.

'Joe,' she said, slightly ruffled, or maybe he was imagining that. 'I thought you'd ring to let me know when you were coming.'

'I told you I'd be here early afternoon, and it's early afternoon,' said Joe, his eyes drifting to the man who had jumped to his feet and taken a step away from Sarah. He knew this guy, who was he?

'You remember Ian,' said Sarah. 'Ian Templeton, he was my cameraman when I was with *Global Review*, remember?'

'Hello Joe,' Ian said, coming towards him with his hand outstretched.

'Sure, Ian, I remember,' Joe said, shaking his hand.

'Ian just arrived in Sydney yesterday,' Sarah explained, suddenly at Joe's side. She reached up to give him a quick kiss on the cheek. She seemed a little flustered.

Joe nodded. 'So what are you doing here, Ian?'

'I just came to say hello to Sarah.'

'All the way from London?'

He looked embarrassed, dropping his head. 'No, no, I'm in Sydney on a bit of a working holiday. I'm just here today to catch up with Sarah.'

'I see.'

There was an awkward pause.

'And I was just about to leave,' said Ian. 'So, good to see you again, Joe.'

'And you.'

Sarah walked him to the door. 'I'll be in touch, Ian, and you have my number.'

She closed the door and turned around to look at Joe, her face flushed.

'Were you expecting him?' he asked.

'He sent an email to say he was coming to Australia,' she dismissed.

'When was that?'

'Oh, I don't know, maybe a week ago. I'm not sure,' she said vaguely. 'Did you have a good time with your family?'

'Yeah,' said Joe. 'And I'd like to get back to them.'

'About that,' said Sarah, a frown creasing her forehead as she paced across the room.

'What?' Joe prompted, watching her.

She stopped, turning to face him. 'Look, the thing is, Joe, I don't know if I should come with you.'

'What are you talking about, Sarah? The family's all waiting to meet you.'

'They've met me before,' she shrugged.

'You haven't met Hilary or Corinne,' he reminded her. 'What's this about?'

'Let's not kid ourselves, Joe, this is an awkward situation for everybody, especially with your dad so ill. I feel like I'd be intruding.'

'Sarah, you're carrying my child, you're part of this family whether you like it or not,' said Joe. 'Dad's anxious to see you. He may not get to see this child, but it will give him some comfort seeing you.'

She clenched her hands together and started to pace again. 'You're placing me in a really awkward position, Joe. I mean, I'm heavily pregnant, and your father is dying, what if something happens while I'm there?'

Joe rubbed his forehead with his hand. 'If you're suggesting we don't spend Christmas with my family —'

'Not "we",' she interrupted him. 'I know you have to be with them.'

'So what are you saying?'

'I don't feel comfortable being there at such a difficult time. I hardly know them.'

He shook his head. 'I don't believe I'm hearing this. You're the one who's been pushing me so hard —'

'Pushing you?' She stopped pacing, her hand on her hip.

'You want us to be a family, part of that is joining in with my family at Christmas, for Chrissakes.' This was beginning to piss him off.

'Well, you're the one who's been keeping me at arm's length,' she said firmly. 'You've made it abundantly clear that you'll only consider us a family once the baby is actually here. And I have accepted that. So let's get this Christmas out of the way, you attend to your family obligations, and then maybe we can get on with our lives.'

He tossed his keys on the table. 'Well now you're putting me in an awkward position, Sarah. Are you trying to make me choose between you and my family?'

'No, not at all,' she insisted. 'Why do you say that?'

'Well I can't leave you here alone at Christmas.'

She took a breath. 'I won't be alone. Ian is on his own, I'll spend it with him.'

Joe frowned. 'What's going on with you two?'

'Nothing, he's a friend. In fact he was a very good friend to me after you left. When I was devastated.'

'How good a friend?'

'Don't be ridiculous Joe. I was pregnant with your child. He was the first to know about it, actually.'

'This doesn't make any sense, Sarah,' said Joe. 'This guy shows up out of the blue and suddenly you don't want to spend Christmas with me?'

'It's not sudden,' she replied calmly. 'I've been reluctant all along to spend Christmas with your entire family under these circumstances. This is the best way to deal with it.' She paused. 'And don't pretend you're not a little relieved.'

He was, he had to admit. But he was also uneasy. Something wasn't sitting right about all this.

'Well, I'm not going to force you,' he said finally. 'Do you want me to stay here tonight?'

'That isn't necessary,' she said, her voice softening. 'But thanks for offering.'

Christmas Day

Jo had slept the night in Caelen's bedroom; it was the preferred option to sharing with the twins, but almost four year olds do not sleep in on Christmas morning, and it was barely 5 am when he climbed on top of her, announcing, 'Santa's been, Santa's been, you have to get up, Arnie JoJo!'

There were a number of things she felt like saying to him, but she restrained herself; it was Christmas after all. Eventually Caelen woke up the whole house and the family gathered bleary-eyed around the Christmas tree, the adults sipping coffee Belle had made to get their hearts started.

Jo stood back a little as the children attacked their presents. She'd forgotten how incredibly excited they could get at Christmas. The twins were barely old enough to comprehend, but still they were beside themselves. It wasn't the presents, per se, it was the magic. Last night they had gone to sleep and there was nothing under the tree. Then during the night, improbably, a big fat man in a red suit arrived on a sleigh pulled by reindeer, delivered their presents, had a sip of the milk left for him, a couple of bites of Christmas cake, and he was off to the next child's house. And they believed every bit of it. That's what made it so wonderful. Too soon these little innocents would be all grown up and they'd find out that Santa was not real, wishes don't come true, and there was no magic in the world.

Jo leaned against the wall, watching them all now; Cascey dancing around through the scrunched-up wrapping paper, sporting a plastic jewelled tiara and waving a fairy wand; the boys vroom-vrooming their toy cars along the carpet, over discarded boxes and legs and anything else in their path. Darren and Belle were bickering as usual, but it had a gentle fun about it today.

'I said *masseur* foot *sandals*,' Belle was saying. 'Not a foot *massager*. When will I ever get the time to laze around with my feet stuck in this contraption?'

'When we're watching telly at night,' Darren suggested.

'What? Between getting up every ad break to stack the dishes or go to the kids?'

'Then I might just have to tie you down one night.'

'Oh, wouldn't you love that,' she grinned, leaning over to give him a quick peck. 'I still want those sandals.'

Even Charlene looked content. It was way too early for her, and she was probably not fully compos mentis, but she appeared happy enough watching the kids play with their toys.

A sentimental Christmas song started to play in the background, about troubles being far away, and the fates allowing us all to be together throughout the years, and suddenly it was all too much for Jo. She slipped out through the kitchen and outside where she could breathe. A few moments later, she heard the doors sliding open behind her. Belle must have noticed her and followed. Jo turned around to tell her to go back inside to her family.

'Mum,' said Jo, surprised to see it was Charlene instead. 'Come out for a smoke?'

'No, it's a bit early for me.'

'Really?'

She nodded. 'I've cut back a bit since I've been staying at your place. It's too bloody inconvenient going down onto the street every half-hour.'

'Well, that's good then.'

Charlene just shrugged. If she didn't want a cigarette, then what was she doing out here?

'Is everything all right?' asked Jo. 'You're feeling okay?'

'Mm,' Charlene nodded, taking a seat at the outdoor setting. 'You?'

Jo blinked. 'What?'

'Are you all right?'

'Yes, of course, I'm fine,' she croaked. 'I just needed some air.'

Charlene nodded again and they fell silent. Why did she have to come out here? Jo had only wanted a moment alone, and now she had to fill in awkward silences with her mother. The music drifted out from inside the house.

'Have you ever had a chestnut?' Jo asked after a while.

'What?'

'We play these songs about roasting chestnuts at Christmas,' she said. 'Can you even get chestnuts in Australia?'

'I dunno,' said Charlene. 'Maybe they import them?' she offered.

'But does anyone roast them at Christmas?' Jo went on. 'I mean, who in their right mind would be lighting a fireplace in this heat? And it's not like you can light one outside, with the total fire ban.'

'Jo, what the hell are you going on about?'

She sighed. 'I don't know.'

Charlene was watching her. 'Belle told me what happened with your boyfriend.'

Jo glanced at her warily.

'Must have pissed you off,' she remarked.

Jo smiled faintly then. Charlene would put it like that. She was right though.

'You know what, I am pretty pissed off.'

'That he chose her over you?'

She bristled. 'No, he didn't really have a choice, she's having his baby.' Jo took a breath. 'What pisses me off is that I feel like I've missed out.'

'Missed out on what?'

'You don't know what it's like to be very, very single, and to be constantly bombarded by images of families gathered around the tree, in mangers in stables, roasting frigging chestnuts.'

'I do have a bit of an idea,' Charlene muttered. 'I never thought you wanted any of that, Jo.'

'Neither did I. Ironic, isn't it?' She looked at her mother. It occurred to Jo that it didn't matter what she said, Charlene was hardly in the position to judge her. She might as well let loose. 'You want to know the truth? I'm so jealous of Sarah, I could spit.'

'Sarah?' said Charlene. 'That's the woman?'

Jo nodded, pacing across the paving, warming up. 'I've never even met her but I'm jealous of her. I want to be the one having Joe's baby, I should be the one having his baby, and I didn't even know I wanted a baby,' she cried, raising her hands.

'You can still have a baby, you're not quite past it yet.'

Jo spun around. 'I don't want *a* baby, Mum. I want *Joe's* baby.'

Charlene looked a little shocked. That was a first; Jo didn't think she could ever shock her mother.

'I don't want the baby he's having with Sarah,' Jo assured her. 'What I'm trying to say is, I found the father of any babies I was meant to have. The one. The guy. And the cosmos laughed in my face. You want to be a real girl? You can't be a real girl. I feel like Pinocchio.'

'Didn't Pinocchio get to be a real boy in the end?' Charlene frowned, thinking about it. 'I'm sure that's how it went.'

Jo shook her head. 'That was a fairy tale, Mum,' she sighed. 'This is real life, you should know better than anyone that it's no fairy tale.'

Charlene let out half a chuckle. 'You can put that in the bank.'

'I don't even know what I'm going on about,' Jo groaned. 'I was never even sure I wanted a baby, I'd probably be a hopeless mother.'

'You're kidding, right?'

Jo looked over at her.

'You've been mothering Belle since you were a kid yourself, I think you've got it nailed.'

Right on cue, Belle popped her head out of the sliding door. 'Are you two coming back in? We have to have the traditional photo in front of the tree, after the presents are opened. Darren's setting up the camera so we can all be in it together.' Then she disappeared again.

'You're to blame for this Christmas obsession of hers,' said Charlene, getting to her feet.

'You can't blame that on me.'

'Yes I can. We wouldn't have had any sort of a Christmas if not for you and your secret operation.'

Jo stared at her. 'You knew?'

Charlene laughed. 'What, did you think I believed it was Santa?'

'Why didn't you ever say anything?' said Jo as they walked over to the doors.

She shook her head. 'You would've been so embarrassed if I sprung you, Jo. You know what you were like, you had your system all worked out, you didn't need any help from me. You did it better than I could have anyway.'

Jo felt a twinge in her chest. 'It would have been nice for you to say that some time.'

'I'm saying it now, aren't I?' said Charlene, reaching for the sliding door.

*

Leura

Christmas had not turned out to be the festive celebration the family had been counting on. Their father was gravely ill; they had hoped he'd make it to the dinner table, even for a brief spell, but he certainly couldn't sit, and it proved too painful even to prop him up so they could join him at his bedside. He had barely been able to take any food by mouth for the last few days, not even a taste of the clove-studded honey-glazed ham Mim had fretted over, painstakingly following their mother's recipe. Sometimes he was so weak he could only type *yes* or *no* with effort; in fact his answers to their polite enquiries had often become a mere *Y* or *N*. But his eyes communicated his pain and despair.

Joe was up early on Boxing Day. He hadn't been sleeping well; he blamed the heat, but he probably didn't need an excuse. As he walked down the hall, a nurse was just coming out of his father's room. He couldn't remember the names of all the different nurses now, and they'd had to use locums over Christmas to fill in for the regulars who had family commitments.

'Your dad's not too bad this morning,' she told Joe. 'We've just had him on the coughing machine for a spell. He's comfortable. He's talking a little, you should go in.'

'Thanks.' Joe walked into the room and crossed quietly to the bed. He wondered if his dad had gone back off to sleep; he was very still, and his eyes were closed. Joe stood back, watching him. He had seen a lot of dead bodies, too many probably, and it always struck him how the body was not the person any more. It was actually reassuring. The body was left behind in death, and with it all the pain and suffering and disease. It seemed like his dad was slowly leaving his body; he was still there, but he was fading, fading from their lives, from this world. Joe was not at all sure there was anywhere to go after death, but at least he was glad his dad would be rid of the burden of his useless body.

He opened his eyes then, and they came to rest on Joe.

'Hey Dad,' Joe smiled, taking a few steps closer to the bed.

'Sit,' he managed to squeeze the word out.

'Don't try to talk, Dad,' said Joe, reaching for his keyboard and attaching it to his seemingly lifeless forearm. He wheeled the table with the monitor closer, and took a seat beside the bed.

'Where's your girl?' he asked with difficulty.

'Maybe she'll come up later,' Joe said. 'I have to call her.'

He began to type slowly. *Is she frightened to come, frightened of me?*

'No, Dad,' Joe dismissed, but he couldn't look at him. 'She's nearly due, she doesn't want to be too far away from the hospital. You know what the English are like, they don't go this far on their annual holidays.'

LOOK AT ME came up on the screen. Joe turned to face his father.

'Are you happy?' he breathed.

'Sure.' But he had to look away again.

I wish I had the strength . . .

'I know, Dad. It's okay, don't upset yourself.'

'. . . to shake you,' he finished.

Joe looked at him, looked into his eyes, and he actually saw anger there.

'Do you love her?' he gasped.

'I'll learn to love her.'

Joe heard the clicking of the keyboard again, and turned back to the screen.

It's not something you can learn.

'There's a child, Dad.'

People think a child brings you together, but that's not how it works. I loved your mother more than I loved you, or the girls, or Will. And still it was hard. She's what kept me coming home. I was only any sort of father because of her. Because I loved her.

Joe looked at him, there were tears pooling in his eyes. He covered his hand with his own. 'Dad, don't worry about this, don't worry about me.'

A tear escaped down the side of his face. He was genuinely distressed, and his breathing was becoming laboured. Joe didn't notice the nurse had slipped back into the room.

'Oh dear,' she muttered. 'You mustn't let yourself get upset,' she said loudly to his father as she approached the bed.

She arranged the oxygen mask over his face while Joe detached the keyboard from his arm and quickly deleted the words on the screen, pushing the stand out of the way.

He looked down at his dad, who was gazing sadly up at him. Joe bent down and stroked his head, and then kissed him on the forehead. 'Get some rest, Dad,' he said, and then he turned away and walked quickly from the room. He didn't look to see if anyone was around as he continued through the kitchen and out the back door, and then off into the bush at the back of the house. He started up the ridge, picking up his pace.

This was getting too hard; his heart felt like it couldn't take much more. What had he come home for? To have his heart broken, to watch his father die? He'd lost Jo, and he was going to lose his dad soon. But he didn't have the luxury of falling apart. He had to keep it together, he had a baby on the way, with a woman he struggled to have any feelings for. His future felt uncertain and unhappy. There, he'd said it, he'd admitted it, if only to himself. He couldn't feel happy, or positive, or certain about anything. In fact, he just felt like shit.

He made it to the flat rock at the top of the ridge and stood there, gazing out to the horizon as he caught his breath. A part of him wanted to shout up at the sky, the way people did in movies. He wondered whether it'd feel any good, or if he'd just feel like a goose . . . throwing his arms open and yelling at the top of his lungs. Nuh, he'd feel like a goose. Joe started to laugh at himself, out loud, and when he heard himself laughing, it made him laugh more, and before long he was laughing so hard he couldn't stop, and tears were streaming down his cheeks, and his stomach ached as he cried like a baby, slumped over on the flat rock.

A sudden squawk and the flapping of wings startled him. Joe looked up to see the pair of black cockatoos swoop past. He took a deep breath in and out again, wiping his face with the sleeve of his shirt. He watched the cockatoos. He felt drained, but oddly at peace.

Joe wasn't sure how long he'd been sitting there when Mim suddenly appeared in his line of sight.

'Mim, is everything all right?' He went to get up but she stopped him.

'Yeah, I saw you head off up the back,' she said, sitting down on the rock beside him. 'I thought you might like some company.'

'How did you know where to find me?'

She smiled faintly. 'This is where the track leads to, Joe.'

They sat there together for a while in silence. Mim was easy that way. There was no need to say anything, you could just sit.

After a time, she leaned her head on his shoulder, and it occurred to Joe that maybe she hadn't come up here to comfort him. He put his arm around her. This must be tough for her. This had been her whole life for the last few years.

'How are you, Mim?'

'I'm okay.'

'Really?' he said, looking at her.

'I'm not the one who's dying, Joe,' she said plainly. 'I don't want him to suffer any more. It's gone on too long.'

'This has been hardest on you.'

'No,' she denied. 'It's been hardest on Dad.'

'You know what I mean.'

'I do,' she said, giving his arm a gentle squeeze. 'But it's actually been a privilege to be with someone at the end of their life. Especially someone you love so much.'

Joe was watching her. 'You didn't have much time with him when you were a kid, did you?'

She shook her head. 'But we've caught up.'

'Is this a private party or can anyone join in?' said Will as he appeared in the clearing.

'Only if you're good-looking,' said Joe. 'But we'll make an exception in your case.'

Mim laughed.

'Don't encourage him,' said Will.

'How did you find us?' asked Joe.

'Mim left a trail of breadcrumbs.'

They shifted across and Will sat down on the rock next to Mim. 'And so this is Christmas,' he announced.

'It's Boxing Day, actually,' said Joe.

'Why is it called Boxing Day anyway?'

'It was traditionally the day employers and landowners gave gifts or money to their employees and the poor.'

'That doesn't explain why it's called Boxing Day,' said Will.

'I think there were boxes involved somehow . . .' Joe mused.

'Well, that's cleared that up then.'

'Were you actually trying to lose us, William?' Hilary declared as she appeared in the clearing above the ridge, with Corinne right behind her.

'If I'd been trying, you wouldn't be here, sister,' he said ominously.

Hilary wiped her brow with the back of her forearm. 'Whoo, I'm getting too old for this. No wisecracks,' she added quickly.

'I'll just say, Joe was up here first,' said Will, 'and he's got at least ten years on you, isn't that right, Hil?'

'Oh, shut up, will you.' Joe reached across Mim and clipped his ear. 'I'm four years older than Hil. Four, okay? Then the rest of you came like an assembly line, every two years.'

'I wonder why they waited the longest after they had you, Joe?' Corinne pondered out loud as she plonked herself on the ground near his feet.

'Because they were worried about spoiling their perfect record, Crinny,' Joe answered her. 'And then they did all right, up until Will came along.'

'Oh, good one, bro,' said Will, affecting a hearty chortle.

'Okay, that's enough, boys,' said Hilary, getting their attention. 'Listen, I wanted to mention . . .' she hesitated. 'I called the college, and Gregory. I told them I wasn't sure when I'd be back. I'm not leaving, until . . .'

Everyone knew what she meant.

'We don't have to get back for anything,' said Corinne, her voice wavering. 'We'll stay too.'

Will clenched his hands together. 'I have to go down to Sydney for the production I told you about, for the fringe festival. I'll have to be away for a couple of days at least, but I might be able to organise someone –'

'It's okay, William,' said Hilary. 'I think we'll have some notice, we can't all put our lives on hold to sit here waiting. You should go, do what you have to do, and we'll keep in touch, constantly, I promise.'

Joe was silent, staring down at the ground.

'Joseph,' Hilary said carefully, 'you obviously have to get home to Sarah. Maybe you can both come back in a day or two, if she's up to it?'

He shook his head. 'She doesn't want to come up here, it's freaking her out. I don't know what to do.'

'Don't worry, Joe, we'll keep in touch,' said Corinne.

He glanced around at them. 'You all understand what happens when Dad goes onto a permanent ventilator?'

Heads nodded around the circle.

'If he is intubated they can stabilise him,' said Hilary, 'make him comfortable, relieve his pain, and he can die peacefully at home, with all of us around him.'

'But he won't be able to speak to us any more,' said Joe. 'He'll slip into unconsciousness, and eventually into a coma.'

Corinne sniffed, and Joe reached over to give her shoulder a squeeze.

'But,' Hilary added, 'the alternative is —'

'I know. Too horrible to contemplate.' Joe sighed. 'I just hope we have some time.'

'For what, Joe?' Will said bluntly. They all turned to look at him. 'I mean, what are we talking about here? He's had enough, hasn't he told you that? Because he's certainly made it clear to me.'

They were all silent as they mulled over his words.

'You know what I think?' Will went on after a while. 'We haven't got over the shock of losing Mum the way we did, so we can't let go of Dad. But it's time. We have to let him go to her.'

'Do any of us really believe that?' Joe asked. 'Dad doesn't even believe in an afterlife.'

'But Will's got a point,' said Hilary. 'Maybe he's not going to be with her, but he doesn't really want to be here any longer without her.'

'He told me the last thing he could do for Mum,' Mim spoke up, 'was to make sure we were all going to be okay.'

'Then we have to let him know that we will be,' said Joe, resolved.

*

Saturday night

It was one of those gorgeous summer evenings, warm and balmy, with a clear sky and a light breeze, so Jo decided to wear flat sandals and walk to the theatre. Angie was performing in Will Bannister's troupe, in a production that was slated to be part of the Sydney Fringe Festival. They were holding a brief preview season, by invitation only, so they could tighten up their act in front of a supportive audience. Angie had been rehearsing constantly in all her spare time over the past few weeks. Although Jo imagined she must be exhausted, every time she had spoken to her she had been struck by her boundless enthusiasm and excitement for the whole thing. Jo couldn't help but be happy for her, and she was not going to weigh her down with her own private miseries. Angie knew what had happened with Joe, of course, but after the initial debrief, Jo had played it down, claiming to be relieved they had not got in any deeper. As far as Angie was aware, Jo had moved on.

As she approached the old workshop it looked much the same from the outside, despite all the working bees Angie had participated in. There was improved signage though, probably provided by fringe festival funds. It looked quite professional, in an indie sort of way. But as she stepped through the door things were quite different. Black partition walls had been arranged to form a kind of foyer, and there was even a reception desk cum box office of sorts. She handed her ticket to a smiling girl with an electric blue slash through her black hair and a stud just below her lip.

'Seats aren't numbered, so sit wherever you like,' she said happily.

Jo walked through into the main area and was genuinely surprised by the transformation. It was actually beginning to resemble a real theatre, of sorts. The grunge had been largely eradicated, along with the smell, thank God, which had been replaced with the lingering odour of fresh paint. Most of the walls had been painted black, and a variety of old theatre posters were hung at intervals around the room. The seating was

arranged in the same right-angle fashion as before, defining the
stage which was still at floor level. But there were many more
seats, and the last few rows were raised. Very flash. Professional
theatre lighting had been installed on tracks above the seating,
and Jo noticed an impressive-looking sound desk positioned
behind the last row.

She wandered on past the stage area towards the back of the
building, where there was quite a crowd milling about, drinking
wine from real glasses, by the looks of it.

Then Jo saw him. And there was a woman standing beside
him. She felt the panic rising in her chest. She wasn't prepared
for this; it had occurred to her that Joe might be here, just not
with *her*. She wanted to turn and flee, but Angie had phoned only
this afternoon, checking to make sure she was definitely going to
be here tonight. She had to stay, so she had to find someone she
knew, anyone. Her eyes scanned the crowd; she didn't suppose
Angie would be out here before the show.

'Jo,' she heard his voice and saw him approaching at the same
moment that she spotted Oliver coming through the entrance.

'Oh there he is,' she said in Joe's general direction without
actually looking at him. 'Excuse me, won't you?'

She dashed headlong at Oliver.

'Well, hello petal, this is a lovely surprise,' he greeted her, clasping her hands.

'I'm so glad to see you,' she gasped. 'Will you be my date?'

'What's going on?'

'I just don't want to be alone.'

He took her arm in his. 'Okay, but no funny business afterwards, I'm not that kind of a fella.'

Jo smiled gratefully. But as they turned around, she saw that
Joe was standing expectantly, waiting for them. And she was still
beside him, naturally. She was quite beautiful; she had dark hair, of
course, and an English rose complexion, and she was much taller
than Jo. Damn, why did she wear these flat sandals? Sarah was
long and slender and graceful, even her baby bump was elegant.
They looked good together, they made a striking couple.

'Hi,' Joe said as they drew closer. He was gazing at her a little
blatantly; he really shouldn't do that.

'Well, hello there, Joe,' Oliver greeted him. 'I wouldn't have picked you for a theatre lover.'

He smiled faintly. 'My brother's in the company.'

'Ahh,' he nodded.

The woman was looking at them curiously. 'Hello,' she said.

'Sarah, these are my friends, Jo Liddell and Oliver . . . I'm sorry, I don't know your last name, Oliver.'

'I don't need one, like Cher, or Bono,' he said, extending his hand to Sarah.

'This is Sarah Parrish,' said Joe.

'Pleased to meet you,' said Sarah, shaking Oliver's hand.

She spoke beautifully, of course. Damned English accents always sounded so classy.

'And Jo, is it?' she said, offering her hand. 'Nice to meet you.'

Jo briefly took her hand, and then looked away, pretending something had caught her attention.

'I didn't expect to see you here,' Joe said, claiming it back.

No, she supposed he wouldn't have.

'Angie's performing tonight,' Jo explained. 'Will didn't mention it?'

'No,' he said. 'But we've, uh, we've been distracted lately.'

'How is your dad, Joe?' she asked, genuinely concerned.

She saw the pain flitter across his eyes as he shook his head faintly. 'Not so good.'

'Oh, I'm so sorry to hear that.'

A sad, meaningful look passed between them. 'What about your mother?' he asked.

'She's doing all right. She'll be finished the treatment this week.'

'Do you think they might have a soda water, darling?' said Sarah, planting a possessive hand on his forearm.

'Would you like a drink, petal?' Oliver asked Jo.

'No, I think I'd rather take our seats,' she said. 'Catch up with you later.' She took Oliver's arm and steered him away.

'I can't wait to hear all about this twist in the saga,' said Oliver under his breath.

'In a minute.'

Jo surveyed the seating options. She didn't want to risk ending up anywhere near them, so she led Oliver into a row where they were virtually surrounded.

When they had sat down he turned to her. 'So what was that about? Is Mr Joe married after all?'

'As good as,' she said.

'Well what do you know,' he pondered. 'I thought he was one of the good guys, but he's been lying to you all along?'

'No, he wasn't,' she shook her head. 'It's a long story.'

'Well go on, out with it.'

Jo glanced around before looking at him directly. 'She was his girlfriend when he was based overseas, but they broke up and he came home. She showed up on his doorstep pregnant . . . I guess it was a couple of months ago now. It's his.'

Oliver's eyes were wide. 'He didn't know about it when he left?'

She shook her head.

'And there's no doubt it's his?'

'Apparently not.'

'Well,' he declared, 'this is like an episode of a bad soap.'

'Tell me about it.'

Oliver became thoughtful. 'He's being very noble and all, but a tad old-fashioned. Does her father have a big shotgun?'

'That's the long story,' said Jo. 'Suffice to say that if they can't make a go of it, she'll move back to England to be close to her family, and Joe's child will be on the other side of the world.'

'Makes weekend access a bitch.'

'Exactly.'

Oliver shifted in his seat. 'Still, surely there must be some other way to deal with this?'

'If you come up with one, let me know,' Jo said wryly.

He touched her arm. 'I'm sorry, petal.'

She glanced at him sideways. 'So am I.'

A gong sounded a few times, and the seats began to fill rapidly. Jo wanted to know where they were sitting but she didn't want to look, or be caught looking, more to the point. She scanned the crowd discreetly, eventually spotting them in the section perpendicular to them, in exactly the same row. She met Joe's eyes before she could look away; he was gazing at her with a yearning she could feel from here. He really had to stop doing that. She glanced at Sarah beside him; she was watching Joe and just then she turned her head to see what was so absorbing him. Jo looked away quickly, linking her arm through Oliver's. She wasn't fooling anyone – Oliver could set off a gaydar at fifty paces – but she was glad she had someone to hang onto.

And she was even gladder when the house lights dimmed and the spotlight hit the stage area. Her heart missed a beat as Angie appeared in the middle of the empty space, alone. And from then on Jo was mesmerised. Her friend, her dear, self-deprecating, modest, beautiful friend held the audience in the palm of her hand as she delivered the most exquisite monologue, speaking of love and loss and heartache, and inviting the audience to come with her on the journey they were about to take.

And the audience went with her; Jo had a feeling Angie could have led them anywhere. She watched in awe as her friend laughed and cried – real tears – and sang, with a sweet, pure voice, and became a child in one scene, an old lady in another. There were other actors sharing the stage, and they were good, very good, this was a far superior production to the previous one, but Jo couldn't take her eyes off Angie. She commanded the stage with a confidence Jo never knew she possessed. It was a revelation.

'Is it just me,' Jo whispered to Oliver during a scene change, 'or is she really, really good?'

'She's really, really good, but then I don't know if it's just me?'

The whoops and cheers Angie received at the curtain call confirmed that they were not alone. Jo tried to catch her eye, but she doubted Angie could make her out in the sea of faces. She would find her later, and hug her, and tell her she was amazing. And in the meantime she would have to try to avoid Joe. But that was going to be difficult, she realised, when she saw him waiting in the aisle as she and Oliver made their way out of their row.

He was smiling, the first genuine smile she had seen on his face all evening. 'Angie was fantastic,' he said. 'I had no idea.'

'Me neither, and she's my best friend.'

'You haven't seen her perform before?'

'Only in ads, mostly.'

'Which one was Angie?' Sarah enquired, appearing at his side.

'She opened the play,' said Joe.

'Oh, yes, the big girl. She was very good.'

Jo gritted her teeth. 'Well, we seem to be blocking the aisle here,' she said, grabbing Oliver's arm and falling in with the stream of people making their way to the bar area. But as the crowd spilled out into the open space, she realised Joe was right on her heels, with Sarah trailing along behind.

Just then Will bounded up, registering a faint but fleeting surprise when he saw them all together.

'Hey, everyone . . .' he said. 'Jo, hi, haven't seen you in ages.' He leaned over to kiss her on the cheek. 'Wasn't Angie great?'

'She was. I'm gobsmacked.'

'What did you think, brother?' he asked Joe.

'Oh, Angie was wonderful.'

'But of the whole thing?'

'It was terrific,' said Joe. 'You guys have really got your act together.'

Will rolled his eyes. 'Very punny.'

'Yeah, well I couldn't help notice they kept you out of sight.'

'Where I was indispensable,' Will pointed out. 'The whole thing would have fallen apart without me.'

Joe nodded with a grin. 'Seriously, it was a fantastic production, and the writing was first-rate. Was it published material, or did someone here write it?'

'It was someone here,' said Will. 'Though everything is a collaborative effort.'

'Don't try and take some of the credit for yourself.'

'Will Angie be out soon, do you think?' asked Jo. 'I'm anxious to see her.'

'Come on, I'll take you back to her dressing room, I have a pass,' he winked, grabbing her hand. 'Catch you, guys.'

'I'll get us a drink,' Oliver called after her as Will whisked her away through the crowd to a corridor at the back of the building and then into a room packed with all the actors and crew.

'When I said her dressing room,' said Will, shouting a little over the excited din, 'I was overstating it. We all share here.'

Jo was swamped, she couldn't see past the person in front

of her. But Will could easily see above the rabble at his height. 'There she is.'

They weaved their way through to a corner of the room just as a champagne bottle popped nearby.

'Jo!' Angie squealed when she caught sight of her. She lurched at her, throwing her arms around her neck. 'What did you think?'

Jo pulled back to look at her, tears in her eyes. 'I thought you were so wonderful.'

'You're not going to cry, are you?' said Angie. 'You'll make me cry!'

They hugged again, as somebody tried to pour champagne into the plastic tumbler in Angie's hand.

'Quick, grab a cup, Jo,' said Angie, but Will was already passing her one. 'We have to make a toast. Everyone,' she said in a loud voice. 'To Will, playwright extraordinaire.'

They all raised their cups, echoing her salute. Jo turned to him wide-eyed. 'You wrote it?'

'Didn't he tell you?' said Angie.

'It was a collaboration,' he dismissed.

'It was not,' Angie berated him.

'We had to workshop it.'

'That's what you do with plays, dodo,' she returned. 'Besides, barely a word was changed, it was too good. He's brilliant, isn't he?' she said to Jo.

'He is. You both are.'

'It's the words, I'm telling you,' said Angie. 'It was a gift for me, this play. For all of us.'

Somebody burst into the circle and threw his arms around Angie. Jo turned to Will. 'Why didn't you tell Joe out there when he brought it up?' she asked him.

'I wanted to make sure he really liked it before I owned up.'

'Why are you being so coy?'

He looked at her with a sheepish smile. 'Everyone in my family is involved in writing, in one way or another,' he explained. 'I resisted it, I wanted to be different, do my own thing with the acting. But you can't escape your genes, I guess.'

'Why would you want to?' said Jo. 'You're so talented.'

'Now you're going to make me blush,' he grinned. Then his expression grew serious. 'How are you anyway, Jo?'

She shrugged. 'Getting by.'

'We missed you at Christmas.'

A lump formed in her throat. 'That's nice of you to say, thanks.'

'If it's any consolation, Joe's miserable.'

'You know what, Will, that isn't any consolation at all,' she said honestly. 'I don't want him to be unhappy, that's the last thing I want.'

'Then you're a better man that I am, Gunga Din.'

Angie rejoined them then, and Will excused himself as someone called him from across the room.

Jo turned to Angie. 'Why didn't you tell me you were so incredibly talented and amazing?'

She just laughed. 'You mean you didn't recognise my elusive star quality in that printing paper ad I did, or my memorable turn as shopper number three in the series of training films on customer communication?'

'Well, at least you won't have to do crap like that any more,' said Jo.

'Of course I will,' Angie chided. 'This is a fringe production with an amateur theatre group, Jo. There were no Hollywood producers in the audience, we'll be lucky if there was an online arts critic out there.'

'But –'

'Angie!' someone grabbed her by the shoulders from behind.

'Listen, I'm going to leave you to it,' said Jo.

'But you won't go yet?'

'I won't, Oliver's waiting for me out there.'

'Oh, he made it?' she said happily as she was dragged away. 'Okay, I'll find you guys when this commotion dies down and we'll have a drink together.'

Jo had a feeling that was going to take a while. She walked back up the corridor to the main space, and stood just inside the doorway, scanning the crowd for Oliver. There seemed to quite a line-up at the bar. She really didn't want to bump into Joe again, and especially not Sarah. Maybe they'd left already; she probably tired easily in her condition.

'Jo?' said a female voice behind her.

She swung around to come face to face with Sarah. Or more like forehead to chin. God, she wished she'd worn high heels.

'Where did you come from?' Jo blurted.

'The loo,' she admitted. 'My second home these days,' she added, patting her belly. Her expression turned serious. 'You're *the* Jo, aren't you?'

'I beg your pardon?'

'The Jo he was having a relationship with.'

Oh God. 'I think calling it a relationship might be overstating it a bit,' she dismissed. 'We had a couple of dates. It wasn't serious.'

'I'm not sure that's how he sees it,' she said wistfully.

Jo really didn't want to be having this conversation.

'I'm sorry,' said Sarah.

Jo looked at her.

'I am. I'm sorry about the way things turned out. It's all a bit of a mess, isn't it?' she said. 'But I didn't know about you, Joe and I weren't in contact at all after he left. I nearly didn't come, I kept telling myself it wouldn't make any difference, but it does, don't you think?' She broke off, gazing out into the crowd. 'I knew he would be the best father for my baby,' she murmured. Suddenly she seemed to snap out of it. 'I couldn't deprive either of them of that. It didn't seem right. I hope you understand.'

Jo didn't know what she expected her to say.

'There you are, blossom.'

Thank Christ. She turned to see Oliver making his way towards her, holding two glasses aloft.

'I best get back to Joe,' said Sarah, and she slipped away into the crowd.

'What's the matter, cherub?' asked Oliver, handing her a glass. 'You're positively white.'

Jo held the glass to her lips, and drank, and drank, and drank some more until there was nothing left.

'My Lord, Josephine,' said Oliver. 'What's spooked you?'

'I have to get out of here,' said Jo. 'I'm sorry, I can't stay any longer.'

'Then we'll go,' he said simply.

'You don't have to –'

'Nonsense,' he dismissed. 'I can't let a date of mine go home alone. I'm a gentleman.'

'Thank you,' she said gratefully.

They made it outside without sighting either Joe or Sarah again, and Oliver led her smartly up the street to the main road where he hailed a taxi. He gave the driver the address of the *Trib* building.

'Where are we going?' Jo asked.

'Back to the café, you need a drink . . . another drink.'

'But your place isn't even licensed.'

'And I won't be charging you,' he said.

They travelled the rest of the way in silence. Well, not exactly, Oliver chatted away to the taxi driver, but Jo tuned out. She kept going over the conversation with Sarah in her head, there was something not quite right about it. Joe was the 'best' father, what did that mean, exactly? And why was she sorry, and why was it all a bit of a mess?'

Bugger, she just remembered. She told Angie she'd wait for her. She got out her mobile phone and sent her a text message.

So sorry, had to go. Explain later.
You were stupendous. Bask in it.

They arrived at the *Trib* building and Oliver unlocked the doors into the café, standing back to let her in. 'Quickly, inside, before anyone gets the idea I'm opening up.'

Jo ducked past him and Oliver locked the door again. 'Take a seat,' he said as he strode off around the counter. 'I'll fetch the refreshments.'

She sidled into a booth, the lights from the street providing enough illumination to find her way.

Oliver returned with a bottle of wine and two glasses and sat down opposite her. 'So what's ailing you, Josephine?' he began as he set the glasses on the table. 'You look like you lost your best friend after you dropped a pound and picked up sixpence.'

'I'm fine.'

'Fine my Aunt Beulah.'

'It's nothing. Nothing I can do anything about anyway,' she said despondently.

'Okay, Jo,' he sighed as he twisted the corkscrew into the bottle, 'you know that game heterosexuals play? The one where the man asks "What's wrong?" and the woman says "Nothing" a certain number of times until someone breaks? Well, I'm gay and I don't know how to play that game, so I give up. What's wrong? What did that fecund woman say to you?'

Jo was thoughtful. 'You know, I'm not exactly sure.'

'What, you couldn't hear her above the din?' he asked as he poured wine into the glasses.

'No, I heard her. I'm just not sure what she was saying.'

'You're being rather cryptic, my girl,' he said, sliding a glass over to her.

'So was she.' Jo picked up the glass and took a mouthful, and then another.

'You really have to stop guzzling your wine, darling, it's most unbecoming. Now focus, what did she actually say?'

She set the glass down again. 'Oliver, do you think it's important to tell the truth, no matter what?'

'I see, so we're going to take the scenic route via the long and winding road of Life's Big Questions,' he said dryly. 'I'm glad I opened a bottle.'

'All right, I'll try to be more specific,' Jo conceded. She leaned forward. 'Just say you heard something, something that could change everything, but you don't really know what you heard, for sure . . . should you tell the person involved anyway?'

'That's being more specific?' He pulled a face. 'What did that woman say to you?' he pleaded. 'Out with it, Josephine.'

'It was more the way she said it. She asked me if I was "the" Jo. She knows Joe and I were together.'

'Awkward,' he remarked.

'And then she said she was sorry about the whole mess, but that Joe was the best father for her child. What's that supposed to mean?'

'Sounds like he was the winning candidate for the job.'

'That's what I couldn't help thinking,' said Jo, her eyes wide. 'I mean, why would she put it like that?'

Oliver sighed, twirling the stem of his glass. 'Because she didn't realise that you would take every word she said and dissect it in the hope of finding some hidden meaning.'

Jo's face dropped.

He leaned forward and took her hand. 'This is not really a bad soap opera, Jo, darling, no one scripted her lines; she just had to get something off her chest. And you desperately want to believe that things may not be as they seem. But unfortunately they usually are.'

'But what if there's even a small chance they're not?' said Jo. 'Listen, I haven't told anyone this, but I did a little research. Do you have any idea how many babies are not the biological child of the man who believes he's the father? Women used to be able to keep it secret quite easily, but now with DNA testing, more and more cases are being discovered, and the statistics are mind-blowing.'

Oliver was just staring at her. 'You do realise you're beginning to sound . . . mm, what's the word I'm looking for . . . Crazy?'

'Just hear me out,' Jo persisted. 'Apparently she was really pissed off when Joe left her, he told me she was angry that she'd wasted all her childbearing years with him. So what's to stop her getting pregnant, then marching out here and claiming it's his?'

'Oh, a few months, at a guess.'

'Pardon?'

'You really are going off the rails now, poppet,' said Oliver, shaking his head. 'In your scenario, she'd only be about three months along, wouldn't she? She looked a lot more pregnant than that.'

Jo's heart dropped into her stomach. Oliver was right. What the hell was she thinking?

'Really, Josephine, clutching at the conspiracy-theory straw?' he went on. 'I would have expected more from you.' He leaned forward on the table. 'Tell me, does Joe strike you as stupid?'

'No, of course not.'

'And he's sure the baby's his?

She nodded reluctantly.

'I'm well aware that many a woman has pulled the wool over the eyes of many a man, and vice versa, but given the circumstances, I'm thinking Mr Joe would have been pretty rigorous about checking the validity of her claim. The way he looked at you tonight, I don't think he'd have done this lightly.'

Jo blinked back tears that crept into her eyes.

'But here's the thing, petal, I don't understand why you both think this is the only way,' said Oliver. 'So she takes the sprog home to Mother England. Joe's a big boy, he's lived half his adult life overseas from what I understand; why not go too, share the parenting from different addresses like half the people with children do anyway?'

'I don't think that's really the preferred option.'

'Not everyone gets their first preference in life,' he said. 'You'd go with him to England, wouldn't you?'

He'd have to ask her. It still niggled that he'd never suggested that.

'Oliver, if there's a chance for them to be a family, isn't that the best thing for the child?'

'Only if that's where they really want to be,' he declared. 'They won't be doing the child any favours sticking it out in a loveless relationship. My mother and father despised each other, but they nobly stayed together "for the sake of the children".'

'What happened?'

'My mother drank herself into an early grave and my father promptly sold the house and everything in it and took off and we never saw him again. My sister and I both have massive commitment issues, she's on her fourth marriage, while I'm so afraid to commit I have trouble buying green bananas.' Oliver paused, taking a sip of his wine. 'If you ask me, sticking it out for the sake of the kids is as bad as getting married just because you're pregnant. Joe's ticking both those boxes. It's a doomed proposition.'

Jo shrugged. 'Look, they loved each other once, there's no reason they can't rekindle that.'

'That's not how it works, Jo. If they loved each other once and something external drove them apart, then yes, maybe, but it sounds like Joe left her quite intentionally. He was over her, I assume. The fire had gone out, so there's nothing to rekindle.'

Jo sighed. 'Well, this is all academic anyway, because the decision's been made. Joe will be an excellent father. Family means everything to him, he couldn't have done this any other way.'

Oliver regarded her thoughtfully. 'Well, we'll have to agree to disagree on that one, petal. But if the die is so cast, what about you? Where do you go from here?'

Jo had no idea.

'Well,' said Oliver after a while, 'moving on, which I strongly suggest you do, let's drink to a new year and new possibilities.' He raised his glass. 'And even, dare we hope, to a new love.'

'I don't think I can drink to that, Oliver.'

'Ah but you must, my dear,' he urged. 'Life without love is like non-alcoholic wine. What the fuck's the point?'

11 pm

Joe drove through the city streets after they left the theatre, absorbed in his own thoughts. He felt on edge. It was difficult not seeing Jo, but it was difficult seeing her as well. She hadn't said goodbye. After Will had spirited her away he'd only caught sight of her once, over by the backstage exit, talking to Oliver. And then he hadn't seen her again. He could still feel the dull ache of disappointment.

He had only planned to come back for the night. He wanted to see Will's play while he was here, but he mainly came to convince Sarah to go up to the mountains with him tomorrow. Joe was still haunted by his father's words, the anger in his eyes. Maybe if he saw Sarah and him together, and the physical evidence of a baby on the way, it would put him at ease, and he'd be reconciled that Joe was doing the right thing.

'Listen, Sarah, you realise I want to head back home first thing tomorrow,' he said firmly. 'You are coming this time, right?'

'Joe,' she hesitated, 'I don't think I should be travelling so far away from the hospital at this stage.' She shifted in her seat, resting a hand on her belly as though to remind him. 'I've been having a lot of contractions on and off lately.'

'They're only Braxton-Hicks, they could go on for weeks.'

She looked at him. 'How do you know that?'

'I've been reading the books.'

'You have?'

He glanced at her. 'That's what you wanted, isn't it?'

'Yes,' she said quietly.

'Anyway, you've still got weeks to go,' he went on. 'But I don't know how long Dad's got. I think you can risk being a couple of hours' drive from the hospital.'

'I could go early.'

'First pregnancy you're more likely to go later,' said Joe. 'I need to get back to Dad. I need to be with my family right now, Sarah.'

'I understand,' she said. 'I do. You should go and be with them. I'll be fine.'

He sighed loudly. 'I can't keep leaving you here on your own.'

'I won't be.'

'Oh right, because Ian will keep you company, I suppose?'

'Well he is close by if I need anything.'

Joe shook his head. 'You know, Sarah, I have to say it, I find this whole thing with Ian weird. I still don't understand what he's doing here, hanging around.'

'He told you, and I've told you, a number of times, he's on a working holiday,' she insisted. 'We were good friends, Joe, we worked together. If he was a woman, you wouldn't be thinking twice about him "hanging around".'

Joe pulled up at traffic lights. 'Whatever, I'm still not comfortable leaving you again.'

There was a pause before she spoke. 'I don't think it's such a bad idea, to be honest.'

He frowned at her. 'What does that mean?'

She didn't look at him; she was staring down at her hands. 'I'm just wondering if we need a break.'

'A break?' he exclaimed. 'What are you talking about? We're not even really together.'

'That's the whole problem,' said Sarah. 'I thought it was going to be different, Joe. I thought this would be our time to bond, before the baby came.' She finally met his gaze. 'But you're not over that woman, I saw the way you looked at her tonight.'

There was the toot of a car horn behind them. Joe looked up to see the lights had changed. He took off again, clenching his jaw as tightly as he was clenching the steering wheel.

'Sarah,' he said in a level voice. 'I told you I needed time. I've been as honest as I can, which is more than I can say for you.'

'What are you implying?' she said defensively.

He glanced across at her. 'We could have avoided all this if you'd told me you were pregnant before I left England.'

'Avoided what? That you were over me, that you wanted to leave me and settle down in Australia without me?'

'I suppose we would have had to work through all that,' he returned. 'But it would have been a hell of a lot less complicated if there was no one else involved, don't you think?'

'Yes, I do,' she said quietly.

He sighed. 'Look, we just have to hang in there till the baby comes, I'm sure it's going to make a difference.'

There was a pause before she replied. 'I don't know if I can, Joe.'

'What?'

'I think that perhaps I made a mistake.'

Joe swerved the car over to the side of the road, pulling up in a no-standing zone. He reefed on the handbrake and turned in his seat to face her. 'What are you trying to say, Sarah?'

'Coming out here to Australia,' she said tentatively. 'I think it might have been a mistake.'

'Well I think you have to give it a bit more time before you decide you can't live here, don't you?'

'I don't mean coming to Australia, I mean coming to you. I'm beginning to think I should have left well enough alone.'

Joe was stunned. 'Is this some kind of a game to you, Sarah? Tell him, don't tell him, come, go . . . are you motivated by what's right at all?'

'That isn't fair.'

'I think it's a perfectly fair question,' he said, raising his voice. 'I don't understand what you're playing at. You came all the way out here to tell me you're having my baby. I never would have known otherwise. And you know what, at first I wished I didn't, that you hadn't told me, that you'd met someone else and the child would never know the difference.'

She was staring at him. 'You actually thought that?'

He nodded. 'It made me ashamed of myself that I even enter-
tained the idea, that I'd prefer not to know I had a child somewhere
in the world. So I decided I had to get over it. And I'm sorry if it's
taking longer than you'd like for me to come to terms with this,
but I'm doing the best I can.'

His voice reverberated throughout the car.

'I know you are, Joe,' Sarah said after a while. 'And despite
what you think,' she said slowly, her voice heavy with emotion, 'I
was trying to do what I thought was right too, so the baby would
have a mother and a father. But if there isn't any love —'

'Are you saying you don't love me either?'

'I don't know any more, to be honest,' she said plainly. 'I know
that you don't love me, Joe, and I don't know if you ever will. All
you can offer me is to wait and see, to hope that when the baby
comes you might feel differently.'

Joe leaned his head back against the seat. This was such a fucking awful mess. He couldn't keep living like this, something had
to change. Ironically it was Jo's words that kept echoing in his
head. What was the point of all this if he didn't put his heart and
soul into it? Then nobody wins.

'I understand how that must make you feel,' he said eventually, attempting to soften his tone. 'But this is all academic, Sarah.
You're due very soon, and I'm not going to let you do this on
your own, so far from home. Whatever you think, I do care about
you, and I'm completely committed to this child. We're going to
have to make the most of this, we're going to have to try, for his
sake. Shouldn't the baby be our first priority?'

She was staring at him, biting her lip. But finally she nodded
slowly.

'All right then,' said Joe. He breathed out heavily. 'I won't go
back up to the mountains until I have to.'

'But you have to now, Joe, I can't let you —'

He held up his hand to stop her. 'The girls will let me know
when it's time. I can make it up there in under a couple of hours.
In the meantime I'll stay here with you.'

Sarah clasped her hands on her belly, her head bowed. 'You
don't have to do this.'

'But I do, Sarah, that's the thing.'

*

New Year's Eve

Jo was settled in for the night. She had a bottle of bubbly chilling in the fridge, though she wasn't at all sure she was going to be in the right spirit to open it at midnight, even though she finally had her place to herself again. Charlene's course of treatment was complete and she was spending New Year with Belle before she headed back home next week. Belle had asked Jo to join them as well, but they were having all the neighbours in for a soiree and Jo would really rather not. Angie had asked her to a cast party; they weren't performing tonight, the preview season was over and they were going to celebrate. Any other time, that might have been fun.

But she wasn't in the mood for fun exactly. She didn't want to be dismal either, but it was difficult to know what to do with herself. She had wandered around the video store for forty-five minutes this afternoon looking for a title that wasn't too sad, or too funny, or too epic, and certainly not too romantic . . . but in the end she gave up. She didn't know what mood she was in, or what mood she wanted to cultivate. She wanted to be hopeful, she really did, but there wasn't a movie that seemed to embody that for her, and besides, she wasn't so sure a Hollywood movie should be her inspiration for the new year. Or her life beyond.

One thing was for sure, she was sick of the sound of her own voice in her head. So she went home and played music on the stereo. Loud, boisterous, headbanging stuff she could bop around to while she pottered about the flat putting things back in place, reclaiming the space now Charlene was gone. But as the clock ticked over to ten, Jo seriously wondered how she was going to make it all the way to midnight, whether she shouldn't just give up and go to bed. The new year only set people up for failure and disappointment. All that bright hope that things were going to be different, funnelled into unsustainable resolutions that nobody ever kept. She'd done her column on that last new year, miserable killjoy that she was.

Jo had not submitted a Christmas or New Year column this year. It wasn't unusual to drop regular features over the holiday period, and besides, she had been totally occupied pulling her investigative piece together. She was glad for the distraction; ever since the night of the play, all she could see every time her mind drifted was Sarah's face, her baby bump, the two of them together . . . So Jo had thrown herself into her work. The weeks before Christmas had been spent gathering information, which presented its own particular challenges at that time of the year. But she knew if she didn't make headway then, she wouldn't have a hope come the January shutdown. So she was persistent to the point of being annoying, and finally she was able to begin connecting the dots.

All roads led to one senior minister, but Jo had to be a hundred percent sure she had it right. She didn't want another debacle like the Andrew Leslie affair. This wasn't personal, however; it was corrupt and possibly criminal. The tendering process had been manipulated in favour of certain preferred contractors, as the original informant had indicated. Appeals from other contractors had been quashed and environmental impact statements buried to ensure the tollways went ahead unimpeded. But even worse, Jo had finally linked the senior minister to various companies investing in the projects, companies that were set to make enormous profits. It had involved untangling a matted web of family trusts and offshore shelf companies, but as Jo had written the piece up and it had begun to take shape, her heart had started to beat a little faster. She'd gone over and over it, fastidiously double-checking every detail, keeping her writing objective and spare. She'd written only the facts; she hadn't embellished a single point. It was a strong piece of journalism, and Jo was proud of it. She was ready to submit it to Leo, but considering the sensitive nature of the material, she had decided to wait to give it to him in person next week. She wasn't comfortable about it floating around in cyberspace, unsupervised.

Suddenly her intercom buzzed and Jo's heart did a small involuntary leap.

'Hello?'

'I knew you'd be there, you big liar.'

It was Angie. Jo had told her she was spending the night at Belle's, just as she'd told Belle she was spending the night with

Angie, so neither of them would feel sorry for her. She had not counted on feeling so sorry for herself.

'What are you doing here?' Jo asked.

'I've come to see the New Year in with you. What do you think I'm doing here?'

'But you have a fabulous party to go to.'

'Been there, done that. And it wasn't fabulous knowing my best friend was spending New Year's Eve on her own.'

'But I told you I was going to Belle's.'

'Lucky I know when you're lying then, isn't it?' she returned. 'Now, I've got one bottle of bubbly, have you got any grog up there or do I have to go pick up some more?'

'I've got a bottle,' Jo said meekly.

'That should do us. So are you going to let me in?'

Jo hesitated. 'Are you sure, Ange? I don't know if I'm going to be very good company.'

'Just shut up and press the button!'

She did as ordered, and skittered out the door and up the hall to wait at the lift. After a minute or two the doors opened and Angie was standing there, and Jo didn't think she'd ever been happier to see her.

'Thank you,' she gushed. 'Thanks for coming.'

'Cut it out, you might be a head case but you're not exactly a charity case,' she said, walking out of the lift. 'Besides, this was my plan all along, pre-New Year's with my new best friends, the main event with my old best friend, no offence intended.'

'None taken,' Jo smiled.

Ten minutes later they were planted on the living room carpet, raising their glasses to each other.

'What should we drink to?' asked Angie.

'I don't think I've got much to drink to, what do you suggest?'

'Well, let me see, I suppose we could drink to Joe and his new baby, seeing as you're *so* cool with all that,' she said, raising an eyebrow. 'Another dirty lie.'

Jo pulled a face.

'You never had me fooled. I just knew I wouldn't have the chance to talk to you properly until the play was over. But I do now. So out with it.'

Jo shrugged. 'There's really nothing more to say. It's over between us, he has a new life.'

'But you're not okay, are you?' said Angie. 'That's why you ran off from the theatre the other night. I bumped into Joe and the woman when I came out to find you.'

'You did?' she asked, trying to be nonchalant. 'So you saw her?'

'Uh huh,' Angie nodded, taking a sip from her glass.

'What did you think of her?'

'Not much, I barely said two words to her. Joe asked me if I'd seen you, he was looking for you as well.'

'Was he?' she said wistfully.

Angie put her glass down on the table. 'You're not fine with this at all, are you?'

Jo stared down at the carpet. 'It doesn't make any difference. You know, seeing him with her was . . . well, it was excruciating, to be perfectly honest. But it also made it real.' She looked up to meet Angie's gaze. 'She's a real live person walking around with Joe's baby inside her. I don't have any choice but to move on.'

'How do you plan to do that?'

'By talking about something else,' she said plainly.

'You mean by avoiding the subject?'

'Yes, actually. Anything to get my head out of this space. I can't keep thinking about him and talking about him. It's too hard.'

'Fair enough,' said Angie. 'So what do you want to talk about instead?'

'Something happy and uplifting for New Year's,' said Jo. 'Your plans, for example.'

'My plans for what?'

'Your plans to capitalise on your new-found fame.'

'I tried to tell you the other night, Jo,' said Angie, 'there is no fame to be found in an amateur theatre group.'

'But you've had a great opportunity here,' Jo insisted. 'You have to build on it.'

'It's not that easy, you know how difficult this profession is.'

'Fair enough, but you still have the main season to go. What's your agent doing to promote it, get you some attention where it matters?'

Angie shook her head. 'I only got this chance because it's an amateur production, and I appreciate it, I really do. I'm having a ball. But no one else is going to look twice at me.'

'So what are you going to do about that?' said Jo, unfazed.

Angie shrugged. 'There's nothing I can do about it.'

'Of course there is. You have to think positively.'

'Jo, all the positive thinking in the world is not going to change the world. I would never even be considered for a part like that in mainstream theatre.'

'Why not?'

'Look at me.'

'I am, and I see an incredibly talented, beautiful woman.'

'Who's overweight.'

Jo paused, considering her. 'So lose some of it.'

Angie blinked. 'Oh, okay, Jo, I'll make that my new year's resolution,' she said sarcastically.

'New year's resolutions don't work,' she said bluntly. 'You need a strategy.'

'Why are you talking like this, Jo?' She seemed hurt. 'You've never talked like this before.'

'Because I'd never seen you act before,' Jo insisted. 'Not really, and I understand what you're saying, I do. I know how bigoted the world is, so never mind that at least half the population is overweight, and you are in fact, quite average – if you won't be considered for roles because of your weight, then you have to lose some of it.'

Angie looked piqued. 'You think it's that easy?'

'I didn't say that,' Jo shook her head. 'I don't think it's going to be easy at all. I imagine it would be really hard. In fact, everything I've ever read suggests it's incredibly difficult.'

'Then why are you giving me a hard time?'

'Because if I had a talent like yours, I'd do everything I possibly could to give myself a chance,' she said plainly. 'I know it's unfair, Ange, but don't hide behind it either. Do you realise how good you are? Did you hear the applause, the praise? You could be really successful. Cate Blanchett-Nicole Kidman successful.'

'Okay, now you're being ridiculous.'

'Why is it ridiculous?' asked Jo. 'You've got the potential. You've got the looks. If it's only your size stopping you, then do something about it.'

Angie chewed on her lip. 'What do you suggest?'

Jo thought about it. 'Stop working around food, for a start.'

She frowned.

'I mean, come on, talk about putting the cat among the pigeons,' said Jo. 'Why make it harder for yourself?'

'What else am I supposed to do?'

'Anything,' said Jo. 'Become an office temp, a receptionist, even a cleaner would be preferable, at least that would be a bit more physical, and you'd be away from food. Save up for a personal trainer, do whatever you have to do.'

Angie was listening intently, Jo could almost hear the cogs turning in her brain. She wasn't too bad at sorting out other people's issues.

'Oh, I almost forgot, I have your Christmas present,' said Jo, jumping up. 'I know it's late but I didn't know what to get you until the other night.'

'What is it?'

Jo dashed over to her computer desk, and came back, presenting Angie with a piece of paper. 'Sorry it's not wrapped,' she said. 'It's a review of the play. I went over Leo's head, or under it, or around it, whatever, I went straight to our theatre critic. And he was very interested; he said if I gave it a bit of a rewrite, he'd run it to tie in with the fringe festival.'

Angie was scanning the page. 'Why did he want a rewrite?'

'He said I should make it a tad less gushing.'

Angie smiled. 'I can see why.' She looked up at Jo. 'I can't believe you did this for me.'

'Oh, that was easy, the hard part's up to you now.'

Angie nodded vaguely, staring back at the paper in her hand. 'Thank you, thank you so much.'

'My pleasure. I'll go get that bottle,' Jo declared, turning towards the kitchen. 'Because now we really do have something to drink to.' She came back a moment later and refilled their glasses, before settling back on the floor opposite Angie. 'So, let's drink to your brilliant career,' she said, holding her glass up. 'You'll still be my friend when you're famous, won't you? Swanning around in limousines and partying with Brad and Angelina —'

'– and George,' Angie swooned. 'And Matt and Johnny, sigh, and James and Rob . . .'

'I'm not sure who all those people are,' said Jo, 'but I'll drink to them anyway.'

They clinked glasses and drank.

So now it's your turn,' Angie said.

'For what?'

'To make your new year's resolution.'

Jo shook her head, taking another gulp from her glass. 'Don't believe in them,' she said.

'All right then, what are your "plans" for the new year?'

'To finish this bottle,' she said, topping up their glasses. 'And get through the next.'

'Jo,' Angie chided, 'stop avoiding the issue. How are you going to move on?'

She met her eyes. 'By putting one foot in front of the other.'

'Jo!' she groaned. 'Be serious!'

'I am being serious,' she replied calmly. 'Putting one foot in front of the other is my strategy.'

'And that's how you're going to get over Joe?'

She looked straight at Angie. 'I'm not going to get over Joe.'

Angie frowned. 'You have to try. If I'm going to try to lose weight, you have to try to move on.'

'I didn't say I wouldn't move on, but that doesn't mean I'm going to get over him. You're the big expert on soul mates. How can you get over your soul mate?'

'You don't even believe in them.'

'I suppose you don't believe in them until one comes along. Like ghosts, and extraterrestrials.'

'Jo Liddell,' said Angie, shaking her head, 'I never thought I'd hear you talk like this.'

'What can I say? I didn't believe in them and then I met mine, and now I can't imagine being with anyone else. I can't imagine even kissing another man,' she shuddered. 'I'm not being hope-less, or helpless, or defeatist, Ange, it's just the way things are. Joe might end up having a dozen babies with Sarah, and live happily ever after, and I hope he does, but I can't see how I can get over him.'

Angie considered her thoughtfully. 'So what are you going to do? Putting one foot in front of the other is all very well, but do you know where you're going?'

'Away from here, I think,' said Jo, hugging her knees. 'I can't hang around and risk bumping into him all the time. With her, with the baby. I certainly can't keep working with him. So I'm going to have to get a long way away from him.'

'Where will you go?' Angie frowned. 'Do you actually have a plan?'

Jo thought about it. 'Not really, I'm making it up as I go along.'

The Tribune

'This is a fine piece of investigative journalism, Jo. It's rigorous, meticulous, compelling. Everything connects, it's as tight as a drum ... and I can't print it.'

'Pardon?'

'At least not until our lawyers are finished with it,' Leo explained. 'And first impressions are that it may have to be handed over to the authorities first.'

'But that's not fair, it's our exclusive,' said Jo. 'My exclusive.'

'In cases like this we usually get the go-ahead to run it on the same day they make their move. Obviously they can't let the story get out beforehand, a lot of incriminating material can be shredded or "lost" that way.'

'And there's a lot of incriminating material.'

'How on earth did you get all this?' Leo asked, indicating for her to take a seat.

'Sometimes being cute and blonde is not such a disadvantage, you know.'

He grimaced. 'So I don't want to know?'

'I didn't do anything untoward, Leo,' she assured him, sitting down opposite. 'I just started at the bottom, which is familiar territory for me, after all,' she said wryly. 'You can get a lot more information than you think from the assistant to the assistant's assistant, and they're a lot less careful about what they tell you, especially around the Christmas party season. Most of the time they don't even realise the significance of the information they're giving you, because they're not aware of the bigger picture.'

'Still, you had to uncover the trail.'

Jo shrugged. 'It was buried in a whole lot of bureaucratic red tape, but anyone who had the patience to sift through it would have found what I did.'

'Now you're just being modest,' said Leo. 'You know Leighton reckons this'll be in the running for a Walkley.'

Jo blinked. '*Mike* Leighton? You showed it to the editor-in-chief?'

'Of course. I would have been hung out to dry if I tried to run it under his radar, but once it was going to the lawyers, the chief had to see it regardless,' he said. 'The *Daily* will probably run it, and they'll give us part two.'

Jo was wide-eyed. 'It'll run in Saturday's *Tribune*?'

'Probably. Not for a few weeks, mind. And until then, this stays in this office, Jo,' Leo stated firmly. 'No one can know anything about it, not a soul. If there's a leak, it's all over.'

She nodded. 'I understand.'

'Once it breaks, I imagine the *Daily* will second you and before long you'll be offered a transfer. That's what you've wanted all along, right?' he prompted. 'To be taken "seriously". Working on a broadsheet is the brass ring, isn't it?'

Jo sat there, speechless.

'Jo?'

She looked at him. 'Maybe not. Could I ask a favour, Leo?'

*

Sydney domestic terminal

'So how do I look?' asked Charlene, getting to her feet as the call to board her plane was announced.

'You look really great, Mum,' Belle said enthusiastically.

Her new beau was meeting her at the other end, so Charlene had insisted she had to look her best. Her spirits had lifted significantly, her eyes were bright and she was clearly excited. So if dressing like a Canterbury Road hooker made her feel good, who was Jo to burst her bubble?

'You know, Mum,' she said, 'you should think about telling this guy, give him a chance to do the right thing. You might be surprised.'

'I sure would be,' Charlene returned dubiously.

Jo watched as she gave Belle a hug, and it suddenly occurred to her that it would be a long time before she would see her mother again, maybe . . . She had a sensation like an icy cold hand closing around her heart. Jo roused herself.

'Bye Mum.' She came forward to give her a quick hug, blinking back the tears she could feel pricking at the corners of her eyes.

'Wish me luck!'

Jo and Belle stood together, their arms linked, as Charlene disappeared down the gangway with a cheery wave but no backwards glance.

'I'm so worried about her,' Belle murmured.

Jo looked at her. 'Mum has made her own decisions for her own reasons, and we have to respect that.'

Belle nodded begrudgingly as they turned around and ambled away. 'I guess we don't have a choice.'

'When did we ever have a choice about what Mum did with her life?'

'Never.'

'So nothing's changed. She has her bloke, that's what makes her happy.' Jo paused. 'Listen, do you have time for a coffee?'

'When?' said Belle.

'Now.'

'Here?'

'Well, yes.'

'But it's so expensive.'

'I don't think it'd be any more than four dollars,' said Jo, confused. 'I'll shout you.'

'No,' Belle shook her head. 'It's the price of the parking that makes it expensive.'

Jo sighed, a little frustrated. 'Then I'll pay for the parking.'

'That's not the point.'

'Belle,' said Jo. 'I have to talk to you. I need to talk to you now.'

She frowned. 'Okay. Then let's just talk.'

They sat on a bench facing a wall of glass where they could see the planes parked in their bays and, further off in the distance, more planes taking off and landing.

'What is it?' Belle asked warily.

Jo took a breath. 'I'm going away.'

'Where to?'

'London, first.'

Belle shifted to face her. 'What?'

'The European bureau for the *Trib* is based in London,' she explained. 'And not just the *Sunday Trib* but the whole organisation. I'm going to be a correspondent for publications right across the country.'

Belle's eyes grew wide. 'You're going to work in London? You're not talking about a holiday?'

'No, it's not a holiday, Belle,' said Jo. 'And I'll only be staying in London until they find a post for me. The French correspondent is leaving, but everyone wants that gig, so depending on who gets it, and the shuffle that happens as a result, I'll end up wherever there's a vacancy.'

'Like where?'

Jo shrugged. 'Well, it might be Moscow. Apparently no one wants to stay there longer than they have to, so there's a big turnover of correspondents.'

Belle leapt up off the bench. 'You're moving to Moscow?' she cried.

'Sit down,' said Jo, grabbing her hand to pull her down again. She was attracting attention.

'How can you do this?' said Belle in a high-pitched voice. 'You . . . you can't . . . you, um . . . you have a mortgage.'

'That's nothing,' Jo dismissed. 'What's more important is that I have a wonderful sister who I'm going to miss like crazy.'

Belle's face crumpled and Jo put her arms around her, stroking her back in a circle the way Belle had done for her.

'You're really going to do this?' she said in a small voice.

Jo held her shoulders to look at her directly. 'This is a fantastic opportunity, Belle. I'd really like you to be happy for me.'

She sniffed. 'I know you've always wanted this, Jo. And I am happy for you, really. I just don't know what I'm going to do without you,' she whimpered.

'You're going to do absolutely fine, like you always have,' Jo assured her. 'I haven't been much of a support to you, or an aunty to those kids. You're running your own show, Belle, with no help from me.'

'That's not true,' said Belle. 'You've always been there for me, Jo.'

'And I still will be, with the Internet and email,' said Jo. 'You'll be able to pick up the phone and talk to me any time. I'll never be far away from you, Belle, wherever I am in the world. You should know that by now.'

Belle wiped her eyes. 'You're going because of what happened with Joe, aren't you?'

'I can't deny that was the catalyst,' she admitted. 'But I worked on this big story around Christmas –'

'Oh? What was it? You didn't mention.'

'I couldn't, I shouldn't even be telling you this much,' said Jo. 'It's going to break soon, and it's a pretty big deal.'

'Wow, congratulations.'

'Thanks,' she smiled. 'Anyway, the thing is, it gave me some bargaining power. There was a good chance the *Daily Trib* was going to offer me a position, so I told Leo how I'd always wanted to be a foreign correspondent, and because there's a bit of rivalry between the papers, and he was probably going to lose me anyway, he was happy to make some calls. It turned out the European bureau chief had the French correspondent's resignation sitting on his desk. It was perfect timing.'

'Serendipity,' Belle nodded, looking a little brighter. 'So maybe it was all meant to be?'

Jo shook her head. 'I don't think that's how things work, Belle. If I was meant to meet Joe in the elevator, only to have him taken away from me, so that I could get this job, then fate is a pretty manipulative old bitch.'

Belle smiled faintly. 'I guess.'

'You know what I do think?' Jo went on. 'I think life just rolls along. Good stuff happens, bad stuff happens. It's what you do with it that matters. Look at you, Belle, you had the same childhood as I did, but you didn't let it defeat you, you didn't let it stop you from going for what you wanted. And you have a good marriage and a happy family. You broke the cycle in one generation, and I'm so proud of you for doing that. I shut myself off from all that, not trusting or believing it could be better for me. And guess what, it hasn't been. That's what they call a self-fulfilling prophecy.'

Belle was listening to her thoughtfully. 'We didn't have the same childhood, Jo,' she said. 'We both had a father who abandoned us, and a pretty useless mother, granted. But I had you as well, and you were so caring and protective and strong, and you helped me trust the world because I could trust you, always. But you didn't have that, you had to protect yourself and you never learned how to trust anyone. Till Joe. I suppose that didn't turn out so well for you.'

'You know what though, Belle?' said Jo. 'I don't regret it. I did for a while, or I thought I did. But if that's all the time I was going to get with him, then at least I had that. I've come to terms with it. And now I have to move on.'

Belle took hold of her hands. 'Maybe it will be good for you to go off and see the world and realise it's not all bad.'

'So I have your blessing?'

She smiled bravely. 'Of course you do, I only want you to be happy.'

They hugged each other tight.

'Just, does it have to be Russia?' Belle said in her ear.

*

The next day

Joe decided to walk home. It was a hot, grimy January afternoon, but he knew the bus was only likely to be hotter and grimier. Work had been uneventful. He hadn't seen Jo all day, she didn't seem to be around much at all lately, so he'd lost even that small consolation. Maybe she'd taken some annual leave, her column hadn't appeared for a couple of weeks and a lot of the staff were away at the moment. The paper was in holiday mode as well, bumper crosswords and the like filling its pages rather than regular features. Joe didn't really need to be there so much, but it gave him a break from sitting around the flat trying to be polite to Sarah. Besides, he used the time to keep up with all the overseas news services. It wasn't summer break in the northern hemisphere, and wars didn't stop for any holiday.

He was beginning to get a little frustrated at the *Trib*. He was going to have to start thinking about his options. With a family to support, he really had little choice but to take a staff position somewhere. He'd had offers ever since his by-line began to appear, and even before that. Sarah didn't want to stay in the flat, and he couldn't blame her, he didn't want to bring up a child in the middle of the city either. But he wasn't sure how she would feel about living up in the Blue Mountains.

She still hadn't come with him to visit his father, and now that she'd gone over her due date, it wasn't going to happen any time soon. Joe had managed to slip away on a couple of occasions, again through the day. His dad was lingering on, but while he still had brief periods of coherence where he could communicate, they were loath to take that away from him. Joe felt constantly torn; he wished he could just stay up there, he wished he hadn't made the promise to Sarah, but there were many things he wished were different, and there was nothing he could do to change any of them.

He arrived at his building, relieved to step into the cool of the darkened foyer. He mounted the three flights of stairs wearily and let himself into the flat. 'Sarah?'

He heard movement from her room and he walked over to the door. It was ajar, so he knocked lightly as he pushed it back.

Sarah was sitting herself up on the bed, wiping her eyes. Ian was standing over at the other side of the bed. He seemed unnerved, even a little embarrassed.

'What's going on?' asked Joe.

'Nothing,' Sarah sniffed.

'It doesn't look like nothing,' he persisted, glancing darkly at Ian.

'I've just been feeling a little homesick, emotional, you know,' Sarah explained. 'That's all. Par for the course.'

Joe felt an uncomfortable churning in his stomach as he looked from her to Ian. 'You'd better stop bullshitting and tell me what the hell's going on.'

'Joe, you're overreacting –'

'We have to tell him,' Ian blurted suddenly.

'Ian!' she said grimly, getting to her feet.

Joe was staring at her. 'Sarah . . . ?'

'It won't change anything,' she said to Ian. 'It doesn't make any difference.'

'Yes, it does.' He looked squarely at Joe. 'I'm in love with Sarah, we love each other.'

'Ian!' she cried again. She turned to look at Joe. 'It's not . . . um . . .'

His heart was beating hard in his chest. 'Is that the truth, Sarah? Don't lie to me now.'

Her shoulders dropped. 'Yes but –'

'Fuck,' he said, almost to himself, as he turned and walked out of the room. He needed some air, he was suddenly feeling very claustrophobic. He crossed to the open window and leaned on the ledge, breathing deeply, in and out. What the hell did this mean? His brain was scrambled with so many possibilities he couldn't think straight.

He turned around. They had both followed him into the living room, and they were standing there like a pair of schoolkids waiting for a reprimand from the principal.

'How long . . . since when?' Joe asked.

'A year, maybe longer,' said Ian.

'What?' He glared straight at Sarah. 'So the baby –'

'Is yours, Joe,' she said.

'And I'm supposed to believe that when this has been going on for over a year?'

'It hasn't,' Sarah insisted. 'Tell him, Ian.'

'She's right,' said Ian. 'I apologise, I put it badly. I have been in love with Sarah for more than a year, but she wasn't interested at first. You two were still together, and she resisted my advances. She was faithful to you. But then you were away so much, she was lonely, we became . . . close. But even so, we were never . . . together, until after you left, for good.'

Joe stood there, feeling numb. Maybe he was in shock.

'I promise you, Joe, if the baby was mine, she wouldn't be here to begin with.'

At least that made sense. He cleared his throat. 'Okay, I think you better go, Ian.'

'What do you want me to do, darling?' he asked Sarah.

'This is my place, and I think you should leave, Ian,' Joe said tightly. 'Sarah and I have to sort this out together.'

'What is there to sort out?' Ian said plainly. 'You don't love her, she doesn't love you, there's no reason for you to be together.'

Joe looked at him. 'Of course there's a reason, the only reason that matters. I'm the father of her child, we don't have much choice.'

Ian went to say something but Sarah interrupted. 'You should go, Ian. We'll talk later.'

He regarded her sadly. 'You'll be all right?'

'Of course. I'll call you.'

He walked over to the door and opened it, turning back. 'The thing is, Joe, you do have a choice, there's always a choice. Doing the right thing is not always the right thing to do.'

And then he left, closing the door behind him. The flat was strangely quiet, even the sound of traffic seemed a long way off. Joe hadn't moved. He was still standing in the middle of the room, his head swimming, trying to make sense of what had just happened.

'Joe?' said Sarah after a while. 'Joe, I'm so sorry you had to find out like that.'

He roused, glancing across at her. She was sitting on the couch now, he hadn't even been aware of her passing by. He cleared his throat. 'How did you want me to find out, Sarah?'

'I didn't,' she said. 'I thought you were never going to find out.'

Joe rubbed his face with his hands. 'So you never intended to tell me that you were in love with another man? Were you planning to continue the affair?'

'No, Joe, you have it wrong, we haven't been having an affair.'

'Then what is he doing here?'

'He loves me,' she said simply. 'He was still hoping to talk me out of this.'

Joe frowned. 'I'm not following you.'

'Like Ian said, nothing happened between us until after you left,' said Sarah. 'We flirted, there was an attraction, but I always made it clear I was in a relationship. The last couple of times you came back from Iraq, I felt like you were growing away from me, but whenever I tried to talk to you about it, about our future, you just brushed it off. All you'd ever say was that you couldn't deal with it with your head in the war.'

She was right. Joe walked around and sat heavily in an armchair opposite her. He'd made that excuse, but that's all it was, an excuse. A cop-out.

'Ian and I became close,' Sarah continued. 'Only as friends though, nothing happened between us. He was a good listener, and he was a good friend, he was my best friend. He finally told me one day he was in love with me. I wasn't all that surprised, I suppose I'd been kidding myself that we could keep it platonic. But I was still in love with you, Joe. Whether from habit, I don't know. I was confused, I didn't know what to do. Then I found out I was pregnant, and after the initial shock, I decided it was meant to be. You and I had been floundering around for too long, we needed to settle down and be a family. I was all ready to tell you when you came home and said you were leaving.' Her voice started to break. 'I fell apart, and it was Ian who helped me get it together again. He promised he'd always love me, and that he would love my baby too, like it was his own. I was so furious with you, I decided I didn't even have to tell you.'

'So you got with Ian out of spite?'

'No, I just didn't tell you, out of spite,' she said. 'Ian was wonderful, he only wanted to make me happy. And I was happy, Joe. For a few months there, I was truly deeply happy in a way I can never remember feeling when you and I were together. No offence.'

'None taken,' said Joe. He knew exactly what she was talking about.

'So what happened?' he prompted her. 'What made you give up all that to come out here?'

'I couldn't keep pretending,' she shrugged. 'Least of all to myself. My conscience simply got the better of me. I knew I had to tell you about the baby. At first I thought I'd write a letter explaining everything, give you time to take it in. But I didn't know how your father was, and what kind of dilemma that would put you in. So then I thought I'd leave it till after the baby was born, so you wouldn't have to feel any obligation to rush over in time for the birth. I went through every scenario and option I could think of, and I still didn't know what to do. I couldn't talk about it with Ian, it hurt him so much that I was even contemplating telling you. He saw it as a kind of betrayal, that I didn't believe he would be the best father for my child. And to be honest, there was an element of truth to that.'

'What do you mean?' Joe frowned.

'I couldn't help thinking that although he said he'd love the baby like it was his own, how could he know for sure? He wanted us to have our own children as well in the future, and I wanted that too, but I was worried about what would happen to this child. It all seemed so complicated and uncertain ... I love Ian with all my heart, but it felt selfish to be putting my feelings, my happiness, ahead of what was best for my child. I don't know if it was hormones or what it was, but I felt I had to come to you. And before I knew what I was doing, I was on a plane.'

Joe was still struggling to understand. 'But you didn't just come here to tell me about the baby, you wanted us to get back together. Why didn't you admit there was someone else?'

'I thought it was over with Ian, I didn't think he'd ever forgive me,' she explained. 'And I meant everything I said to you back then, Joe.'

'Including that you still loved me?'

She sighed. 'I really believed we could make a fresh start out here. But I had no idea what I was walking into. I hadn't even considered you would have met someone so quickly, it didn't cross my mind, the state I was in. It was naive I suppose. The only thing I knew for sure was the kind of man you were, that you'd always do the right thing.' She shook her head. 'You know, Joe, despite all the chaos you've witnessed in the world, you have a very black and white moral code.'

To a fault, apparently. 'Then Ian followed you out here?' he prompted.

She nodded. 'He was devastated when I left. He kept calling me, it only took one conversation where I got a little teary and admitted that things were not as I'd hoped, and he was on the next plane. He didn't hesitate, he loved me enough to follow me across the world, even though I was having another man's baby. You were barely interested, Joe. I know you were trying,' she said when he went to interrupt. 'But I could see how unhappy you were. My God, you were in love with someone else. And so was I. I just wanted to turn back the clock, especially after you said you wished you'd never found out. Everyone could have gone along as they were, everyone would have been happy. I just kept thinking, why did I do this?'

Her words echoed in the space between them.

'Because despite everything,' Joe said eventually, 'this is still my child, and I had a right to know.'

Sarah winced.

'Are you okay?' Joe frowned, watching her.

'I'm just uncomfortable.' She shifted her position. 'Of course, you're right, Joe. Back home, I kept casting my mind into the future, with a sixteen year old who didn't know that the man who had brought him up was not his biological father. I would have had to tell him, probably long before, I couldn't keep up a deception like that. And there would be every chance that he'd want to find you. I imagined the damage that would be done then. It was one of the reasons I boarded that plane.'

Joe was shaking his head. 'I thought about the sixteen year old too.'

'I'm sorry?'

'I really didn't want to give Jo up, but I kept seeing this sullen teenager who was going to resent me for giving him up.'

Sarah winced again. Joe looked across at her, she was pale, and there was a film of sweat covering her face.

'You don't look so good, Sarah. How are you feeling?'

'I haven't felt well at all today,' she admitted. 'It must be the heat.'

'Can I get you something? Do you want to go lie down?'

She shook her head. 'I might just go to the bathroom.'

Joe got up to help her to her feet. She met his eyes directly. 'I'm so sorry, Joe. About everything.'

'It's not your fault, Sarah,' he said honestly. 'We're all in this together.'

He watched her walk through to the bathroom, before wandering over to the window to stare out at the skyline. The traffic was louder now, the air oppressive. So what now?

'*Joe!*'

He rushed across to the bathroom door. 'Sarah? Are you okay?'

'The door's not locked, you can come in,' he heard her cry weakly.

He opened the door gingerly, peering inside. She was slumped back on the toilet, but he could see what had happened.

'I think my waters broke,' she whimpered.

'I think you're right about that,' he said, sidestepping the puddle on the floor to get to her. 'Come on, we have to get you to the hospital.'

He took hold of her arms to help her up, but she grabbed one of his hands. 'Joe,' she said plaintively, 'can you phone Ian? Please?'

'Sure, I'll call him, but let's call the hospital first, okay?'

Joe was sitting on a bench in the corridor outside the delivery rooms when Ian appeared around the corner, almost running towards him.

'Take it easy,' said Joe, getting to his feet. 'Nothing's happened yet, they're just making her comfortable, checking her over.'

'Was she in much pain?' he asked, breathless.

'The contractions started after her waters broke, but she seemed to be handling them all right so far.'

He nodded, grasping his arms to himself. 'It's not unusual, the waters breaking first, I read about that. It shouldn't affect the baby. Did they say anything about the baby? They're not worried?'

Joe shook his head, moved by his obvious concern. 'Everyone was acting like it was routine, I don't think there's anything to worry about, Ian.'

A nurse came out of the door opposite. 'Ms Parrish wanted to know if a Mr Templeton has arrived yet?'

'Yes, tell her I have,' said Ian.

'You can go in.'

Ian glanced at Joe. 'Oh, no, I don't think so . . .'

'Go ahead,' said Joe. 'She wants to see you.'

'Are you sure?'

'Of course.'

It was a full half-hour before Ian reappeared, looking flushed and not a little awkward. 'Sorry, Joe,' he said. 'Time got away. You should go in now.'

Joe regarded him, frowning. 'Is Sarah asking for me?'

'Oh, well, um,' he stammered, 'not specifically. She's got other things on her mind, after all. But you should go in, she needs someone to be with her,' he added, glancing anxiously back at the door.

Joe sighed. 'I don't think that someone should be me.'

Ian looked a little startled. 'But it's your baby, Joe.'

'I'm not going anywhere,' he assured him. 'But you should be with Sarah, she needs you.'

After a few more half-hearted protests, Joe persuaded him to go in, and Ian promised in return that he would come out with regular updates. Joe wandered into the waiting room and sat on one of the vinyl lounges.

His child was about to be born, not more than a few metres away, and another man was going to witness it. But it felt right somehow. He knew Sarah would want the man she loved in there with her. If Jo were having a baby, anyone's baby, he'd want to be with her. He wished it was Jo in there now, having his baby. It was an absurd and pointless fantasy, but he indulged in it anyway.

Any baby he was going to have should have been with Jo. How the hell had things turned out this way? How could this child feel loved and secure with two unhappy parents who wished they were with someone else? It was untenable.

Eight hours later

'Joe . . . Joe . . .'

He lurched up suddenly. He'd fallen asleep, slouched sideways on the lounge. His body felt stiff, his mind disorientated, as he blinked repeatedly to bring Ian's face into focus.

'It's a girl!' He was beaming.

Joe swallowed, his throat was dry. 'A girl?' he croaked.

'And she's beautiful, Joe,' he went on. 'She's absolutely perfect. You have to see her. They're just getting her cleaned up now and then Sarah said you should go in.'

The fog was gradually lifting. 'Sarah, is she okay?'

Ian sat on the lounge opposite. 'She's wonderful. She was incredibly brave and strong . . . just wonderful.'

Joe nodded, taking it all in. It was a girl, he had a daughter. He was a father. It didn't really mean much yet.

He stood up to stretch, giving his head a good rub to scatter the cobwebs. 'You must be tired,' he remarked to Ian as he crossed over to the water dispenser and pulled out a paper cup.

'No, I'm still pretty keyed up, actually,' he said. 'It was an amazing experience.'

Joe filled the cup with water and offered it to Ian, but he declined. He drained the cup himself and tossed it in the bin, just as a nurse appeared around the corner.

'Mr Bannister? Joe Bannister?' she said, glancing from one to the other.

'Yeah, that's me.'

'Sarah said you can come in now.' She turned away and Joe went to follow her.

Ian stood up and put out his hand. 'Congratulations, Joe.'

He shook his hand, nodding vaguely. He hadn't really done anything, but he said 'Thanks' anyway. He walked around the corner. The nurse was standing a little way up the corridor, indicating the door. 'You can go right in.'

Joe walked past her into the room. Sarah was lying in the bed, propped up with pillows. She looked tired, but there was an expression on her face he could only describe as blissful. 'Hi Joe,' she said.

'Hi.' He came closer, but his gaze was inexorably drawn to the perspex crib on the other side of the bed. 'How are you feeling?' he asked, his eyes fixed on the tiny bundle wrapped in a white sheet, the top of her little pink head poking out.

'I'm fine,' said Sarah, watching him. 'Go and introduce yourself to your daughter.'

He glanced at Sarah then. 'I don't know if I'm ready for this.'

'She won't realise,' she smiled.

Joe walked slowly around the bed. He was nervous, his stomach was churning and his heart was beating hard in his chest. He drew closer to the crib; he could see her face now, her dear, little perfect face. A lump rose in his throat.

'You can pick her up, if you like,' Sarah was saying.

No way was he ready for that. He didn't even know how to go about it. No, he didn't want to disturb her. He bent right over the crib, staring at her; her eyes were closed, but she had a perfect miniature nose, and perfect miniature rosy lips. She was exquisite.

'Don't be afraid,' said Sarah. 'You can touch her. She won't break.'

Joe reached in and carefully let the back of his fingers connect with the skin of her cheek. She was real, she was warm, and she was so very soft. He swallowed back the lump in his throat.

'She's beautiful,' he managed to say.

'Isn't she?'

He nodded. He couldn't take his eyes off her. He suddenly felt protective, and proud, and a whole lot of feelings he couldn't even name because he'd never experienced them before. She was part of him, part of his family. He wanted her to know her amazing aunts, her Uncle Will. He wanted her to know all about her grandfather, even though he wouldn't be around long enough for her to know him. Joe wanted to give her everything it was in his power to give. He wanted her to be happy, to feel loved and secure. And he realised, gazing down at her, that there was a way he could give her all those things.

'Does she have a name?' he asked.

'She didn't come with one,' said Sarah, smiling.

He looked across at her then. They had not talked about names. When Sarah had tried to bring it up, he'd been disinterested, it made it too real, and he wasn't ready. But she was a person now, lying there in the crib, and he needed to know what to call her.

'What did you have in mind?' he asked.

'Well, we should discuss it.'

'What did you have in mind?' he repeated with a faint smile.

She hesitated. 'Well, my father's mother, I never got to meet her, she died before I was born. He always spoke so fondly of her . . . her name was Julia.'

'You want to call her Julia?'

'What do you think?'

'I don't think it's up to me, Sarah.'

'Joe, she's your daughter too.'

'I know that.' He gazed down at his little girl. 'Julia it is then.'

'Thank you,' said Sarah, her voice catching in her throat.

Joe straightened, perching on the end of the bed to look directly at her. 'What were we thinking, Sarah?'

She seemed taken aback by that.

'We never had a chance, you and I,' he went on. 'We kept saying we had to put the baby first. Well, I think I'm finally putting her first, ahead of my ego and everything else that has gotten in the way. She needs a mother who has the love and support of a good man. She needs two parents who are committed to each other, and who have a better than average chance of staying together and giving her a happy childhood. I'm her father, nothing can change that, and I want to be a part of her life. But you should be with Ian, Sarah.'

Her eyes filled with tears. 'What are you saying? Do you want us to stay in Australia?'

'No,' he assured her. 'I don't expect you to do that.'

'Then what?'

He sighed. 'I guess I'm going to build up a lot of frequent flyer points in the next few years. Or probably I'll live some of my time overseas, I don't know. We'll work it out.'

'Joe, are you sure? You always wanted to settle here.'

'It doesn't matter,' he said. 'Julia comes first from now on, okay?'

When Joe walked out of the room a short time later, Ian was anxiously pacing the corridor.

'Go on in,' said Joe. 'Your family's waiting for you.'

He looked a little startled. 'Joe, I would never presume . . . she's your daughter –'

'I know she is,' he said. 'So I'm going to expect you to take incredibly good care of her when I'm not around. Are you up for that?'

He blinked. 'Yes, absolutely.'

'Okay then. What are your intentions with Sarah?'

'I'm sorry?'

'Are you going to marry her?'

'Why, yes, if she'll have me.'

'I don't think you have to worry about that,' said Joe. 'So, if you're going to be married to the mother of my child, I guess that makes us some kind of in-laws.' Joe offered him his hand and Ian took it, still a little wary.

'It's okay, Ian, I'm not going to move in with you or anything,' Joe reassured him.

Ian finally smiled, shaking his hand.

'So, could you say goodbye to Sarah for me?' said Joe. 'Tell her I'll see her later.'

'Are you sure, Joe?' said Ian. 'You don't have to go, you know.'

'I do actually. There's something important I have to do.'

Joe walked away down the corridor, and although he felt as if he was leaving a piece of his heart behind in that hospital room, he had no regrets. This was the right thing to do, the only possible way to proceed. It wasn't going to be simple, he didn't really know how it was going to work logistically, but for the first time he actually felt happy about bringing this child into the world. His daughter was going to have a good life, surrounded by an amazing array of people, near and far, who loved her very much and who only had her best interests at heart.

He wondered if Jo would be prepared to be one of those people. He got into the lift and pressed the button for the ground floor. Was it too late though, what if she'd moved on? Could he expect her to have feelings for him still, and not only that, to want to take this complication on board?

He had to try, what did he have to lose? He checked his watch; it was early, just coming on six. Was that too early to call? His heart started to race at the thought of hearing her voice, seeing her. Maybe he should just go straight to her place, that'd take twenty minutes or so . . . But what if she wasn't there? God, he hoped she wasn't away somewhere on holidays. Bugger it, so what if he woke her, he had to know where she was and if she was prepared to see him. Suddenly he couldn't wait another minute.

The lift doors opened as he took out his phone and turned it on. As it came to life, it started to beep repeatedly. He stepped out of the elevator frowning at the screen. There were six missed calls, all from Mim and Hilary.

He called Hilary. 'Joe,' she said when she picked up. 'Thank God, we've been ringing you all night, at home, on your mobile. Where have you been?'

He couldn't explain everything now. 'Never mind, what's going on?'

'You have to come, Joe. You have to come as fast as you can.'

*

J O   L I D D E L L
B I T C H

You know what? I'm tired of bitching. That's right. I've had enough. I don't see the point any more. Bitching, harping, carping, moaning, groaning, whingeing, whining. It's all the same, and I've learned that it doesn't get you anywhere. In fact it just drags you down into a pit of self-righteous self-absorbed self-pity, which is a pretty dark smelly pit, let me tell you.

But I want to share with you what else I've learned – and this is of far greater value. If you can't say anything nice, don't say anything at all. You've heard that before, haven't you? Your mother probably said it all the time. Well listen up, she was right. If you can't say anything nice – read pleasant, encouraging, positive, kind – then keep your trap shut. You're not doing anyone any favours, least of all yourself.

So, in the spirit of practising what I preach, this will be my last column, and it's a short one, but this is all I have to say. I need to move on and start smelling the roses instead of complaining about their thorns.

Thank you for having me at your breakfast table these past few years, but I'm kind of hoping you're glad to see the back of me. That you're relieved there's finally an end to the griping, sniping and sneering, at least in this space.

Look out for my by-line in greener pastures. By that I don't mean I'm going soft and heading for the gardening pages. It's just that I want to write about things that matter, things that will inform, educate, perhaps even make a difference. I hope you'll consider joining me from time to time.

bitch@thetribune.com

It was Jo's last day at work. She had spent the past week slowly packing up her desk, doing the odd article, just writing up news off the wire. No one really expected anything of her.

She hadn't seen Joe at all around the office, but she hadn't asked after him. She didn't want to hear he'd had the baby. She didn't want to know, even though she was painfully aware that had to be what was keeping him away.

'So, was it a boy or a girl?' Oliver asked at breakfast. He actually joined her and Angie at the table, for a good half an hour. It was Angie's last day at Earl's as well, and so probably the last day they would have breakfast at Oliver's. But he swiftly quashed any whiff of sentiment.

'If you're asking about Joe's baby, I don't know anything,' Jo replied. And hopefully she would leave the country without finding out anything, before the congratulations started flowing around the office or, God forbid, he brought the baby in to show it off.

'Well, there must be someone you can ask?' Oliver persisted.

'Hey Oliver,' said Angie, 'maybe she doesn't want to know.'

'A prize to the girl in the navy blue tracksuit,' said Jo, talking into her spoon. 'Hey, looking the part, Ange.'

'I don't just look the part,' she said, consulting her pedometer. 'I'll have you know I've walked almost six thousand steps already this morning, which puts me well within range of reaching my ten thousand step daily target, especially as I'm going to do a circuit class tonight.'

'You do understand the main reason people lose weight when they're on a fitness kick?' Oliver said wearily. 'Their friends stop asking them to dinner because they're so boring. Word to the wise, Angelina, find something else to talk about.'

'Okay,' she took the hint. 'I do have some news actually. I got a job.'

'Well done you,' said Jo.

'I don't start till after the fringe festival, but I wanted to focus on that anyway.'

'So, don't keep us in suspense,' said Oliver. 'What is it?'

She smiled serenely. 'I'm going to be cleaning the theatres down at the Wharf.'

'Well, you always wanted to work in the theatre,' said Oliver.

'I figure at least I'll enjoy the surroundings,' said Angie. 'And I'll probably get to be around during rehearsals, who knows what contacts I can make. And like you said, Jo, it's more physically active.'

'I think it's fabulous,' said Jo, holding up her orange juice in a toast. 'To all of us in all our fabulousness.'

'Easy for you to say, Josephine,' said Oliver. 'Swanning off to
Europe and abandoning us all.'

'I thought you said we weren't allowed to get sentimental?' Jo
reminded him.

'I'm not getting sentimental,' he maintained. 'I just want to
know why you're not taking me with you.'

By ten o'clock, Jo was at a total loss as to what to do with herself.
So she decided to make her way up to see Leo.

'Hello Jo,' said Judith warmly as she approached her desk.
'It's your last day! How do you feel, heading off into the great
unknown? Nervous, excited?'

Jo shrugged. 'Both, I guess.'

'I should think so!'

'I don't suppose he's free?' asked Jo, cocking her head in the
direction of Leo's office.

'Well, there's no one with him,' said Judith, 'so you might be
in luck.' She pressed the intercom on her phone. 'Jo Liddell to
see you.'

'Okay, send her in.'

Judith smiled. 'Go ahead.'

Jo walked over to the door and let herself in. Leo was staring
at the computer screen, but he looked up as she approached his
desk.

'So, are you all set?' he asked her, sitting back in his chair.

She nodded. 'I am. You got my column?'

'Yeah, but I won't be running it.'

Jo blinked. 'Oh.'

'Don't be offended,' he said, 'It's just that the way it reads, you're
stopping anyone else from doing the column either.'

'You want to keep the column?'

'I don't see why not,' said Leo. 'It's a good column, people
respond to it.'

'Do you have anyone in mind to take over?'

'I've already asked Carla.'

Of course. 'Good choice.'

'Look, if you want to have another shot at a farewell piece –'

'No,' Jo shook her head. 'I think I'll just disappear mysteriously.'

'When do you fly out?'

'A week from today.'

'You're going to miss all the hoopla then,' he said. 'It looks like we'll be clear to run your piece the following week.'

'Really?'

He nodded. 'I was talking to the subs about the headline only this morning.'

'Did you settle on anything?'

'Probably *HIGHWAY TO HELL* for the banner, then *Minister forced to hit the road.*'

Jo smiled faintly. Bloody subs and their obsession with wordplay.

'Well, I wanted to thank you for everything, Leo . . .'

He gave a dismissive wave of his hand. 'Just don't make a fool out of me for recommending you.'

'I won't,' she said. 'I promise.'

He nodded. 'So, apparently there's a cake later.'

'I don't want any fuss, Leo.'

'It's not a fuss, Jo, it's a cake,' he said. 'See you then,' he added, returning his attention to the computer monitor.

Her audience was clearly over. She turned to walk out.

'Oh, by the way, Jo –'

She stopped at the door and looked back.

'– did you know that Joe Bannister passed away?'

The blood drained from her face and she couldn't take a breath.

'His dad, I mean,' Leo said quickly. 'Joe Senior.'

She managed to breathe then, which was just as well or she might have passed out.

'Are you all right?' he asked.

'Sure, of course.'

'Anyway, the funeral's today. I'm not going to be able to get up there, bloody board meeting. We sent flowers from the office, and more from the corporation. He was hugely respected in the industry. They're running a big piece in the Obits in the *Daily*. I daresay all the dailies will be running something.'

Jo nodded. 'Thanks for letting me know, Leo.' Her hand was still shaking as she fumbled with the doorknob and left the room.

'See you later for the cake,' Judith said brightly as Jo came out of the office.

'Judith,' she said, approaching her desk. 'You don't happen to have the details for Mr Bannister's funeral, do you?' she asked.

'Of course, I had to send flowers.' She glanced around her desk. 'I did it yesterday.' She reached into one of the trays. 'Here we are. There will be a graveside service at Katoomba Cemetery at noon today.'

'Thanks.'

Jo hurried to the elevators. She had to do this. She didn't know why exactly, but she had to do it. She got back to her desk, grabbed her bag and jacket and headed out to the elevators again, taking a lift down to the basement. She'd sign a car out, no questions would be asked, they took the journalists at their word. What were they going to do anyway? Fire her?

Katoomba Cemetery

Joe was glad his father had decided on this form of service. They were not religious people. His parents had seen too many wars waged in the name of too many religions to want to be buried in the name of any particular one. Their mother had never had the chance to make any requests about her own funeral, so they'd had a simple secular service at her graveside. Their father had asked for the same. It was a beautiful, bright summer day, which was incongruous, but was nonetheless preferable to a grey and miserable one.

Although they were a family of wordsmiths, no one had felt up to the task of speaking, but their father had made only one specific request, that Mim read one of her poems. And she had done so, with such exquisite poignancy that not an eye was left dry by the end of it, not least amongst her siblings.

As the grandchildren stepped forward to lay flowers on the coffin, Joe lifted his eyes to gaze across the vast assembly. His father had never been a proud man, but he hoped he would be proud that so many had come to pay their respects.

And then he saw her. Standing back, her head bowed, away from the main congregation of people. And suddenly he couldn't concentrate on anything else. The proceedings were drawing to a close anyway; he became aware that people were dispersing, coming forward to shake hands, embrace his sisters, but he could barely focus on who they were or what they were saying. He had to get to her, before she left. Joe started to weave his way through the crowd, his heart racing, fixing his eyes on her so she'd notice him, so she'd look up and realise that he'd seen her. And finally she did. Their eyes locked across the sea of people, and she acknowledged him with a faint nod. She'd wait for him now, he was sure, and he accepted the condolences of people mostly unknown to him as he pushed his way on towards her. And then there was no one else in his way, and she was still standing there, waiting for him.

'Jo,' he said as he approached her, 'it's so good of you to come.'

That sounded lame, like she was just someone who'd showed up. But she wasn't just someone. What had made her show up? Did she know about him and Sarah, about the baby? But how could she know the whole story, and how could he explain it to her now?

'Hello Joe,' she was saying, 'I was so sorry when I heard . . .'

'Thank you.' He was standing right in front of her now. He wanted so badly to take her in his arms and hold her close. But he couldn't, not now, not here, not till he had a chance to talk to her. He had to find a way to make her stay, somehow.

'How are you coping?' she asked.

'Okay, we're doing okay.'

She glanced around, as though she was looking for who else he meant by 'we'. Damn.

'I'm so glad to see you, Jo,' he said.

She smiled a little awkwardly. 'Did he die peacefully?' she asked.

He nodded. 'But I didn't make it before he lost consciousness. I didn't get to speak to him.'

She reached for his hand instinctively. 'You two said everything you had to say throughout your lives, you were lucky you had that kind of relationship, Joe. And he would have known you were there.'

He took a deep breath, feeling the comfort of her hand in his. 'I'm so glad you're here, Jo.'

She dropped her head then, breaking eye contact, and he felt her hand slip away, but he gripped it tight. 'Can you come back to the house?'

She shook her head regretfully. 'I have to go. It's my last day at work, I shouldn't even be here.'

'Your last day?'

'I'm going away, Joe,' she said, meeting his gaze again.

'Where to?' he frowned.

'I'm finally going to be a foreign correspondent. I'm off to London first, then they're going to find a post for me in Europe.'

She was going away? His heart was twisting painfully in his chest, his head was spinning. He had to talk to her. 'That's . . . that's really great, Jo. It's what you've always wanted.'

She nodded faintly, staring up at him. 'Yeah . . . yeah, it is.'

'The car's leaving now, Joseph.'

He turned. It was Hilary. She smiled at Jo. 'Hello, thanks for coming,' she said, before walking on. He would have liked to introduce them, to tell Hilary this was Jo.

'I'll let you go,' she said, sliding her hand out of his finally.

He wanted to say something, anything, to make her stay. 'You're sure you can't come back?'

She nodded. 'All the best, Joe.'

And then he couldn't help himself. He brought his arms around her, but she didn't resist. She hugged him as hard as he was hugging her. He didn't want to let her go, but he felt her pulling back after a while.

She looked up at him, her eyes glassy. 'Bye Joe,' she said, and then she turned and walked away.

He was still in a daze an hour later back at the house. People kept coming up and speaking to him, though now it was mostly people he knew at least. But Joe still didn't know what to say to them. He didn't really feel like talking to anyone. He had an urge to walk out the back door and beyond through the bush and up to the top of the ridge, and sit on the flat rock and watch the black cockatoos. He didn't want to be with these people, he wanted to be with Jo. But he didn't know how that was going to happen now.

Will came up behind him, laying a hand on his shoulder. 'Was that Jo I saw at the cemetery?'

He nodded.

'Is she coming back here?'

'No, she couldn't.'

'Why not?'

'She's going away.'

Will came around to face him. 'She's going away? Where to?'

Joe sighed. 'Europe.'

Will took a moment to process that. 'Does she know?'

He shook his head.

'So what are you still doing here?'

'Will, it's our father's funeral.'

'Yeah, I realise that. Why are you still here?'

Joe looked at him directly. 'It's Dad's funeral.'

'And so I'll ask the question again, why are you still here?'

'Because it's Dad's funeral,' Joe repeated firmly.

Will folded his arms, shaking his head. 'And where do think he'd want you to be right now?'

Joe just stared at him.

'God, Joe, have I taught you nothing? Grand gesture! It's time for the big one, brother, before she gets away for good.'

The Tribune

It was going on four o'clock when Jo arrived back at work. She was pretty sure she must have missed her cake; it didn't bother her, she just hoped it hadn't bothered anyone else.

She had cried on and off the whole way home. She was glad she'd gone, glad she'd had the chance to say goodbye to Joe. But it had been so hard, especially when he'd hugged her at the end. He'd held onto her so tight, like he didn't want to let her go. And perhaps he didn't, but that didn't change anything. She had searched the crowd when she'd arrived, spotting Joe straight away, and Will and Mim, and the other two sisters, she assumed, tall and attractive like their brothers. But she couldn't see Sarah anywhere. Surely she'd be standing with the family? Jo had decided in the end that she was either too heavily pregnant, or else she was still in hospital after the birth, which would be truly awful for Joe. What if the baby had been born close to when his father died? He'd said he didn't get the chance to say goodbye . . . It was too sad to think about. She parked the car in the basement and signed it back in. She took the elevator up to the news floor, and as she walked back to her desk, Hugh Moncrieff was coming towards her, cradling a piece of cake in a paper napkin.

His faced dropped when he saw her. 'Oh, we've just had your cake, Jo. When you didn't show . . .'

She smiled reassuringly. 'That's fine, Hugh. I'm sorry, I was called out unexpectedly.'

He looked embarrassed.

'Is it any good?' Jo asked.

'I have to say it's not bad,' he said. 'It's from that patisserie in the arcade. It's a five-layered almond torte interspersed with a crème fraiche filling and smothered in dark chocolate ganache. Quite delicious actually. I think there's still some left.'

'Thanks, Hugh,' she nodded. 'Well, it was nice knowing you,' she said, offering him her hand.

He almost blushed, wiping his fingers on the napkin and reaching out to shake her hand. 'All the very best to you, Jo.'

She proceeded to her cubicle and dropped her bag on her desk. That was it, she supposed. She could go now. Though there was one more person she really should say goodbye to, despite everything. She walked over to Lachlan's office. The blinds were closed, so she knocked on the door.

'Just a minute,' she heard his voice from inside.

A moment later the door opened and Carla strode out past her, slightly flushed. 'Oh, Jo, I thought you'd left already,' she said.

'I'm on my way,' she said. 'Good luck with the column, Carla.'

'Thanks,' she said breezily, walking away.

Jo stepped into the office. Lachlan was sitting at his desk, a sheepish expression on his face.

She shook her head as she closed the door behind her. 'Lachlan, really,' she winced. 'Carla?'

'What can I say,' he said, getting up and coming around the desk. 'I'm incorrigible.'

'Unconscionable more like,' said Jo, folding her arms. 'Sandra deserves better, and so do you, I might add.'

'I don't know about that,' he shrugged, leaning back against the desk, facing her. 'Maybe I've found my match.'

He had a point.

'Anyway, I just wanted to say goodbye,' said Jo.

He nodded. 'Listen, I realise things didn't work out for you and Bannister.'

She shrugged.

'Are you sorry we broke up?'

Jo smiled. 'No.'

He grinned then. 'Fair enough.' He stood up. 'Do I get a kiss goodbye at least, for old times' sake?'

'Sure,' she said, but she only lifted her cheek towards him. He bent to kiss it, giving her arm a gentle squeeze.

'I'll miss you,' he said.

'No you won't,' she returned. 'You'll barely notice I'm gone.' She turned back to the door. 'Try to be good, Lachlan.'

'Try to be happy, Jo,' he said as she walked out the door.

She went back to her desk and gathered up the last of her things into a small cardboard box, switched off her computer, and picked up her jacket from the back of her chair, slipping it on. She placed her handbag on top of the box, and then hoisted it onto her hip as she walked out of her cubicle. Jo was relieved no one paid any attention as she made her way across the news floor to the elevator bay.

The receptionist was munching on cake as she went to walk

by. 'Oh, Jo, we missed you at afternoon tea. Did you get some cake?'

'It's okay . . .' Then she frowned. 'I'm sorry, I've forgotten your name?'

'That's all right, I've only been here a few weeks. It's Marianne.'

Not Elizabeth, or Louise . . . Jo couldn't remember all the names of the receptionists who had come and gone during her time here. People moved on every day, Jo realised, and they survived. So would she.

'Well, bye Marianne,' she said.

'Goodbye Jo. All the best.'

She walked out to the lift bay and pressed the button for down, then stepped back, waiting in front of the second elevator on the right. For old times' sake. The ping sounded at the other end, behind her; Jo glanced back at the indicator light, but it was going up. Another ping, and the doors in front of her were gliding open. She stepped in.

'Hold it! Hold the lift.'

She turned around and her heart stopped. It was Joe, striding towards her. Somehow she found her voice. 'What are you doing here?'

'I had to see you.'

'You just saw me,' she said, stunned. 'Joe, you left your father's funeral?'

'I did,' he said, stepping into the path of the lift doors so they wouldn't close. 'There's something I have to tell you, Jo, something you should know before you leave . . . Can we talk?'

'I'm . . . um, I was just on my way out.'

'Can I ride down with you?'

She was staring at him in disbelief. 'Sure,' she said in a small voice.

He stepped into the elevator and pressed the button for the ground floor.

'What is it, Joe?' she asked. 'What do you have to tell me?'

He took a breath. 'Sarah and I . . . we're not together. She's in love with someone else. Same as me.'

The box slid out of Jo's arms but he caught it before it dropped to the floor, setting it down. He straightened up again to face her.

She seemed to be in shock. 'But . . . the baby?' she said, her voice barely making it out of her throat. 'It's not yours?'

'No, it's mine. She's mine. Julia. She was born just over a week ago.' He glanced up at the numbers rapidly descending. Damn, this thing was moving too fast. He reached over to slam his hand on the emergency stop.

That roused her. 'What are you doing?'

'Sorry. I'm sorry, Jo, I know you get nervous in confined spaces, but I just need another minute.'

'It's okay,' she said calmly. And it was. Jo didn't feel anxious, she felt safe. With him. Like in her dreams.

'It's over with Sarah,' he was saying. 'It never really got started this time around, but it's certainly over.'

'I don't understand. If the baby's yours . . .'

'Jo,' he took a breath. 'I'm the biological father of the baby, nothing's going to change that. But Sarah's in love with someone else. And he's a really decent guy. He followed her all the way out here; he'll be a good father, because he loves Sarah. And he loves the baby, even though she isn't his. I'm prepared to step back and let him do that. Because the right thing is for that little girl to have two parents who love each other and are committed to each other.'

'So you're giving her up?

'No, not at all,' said Joe. 'I'll have a relationship with her, I just won't be there day to day. But I'm going to make sure she knows I love her and that we did the right thing by her.' He paused, thinking about what to say next. 'Jo, it was never going to work. I can't be a good father, I can't be good at anything if I'm not with you.'

She stared up at him, her eyes glassy. 'But I'm leaving the country, Joe, I told you.'

'I know, and I want you to go, I want you to do whatever you need to do, Jo, I'll never stand in your way.'

Now she looked confused.

He took hold of her arms. 'It's just . . . I want to come with you.'

'Oh,' she said, her eyes wide. 'But . . .' She seemed hesitant. 'But you said you don't want to live overseas any more, you said you wanted to settle down.'

'That's all changed. I'm going to spend part of the year overseas now anyway. And I want to settle down with you, wherever that is.'

She was breathing hard. 'I don't know where I'm going to be yet, they haven't appointed me.'

'I don't care.'

'It might be Moscow.'

'I'll bring a coat.'

Her heart was racing. 'But what will you do?'

He shrugged. 'Well, I was thinking, I might write a book about my dad.'

She smiled faintly. 'So you have a plan?'

'Not really. I'm making it up as I go along.'

She looked at him. 'You'd really up and leave everything, just like that?'

'In a heartbeat,' he said without hesitating. 'I love you, Jo. I never stopped loving you this whole time. When I sorted things out with Sarah, the first thing I wanted to do was find you and tell you, see if there was any chance you'd have me back. I didn't know if you'd ever want to have anything to do with me again. And then you were there, today, and I can't let you go again . . . not without me.'

There was silence, she wasn't saying anything. Maybe it was too late, maybe she couldn't understand . . . but something in her eyes, gazing up at him, wide and glassy, gave him hope.

'What are you thinking?' he asked tentatively.

'I'm thinking . . .' she said slowly. '. . . Okay.'

He breathed out. 'Okay?' he said. 'You're saying okay?'

She smiled then. 'I'm saying okay, Joe.'

And he smiled too, and they drew into each other's arms, completely in sync, like it was a movie or something. And their lips met, with no bumping of noses or knocking of teeth, in a perfect, wonderful, exhilarating kiss.

'Is everything all right in there?' the intercom crackled into life.

They drew back to smile at each other.

'Everything's just great,' said Jo.

CARLA DELACQUA
BITCH

Novelty weddings, is there anything quite so absurd? Reciting solemn vows as you parachute out of a plane or ride a surfboard, or even hang by a bungee rope. At least I can recognise the inherent, if lame, romance in the notion, if you go for that kind of thing.

But here's one that takes the idea to a whole new level – excuse the pun – of inanity. Two former employees of this newspaper, who should know better, decided to tie the connubial knot in – wait for it – an elevator of all places. And why? Because they met in an elevator that broke down. Aww, I think I'm going to puke. Lucky they didn't meet in an STD clinic.

If this trend takes off, are we going to be confronted anywhere and everywhere with a new breed of reality weddings? The line at the post office could suddenly become the conga line at someone's reception; people will get stuck behind wedding car processions at their local McDonald's drive-thru; every second pickup joint will become a tacky reception venue.

The fact is, most people meet on the Internet these days, so some entrepreneurial person ought to get onto this and offer weddings online, with virtual food, virtual guests, virtual speeches. It would be a lot less boring, considerably cheaper, and the happy couple wouldn't even have to be in the same room. Should get them used to the rest of married life.

See, this obsession with novelty weddings is just to distract the players from the main game, the fact that they're committing to each other for the rest of their lives and that neither of them probably believes it for a second, deep down. If they did, why are pre-nups under 'essential' on every wedding planner's to-do list these days?

Divorce is now wedded to the paradigm of marriage. That might sound ironic, but the facts are, thirty-four percent of couples who say 'I do' today will not last ten years, giving a whole new meaning to the phrase 'till death us do part'. That is, you're more likely to divorce each other if you don't kill each other first.

Truth is, it's all stuff and nonsense. And that's a bitch.

Editor's note: Despite the opinions of this columnist, the staff at the Tribune *wish the aforementioned couple every happiness.*

ALSO BY DIANNE BLACKLOCK IN PAN MACMILLAN

Call Waiting

Ally Tasker feels trapped. Her dreams of a fulfilling life after art college didn't include cleaning up after bored school children and being a doormat for her high-flying boyfriend. Ally envies her friend Meg who has turned her art training into a lucrative job in graphic design, not to mention having a doting husband and a gorgeous baby to complete the package.

But when Ally's grandfather, her sole relative, dies, she returns to the Southern Highland home of her childhood where she must confront painful issues from her past that her safe life in the city has allowed her to ignore. Meanwhile Meg is not as happy as Ally imagines . . .

Sometimes you have to risk all you have to realise what is worth saving.

'It's funny, it's genuine and it will resonate in the lives of women everywhere'
AUSTRALIAN HOUSE & GARDEN

Wife for Hire

When she was a little girl, all Samantha Driscoll ever wanted was to be somebody's wife. She would marry a man called Tod or Brad and she would have two perfect children. But instead she married a Jeff and he's just confessed to having an affair.

Spurred on by supportive friends and her unpredictable sister Max, she finds the job she was born for: *Wife for Hire*. Sam manages everything from renovations to social events, for many satisfied customers.

However when Hal Buchanan is added to her client list but claims not to need her services, Sam realises that while she can organise many things in life, she is not so businesslike when her emotions are involved.

'Think Maeve Binchy, Marian Keyes and Cathy Kelly'
GOLD COAST BULLETIN

Almost Perfect

Georgie Reading runs a successful bookshop – with a name like that, she was born to. A fun-loving friend, loyal sister and adored aunty, life's pretty good for Georgie. Except her love life, that is. Nothing seems to go right and she's ready to give up.

On the other side of town, Anna and Mac appear to have the perfect marriage. But with every failed attempt at IVF their relationship suffers further and Mac doesn't know how much longer he can cope with Anna's pain and disappointment.

So when a stranger walks into Georgie's bookshop and they strike up a friendship, events are set in motion that no-one could imagine. What is the connection between the stranger, Anna and Mac? And what will the consequences be for everyone involved if Georgie allows herself to fall in love with him?

False Advertising

Helen always tries to be a good person. She recycles, obeys the water restrictions, she is even polite to telemarketers. As a mother, wife, daughter and nurse, Helen is used to putting everyone's needs before her own. But it only takes one momentary lapse of concentration to shatter her life forever.

There was no such momentary lapse for Gemma. Her customary recklessness leaves her pregnant, alone and estranged from her family, with her once-promising advertising career in tatters.

So when Gemma barges unceremoniously into Helen's life, things will never be the same again for either of them. Two very different women who have one thing in common – their lives have fallen short of their expectations. But is fate offering them a second chance?

Author photograph: Pat Naoum